THE CHINGLES GO WEST

PATRICIA MURPHY

POOLBEG

This book is entirely a work of fiction. The names, characters and incidents portrayed in it are the work of the author's imagination. Any resemblance to actual persons, living or dead, events or localities is entirely coincidental.

Published 2006
by Poolbeg Press Ltd.
123 Grange Hill, Baldoyle
Dublin 13, Ireland
Email: poolbeg@poolbeg.com

1 3 5 7 9 10 8 6 4 2

A catalogue record for this book is available from the British Library.

ISBN 1-84223-218-5

Typeset by Patricia Hope in Goudy 12.5/18.5
Printed by Litografia Rosés, Spain

www.poolbeg.com

About the Author

Patricia Murphy grew up in Ballygall, Dublin, the eldest of six children, and turned to storytelling to amuse her brothers and sisters and sixty cousins. After reading English and History at Trinity College Dublin, she worked in television as a reporter and documentary maker and got to travel the world from the Arctic Circle to the Amazon Jungle. She is now a producer/director and has made a number of acclaimed documentaries for the BBC and Channel 4, including several on children's lives. She is married and lives in Oxford.

The Chingles Go West is the second book in a trilogy. Her first children's novel, *The Chingles from the East*, was the winner of the Poolbeg "Write a Bestseller" Competition 2004.

This book is dedicated with love to
Daniel, William, Ivan, Louis, Molly, Alice,
Kitty, Elsa and Edward

CHAPTER 1

It was hard to see through the thick glass but there were tears of blood on the woman's face. She looked beautiful but forlorn and on her back were swan's wings, whiter than snow. Then Cassie caught her own reflection and that of her brother Thomas and sister Nancy rippling like water across the glassy surface. In a heartbeat, a dark, shifting shadow clouded the scene. A monstrous bird with the body of the Corra and the head of an old hag with hideous fangs flew down on leathery wings. The creature tore into the glass with talons sharp as knives. The Swan Maiden, Cassie and her brother and sister were each split in two. A screech shattered the air and flying shards of glass obliterated everything.

All that was left was a white swan's feather.

"It's alright now, Cassie . . ."

Cassie heard her grandmother's voice soothing her and felt her soft hand stroking her hair as she floated up from sleep.

She sat up in the bed and shuddered. It was hard to believe she wasn't in some icy hell but in a comfortable berth on her grandparents' houseboat in Ireland.

"It was just a bad dream," she reassured her grandmother as she got up and dressed quickly, in a hurry to join her brother and sister on the deck of the houseboat.

"Is it because of the new arrivals you've been having these bad dreams?" asked her grandmother, for what seemed like the thousandth time.

The children's mother had just given birth to twins who had been born early and their grandparents kept harping on about it. They were acting like Cassie, Thomas and Nancy had been turned into orphans. Actually, when Cassie thought about it, this was partly true.

"It's a big upheaval for you three older ones, having new babies in the house," continued Gran.

"Matthew and Matilda nearly died, so it's understandable that Mum and Dad are anxious about them," said Cassie, trying to sound grown up.

She obviously succeeded because her grandmother said, "Cassie, sometimes you seem so mature."

But Cassie didn't really feel mature. She felt confused and lost, just like she did in that horrible nightmare. She didn't tell her grandmother how her mother did nothing but snap at her these days. In her secret heart, Cassie was glad that she was spending the summer away from home. Her secret fear was that her parents felt the same way.

Out on deck, Granddad McColl sat at the wheel with Cassie's sister Nancy on his knee. Nancy, who was nearly four, gave her a big smile. But Cassie saw with a flash of annoyance that Thomas, her ten-year-old brother, was *still* pretending to be blind. He was shambling around on deck, clutching a stick with his eyes closed. It was bad enough, the day before, when he'd pretended he had no hands. He'd even painted a picture using his mouth. But then everything Thomas did was calculated to wind her up. She was only a year and a half older than him and the worst thing anyone could say to her was that they were like twins.

Cassie tried to put the nightmare out of her mind. She'd been having it all year since her last visit to Inish Álainn, the island off the west coast of Ireland where they were due to spend their summer holidays with their Uncle Jarlath. Now that their grandparents were taking them down Ireland's waterways in their houseboat to the ferry, there was a new urgency about the dream. She still felt shaky but here in the bright sunlight as the canal boat drifted lazily on, it was easier to forget the sickening panic caused by the images.

"Isn't Nancy the gas ticket?" said Granddad McColl, tilting the helm. "She's only telling me a great story about how you all defeated an evil giant on Inish Álainn last year. And you being the Changles."

"*Chin*-gles!" corrected Nancy in a singsong voice.

"Don't mind Nancy," Cassie said quickly. "You know she has an over-active imagination." She looked worryingly at her brother Thomas but he was too engrossed in his game of blindness, which chiefly involved bumping into things, to notice her.

"She must be thinking of that horrible fella, what's his name, Dignum Drax, who tried to buy up the island and blew himself up," said Granny.

"She almost had me convinced," laughed Granddad McColl and chucked Nancy under the chin. "So why do they call you the Chingles?"

"It's our nickname on the island," said Thomas. "Last year when Nancy couldn't say 'children' properly she told everyone that we were 'Chingles from the East' instead of children from East Croydon. But there was a prophecy about Chingles who were supposed to be legendary warriors who'd come to rescue the island from Balor of the Evil Eye. So –"

Cassie gave him a hard look and he shut up. "It was just an old story," she added quickly, "but the nickname stuck."

Nancy winked and crossed her fingers behind her back. "Just pretend," she said. "And I can say 'children' now but I like being a Chingle."

"I'm more worried about Cassie's nightmares," said Granny McColl.

"It's just a book I was reading," Cassie said, avoiding her grandmother's eye. Then, as soon as she could without being noticed, she pinched Thomas and leaned in close. "I've had that dream again," she whispered.

He followed her down to the cabin so they could discuss it in private.

For Nancy had been telling the truth. Nancy always told the truth – except when she was crossing her fingers behind her back.

Last summer, they had indeed saved the island from an evil developer called Drax who was the reincarnation of the giant Balor of the Evil Eye. He'd returned to look for a magical stone called the Star Splinter that could give him the powers to take control of the sun. Luckily, with the help of Áine, who was really the Sun

Goddess, and other magical beings, the children developed special powers that helped them save the island. Or so they had thought. Such was Cassie's sense of foreboding, she wasn't sure any more.

"So more dreams of Finnen the Swan Maiden," Thomas said, closing the hatch behind them. Finnen was Áine's sister, a Swan Maiden who had disappeared in an earlier battle with Balor, the First Battle of the Skies. "She's been lurking in your nightmares all year since you had that vision of her hidden among the stars."

"This time we were trying to rescue her but a creature like the Corra attacked us and we were each split in two," said Cassie. "I'm worried that something terrible is going to happen. Something to do with Balor."

"Relax. We obliterated him to nothing and you saw off the Corra," said Thomas, his eyes clenched shut, playing blind again.

The Corra was a hideous water monster, like a prehistoric bird, that Cassie had defeated in battle.

"But remember what Áine said about only being able to defeat his evil for a time? Evil forces can always come back," said Cassie, her forehead creased with frown lines

"Oh, Balor, come and get us!" jeered Thomas, waving his stick around for emphasis.

To their horror the boat convulsed to a stop, they

were knocked around the cabin and there was an ear-splitting sound. A mirror over the washstand crashed to the floor, its shards splintering into fearful daggers. Knives sprang from the drawers and pinned Cassie's skirt to the wooden bench.

"See what you've done now?" shouted Cassie in a fury at her brother.

"I didn't touch anything," he moaned. He held up his arm and tiny needles from his grandmother's sewing box had pierced his flesh. Beads of blood stood out on his arm like ruby jewels.

Their grandmother and grandfather hurried down the stairs and looked horrified at the devastation in the cabin.

"It wasn't me, I swear it!" moaned Thomas.

"There, there," said their grandmother. "Thank God nobody is badly hurt." She set about taking the needles from Thomas's arm while Granddad McColl freed Cassie from the prison of knives. The needles left a curious curling C-shaped scar in Thomas's arm.

"I'm damned if I know what caused that," said Granddad as he swept up the debris. "We must have hit a rock or something."

There was no time to dwell on it because they had to go through a lock that joined the canal to the River

Shannon. The lock was a narrow man-made channel linking the waterways, big enough for a boat to get through. It had large metal gates on each end and helped the barge to move smoothly from the canal to the river, which was on a slightly lower level. Thomas and Cassie were fascinated by the lock with its system of gates and changing water levels. They perked up and, grabbing the ropes at either end of the boat, jumped on to the bank.

The lock-keeper opened the gates to the lock by pushing the huge wooden beams on top of the gates. As they opened, the children could see stone walls and other gates in front of the boat. The water flowed through, filling the lock and when it was at the same level as the canal, Granddad McColl steered the boat in and stopped the engine. On the bank, Thomas and Cassie wrapped the ropes at either end of the boat around the bollards. The lock-keeper closed the gates behind the boat. Then he went to the gates in front and using a large "L" shaped bar, lifted up panels at the bottom of the gate. Water began to sluice into the river in front of the boat. Thomas let off the ropes as the boat was gently lowered down to the level of the river. He enjoyed the sensation of the rope tugging in his hand as if the boat was an animal chafing at the bit.

"It's ready!" he called as the water level in the chamber reached the level of the river.

The lock-keeper helped Cassie open the gates between the lock and the river. Then Cassie and Thomas jumped back on board and grandfather powered up the engine.

As the lock-keeper closed the gates behind them, Granddad explained about their crash. The lock-keeper looked mystified but said he'd investigate it in case there were any other accidents. They continued on their way.

The closer they got to the sea and the ferry terminal, the more excited the children got about their journey to the island and they soon forgot about the strange incident with the broken mirror.

Soon they arrived at the sea.

Just as they were about to get on the ferry, Granny McColl handed Cassie a basket full of goodies. Then she produced a bundle wrapped in brown paper, saying, "Here's a gift for Jarlath. And tell him to eat his greens."

"And wash behind his ears," Thomas laughed, interrupting her.

Granny McColl always behaved towards their Uncle Jarlath as if he was still a baby, which was probably about right in the children's opinion.

Granddad added, "And tell Jarlath all that business with Áine will blow over."

Cassie pricked up her ears. Granddad was being mysterious. "What business?" she asked.

Jarlath and Áine were supposed to be getting married. So what did Granddad mean? Had Jarlath and Áine called off the wedding or were they in some trouble? She couldn't help worrying that it had something to do with her nightmare. But Granny gave Granddad a warning look and there was no more information. Clearly something had happened and Cassie had that sickening feeling in her stomach again. But she would just have to wait until she got to the island to find out more.

Getting on to the ferry was complicated by the fact that Thomas was now pretending to be lame. But soon they were on board with their bikes and baggage, greeting Podge the captain as an old friend. They also recognized some of the islanders. Mrs Moriarty, the local craft-shop owner, told them she was bringing back a llama and an angora rabbit so she could have different sorts of wool for her knitting. Nancy immediately insisted on seeing them and dragged Cassie and Thomas below deck to the hold. She started an animated conversation with the animals. She had always had a special touch with animals but since she'd swallowed the Star Splinter last year she'd become a master animal linguist. The llama and rabbit just grunted a little and looked rather seasick.

But there was also another strange animal in the hold, with shaggy red hair. It looked like a cross between a stubby Red Setter dog and a miniature orang-utan. Cassie reached out and stroked the long silky hair on its head.

"I'm worried about what Granddad said about Jarlath and Áine. I wonder what's going on?" She frowned as she patted the strange creature.

Áine and Jarlath were a strange match. Jarlath was a scientist and had no idea he was marrying a goddess. As far as he was concerned, she was a herbalist.

"Maybe Áine's been kidnapped and Jarlath hasn't got the ransom," Thomas said.

"That's stupid," retorted Cassie.

"Yes, that is stupid!" said a familiar voice.

They looked around, startled by the interruption. There was nobody else in the hold.

The strange animal suddenly stood up on its hind

legs. It was smaller than Cassie. Thomas nearly fell out of his standing. He could have sworn the creature smiled at him. Then he looked more closely at its face. Underneath the shaggy growth of russet-red fur, the glinting green eyes were unmistakable.

"Connle!" cried Nancy, throwing her arms around him.

"But what's happened to your face?" asked Cassie, embracing him in her turn.

It was indeed their old friend from the island, undoubtedly hairier, but his eyes twinkled just the same.

"Since I've been living outdoors I've returned to my natural state," he said ruefully, shaking his hairy head.

For Connle, the caretaker at the summerhouse, had a secret. He was really a five-hundred-year-old half human and half fairy, known in Irish as a *gruagach* – a "hairy one".

"But why are you living outdoors?" asked Thomas.

"First things first," said Connle. "As you know, despite my advice Jarlath went ahead and asked Áine to marry him." He continued in a low voice, checking over his shoulder to make sure there was no one around: "I tried to warn him there would be difficulties with her being – a bit different. But he wouldn't listen and neither would she. Well, the gods of the Tuatha Dé Danann got wind of it and they've summoned her to a judgement."

"But that's ridiculous in this day and age!" said Cassie with indignation. "What have they got against Jarlath? What's wrong with the McColls? You've worked and lived with the family for years!"

Connle looked at her with great affection. "You are the finest family in Ireland but fierce contrary. And Áine's not helping by flatly refusing to tell Jarlath she's a goddess. I'm afraid Jarlath and I have fallen out over the whole business," he said sadly.

A howling wind suddenly whipped up out of nowhere and died down just as quickly.

"There are rules about humans and gods," continued Connle. "Don't forget I'm the product of a mixed marriage myself. Áine doesn't only run the risk of their displeasure – she and Jarlath might die if she disobeys the gods."

The seriousness of the issue struck them.

"But why are you living outdoors?" persisted Thomas. "Did Jarlath throw you out of the house?"

"Well, I'm so busy looking after the trees of the Sacred Grove that I –" The hooter of the ferry interrupted him, indicating that they were coming in to land. "But that's another story. Listen carefully. We haven't much time. The gods have summoned Áine to a gathering at Tara tonight. Be sure you get to Áine's cottage before midnight. It's Midsummer's Day and one of the few times we can enter through the crack between the worlds. Now, I have to sneak off and avoid Jarlath." He bustled them back up on deck before they could say anything.

Despite Connle's bad news, the children were excited about their first glimpse of the island. Cassie was hardly able to stay still and craned over the side. Thomas naturally couldn't move much because of his lame game. Several of the islanders looked sympathetically in his direction, thinking he really had an injured leg.

As they approached the harbour, they could see Mr Mulally running down from the pub with a beer barrel and Muiris the postmaster freewheeling down on his bicycle from Stag's Cliff. Then they spotted the figure of their Uncle Jarlath pacing the pier. He looked more unkempt and dishevelled than usual.

When they got on shore they encircled him in a big hug. He seemed genuinely delighted to see them but soon became quiet and morose.

After they got their bicycles on shore, they put their baggage onto Derry the Donkey in silence. Then

Nancy who had climbed on his back began to converse with Derry in a series of brays and hee-haws which Cassie and Thomas knew to be fluent Donkey. In fact Nancy's Donkey was better than her English.

As they pushed their bikes up the hill, Cassie and Thomas tried to cheer Jarlath up by talking about the significance of the number 9, which he'd been working on the previous summer. He looked marginally more cheerful.

"I've tried the number 10 and the number 8," he said moodily, "but they're not the same . . ."

They listened to him as if he was a radio in the background with a very boring adult programme on. But they were just glad that he was talking. Cassie decided to risk asking him about Connle.

"Do you miss Connle now he's no longer living at the house?" she asked.

"Never speak that man's name in my presence again," said Jarlath curtly.

"But he's your best friend! Did you throw him out?" asked Cassie, puzzled.

But Jarlath just stared resolutely ahead.

What has happened to Jarlath? Cassie wondered. He had always been so light-hearted and not serious and bossy like so many adults.

They trooped on in an uneasy silence. Cassie was sorely tempted to ride off on her bike but it seemed rude to leave Jarlath trudging morosely beside the donkey.

"What does the poor man have and the rich man want?" asked Thomas suddenly. He had become obsessed with puzzles and crosswords recently, as well as experimental ailments.

"Eh, time?" ventured Jarlath.

Cassie stayed silent. She'd heard this one before.

"Nothing," chimed Thomas. "The poor man has nothing and the rich man wants for nothing."

Jarlath smiled and Cassie inwardly thanked Thomas for lightening their uncle's mood.

As they were passing the Fairy Field near the house, all the children coughed and said hello under their breaths to the little people. The fairies were contrary and the children didn't want to get on their bad sides by being impolite.

"I think Jarlath threw Connle out no matter what he says," Cassie whispered to Thomas as they left their bikes in the shed.

"We'll just have to check it out with Granny Clíona," he replied, speaking of the ghost who haunted the house.

Fairy Fort House was looking a bit more sad and dejected than they remembered. Inside, it felt lonely and untidy. Worse still – it smelt! Of dirty socks and stale food and as if it hadn't been cleaned in a month and nobody ever opened the windows.

Jarlath grunted at them when they got in the front door and, saying he had a headache, went off to his own room.

"Some hero's welcome this is – after all we did for the island!" Thomas sighed. "I'm starving."

They scratched around the kitchen looking for food and all they could find was an empty jar of peanut butter and some stale bread. They were about to go to bed hungry when Cassie remembered Grandma McColl's food basket! They were delighted to find it contained a fruitcake, pork pies and a quiche. They knew the brown paper parcel contained some of the strange knitted hats that were Grandma McColl's speciality.

They ate everything in no time at all.

"Let's see if we can find Granny Clíona," said Thomas then, wiping the crumbs off his mouth.

Granny Clíona was a sixteenth-century witch whose ghost had been captured in a bottle. She was also a McColl, their ancestor.

So they rifled through the house, looking for the silver bottle with a stopper in it where Granny Clíona spent her days when not haunting the house.

They found the silver bottle under Connle's bed and sneaked back up to their attic bedrooms. Checking the coast was clear, they released the stopper. The very tall ghost of an imposing old woman dressed in sixteenth-century clothes oozed out. She wore a black hooped dress and a shawl.

"Ach, me grandchildren!" she said in her weird Scottish-Irish accent. She gave them all a ghostly kiss that made Nancy laugh. "Oh, 'tis a joy surely to hear the sound of laughter in this house again! Jarlath has been so cross and quarrelsome with poor Connle."

"I just don't understand how Jarlath could fall out with Connle," sighed Thomas. "Why did they quarrel?"

"Jarlath got it into his head that Connle turned Áine against him. When Connle tried to persuade him to leave Áine to sort her problems out with her own people, Jarlath the poor soul went astray. He was shouting one minute and crying the next. He wouldn't talk to wee Connle and the silence was like a knife in his heart."

"Jarlath's gone mad," said Thomas.

"No, he's just in love," said Granny Clíona wistfully.

"Well, I'm never going to be in love if it makes you so stupid," said Cassie with determination. "But, Granny Clíona, *did* he throw Connle out of the house?"

"Connle left of his own accord," said Granny Clíona. "He's spending so much time looking after the trees of the Sacred Grove that he doesn't have time for sleep!"

"He did say something about the Sacred Grove," said Cassie. "Are the trees growing back already?"

Last summer Sir Dignum Drax had destroyed the magical trees in a fire. But the children and Áine had rescued the seeds and replanted them.

"Well, you know how the trees are a mixture of human spirit and tree," said Granny Clíona. "Now that they've been reborn they're a bit of a handful. Imagine trees with the behaviour of wild wee bairns about two. They're running wild around the island like youngsters."

In fact, the children couldn't imagine anything more unlikely than the likes of stately Dair the Oak and solemn Saille the Willow behaving like two-year-olds. The origins of the trees of the Sacred Grove were mysterious but they were thought to be the souls of ancient warriors who had been turned into trees.

The children started at a sudden noise downstairs. Then they heard Jarlath cough.

"We have to meet Connle tonight," said Cassie.

"Bring me with you," whispered Granny Clíona and she slipped back into her bottle.

Their attic bedrooms, that they'd remembered as snug and warm, felt damp and draughty. Nancy and Cassie got into the cold double bed where the sheets felt like uncooked pastry. Thomas's single bed, in the bedroom adjoining their shared bathroom, was as freezing as a slab of marble. At least, they were fully clothed.

"What question can you never honestly answer yes to?" Thomas called from his bedroom.

"Shut up, we're supposed to be asleep," said Cassie.

"Are you asleep?" said Thomas.

"No," she admitted.

"See, that's the answer," Thomas replied.

"You can never answer yes to the question 'Are you dead?'" said Cassie, "which is what we will be if Jarlath hears we're still awake!"

"Unless you're a ghost!" quipped Thomas.

Moments later Jarlath crept into the room and kissed them all on the cheek. "I'm so sorry," he said, and left the room in tears.

Oh dear, Cassie thought, some holiday this is going to be!

CHAPTER 2

At a quarter past eleven, they heard Jarlath go into his room. Once they heard his snores, they promptly got up and legged it down the drainpipe. Cassie had the silver bottle containing Granny Clíona in her pocket.

Outside, the bright moon showed the twisty turny road to Áine's home. They were startled by an urgent bray from Derry the Donkey.

"Connle told him to take us," said Nancy so they all clambered onto his back.

It was a tight squeeze and they hung on for dear life as he burst into an amazing gallop as if competing in a donkey derby.

Soon they'd passed Tadgh's Tower and were heading down to the cottage. In the distance they saw a big fire blazing and the flickering shadow of Connle running around like a madman. Cassie noticed trees growing on the roof of Áine's cottage and guessed they were the saplings of the Sacred Grove.

Connle was collecting dew that had gathered on the grass into two bowls.

"Thank God Derry got you here quickly," he said. "Time is tight." They dismounted and Derry went to graze, exhausted, in a nearby field.

Cassie tossed him the silver bottle. He opened the stopper and Granny Clíona squeezed out.

She turned to Connle. "You've managed to calm the saplings down."

"Áine has spread some sacred soil from Cnoc Áine on the roof. But they'll get bored later on and start moving round again. I'm at my wits' end figuring what to do with them."

"I'll stay and control them through a vortex," said Granny Clíona. "Up here at the far west corner of the island we shouldn't be noticed."

"That would be a great help," said Connle. He was now distractedly shaving himself with a rusty old razor, using one of the bowls of dew he'd collected and a cracked mirror propped up on a window ledge. "Áine is replenishing her energies on her crystal bed, for fear the stress of the night might drain them away and she might turn into an old hag in front of all her relations. And I don't want to appear as a hairy fairy. Next time you come, bring my good razor from under my bed."

All day, Áine was a beautiful young woman. But when the sun died in the heavens at night she became old and worn. By resting in her crystal bed, she was reborn each dawn as a beautiful young woman again. Only by taking human form could she ensure that Jarlath never found out her secret.

Connle was flustered and only half shaved when Áine appeared in the doorway. She looked stunning. Her golden hair was plaited with finely wrought jewelled hair-slides. Her gown was woven with sun symbols and gold and silver threads that shone with their own light.

"You look beautiful," said Thomas.

Áine's face lit up with a smile. "How is . . . everything at Fairy Fort House?" she asked.

"Jarlath just spends all his time moping and sighing and there's no food in the house," Thomas said.

"And it smells," added Nancy.

"Oh, how terrible for Jarlath!" said Áine.

"Not as terrible as it is for us," muttered Cassie.

A tear ran down Áine's cheek and a light shower began outside.

Connle looked at the moon. "We must hurry," he said, removing the rush matting from inside the doorway and revealing a crack in the floor.

Áine was jolted out of her trance and, picking up a small basket, she sprinkled herbs at the door's threshold. "*Here's vervain, at the threshold, the crack between the worlds, the place that is neither here nor there!*"

Connle took the other bowl of dew he'd collected and sprinkled it on the threshold. "*Here is moonglow dew, to soften our path!*"

The trees from the Sacred Grove stood stock still on the roof, Granny Clíona keeping a watchful eye on them, ready to create a vortex should they step out of line.

At one minute to midnight, the stars burned more brightly than usual. Áine ventured towards the crack.

"Now Thomas and Cassie, Nancy and Connle, repeat after me:

I am

A rain shower in sunlight,

A whisper in a breeze,

A shout in a storm,

I am between things,

Neither here nor there.

I pass between worlds."

They repeated her words as she said them, then joined hands and raised them up.

Suddenly, Áine was suffused with a surge of crackling light that passed through them all as if they'd been electrified. Then there was a feeling of being sucked into a dark tunnel by some powerful force of gravity. They felt like frost, like smoke, like rain in sunlight, neither here nor there.

"Open your eyes," commanded Áine.

They felt an intense heat on their faces and when they opened their eyes, they saw a green hill on which blazed a gigantic bonfire. The flames crackled gold and russet, licked with green and silver. Tending to the fire was a tall woman with bright red hair, the tendrils like flames themselves. She was dressed in red, the colour of molten metal.

"That's Brighid, Goddess of Fire," explained Áine.

The sun and the moon were out and the stars shone like fairy lights even though it was a blue daylight sky.

Near the hill was a great wooden structure, the size of a cathedral.

"That is the Great Hall of Tara," explained Áine.

Áine made her way to a wooden shelter, decorated with banners of sun symbols, near the Great Hall. "I will rest here a while," she said, "but, children, feel free to roam. You are honoured guests here."

"I can't believe I'm here. I've dreamed of this for years!" Connle exclaimed.

Just then a fabulous chariot of gold and silver inlaid with diamonds streaked down from the sky. It was pulled by two magnificent horses, one a chestnut and the other coal black. A powerful man got out carrying a huge club.

"That is The Daghda," said Connle, awestruck. It sounded a bit like The Die-dah but as if Connle was gargling the name. Irish words often sounded musical to the children but also gutteral, as if you were clearing your throat. "He's my hero. He is known as the Good God, because he is famously kind-hearted and excels at so many things."

They tiptoed nearer to get a closer look. Surprisingly he was somewhat uncouth and was dressed like a medieval peasant in a tunic with a leather belt and leggings of rough cloth. When he turned round to pat the horses he bent forward slightly and they saw that the tunic barely came to the top of his breeches, exposing his rump.

"The Daghda has a builder's bottom," sniggered Cassie.

The Daghda summoned two servants to help him lift a huge cauldron from the chariot and he supervised them carrying it into the Great Hall.

Then the most heavenly music started up. Connle stood there as if in a dream.

They found themselves drawn towards the Great Hall. Outside hounds as big as horses lay waiting for their masters.

Immediately at the entrance was a huge flat-topped stone set into the ground, about four metres high.

"That's the Lia Fáil," explained Connle, "the Stone of Destiny. It has many magical properties and reveals hidden things."

The outside of the hall was magnificent with large trunks of oak trees for walls. The roof was made of slanting silver birch trees interwoven with red willow branches.

Inside, it was dark and lit by tapers and seemed to shine with a thousand jewels. On both sides of the hall were rows of wooden thrones inlaid with sparkling rubies, diamonds, crystals and emeralds. Even more sumptuous were the thrones of crystal and diamonds at the far end of the hall. In front was a crystal table on which lay the copper cauldron. In one corner sat an old, blind harper and a dark-haired, pale woman accompanying him on uileann pipes. The sound they made was eerie and otherworldly.

So far only one god had taken his seat, just to the left of the table. He was thin-faced and ugly, not like they imagined a god at all. Connle said that he was Cairbre, the satirist, whose biting verse could turn battles.

Connle and the children stayed close to the entrance as the gods and goddesses of the Tuatha Dé Danann took their seats. The Daghda, who seemed to be quite important, took his seat at the top table beside his cauldron. His massive club was laid behind his throne. Beside him sat Brighid, the fire goddess, and on her left was The Daghda's brother, Oghma.

"He is a great friend of Áine's," said Connle, pointing him out. "He is so fine an orator he is called 'honey mouth'. You should hear him talk. He invented Ogham, the secret druids' writing."

"I hope we don't have to remember all their names," whispered Cassie, somewhat overawed by the occasion.

Along the other side of the wall, there was a throne

carved from black onyx and swathed in a black cloth. Connle shuddered and said that it belonged to the mysterious God of the Dead who never came to the gatherings, preferring to stay aloof in his own kingdoms. He whispered his name, Donn, and said even the Immortals feared him.

But it was hard to dwell on the gloomy god Donn as the enchanting music played on in the dazzling hall of jewels. Most of the goddesses and gods wore the most opulent clothes and shining crowns, but when Áine made her entrance she easily out-dazzled everyone in the room. She looked surprisingly nervous as she took her throne at the top table.

The musicians ceased playing and Oghma stood up. He smiled broadly and, when he opened his mouth, his voice was deep and sweet, just like honey, and it was almost as if he hypnotised the listeners.

"Welcome, my kith and kin – you are the wind blowing on the sea, the roar of the surf, a dewdrop falling on sunlight."

"I don't know what he's on about," whispered Thomas, "but it sounds good."

Then Oghma went to Áine and bowed low.

"We are here to vote if our Sun Sister can quit the skies to become mortal. Áine, it is you who traces the path of the sun and drums out the rhythm of the moon. Are you sure you wish to leave us for the lifetime of a mere man?"

Áine nodded her head in agreement.

Cairbre the satirist stood up. His face was sharp and his long pointy nose seemed to be constantly twitching at a bad smell in the room.

"You are the flightiest of women. You shine when it pleases you. Nothing in Ireland is as inconstant as the sun!"

"He does have a point," whispered Cassie.

"Do you want to be a flowergirl or not?" hissed Thomas.

"I'm just saying," whispered Cassie quickly.

"Áine's not flighty. She always does as she says," Thomas said out loud. Cairbre spun round and glared, then on seeing it was Thomas who spoke, he burst out laughing.

"So the Sun Goddess has only a mere child to defend her!" he sneered. Áine coloured and a fiery look came into her eye. "That mere child, together with his two sisters," she said indignantly, "defeated Balor in a mighty shapeshifting battle. They are known as the Chingles."

Cairbre grimaced.

"So, hatchet-face, just get your facts straight before you start making accusations," Cassie said vehemently.

They glared at each other across the hall.

Cairbre swivelled on one leg like a crane, closed one eye and held out his arm, pointing at Cassie with his long bony fingers. The whole hall took a sharp intake of breath.

"Oh no, not the poet's curse!" exclaimed Connle, jumping in front of Cassie.

"You and your big mouth!" hissed Thomas to his sister.

Oghma laid his hand on Cairbre's shoulder, causing him to spin round quickly, lose his balance and plummet with a flurry to the floor, his black cloak rising around him like the wings of a bird shot from the sky. Some of the deities began to snigger but the mean expression on Cairbre's face when he picked himself up stopped them dead.

"Cairbre, your weapons are too heavy for the slight offence. Let everyone speak their piece," said Oghma softly.

Then Oghma called the children and Connle forward. Trembling, they went to the centre of the room and held hands.

"Please let Áine marry Jarlath," Cassie began, "because

even though they are totally different, they were made for each other."

"He wouldn't be the first one," quipped a sour Cairbre.

"What do you mean?" asked Cassie sharply.

"Áine has many times taken human form to marry a mortal man. Fifty-seven at my last count."

"So what!" said Cassie though she was a bit taken aback by the number. "Anyway, why should we believe you, you sour old goat?"

"I think you'll find it's only fifty-five," said The Daghda, counting on his fingers uncertainly. "Or is it fifty-eight?"

The children's eyes opened wide. It was still an awful lot of husbands. They looked over at Áine, who was so busy glaring at Cairbre she singed the hairs on the back of his neck.

"That's only one every few centuries if you're as old as time itself," said Connle.

The gods and goddesses nodded in agreement.

"Just because you have a face only a mother could love!" sniped Cassie at Cairbre.

"In truth, I think he is fierce ugly," said a tall, handsome woman.

"That is his mother," whispered Connle.

"So even she doesn't think much of him!" observed Thomas in glee.

"And this Jarlath?" asked The Daghda. "What does he profit by this union? Does he seek worldly powers?"

"Jarlath is from another planet," said Thomas. When the gods looked puzzled he added, "I don't mean that literally, just that he has his head in the clouds." This made them even more confused.

"Jarlath is a mathematician and he likes inventing things," said Cassie. "Like fog-busters."

"He is a conjuror?" asked Brighid, confused.

"He is a maker and a man of numbers," said Connle, "and he seeks not to profit by their union. He believes Áine to be a herbalist and she wishes it to remain so."

"That's what they all say," commented Cairbre, wincing from his singed neck. "Believe me, Áine's dalliances cause trouble."

"Why should we believe you, sourpuss?" said Cassie.

"Blow on that conch shell if you don't," he said, pointing to a large shell like a trumpet that appeared on the crystal table.

Thomas immediately grabbed the shell and obliged. To his amazement a sea mist rolled out of the shell and filled the whole room. A towering figure rose up before them on a jet of foam. He had long rolling hair like the white horses on waves. His eyes were the aquamarine of oceans and he was seated astride a curling wave. They felt his power in the room as a swimmer at the turn of the tide feels the power of the ocean.

Áine went pale. It was none other than her father, Manannán Mac Lir, the God of the Sea.

"Once more my daughter's fancy has caused trouble in my realm," he boomed, his voice like the crash of waves on a stormy night.

"How so?" cried Áine with passion. "Jarlath and I have nothing to do with the sea."

Manannán opened his great hand and seated upon it were the three Merrows, Fand, Mara and Sionna, who smirked and simpered at the assembled company. They were wearing a great deal of pearls and coral and their hair was in more elaborate styles than usual. The children grimaced. As far as Cassie was concerned, these Irish mermaids were troublemakers. They'd tried to lay claim to Jarlath when Balor tossed him in the sea and he'd nearly drowned.

Áine glared at them. "I might have known," she said through gritted teeth.

"If you please, your ladies and lordships, it's quite simple," said Fand the dark-haired Merrow in a voice as sweet and as sickly as sugar. "As you know it's the rule of the sea that we claim every drowning man we rescue. During the battle with Balor, we rescued Jarlath from certain death. So he's ours."

The three Merrows couldn't resist making impudent faces at Áine.

"Yer one – Áine – just came and grabbed him from us, after us going to all that trouble to save him," complained Sionna.

"And not so much as a by-your-leave, the hussy!" Mara joined in, tossing her blonde curls. "Just because the sun shines out of her backside!"

"But if ever Jarlath claps eyes on her crone's face at night, he'll go and drown himself!" jeered Fand.

Áine paled. This was her own worst fear and what she was hoping to avoid by becoming mortal for the duration of Jarlath's life.

"Quiet!" roared Manannán, who quivered with annoyance so that spumes of foam lathered some of those near him.

He addressed the company again.

"My daughter has broken the laws of the sea by claiming this man who by right belongs to the Merrows."

"I'm sure he'd rather blow himself up with one of his own inventions than fall into *their* hands," whispered

Thomas. The Merrows overheard him and flicked their tails at him, covering him in salty spray.

"But this case is different," urged Áine. "He was only in the sea because of a battle between the gods."

"And we don't know if he would have drowned," said Connle. "If the sea hadn't been enchanted, he might have made it to shore."

The Merrows launched into a flurry of objections, cackling like seagulls.

"What's so special about this one?" The Daghda asked them. "There are many more drowned men in the sea."

"We normally get some wrinkly oul' sailor. This one's a beaut," said Mara.

"You just want him because you know he prefers me," said Áine.

"But, daughter, your entanglements with humans are not always wise," tutted Manannán.

"But this Jarlath is a maker of things," argued Oghma. "No doubt a steady man. He wants neither magic nor power."

"That's what they all say," said Cairbre.

"We do not know that he is worthy of Áine," reasoned Brighid. "And she could lose her divinity and end up unhappy."

The Merrows all smirked at each other, pleased that the tide seemed to be turning against Áine.

A sudden sharp ringing sound cut through the clatter of discussion. The Daghda had struck the cauldron with his club.

"Time for us to cast our votes," he said.

Those who supported the match dropped a gold ring into the copper cauldron, those who opposed a pebble. Everyone waited with bated breath as The Daghda counted the votes. He seemed to take forever. Cassie got the impression that though he might be good at many things, maths wasn't one of them.

"Those against the match have one more vote," he pronounced eventually.

The Merrows let out a shrill cry of triumph.

Then a heavy knock at the door cut through the crowing of the Merrows. The hall grew hushed.

"Ah, yes, we still have to wait for Lugh's vote," said Oghma.

A tall, good-looking warrior with golden hair dashed in, carrying his spear. The children recognized him. He was one of the Sean Gaels who was meant to have saved the island from Balor the year before but turned up too late. He was obviously a bad timekeeper.

"I am Lugh of the Long Arm, thanks to my trusty spear!" He held it aloft and the Merrows recoiled. "I am also a builder, a smith, a harper, a warrior, a poet, a historian, a magician, a healer, a cup bearer and a silversmith! I daresay if I put my mind to it I could even be a Merrow."

Everyone laughed around the room except the Merrows and Cairbre, who gave him filthy looks.

"Yes, I am also known as Lugh of the Many Talents!"

"Except the talent to turn up on time," Cairbre cut in sourly. "Quit boasting and just cast your vote."

Lugh dropped a gold ring into the cauldron in favour of Áine marrying Jarlath.

The Daghda shook his head. "It is no use. We are evenly split."

Cassie suddenly had a burning vision of the Swan Maiden trapped behind glass.

"Aren't you forgetting somebody?" she asked timidly.

"Finnen!" Áine cried. "My sister hasn't voted!"

"Oh, we all know how she'd vote!" sniped Mara.

"I would not be too sure," said Manannán Mac Lir. "Finnen is sensible and doesn't approve of her sister's behaviour."

"I fear my father may be right – Finnen may blame me for her disappearance, as I failed to slay Balor in the First Battle of the Skies," cried Áine hotly. "But my heart is torn, as I long to see her. I hope she has forgiven me! And now that Balor is dead, surely she could return to Inish Álainn if we could find her."

"Whatever your feelings, Finnen still has the deciding vote," said Oghma thoughtfully.

"But we don't know where she is," said Áine sadly. "The last news we had of her was Cassie's vision of her hidden among the stars."

"Oh, a very reliable source!" sneered Cairbre.

Cassie thought of her latest nightmare of Finnen trapped behind glass. But she said nothing, fearing Cairbre's ridicule.

"Perhaps Lugh of the Many Talents can think of a solution," said Cairbre nastily.

Lugh raised himself to his full height and he was imposing, even in this company. He seemed to blaze with light.

"I do have a solution!" he cried. "I propose the Chingles find the Goddess Finnen of Glimmering Lake – since she has the casting vote she can decide if Áine can marry Jarlath."

All eyes in the hall turned on Cassie, Thomas and Nancy.

"And if we fail?" asked Thomas in a small voice.

"If you fail we get Jarlath!" gloated Fand.

"But are the young Chingles equal to the task?" worried The Daghda. Thomas was beginning to have the same doubts but bristled at this querying of his talents.

Lugh strode over beside the children and addressed the company. "I should know how hard it is to defeat my grandfather Balor! Don't forget I slew him at the Second Battle of Moytura."

The children looked at him in astonishment. His grandfather!

Lugh turned towards the towering figure of Manannán Mac Lir. "It is for my sake that you imprisoned my grandmother in a glass tower on Tory island – for swearing vengeance on me. It was you who raised me as your own son and Áine is like a sister to me. I appeal to you to accept this bargain."

Thomas and Cassie were now even more open-mouthed. His *grandmother*!

"Imagine both your grandparents being so wicked!" exclaimed Thomas. "You *have* been very unlucky!"

Lugh looked at him kindly, then turned to address the company once more. "Ah but I was lucky in the Chingles! When I and my fellow warriors Sennan and Scáthach turned up too late to save the island, these children took our place and vanquished the resurrected Balor. They are of the stuff of heroes."

The Merrows raised a clamour of objections.

"Be quiet!" roared Manannán. "That is a fair bargain. The children find Finnen, and she will decide if Áine and Jarlath can be wed. Lugh can take over her duties to the sun. If not, Jarlath returns to the sea. We accept." Lugh smiled in agreement.

"They must be mad to let Lugh take over Áine's job!" muttered Cassie in astonishment to Thomas.

"With his timekeeping the sun will be rising in the middle of the night," whispered Thomas.

But Connle and Áine were more concerned about the other part of the bargain. They looked at the children with a mixture of concern and pride. Áine began to speak but Mara jumped in before her.

"We don't think Áine should help them all the time," fumed Mara.

"Áine will be placed under *geas* to behave like a human, which means she cannot use magic to intervene," said The Daghda. "Remember a *geas* is a solemn promise. The punishment will be worse than death if broken!"

"But I can still use my healing powers? Humans have those too," she insisted.

The gods murmured their consent.

"You can use your healing gifts in moderation," The Daghda decreed.

"This waiting period will give you time to consider if you really want once more to be only flesh and blood," added Manannán sternly.

Áine looked at him askance.

"Remember, daughter," he continued more kindly. "You are in an in-between state. Neither human nor godess. It would be wise to stay close to your home. You may need to replenish your energy on your crystal bed."

Áine smiled at him briefly, thankful for his concern, then nodded her head.

"We don't really need Áine's or anyone else's help," said Thomas defiantly, instantly regretting it as Connle threw him an alarmed look.

Cairbre the satirist looked slyly at them. "Oh yes, they are so gifted themselves. What about your fabled shapeshifting powers? Give us a demonstration."

The gods applauded this suggestion.

Cassie and Thomas looked at each other nervously. During their battle with Balor, Thomas had excelled at the magical skill of shapeshifting into different animals. This was thanks to the magic apple given to him by Quert, the spirit warrior tree from the Sacred Grove. He wasn't at all sure he could produce such magic on demand. Cassie and Nancy had also learned the practice but were far less skilful.

"We're very rusty," blurted out Cassie. "We've been away at school all year."

"Chingles, it's action we need, not excuses!" said Brighid irritably.

Cassie blushed red to the roots of her hair and Thomas was white with anxiety. They held hands and closed their eyes under the gaze of the gods.

"*With all the powers that are strange*," intoned Cassie in a small, faltering voice, "*change, Chingles, change!*"

They tried to enter into the soul of their favourite animals. Thomas imagined he was a stag with a magnificent crown of antlers. Cassie tried to feel her way into the leaping grace of the salmon and Nancy held out her arms pretending she was an eagle. But nothing happened.

"Keep breathing in and out," Cassie said in a tremulous voice.

Seconds passed like minutes.

They opened their eyes.

"We can't do it if everybody is looking," Thomas said sheepishly.

"You just can't get decent heroes any more!" said Cairbre scornfully.

The Merrows looked delighted.

"Perhaps they ought to be permitted to try outside," Connle intervened.

The Daghda waved the children away dismissively.

Outside, a great yapping and barking started up among the hounds.

"Now what do we do?" asked Cassie desperately.

But Thomas had drifted away towards the Lia Fáil, the Stone of Destiny.

"Thomas! What are you doing?" cried Cassie impatiently.

Thomas hardly knew. He just found himself drawn to the great stone.

Suddenly, a drop of water splashed onto his forehead. He looked up. The icy water had fallen from the stone. He felt a sudden compulsion to climb it. He circled around it and noticed toeholds and climbing places.

"Come on!" he called to his sisters as he scrambled up the sides.

Cassie and Nancy found themselves following him, almost in a trance.

The children discovered a shallow pool in the broad

flat top of the stone. Their gazes were drawn to the water as if pulled by a magnet.

"*With all the powers that are strange, I'm so annoyed with this blasted lot!*" fumed Cassie, her breath feathering the water.

As the ripples settled, an image floated to the surface.

They saw a glass tower with a figure inside. As Cassie leaned in to get a closer look, the crooked face of an unpleasant-looking woman floated on the water. It was the hag's face of the Corra in Cassie's nightmare. The woman parted her lips in a contemptuous smile, revealing large crooked teeth like fangs. They thought they saw something glint in her mouth as if she had a diamond tooth. Shards of glass flew up from the water. One caught Nancy under the eye and she screamed. Then the glass fell back into the pool and melted like snow. For a moment the children's reflections stared back at them. But they were unpleasantly changed. Cassie had a bull's head, Thomas a donkey's and Nancy a lamb's. The water rippled and their reflections changed to normal. The hounds bayed frantically and tried to climb up to the top of the stone.

Lugh dashed out, closely followed by Áine and

ugh jumped straight up on to the Stone of nd snatched Nancy up in his arms.

"I sawed her," said Nancy, pointing at the water.

Lugh wiped the blood away from under her eye. It was only a nick. Lugh looked into the pool but all he could see was the stone visible through the water.

"She had funny teeth and I screamed and the glass went everywhere," trembled Nancy.

Lugh looked concerned. "You saw my grandmother – Caitlín of the Crooked Teeth – imprisoned in the Tower of Glass. She must have shattered the glass and broken the spell!"

The children gasped in horror.

Áine and Connle helped them down from the stone as more gods and goddesses came out to see what all the fuss was about, including The Daghda who still held his goblet in his hand.

"Caitlín has shattered her glass tower!" Lugh exclaimed.

"This is a disaster!" roared The Daghda and the gods and goddesses erupted into a flurry of chatter and speculation like a flock of noisy starlings.

Cassie was feeling decidedly strange among the clamour. Something was happening to their appearance. Thomas's ears seemed to have grown rather like a donkey's. Cassie was alarmed to find she had a tail. And Nancy's hair was curling into lamb fleece.

Oghma joined them.

"Could somebody please explain to us what is going on!" bellowed Cassie in an alarmingly deep voice.

Everyone fell silent.

"Caitlín of the Crooked Teeth vowed vengeance on Lugh after he defeated Balor in battle," explained Oghma, "so we imprisoned her on Tory Island, placing a spell on her that she could never escape from the Glass Tower."

"But why is she appearing to us?" gasped Cassie. "Have we broken the spell?"

"There was obviously a flaw in our magic," said Oghma. "We did not foresee that she would wish to have vengeance on anyone else. That Balor would return and you would kill him. The spell protects Lugh and us only. Her appearance bodes ill."

"So she is going to try to kill us now?" Thomas asked, his voice quavering in fear.

"We do not know that yet," said The Daghda. "Hers is a bitter and twisted nature but she may not yet have the strength."

"That's why we've had all those accidents with glass and mirrors," said Cassie. "It's her, the Corra with the hag's face. I've seen her shadow in my vision." Cassie described her nightmare of the Swan Maiden trapped behind glass.

"Caitlín takes the shape of the Corra in her monster state," confirmed Lugh. "She may intend to capture or kill Finnen, who disappeared before Caitlín's imprisonment and so was not protected by the spell."

"Perhaps Finnen is summoning you to rescue her," said The Daghda, looking at Cassie as if she had two heads.

Cassie caught sight of her reflection in the gold goblet that he held. At first she thought she looked freakish because of the curved reflection in the goblet. But then she saw the look of horror on Thomas's face. She had distinct bull's horns and alarmingly had grown a bull's tail. That's why The Daghda had given her a funny look.

Caitlín had put a spell on them, making them change shape without wanting to.

Lugh looked at them with concern. "I fear she has already tried to capture their souls," he said to The Daghda. "Now that she is seeking vengeance, their task of finding Finnen will be doubly difficult. We need to prepare them to face her. We of the Sean Gaels owe them a debt."

The Daghda, Oghma and Manannán Mac Lir, who seemed to be the senior gods, went into a huddle and had a whispered discussion.

"Chingles, you will need greater powers to defeat Caitlín. To help you in your task we permit Scáthach to teach you battle craft and Sennan cunning and mastery of druid skills," pronounced The Daghda.

"But how will we know if they are real heroes if the Sean Gaels are always going to their rescue?" argued Fand querulously.

"We permit them to have only so many days' instruction," ruled The Daghda. He counted on his fingers uncertainly. "Eh, five times they can meet." But he held up six and then seven fingers.

He really had terrible maths. Cassie was about to correct him but Thomas shot her a warning look.

"With Lugh they can only have limited contact for his own protection," pronounced Oghma.

Lugh protested at this but The Daghda overruled him.

"If Caitlín comes looking for the Chingles and he is with them, Lugh's presence will only enrage her further and make it worse for them," he said. "I fear she has already escaped. If so, Lugh must go to Tory Island to cleanse it of her evil magic."

"We also permit the Chingles to have the use of the Crane Bag," added Manannán Mac Lir. "It is still in your keeping, Lugh?"

Lugh nodded and waved his hand through the air. The Crane Bag appeared out of nowhere and hung in the air. It was a wrinkled old hide and shook like a bag of old bones.

Thomas peeked inside it. It was indeed full of old bones and scraps of metal. He couldn't imagine it would be much use.

Then it disappeared into thin air.

The Merrows splashed foam at the children. In annoyance, Thomas picked up the conch shell, blew into it and in a moment Manannán, Merrows, foam and sea mist were all sucked back into the shell.

The hall erupted into a buzz of discussions.

But Áine came to the Chingles and said, "Children, we must be away."

"But what about our weird shapes?" asked Cassie in alarm.

"There is no time and only you yourselves can remedy the problem," Áine said.

"But Jarlath will have a fit!" said Thomas slyly.

Áine looked stricken. "I cannot change what has come to pass."

Before they left, the gods and goddesses of the Tuatha Dé Danann gathered around the Chingles.

"We bless you on your latest task. Seek help from the sacred trees," said Brighid. "And fear mirrors."

"And I will give you the gift to understand other dwellers in the Otherworld," said Oghma, handing Cassie a ring. "Here the Tuatha Dé Danann are under my rule to communicate with you in your own tongue and I have given them the gift. But not all the folk you encounter in the Otherworld will be so obliging or so blessed." The ring was a Celtic knot studded with stones, the colours of the rainbow. "It can also summon the Sean Gaels in an emergency," he added. "Blow on it when you need its help."

All went quiet in the Great Hall. Áine covered the Chingles with her cloak, which was as light as gossamer silk yet as dark as deepest night. The light was snuffed out.

They found themselves back outside Áine's cottage.

All was peaceful. Granny Clíona had managed to baby-sit the saplings successfully – they were all asleep.

"Let's get you home," said Connle. "I'd better stay here and keep an eye on the saplings. Can you leave

Granny Clíona here for a while? I could do with her help."

He whistled and Derry the Donkey trotted up to the cottage. He nuzzled Thomas when he saw his ears.

When the children were settled on Derry's back, Connle slapped him on the rump and waved them goodbye. They set off back towards Jarlath's house.

"Let's hope it all goes to plan," said Cassie, crossing her fingers. "I really want Jarlath and Áine to get married so I can be a flowergirl."

"But I'd rather die than be a pageboy," said Thomas.

"With Caitlín out for our blood, you might just get your wish," mumbled Cassie.

But a steady drone interrupted the children's talk. They shuddered, fearful that Caitlín was already on their trail.

CHAPTER 3

There was a sudden rush of air that blew their clothing hard against their bodies, as the low drone drummed in their ears. But the sound was familiar.

"It's a helicopter," said Thomas. To their alarm they realised that it was about to land on the sacred ground of the fairies. There was a sudden eclipse of the sun as the moon passed over it, leaving a thin sliver of silver light like a fingernail in a darkening sky. The helicopter's beam circled menacingly around the house as if trying to prod them out of their hiding place.

Smelling danger, the children's new animal natures came to the fore and all their senses went on high alert. Panting with fear, they dropped off Derry's back on to all fours and scampered behind the hedges. Derry ran off to a neighbouring field. The scummy water of the damp ditch seeped through the children's clothing. But they crouched into the ground as the helicopter's powerful searchlight combed the countryside.

"What's going on?" they heard their Uncle Jarlath shout. "Children, where are you?"

The noise was deafening to their keener animal hearing.

They heard their Uncle Jarlath run over towards the helicopter. Through a gap in the hedge, Cassie watched nervously as the helicopter door panel swung open. Two men dressed in stiff black suits with walkie-talkies jumped out. She stifled a cry. They looked like bouncers or the secret servicemen that she'd seen on television – the type that guarded American presidents.

"You have to carry me," they heard a boy say in a high-pitched whine. He had an American accent.

A terrifying man with a buzz haircut turned back towards the helicopter and hoisted a gangly, pinched-faced boy in a snow-white tracksuit over his shoulder.

The children looked at each other, mystified.

The boy was about Cassie's age. "Be careful now," they heard him moan. "Don't get any dirt on my clothes!"

"What on earth!" exclaimed Jarlath, obviously equally mystified.

Ignoring his high-pitched squeals, the bouncer dumped the boy on the grass.

"It's all wet," the boy yelled in a shrill voice. "I'll sue you if I get grass stains on my trainers!" He took out a mirror and regarded his face. His hair was so gelled it looked glued to his head.

The heavies turned to help a good-looking woman dressed in an old-fashioned nanny's uniform out of the helicopter.

"Why, Angel!" Jarlath exclaimed in a delighted voice. "What a complete surprise!"

It was their Aunty Angel who the children were very fond of and it was all they could do to stop themselves running to her.

"Didn't you get the letter? Too busy changing the face of mathematics, I suppose," she said in her deep, rich voice.

"I didn't get any letter but it's great to see you," Jarlath said. "But who is this?" He indicated the boy.

The sudden screech of a night owl cut through the air and the children didn't hear the reply.

They watched as the secret servicemen unloaded a number of huge crates and a brand new deluxe motorised scooter from the helicopter and hauled them into the house. Thomas gazed at the scooter with longing. They could hear the boy's high whining voice complaining, "You have to carry me into the house!" But the heavies were too busy and ignored him.

"But where are the children?" asked Angel.

The light was brightening as the sun slipped out from behind the moon but it was still gloomy. The boy stood at the doorway and grabbed a huge torch from one of the heavies. It had a powerful beam like a car's.

"Over there," he said in his nasal voice.

The children were caught peeping over the hedge in the full beam, their freakish heads for all to see. The gangly boy put a hand over his eyes. "Puleeze, can't I go anywhere without some no-mark kids trying to impress me with their lousy theatricals?" he complained.

"Children!" cried Jarlath. "What are you doing out of bed?"

"What's going on?" said Angel, concerned and rushing forward to hug them.

For a brief second, Cassie wanted to slap the boy's bad-tempered face but then his words gave her inspiration. She held up her hands to halt Angel and looked quickly at her brother and sister.

She began to sing off-key:

"*Oh welcome, Aunty Angel and Clean Boy too!*

We've prepared a play especially for you!

I'm Cassie the Bull with a . . ."

She hesitated for a moment. Nancy pulled her tail.

"*With a flicky long tail!*" roared Cassie with more gusto than singing ability. She nudged Thomas.

"*And I'm Thomas the Mule*," he began uncertainly,

"*And I bray without fail!*"

He let out such a thoroughly convincing bray that Derry the Donkey shot out of nowhere to nuzzle him.

Cassie kicked Nancy on the bottom.

"*And I'm a little lamb,*

And I lick your face!" sang Nancy.

She leapt up out of the ditch and jumped up to lick the boy's face. He pushed her off in disgust.

Angel's face lit up and she clapped her hands delightedly. "My children, you are spectacular! You have inherited my acting talent. Okay, the singing needs some work. But the costumes and your physical transformation! Uncanny!"

"Sure they've inherited your acting talent, Angel. As in lack of it!" scoffed the boy. "Just because my pa is the most powerful mogul in Hollywood, I can't even go to the back of beyond without some talentless kids auditioning on the spot."

"These aren't some talentless kids – these are Cassie, Thomas and Nancy," Angel said with dignity, embracing each of them in turn. "This here is Lardon B Hackenbacker the Third. I'm his nanny. We're here to spend some time with you this summer."

Jarlath nearly fell out of his standing. "Well, I guess it's your summerhouse too," he muttered. "But of course it's great to see you!" he added hastily. He gave his sister a hug.

Angel looked mystified. "But the letter explained everything."

"I told you I didn't get any letter. I thought you went out to Hollywood to audition for a film?"

"I didn't get the part so I had to take a job," said Angel. "It's just temporary," she added quickly.

"But you gave up your theatre tour of Europe with the Ham Players in pursuit of a Hollywood career," said Jarlath. "Shame to give up the tour after you'd put so much work into planning it!"

"Oh, the Ham Players promised to send me postcards from each venue," said Angel. "It will be almost as if I was there myself." But she didn't sound convinced.

"I'm cold," interrupted Lardon, sneezing. "This fresh air is setting off my allergies."

Jarlath gave Cassie, Thomas and Nancy a conspiratorial look that echoed their own growing annoyance at the stranger. Then Jarlath did a double take and took in their animal features and their damp and muddy clothes. Before he could say anything, Cassie bustled her brother and sister into the house.

Lardon came into the kitchen with a litany of complaints just as the children were struggling to co-ordinate their animal limbs and climb over his luggage. "I sure hope this dump has central heating," Lardon moaned. "And air-conditioning and satellite TV and . . ."

But the children had bounded ahead up the stairs to their attic bedrooms.

When they took off their damp clothing, Cassie was dismayed to see that her and Nancy's bodies were growing downy hair.

"What are we going to do?" said an alarmed Thomas coming in from his own bedroom and holding up his T-shirt to show them his own hairy belly.

"We'll just have to get into bed and not appear downstairs again tonight," said Cassie. "Hopefully by morning we'll be ourselves again."

They heard Jarlath, Angel and Lardon coming into the hallway and they strained to hear what they were saying.

"I thought you could share a bedroom with Thomas," said Jarlath. "I could make you up a camp bed."

"No way, José, am I sharing anything with those

freakos," Lardon insisted. "Don't you have some barn they could sleep in?"

Their footsteps echoed on the stairs as they climbed to the first floor.

"I want that room there. It has a nice big mirror in it," Lardon said on the first landing.

"But that's Connle's room . . . he's away." Jarlath hesitated. "I mean he might . . ."

"I'm sure he wouldn't mind Lardon using it in the meantime," said Angel. "I'll take the living-room."

"No, you take my room here on the first floor and I'll sleep in the box-room," said Jarlath decisively.

"Thanks," she replied. "It's good if I can be near Lardon. Sometimes he gets bad dreams. Sometimes he thinks aliens –"

"Why don't you just shut your face?" cut in Lardon rudely.

There was an embarrassed silence.

"I'd like to punch him for being rude to Angel!" whispered Thomas. "And, by the way, we never got Connle's razor."

"No," replied Cassie. "But did you notice how Jarlath didn't want to give up Connle's room? That means he hopes he'll come back."

"I don't like this kid," muttered Thomas. "Don't you

think it's suspicious the way he's turned up after last night?"

"But he was coming with Angel. It might be just a coincidence," said Cassie, going into the shared bathroom between the two partitioned bedrooms.

"And he wanted a room with a mirror. Caitlín works through mirrors. I'm going to keep my eye on him," said Thomas darkly, scratching behind his ears.

There was a rustle outside the main bedroom door.

"What are you doing in there?" asked Angel sweetly. They hadn't heard her come up the stairs to the attic.

"Oh, just helping Nancy have a bath," said Cassie casually, running the taps.

"That's not true – we're hiding!" said Nancy.

"*Oh no, we're not!*" said Cassie in a pantomime fashion, glaring at her little sister.

"*Oh yes, we baaah!*" laughed Nancy gleefully.

Angel just laughed and called back, "See you at breakfast!"

As they struggled to get into their pyjamas, they heard the mighty rattle of a tray crashing to the floor and Lardon's voice rising peevishly. "I don't want to stay on stupid Inishawful! What do you mean there are no electrical sockets? Is this the Stone Age? Get on the satellite phone immediately and get my pa to come and rescue me. What do you mean there's no satellite phone? I hate you!"

They heard their Aunty Angel make soothing noises and soon Lardon settled down to a snivelling moan.

"Now, Lardon, remember, sweet dreams tonight. At least there are no aliens on Inish Álainn. I don't want to have to come and rescue you again," she cooed.

"You are absolutely not *never ever* to come into my room again. Even if I ask you. In fact even if I beg you!" shouted Lardon.

"Have it your way," said Angel, closing the door behind her. "And don't spend too much time talking in the mirror."

Thomas's ears pricked up. Why would Lardon talk in the mirror?

"He's quite the most spoiled child I have ever come across," said Cassie as they brushed their teeth.

"Lardass B Hackenbummer the urd!" brayed Thomas.

Cassie sniggered.

"But seriously," Thomas continued, "I'm worried. Angel told him not to talk into the mirror. He could be an enemy communicating with Caitlín. "

They tiptoed downstairs and listened outside Lardon's door. They got a fright when they heard a muffled conversation.

"He's got someone in the room with him," whispered Cassie hoarsely. They strained their ears.

"You tell me," said Lardon in a tough-sounding voice. "It's your move."

Then a high-pitched woman's voice. "Here's looking at you, kid!"

"He's talking to Caitlín!" said Thomas. "He's here to spy on us!"

"I don't know," Cassie said worriedly, "but he is talking weirdly."

"I think we should interrogate him," said Thomas.

"But maybe we shouldn't reveal that we know who he is," said Cassie. "And then we can give him false information."

"Angel said he's afraid of aliens," said Thomas wickedly. "Let's give him the fright of his life."

Nancy had already fallen asleep. Trying not to wake her, Cassie and Thomas covered themselves with sheets and then listened to make sure Angel and Jarlath had gone to bed.

"We look more like ghosts than aliens," whispered Cassie.

"Let's pretend to be the ghosts of aliens!" Thomas replied.

They tiptoed down the stairs to Lardon's room and

realised that the door was off the latch. Thomas gave it the faintest push. Through the widened crack they saw him facing the mirror with his back to the door, wearing a pair of sparkling white silk pyjamas. They were puzzled to hear munching sounds and a pleasant, familiar smell. And then in the mirror they saw he was stuffing his face with two chocolate bars at a time.

They waited a beat and then leapt through the door, Thomas making a low hum that he hoped sounded like an alien growl.

Lardon turned around, horrified. "Oo r ooh," he stammered, his mouth full of chocolate. But then he turned back around and watched them through the mirror as if he wasn't bothered.

Irritated, Thomas unhooked the mirror from the wall.

"We are the ghosts of aliens," he sniggered, trying to speak in a computerised voice through his mule's teeth. "Stay quiet. We wish to question you. If you don't co-operate we will break this mirror."

Lardon froze and they led him to the bed where he meekly sat down. "Don't touch me," he pleaded in a small voice. "I don't want to get my hair mussed up."

Thomas noticed something glinting in Lardon's mouth.

"Smile," he commanded.

Lardon painfully bared his teeth in a grin. A diamond glinted in one of his teeth.

"Why, human child, do you have a diamond tooth?" he asked in his robotic voice.

"It costs a lot of money and looks kind of neat," Lardon muttered.

"I think it looks kind of stupid," Thomas sniggered, sounding more like a donkey than a robot. He looked significantly at Cassie. They'd noticed something glinting in Caitlín's mouth.

Cassie rummaged around the room looking for Connle's old-fashioned razor, which was difficult because the room was now bursting with Lardon's possessions. There were about fifty identical gleaming white tracksuits hanging in the wardrobe and the same number of brand new pairs of trainers still in their boxes piled up around the room. The top of the chest of drawers was crammed with expensive-looking bottles of hair gels and creams. Cassie clumsily reached up to examine them.

"Be careful with my things," said Lardon peevishly.

Just then, Cassie accidentally knocked over a bottle of hair gel that oozed down onto a pair of trainers.

"Oh no!" Lardon was nearly in tears. "I need to have

a new pair for every day and now I might have to wear the same pair twice!"

Cassie, who thought herself lucky to have one new pair of trainers, ignored him and continued searching. She eventually found what she was looking for under the bed – Connle's old-fashioned cutthroat razor was in a shoebox that contained his few possessions.

"What kind of stupid name is Lardon anyway?" asked Thomas.

"It's French. I'm named after my dad and grandfather and my mother thought it was kind of cute."

Thomas giggled and picked up a face cream labelled, "*Zit-zapper*". He toyed with it then held it over a gleaming day-glo tracksuit in a threatening manner.

"Please don't mess it up, I'll give you anything," moaned Lardon, his diamond tooth glinting. He suddenly became animated. "A part in a horror film – you got it! Your own sci-fi series, it's yours, aliens! The ghosts of aliens is a neat idea. You can have twenty per cent of the gross. OK, thirty per cent. You're killing me – ninety per cent! But that's my final offer. It's not worth staying alive for any less."

"Who is your mistress?" intoned Thomas with all the menace he could muster, which wasn't very much considering his mule state.

"*Lardon!*" came a voice. "Please go to sleep this instant!" It was Aunty Angel.

The children froze.

"If you don't stop your playacting, I'll confiscate those chocolate bars you think I don't know about. Or I would if I was allowed in your room!" continued Angel.

"You've got to come and rescue me!" he whimpered. "I'm being held captive by two freakoids who think they're alien ghosts."

"Now, Lardon, you told me earlier I wasn't to come in even if you begged me. Go to sleep!"

"I *am* begging you!" he pleaded. "'*Elp, eh!*" He groaned as Cassie placed a hoof over his mouth.

"That's better," said Angel. "And no more dreams."

They heard Angel's footsteps retreat. Cassie casually spilled some more gel on another pair of trainers. Lardon started snivelling. She whispered in his ear: "If you rat on us, we'll ruin every last thing you own!"

They left him stupefied on the bed and returned to their own rooms.

Cassie took off the sheet and instantly felt slightly ashamed of herself. If Lardon hadn't been so unpleasant earlier she might have felt sorry for him. He was just a spoiled, pathetic wimp.

And wasn't she behaving like the cheapest kind of bully she hated at school? She caught a glimpse of herself as she brushed her teeth in the mirror and her gaze was caught and held by a cold pair of eyes. Now, she thought, it was her turn to push someone around. But remember what it's like, a little voice reminded her – you don't like it when people pick on you. Her features flickered between her normal appearance and that of a bull as she struggled with her conscience. But what fun it was going to be to tease Lardon! She smiled at herself and left the bathroom, her face more bullish than before.

Thomas also had a flicker of shame as he brushed his teeth. Normally, he was the one who defended the smaller boys against the bullies. Even if Lardon was a creep, he was still a human being. Thomas looked into his own face and saw a grinning mule. No, Lardon deserved it. He was rich and spiteful and didn't deserve to have a deluxe brand-new scooter. Thomas left the bathroom with a feeling of jealousy raging in him.

Neither of them noticed the cold pair of eyes in the mirror glitter in triumph.

CHAPTER 4

Next morning, Cassie looked in the mirror and recoiled to see she was looking more like a bull than ever.

"We are still under Caitlín's enchantment," said Thomas, bounding into the room and playing with his donkey ears. "We ought to get to Áine's as soon as possible to get help."

"Jarlath wants to take us to his workshop this morning, remember? We'll have to find a disguise."

She cast her eyes around the bedroom and noticed the parcel given to her by Granny McColl that she'd forgotten to pass on to Jarlath. She grabbed it and ripped it open.

"Quick, put these on!" she told the others. They were the peculiar-looking hats that their granny had made for Jarlath.

Nancy pulled on a bizarrely shaped, striped balaclava in purple and mustard wool. Cassie had to adjust it around the right way so she could see out through the eye-sockets and there was a breathing hole for her mouth. It was such a lumpy design that it didn't matter that Nancy's lamb's ears poked up.

Thomas's jester's hat luckily had two big floppy ears with bells on the end that went over his donkey ears. Cassie found a large round hat like a turban in day-glo orange and green that concealed her bull's horns. She wrapped her bull's tail around her like a belt.

They trooped down to breakfast wearing the peculiar hats. Jarlath seemed to be in a better mood after some sleep.

"The hats are, eh, interesting," said Jarlath, suppressing a laugh. He opened a drawer in the hallway with numerous hats inside. "I'll add them to my collection when you're bored with them. I did once like them, when I was about Nancy's age. I'm too old for them now but your gran thinks I'm still about four years old."

"We love them," said Cassie stoutly, "and we're going to keep them on all day."

Jarlath just shook his head. To their relief there was no sign of Lardon.

Outside, the sun burned through the early morning mist that frequently shrouded the island. Cassie and Thomas cycled to the workshop while Nancy travelled sitting on Jarlath's handlebars.

Cassie and Thomas careened ahead along the narrow lanes called boreens that criss-crossed the island.

"I've been trying to think what to do about our heads," Cassie said as they stopped to wait for Jarlath to catch up. She was about to say something else when she heard a strange, strangled cry and the nervous head of a white woolly llama popped up over the hill ahead of them. Beside it appeared an angora rabbit whose fur looked rather crestfallen in the morning damp. It was Mrs Moriarty the knitter taking her newest pets for a walk. She was munching a potato cake while holding their reins in one hand. A hungry Thomas fixated on the food with the intensity of a starving animal.

"What lovely hats!" Mrs Moriarty exclaimed. "I'd love to sell those in my craft shop."

"Thank you," preened Cassie.

"Could I try one on?"

"No," Cassie replied quickly. "We all have colds and nits and Jarlath told us to wrap up warm."

Thomas obliged with a massive fake sneeze that turned alarmingly into a bray and scratched his head. The nervous llama jumped and the even more nervous rabbit tried to run away.

Mrs Moriarty looked so genuinely upset it gave Cassie a guilty conscience.

"We've got loads more," she said kindly. "We'll bring you some soon." Moments later they were joined by Jarlath with Nancy on the handlebars. Mrs Moriarty regarded Jarlath with a pained expression of sympathy.

"I've got some good lotion for their hair if you want," she said meaningfully, signalling and scratching her head.

Jarlath looked at her as if she was nuts. He muttered goodbye and set off at a cracking pace.

In no time at all they were at the bottom of the meadow where Jarlath's workshop lay. It was a large barn painted a fiery red. It was crammed with all manner of mechanical equipment. There were lathes, hammers, Bunsen burners and a freestanding drawing-board covered in plans and diagrams. Huge old-fashioned blackboards covered every inch of available wall space. One side was covered in a very long equation written in white indelible ink, another one of Jarlath's inventions The other was covered with mechanical drawings, diagrams and calculations. Cassie peered at the drawings.

Laid out in a line in one corner of the barn were some large balls together with some short boards. There was a harness hanging from the rafters, several huge cylinders lined up and curiously shaped pipes. The children assumed all this weird equipment had something to do with Jarleth's latest crackpot invention.

"So, children, would you like to help me in pushing forward the frontiers of science?" said Jarlath with enthusiasm.

"*Yay!*" hollered Nancy and Thomas. But Cassie gave him a cautious look. She was worried about the risk of them exposing their alarming animal features.

But there was no stopping Thomas and Nancy, who followed Jarlath over to the balls and the short boards.

"Now, children," Jarlath waved at Cassie to join them, "I'm going to teach you how to use your centre of gravity."

Cassie thought this sounded innocent enough so she joined the others. Jarlath instructed them to each place a short board on top of a ball, while he did the same.

Jarlath stood up on his board and balanced on the ball. He'd obviously been practising and was quite good at it. He adjusted his stance on the board as if he was surfing on dry land.

"Your body instinctively finds balance," he said. "Your sense of gravity is built into your joints, tendons and muscles."

"What's gravy got to do with it?" Thomas asked.

"It's gravity, you moron, not gravy!" Cassie looked all superior.

Thomas hated when his older sister showed off just because she was a year older than him. He picked up the board and would have whacked her on the backside if Jarlath hadn't intervened.

"Thomas, no more of that," warned Jarlath. "Go on, Cassie, explain gravity."

"There's this big magnet at the centre of the earth and it's what keeps us from falling off. It's why we don't fly away into space," she pronounced.

"Nearly right, Cassie," Jarlath said. "It's the attraction of objects to a large mass and, yes, it's what stops us from falling off the earth. But let's get you all started." He helped Thomas back onto his board.

Nancy, despite her age, was having no trouble at all keeping her balance.

"Try pressing down on your toes to tip yourself back," urged Jarlath as Thomas crashed to the floor.

His T-shirt rode up as he fell and Cassie was alarmed to see that his belly was now very hairy. She quickly staged a crash-landing and joined him on the floor.

"Keep your T-shirt tucked into your trousers!" she hissed.

Thomas did as he was told but was surprised to feel his belly covered in coarse donkey hairs. Luckily Jarlath didn't notice because he was too busy talking to a delighted Nancy who was enjoying balancing on the ball.

"This is just a stupid game," complained Thomas, fed up of toppling off. "So much for advancing the cause of science!"

"It's advancing flying," said Jarlath.

Cassie gave him a pitying look. "The balls and boards don't actually leave the ground, Jarlath," she said in a slow voice as if talking to an idiot.

"But I'm talking about a personal flying-machine with knobs on!" exclaimed Jarlath, leaping over towards the harness.

"What? Like a bicycle that can fly or something?" said Thomas, suddenly interested. "Cool."

"Better than that," said Jarlath, climbing up a small ladder at the side of a large, circular steel container. He indicated to Thomas to follow him up the ladder and for Cassie to climb up the one on the other side.

The container was almost full of water. Floating on it was a ramshackle craft consisting of a metal platform balanced on a large doughnut-shaped lifebuoy. Jarlath leapt aboard.

"Is that it?" asked Cassie in a disbelieving voice.

"It's just a rubber dinghy with a metal frame on top," said Thomas, disappointed.

"It may not be much to look at but this is the revolutionary 'Flying Marine' – a vehicle that can not only fly but travel on water," Jarlath said defensively.

"But why are we learning balancing tricks?" asked Cassie.

"Because you'll need body control to fly my craft," explained Jarlath. "To travel in the air, you'll need to learn to lean in the direction that you want to go."

"Just like on a bicycle," said Thomas, willing to try again. He got down from the container and once more mounted a board.

Nancy was a natural on the board, as nimble as a gymnast. She beamed with pleasure as she jiggled from one foot to the other, pressing down her toes to tip herself back and pushing down her heels to swing herself forward.

Soon Thomas was also looking confident. Cassie was

having a harder time staying on the board. But just as she was about to give up, she suddenly managed it. Without thinking, her body tried to balance. It was like walking on a tightrope, surfing on the sea or indeed riding a bicycle. First you had to really, really concentrate but once you got the hang of it, it began to come naturally.

As she jumped to the floor, Cassie felt her shirt flopping around her bottom.

"That's a very odd belt," said Jarlath, who came over to help her up. She caught her reflection in the steel container. It was her bull's tail. She tucked it hastily around her waist. Oh dear! The bewitchment wasn't wearing off at all.

"It's all the rage in Croydon," she bluffed.

"Yes, that centre of the fashion universe," said Jarlath wryly.

"We're turning into animals," said Nancy. "My tummy is all furry. But I can't show you because it's a big secret."

Cassie glared at her little sister and bounded over to the freestanding drawing-board. "This looks amazing," she said excitedly. "Quick! Come and tell us all about it!" She was banking on Jarlath having a one-track mind and she wasn't wrong.

He joined her at the board and showed them illustrations of stick men standing on air jets. Then he led them to the centre of the barn.

"I am now going to demonstrate the principle of flying on a stream of air," he announced.

A safety harness hung from two beams in the rafters. Below it, a rectangle of wood, like a surfboard with straps for feet, rested on a wooden table that had two holes cut out in its top. Through the holes protruded the nozzles of two air-hoses, which were connected to air cylinders underneath the table.

Jarlath climbed onto the table and slapped his feet into the surfboard contraption. Then he strapped himself into the safety harness. He told Thomas to press a button in a switchboard on the wall and immediately an automatic pulley hoisted him into the air. He dangled from the beams of the rafters, several metres above the table with the air hoses – like a parachutist caught in a tree.

"Stand well back, Nancy," he commanded. She scampered over to the big container. Jarlath told Cassie and Thomas to position themselves by the table with the air cylinders, which he explained would create a jet of air that would lift the board into the air.

"Switch them on when I give you the word," he

instructed them. When they were in position, he shouted, "Release the air!"

Soon, air hissed up the hoses and the wooden table shook and vibrated.

To the children's amazement Jarlath rose high up into the rafters of the barn, nearly banging his head off the roof.

The ropes of the safety harness were dangling slack. Twin currents of air were shooting up from the wooden box and supporting Jarlath!

"*Eureka!*" exulted Jarlath, dancing on the spot. "It's working!"

"You really are standing on air!" squealed Thomas excitedly.

But then there was a big belch and Jarlath dropped down taut in the harness. The air stream had died and Jarlath was once more relying on the ropes to support his weight. He rubbed his eyes as he dangled several metres above the table.

"Get me down," he said. "I'm feeling light-headed. I keep thinking Nancy has a lamb's head." He laughed.

Cassie saw her sister reflected in the smooth steel of the big container. A magnified Nancy, distorted like in a fairground mirror, loomed back at her. Nancy had wrenched off her balaclava and was scratching her woolly head. Cassie leapt over and, grabbing the balaclava from Nancy's hand, jammed it back on to her head.

Cassie surveyed her brother and sister. There was no doubt their animal shapes were becoming more pronounced. She had to do something fast.

"You'd better press the button, Cassie, and let me down," said Jarlath, sounding very disappointed.

Cassie went over to the switchboard for the automatic pulley. "It's not working," she said.

Thomas bounded eagerly over to the board but Cassie pinched him hard on the arm.

"I'll do it," she insisted, trying to disguise her alarmingly deep voice. "No, it's not working, Jarlath! We can't get you down!"

"No problem," he said, reaching for the harness catch. "I'll jump it."

"Oh, no! Don't jump!" boomed Cassie. "You'll hit the table beneath you and hurt yourself! We'll go and get help!"

"Cassie, what's wrong with your voice?" asked Jarlath. But then he was distracted by the fact he couldn't open the harness catch. "This is jammed! I can't open it!"

Snorting with relief, Cassie bundled her brother and sister outside before Jarlath had time to react.

"We're due to have lunch at Prendergast's teashop with Lardon and Angel," shouted Jarlath after them. "Get someone to fetch the Mulally twins!"

Outside, Thomas turned on Cassie and even Nancy tried to kick her on the shins.

"What's all this about?" shouted Thomas.

Cassie held them off. "Have a look at your belly, Thomas – and, Nancy, look at your legs."

Thomas now had coarse brown and white hairs like a donkey. Nancy's legs had tight little white curls, like a lamb's. Cassie swung her bull's tail around and showed them her brown hairy stomach.

"We're half human and half animal!" exclaimed Thomas, munching on a bush. "So that's why we've left Jarlath hanging in the barn!"

"He'll just have to stay there until we're normal children again," said Cassie.

"He'll be waiting a long time," said Thomas, sagely.

"We'll have to use up one of the sessions with the Sean Gaels right now," said Cassie.

"But I want to eat now, I'm hungry," Thomas said stubbornly.

"So am I. Race you, freak heads!" shouted Cassie, all

thought of Jarlath, their own startling transformations – and their bicycles – out of her mind.

They scrambled on all fours past the dry stone walls that edged the fields on the island and each discovered they felt more comfortable that way.

They moved quickly, as they were now part animal, but they were cautious about encountering people. They ducked behind a big bush when they saw Donnacha the bodhrán-maker approaching. He was trying out a new bodhrán – a drum made of goatskin.

"All these loud noises are making me hallucinate," they heard him say as he passed on.

As they came in sight of Mulallys' pub, they took the fork to the teashop instead.

The bright yellow exterior of the teashop loomed ahead of them and the smell of baking carried on the wind.

The teashop was empty. When they got to the front door they soon realised why. A big sign decorated with skull and crossbones read:

"*No dirty boots*,

No backpacks,

No children under three,

No picky eaters,

No men with moustaches,

No smart alec twins (called Mulally),

No animals,

No fiddlers,

No bodhráns,

No people with peculiar headgear."

Despite being excluded on at least three counts, the children barged in.

"I'll be with you in a moment," called Mrs Prendergast in a tight little voice from the kitchen. "Typical – no patience!"

"Can we see a menu, please? We'd like to buy some cakes," said Cassie politely. Her voice was almost as deep as a man's.

"You don't have a moustache, do you?" called out Mrs Prendergast suspiciously. "It's plain bread and butter or nothing. I've had one grand customer, a nice clean American boy with his nanny, who's eaten my whole menu. You could tell he came from money, not like some of the ragged, hooligan children who come to this island. And he left me a tip!"

"That would be Lardon," muttered Thomas.

"Just as well we missed them," said Cassie.

"I could eat a horse!" Thomas brayed.

"I hope there are no animals with you!" shouted Mrs Prendergast.

"What about *those* cakes?" asked Cassie as she leapt towards a display cabinet filled with luscious cream cakes and buns, knocking several chairs out of the way.

"You sound like a bull in a china shop!" roared Mrs Prendergast. She glared out at them through a serving hatch. But luckily she was wearing big thick glasses like the bottoms of jam-jars and couldn't make the children out clearly.

"Cakes," demanded Cassie. "We want cakes."

"Those are afternoon cakes. It's still lunchtime and too early for afternoon tea," Mrs Prendergast pronounced firmly.

Nancy started to baah.

"Is that child under three?" Mrs Prendergast asked.

"I'm a quarter to four," said Nancy.

"She's nearly four," said Cassie. "We'll be happy with bread and butter."

Mrs Prendergast harrumphed.

As they waited, the children found it difficult to control their appetites. Each table held a little vase with daisies and, before he knew he was doing it, Thomas was munching on the flowers. Nancy went to the window and grazed among the ornamental grasses in the planter pots. Unable to control herself, Cassie charged over to the glass cabinet and broke into the cakes.

They were all stuffing themselves uncontrollably when Mrs Prendergast came out bearing a plate of three tiny fingers of bread and butter, with the crusts cut off.

"Merciful hour!" she exclaimed, dropping the plate to the floor, whereupon Nancy scampered over and scoffed the bread and butter fingers. Mrs Prendergast looked around at the devastation. All her plants had been eaten, tables and chairs were upended and cutlery was strewn all over the floor. Thomas was now chewing her flowery chintz curtains.

"You, you . . . children are worse than animals!" screamed Mrs Prendergast. "Get out of here!" She picked up a sweeping brush and tried to herd them all out with flicks to their bottoms.

Cassie turned and stamped her foot as if to charge but Thomas head-butted his sister out the door. He caught hold of Nancy and pulled her free, just as Mrs Prendergast was about to catch her.

"Run!" he cried.

They ran until they could no longer hear Mrs Prendergast's screams and collapsed in a field of buttercups.

"That was a laugh," grinned Thomas.

"No, it wasn't," said Cassie sternly. "This is getting serious. Maybe when we get the Sean Gaels' help, we'll be all right. Can you remember how to contact them?"

Thomas looked at her blankly. "We'd better get the Mulally twins to tickle Jarlath," he said.

"No, it's to rescue him, silly," mooed Cassie.

The changes were stopping them thinking straight.

They approached Mr Mulally's pub by hiding behind hedges and walls, as if they were crack commandos on a special mission in enemy territory. From behind a hedge at the crossroads they watched Mr Mulally roll out a barrel. Nancy immediately started to gambol towards him.

"Sit down," hissed Cassie. Nancy squirmed and evaded her.

"What was that?" piped up Mr Mulally.

His face lit up when Nancy darted towards him and he scooped her up in a big bear's hug.

"Let me see your lovely face," he said to her.

Nancy shook her head. "Can't! I have a lamb's head."

"Of course you do," laughed Mr Mulally. "So where are your brother and sister?"

Nancy pointed at the hedge.

"Come out," cried Mr Mulally.

"We mustn't let him see our faces," whispered Cassie.

"I know what to do," said Thomas. "It's a game we are playing," he hee-hawed, standing up with his back to Mr Mulally. "We're pretending to be animals and doing everything backwards."

They explained that they had been sent to fetch Macdara and Conán to help rescue Jarlath. Then they were going to go straight home.

The twins set off immediately.

Mr Mulally asked the children in for something to eat but Cassie said they'd already been to Mrs Prendergast's café.

"Why anyone would want to go to Mrs Sourpuss's cafe is beyond me," observed Mr Mulally.

Cassie grabbed Nancy from his arms and pulled her away quickly.

"We have to go now," she said briskly. "See you soon." They trotted away from the pub, leaving Mr Mulally even more bewildered than before.

As they got down the road, Cassie turned on Nancy.

"Silly, stupid, mangy little lamb! I could bite you! Could you please stop telling everyone all our business!"

"But Mummy says to always tell the truth," bleated Nancy.

"Leave her alone. She's just a kid," intervened Thomas.

"I'm a lamb," said Nancy stoutly.

"It's not telling lies to have a secret," explained Thomas kindly. "You see, grown-ups don't always understand. It's our game and our secret." Nancy gave him a hug and Cassie felt really bad about being so mean to her little sister. "Sorry," she grunted.

They continued back up the main road. At the fork to the boreen to Glimmering Lake they got a shock to see Muiris the postmaster pedalling hard up the road. They immediately turned on their heels like inelegant ballet dancers.

"Thomas, Cassie, Nancy!" he called out breathlessly.

They stood still, their backs to him, like statues.

"Don't turn round," instructed Cassie.

Muiris pulled up alongside them. "I'm glad I caught you! I've got this letter for Jarlath and a postcard for Nancy and Angel."

Nancy got very excited. "That's for me!" she exclaimed. She was about to put her hoof out for the letter but Cassie quickly linked her by the arm.

"Could you just put them in my pocket?" Cassie bellowed. "We're playing a game where we have to do things backwards and we're not allowed touch anything."

"And we're animals," Nancy bleated. "I'm a lamb, Cassie's a bull and Thomas is a donkey!"

Muiris just laughed and did as he was asked.

"Nancy wants to go to the toilet," Cassie said. She was finding lying easier and easier. "We must hurry."

"No, I don't," said Nancy.

Cassie glared at her little sister.

"Right so," said Muiris.

"We have to go," gasped Cassie in her new deep voice and pulled her little sister roughly along the boreen that led to Glimmering Lake, Thomas trotting beside them. "Nancy is about to wet her knickers!" she called back.

"I am not," wriggled Nancy.

"Come and see Róisín and myself soon," Muiris called after them, getting back on his bike.

But when Thomas looked back, he was still staring after them.

"Do you think he saw through our disguises?" he asked, alarmed.

"If he did it's stupid Nancy's fault!" said Cassie.

Nancy began to bleat.

"Just leave her alone!" brayed Thomas. "Pick on someone your own size!" Cassie snorted through her nostrils and would have head-butted Thomas if he hadn't already run off.

When they got to Glimmering Lake, they drank greedily from the water, lapping it up with their tongues. They looked around cautiously and quickly took off their hats to check their reflections in the smooth surface of the lake. Nancy's head was still completely lamb-like. Thomas had the buckteeth and flaring nostrils of a mule but was otherwise recognisably Thomas. Cassie surprisingly had three horns and the turned-up nose of a bull.

If standing on two legs, they passed for human, but up close they looked like laboratory experiments that had gone wrong.

"Right," said Thomas. "We've got to summon the Sean Gaels."

"But how?" Cassie just couldn't remember. An image of a bull's nose with a ring through it floated through her mind. "Do we have to go to a bullring?" she asked.

"The ring!" said Thomas. "Oghma's ring, stupid!"

So Cassie blew on Oghma's ring, which luckily she was wearing. For a moment the multicoloured inlaid stones glistened and pulsed but nothing happened.

The Chingles stood for a few minutes.

"Let's go home," Thomas shrugged. "You just can't rely on those Sean Gaels."

Just as they were about to leave, a glint of gold flashed in the water. Cassie thought it looked like the reflection of a fiery sunset in the lake. But it was still only the afternoon. Then she felt an intense heat on her cheeks, like standing too near a fire. She looked up and fell back, amazed, clutching her brother and sister.

"Wow!" said Thomas.

They stood back in awe. A ball of flickering gold and blue flames hovered over the enchanted waters of the lake. Around it the three Sean Gaels – Lugh, Scáthach and Sennan – stood on the water.

"Stay," commanded Scáthach in her low, husky voice as the three warriors strode across the water and joined the children by the lapping waves of the shore.

Scáthach ran her hands over their heads and felt their hooves and Cassie's tail. "You must walk around the cleansing fire three times."

The children felt compelled to obey but an equally strong urge to escape.

"Brighid has sent you this fire," said Sennan. He looked at them kindly. "The cleansing power of flames often banishes enchantment." He held out his hand to Thomas.

Scáthach led Cassie and Lugh carried Nancy. But suddenly, each child refused to co-operate. Thomas dug his heels in and wouldn't budge, Nancy struggled in Lugh's arms and Cassie roared and nearly pulled Scáthach's arm out of its socket.

"Come now, children, do not refuse your own good," Lugh insisted. He looked levelly at each of them and it was as if a blaze of light seared into their brains.

Transfixed, the children allowed themselves to be led by the Sean Gaels to the blazing fire. They all walked over the water and then, as they approached the ball of flames, rose in the air.

"I hope they won't chuck us in," quaked Cassie.

Sennan bid them circle the fire three times, in a clockwise direction. They did so, holding the Sean Gaels' hands, their limbs feeling like lead, their cheeks burning from the fire.

But Cassie also felt as if her cheeks were burning from embarrassment. Her feelings churned and boiled. Images of her behaviour in the last day floated through her mind, her ruining Lardon's trainers, her lying to Jarlath. Thomas likewise felt Lardon's loneliness, Mrs Prendergast's shock, Jarlath's discomfort. It was the burning sensation of shame in each of their minds that hurt the children most of all.

"Gaze into Glimmering Lake to see what lies within," said Scáthach in her rasping voice.

They circled round it, hovering in the air. The lake's surface was as smooth and unforgiving as a mirror.

"Cassie, you have second sight," said Sennan. "Behold your reflection and see if your sight can become insight."

Cassie looked at her reflection in the water. Her own face with bull-like features gazed back at her. She grew angry at the stupid trick Caitlín was playing on her. And as she gazed, her face became even more like a bull's. She breathed heavily out of her upturned nostrils and ruffled the water with her snorts.

"See what happens when you get angry," said Sennan patiently.

Cassie looked into her own eyes.

I am angry as a bull, she thought. She remembered all the times she had been angry in the last day, at Mrs Prendergast's teashop, with Thomas and Nancy and the insufferable Lardon. She felt annoyed at herself now and somewhat ashamed of her hasty temper. To her amazement, her face became less bull-like.

"Since Tara, every time I get angry I grow more like a bull," she said. It was as if a light had gone on in her head.

"It is Caitlín's enchantment. She has put a spell on you to bring out the worst in your nature. She has a spiteful sense of humour and so it takes physical form," said Scáthach.

Cassie felt embarrassed. "I guess my bad temper puts me in Caitlín's power. I'm not going to make it so easy for her again."

Thomas tweaked her arm and smirked at her. Cassie felt a flash of annoyance but then she swallowed her anger.

Scáthach smiled at her. "You are learning. Look into the water," she said.

Cassie was pleased to see that she had lost her bull features. She felt for her tail but it had gone.

"Each time I control my temper I am more like a human being than a bull," she realised.

"By facing the truth about yourself you are turning Caitlín's enchantment to your own advantage," agreed Lugh.

Next it was Thomas's turn to glance into the truth-telling waters. But he stuck out the lip on his lower jaw.

"Don't want to," he said sullenly.

"Don't be such an ass!" scolded Cassie.

"Surely you are not afraid," said Sennan. "Your sister had the courage to look within. Follow her example."

"No chance," said Thomas even more mutinously. So the Sean Gaels ignored him and continued to hover. When he thought they weren't minding him, Thomas stole a look. He saw his stupid ears, big yellow teeth and mule's face. He looked weird and ugly.

"Are you seeing beyond the surface?" asked Sennan.

A red mist clouded Thomas's brain. He felt stubborn and annoyed at people always bossing him about. "I really, really don't like being told what to do!" he mumbled vehemently through gritted teeth

"Even when it's for your own advantage?" asked Scáthach.

"I don't care. I just don't like it!" he brayed.

"Not many people do," laughed Sennan. "But why do you object so strongly?"

Thomas felt puzzled. He realised he'd never tried to understand why it made him feel so sullen.

"It makes me feel like people think they own me," he said in a small voice. "Just because I'm a kid and younger than Cassie."

"But sometimes it is in your interest to do as you are told," said Scáthach. "There's no use in cutting off your nose to spite your face."

"He's not always like that," said Cassie loyally.

"Yes, I am," he said but this time when everyone laughed, he did too. He stole a look at his face and was relieved to see he looked like Thomas again.

"Stubbornness can be a good quality," observed Sennan. "But not when it's against your best interest."

Then Lugh held Nancy up to the water. "Nancy is too young to understand her strengths and weaknesses," he said. "She is a lamb because she is gentle and giddy and can't help being these things. But it is right sometimes to hide your gentleness and right sometimes to show it. These will be things she will face in the future."

Nancy looked into the water and her laughter ruffled her reflection. When the ripples subsided, it was once more her own face that looked back at her and she smiled to see it.

"The healing fires can only help you once," said Scáthach. "Next time you must fight her enchantment by yourselves."

"That's going to be hard," Cassie said.

"We have no choice," said Thomas. "I don't want Caitlín getting power over me again."

"Remember, Nancy is younger than you and it is your duty to protect her," said Sennan to Thomas and Cassie.

"Sometimes we can barely look after ourselves," said Cassie humbly.

"But why did these things happen to us?" asked Thomas. "Is it because we're very bad?"

Sennan laughed. "The opposite. It's because you have the power to be good, great even. You have turned Caitlín's enchantment to your advantage. Getting stuck in animal shapes has helped you to learn how to control your own natures." He patted them good-naturedly on the head.

"And remember, keep trying to discipline yourselves," said Scáthach. "It will get easier. A child only learns to walk by constantly falling over."

As Scáthach spoke, the ball of fire descended back into the lake. Cassie thought she saw something take shape on the water – a deep red planet spinning in space and then a map – of the Northern Hemisphere of the world – with a number of places lit up. But when she blinked the image was gone.

The children walked back across the water with the Sean Gaels. It was like walking on smooth glass. As they reached the shore, Thomas was amazed to see his feet weren't even wet.

Just then the sky split with a scream and three black hooded crows flew over the horizon. They swooped over the waters and fell to earth as three terrible hags. They wore black clothing of crow's feathers, all mangy and dusty. One of them had an eyeless face like a skull, so close did the skin cling to her bones. Another was toothless. The tallest of the three had pockmarked skin and huge jaws like a wolf's and spoke in a rasping voice that chilled their hearts.

"I am The Morrigan," she said. "These are my sisters Babh and Macha. We are the War Goddesses. We have come to warn of a great battle. Now Caitlín has a new enemy!"

They changed back into birds and alighted on the shoulders of the three children. A cold clammy feeling penetrated each of them to the marrow. "I see a battle," cawed The Morrigan, "where you will all be slain!"

And with that the birds flew into the sky, casting a fearful shadow.

Cassie, Thomas and Nancy clung to each other.

"We are doomed," said Cassie fearfully.

"We're going to die," said Thomas in a small voice.

"Courage," said Sennan firmly. "Prophecies are not to be taken literally. They can have many interpretations."

"It may be a warning," said Lugh. "If you change, the future can change."

"But they have foreseen our deaths," said a deeply worried Cassie.

"The Morrigan has seen just one of many possible futures," said Sennan. "You will be learning new skills. It will be a very different Cassie, Thomas and Nancy who face Caitlín in battle."

But the children didn't look convinced.

"You also have visions, Cassie," said Lugh. "Do they all come to pass the way you see them?"

"No," said Cassie. "I saw the Sacred Grove burn down. But I didn't see that it would be reborn."

"The same applies to The Morrigan's prophecies," said Lugh.

"I'm going to show that Morrigan she's rubbish!" said Thomas resolutely.

"That's the spirit," smiled Sennan.

"Meet me tomorrow for your first lesson in battle craft!" commanded Scáthach. "And don't be late."

The children set off home, glad to be back on two legs. They enjoyed the new-minted sensation of being in their own skins. For the moment their fears of Caitlín were banished by the confidence that the Sean Gaels had in them.

When the children were gone, Lugh's face darkened. "I fear this prophecy and their animal shapes are a foreboding that Caitlín already has a hold on them," he said to his fellow warriors.

"We must hope the prophecy has a hidden meaning. We do not have a lot of time to help them," said Sennan.

"They have a lot to learn," observed Scáthach. "They may master the skills but lack the discipline."

"The Chingles haven't let us down yet," said Lugh stoutly.

"But I do not think the Tuatha Dé Danann have realised the real danger of an awakened Caitlín," said Sennan. "The old gods have grown fearful and out of touch."

"Then we may have to risk their wrath," said Lugh grimly, "and contemplate the worst. My grandmother will not stop at destroying the Chingles. She has always lusted after power. We owe the Chingles even at the risk of our own annihilation."

His companions nodded their agreement and the three warriors joined hands to seal the pact.

CHAPTER 5

The next morning, Cassie decided to wear her new trainers for her first lesson in battle craft. As she bent down to put them on, she tried to banish her fear of The Morrigan's prophecy. They had to concentrate on finding Finnen. But she got a nasty surprise when she put her foot into the shoe and touched something sticky and wobbly.

"It has jelly in it!" she cried.

She went into the bathroom to clean out her trainers. She blinked. "*THIS IS WAR!!!*" was scrawled on the bathroom mirror – in blood. She called Thomas, who looked at it with alarm.

"Could this be a message from Caitlín?" he asked. He dipped his finger in the writing and smelled it. "It's not blood," he said.

Cassie picked up a tube of red lipstick that was lying on the floor, all squashed up. "This is Lardon's doing. Maybe you're right, Thomas, about him working for her."

She didn't hear the slight rustle outside the door.

"Caught red-handed! Cassie, I'm shocked," said an indignant Aunty Angel from the doorway.

Cassie's face went red. "It wasn't me!" she bleated. "My new trainers are ruined."

Lardon loomed from behind her aunt and smirked at her. "Gee, why don't you just wear another pair? Oh I get it, you're poor people and only have one rotten pair," he gloated.

Cassie picked up her trainer and hurled it across the room.

"Temper, Cassie! I know you're upset but trainers can be cleaned," Angel said.

"Why don't you ask Lardass Hackenbummer the Turd what happened to your lipstick?" Cassie said to her aunt. "We weren't even here –" She stopped herself as her aunt gave her a hard look.

"What kind of name is Lardon any way?" asked Thomas.

"I told you it's French," said Lardon.

"It means little strips of bacon," chimed in Aunty

Angel. "But it's also a term of endearment meaning 'little one' or 'chip off the old block'."

"We could call you Streaky Bacon as a term of endearment," sniped Thomas.

"Long streak of misery, more like," snorted Cassie, collapsing into uncontrollable laughter.

"And I could call you Bum-head and Pus-face," retorted Lardon. "Or maybe just 'poor people'!"

"Children!" shouted Aunty Angel.

Lardon put on a tiny little humble voice. "Gee! People are so cruel to me. Bullying me is a sign of their own weakness, my psychiatrist said, but it's sure hard to take."

"There, there," said Angel soothingly as if she was talking to a two-year-old who'd grazed his knee. "Having to defend an unusual name is character-building. But there's no need to call other people names." She turned her gentle eyes on Cassie and Thomas. "I'm so disappointed in you. You can wash up all the dishes as a punishment. My favourite lipstick – 'Rampant Red'!" She threw it in the bin, looking disappointed.

"But we have to go somewhere," Thomas stuttered.

"You will do as I tell you," said their aunt sternly, "and you can take Lardon on a tour of the island after breakfast as an apology."

"You mean I have to go outside!" exclaimed Lardon. "It's really awesomely dirty out there and it's full of creepy crawlies and stuff."

"The fresh air will be good for you," said Angel.

"But I never do any exercise without my personal trainer. I might get an injury," moaned Lardon. "And all that green stuff will set off my allergies. And the wind will muss my hair and there are no hair salons here. And I can't go to the mall to get some more products. And . . ."

"Why don't your try out your nice new scooter," interrupted Angel. "You could let Thomas and Cassie have a go."

Thomas's face lit up with expectation. If Lardon would let him have a ride on his scooter, he could manage being nice to him for half an hour. He smiled encouragingly at Lardon.

Lardon's eyes brightened maliciously. "No deal. I'm the only one who's insured and I don't want to be sued."

Thomas looked crestfallen. He snuffled like a pig to wind up Lardon. Lardon put on his headphones and switched on his expensive headset.

"It's not working," he said with a sour expression.

"Things like that have a tendency not to work on the island," said Cassie airily.

"You broke it," Lardon accused her.

"Cassie's right. Modern equipment tends to fail on the island. Now out, children," ordered Angel, "and no more bickering."

Grumpily, Cassie pushed her hands down into her pockets and felt the letter and the postcard Muiris had given them. She was about to hand them to Angel but instead she stuffed them hastily in a drawer. She didn't want to get into more trouble and have to explain why she had forgotten to give them to Angel and Jarlath. Cassie was in such a hurry, she didn't notice Lardon observing her hiding place with narrowed eyes.

After breakfast, they set off on their bicycles, Nancy perched on Thomas's crossbar. Lardon whizzed ahead on his super sleek scooter, squealing at the top of his voice. At first, Thomas was really jealous. But the scooter wasn't built for Irish boreens and kept getting stuck in potholes while Cassie and Thomas were enjoying freewheeling, feeling the wind through their hair. Thomas especially relished passing the scooter, stalled in yet another pothole. Lardon got frustrated and against Thomas's advice increased the speed. They pelted after him in hot pursuit.

"*Look out!*" shouted Thomas as Lardon revved towards the crossroads at Tadgh's Tower, oblivious to

Mr Guilfoyle's tractor that was coming from the opposite direction. Stephen Guilfoyle managed to swerve into a ditch but his vegetable trailer overturned and Lardon found himself and his scooter covered in a mound of Brussels sprouts.

"Holy moly, guacamole!" he moaned. "It's the attack of the killer green marbles! What the hell are these things?"

"They're Brussels sprouts," said Cassie, hauling him out of the mound with a firm grip.

He squealed in pain as if he'd been stabbed. "You're hurting me! And I'm getting marks on my clothes from those meany greenies," he whinged.

"I love them," said Nancy. "They're the best food in the whole world."

Lardon held one up between his thumb and forefinger and regarded it with interest. "Did you know my grandfather was a master chef? I have awesome taste-buds." Gingerly, he popped it in his mouth, then spat it straight out again with disgust.

"You're supposed to cook them first, moron, not that it makes much difference – they're still yeuch!" said Thomas.

"I'm the gourmet round here – I can get a table at Zak's like that!" Lardon crowed, snapping his fingers.

"They're yummy," said Nancy.

"Nancy's the only known child in the world who loves them. She calls them 'baby cabbages'," said Cassie.

"Baby cabbages," mused Lardon. "That gives me an idea." He fingered them like they were gold. "Farmer guy, I'll buy the lot!"

"Well, I don't normally sell them," stuttered Mr Guilfoyle, who was busy righting his trailer and shovelling the vegetables back into it. "I only grew them because Mrs Prendergast said she wanted them. I end up giving the rest of them to the pigs."

But Lardon wasn't listening to him. "I'll give you ten per cent more than your usual buyer," he said decisively.

"Well, apart from Mrs Prendergast and the –"

"Thirty per cent," said Lardon quickly.

"Even Mr Mulcahy doesn't –"

"Fifty per cent. You sure drive a hard bargain."

Mr Guilfoyle looked at him with incredulity.

Lardon stuffed two hundred-dollar bills into his hands. "Here's a down payment and I'll pay double and that's my final offer."

Mr Guilfoyle looked gratefully at the money, then spat on his hand and offered it to Lardon, who disdainfully covered his in a hankie before taking it.

"He's such an idiot," whispered Cassie.

As they continued on their way on foot, pushing the bikes, Lardon kept chuckling to himself in between picking out Brussels sprouts that had got jammed in his scooter.

"Well, aren't you wondering what my latest brilliant scheme is?" he asked, then added before they got a chance to answer, "You are looking at the first bonsai millionaire." He clapped his hands. "You kids ever been to Japan? Didn't think so. You're small-town hicks. *I* flew there in a private jet! Well, anyhow, those Japanese love small and dainty things. They've got all these dinky little trees called bonsai. Well, I'm going to market them there Brussels sprites as bonsai cabbages and win my little ol' self a bonsai bonanza."

Cassie and Thomas regarded him as if he had two heads.

"Can't wait until I'm on the cover of *Time* magazine. The Bonsai Billionaire!" he crowed.

"Is that before or after you win the Oscar for the best children's film ever?" asked Cassie sarcastically.

"The boy can't help it! It's not going to be a children's film but a cross-over adult documentary art indie movie." He revved up his scooter as they crested a hill and roared, "Look at me, Ma, I'm on top of the world!"

"We've got to get rid of him," Cassie said in exasperation as they paused for breath at the top. "We're supposed to be at Áine's for our first lesson in battle craft."

"The way he's driving he'll soon crash," said Thomas and yelled out a warning: "*Slow down!*"

But Lardon was going so fast he didn't hear him as he streaked downhill. As he rounded the turning that led to Glimmering Lake, he took the corner so sharply he lost control. The scooter careened down the hill and Lardon was thrown into the marshy ground near the lake.

"Holy moly, guacamole! It's quicksand!" he screamed. "I'm being sucked in!"

Thomas and Cassie pulled him free with much heaving and panting. But in the process he'd managed to lose his gleaming white tracksuit bottoms. He stood shivering and snivelling at the water's edge in boxer shorts decorated with miniature teddy bears with angel's wings. Cassie and Thomas exchanged a smirk but Nancy gave him her tissue to wipe off the oozing mud.

Lardon wiped his face, then took out a small mirror and looked at himself His hair stood in a stiff muddy peak on his head. "My hair! I'm filthy!" he cried, on the verge of hysterics.

"Why don't you wash off some of the mud in the lake?" suggested Cassie. Lardon tiptoed over to the water's edge as if trying to avoid stepping on landmines. He dipped his toe in the water and then screamed as if he'd had an electric shock. "It's f-freezing!" he yelled. He slumped on the bank and then jumped up squawking, complaining the reeds were too itchy.

Cassie handed him her sweatshirt and he tied it around his waist.

"I demand to sit down somewhere clean! I'm not sitting on grass!" Lardon stamped his muddy trainer.

Thomas spotted a currach at the water's edge. It was overturned and looked like a black beetle. He righted it and gestured to Lardon to take a seat in it. As Lardon clambered on board, he turned to Thomas and said, "Don't even dream about ever getting on my scooter, you bum! I'm going to tell Angel you broke it."

"You do that, Lardass the Turd, and you'll regret it," said Thomas in a cold voice. And with a great heave he pushed the currach into the water.

The boat began to slip away from the shore.

A bewildered Lardon stood up, causing the boat to nearly tip over. "There's no engine thing!" he bleated as he hurriedly sat down again.

The currach was now quite far from the shore.

Thomas picked up the oars that were lying on the bank. "Oh silly me," he said, mock innocent. "You stay here while we go for help. And don't make a sound. There's a white worm monster in that lake whose favourite snack is Lardons dipped in mud."

He signalled to his sisters and they jumped on their bikes and cycled back up the path, towards the boreen leading to Áine's house.

Soon Lardon's cries of "Ratfink!" and "You no account Injun!" faded away.

"Are you sure he's OK?" Cassie asked guiltily as they caught their breath at the crossroads.

"You're the one who wanted to get rid of him," said Thomas defensively. But Cassie still felt mean. She checked her head to make sure she hadn't sprouted bull's horns.

She was relieved when they bumped into Muiris and he promised to fetch Jarlath immediately so he could collect Lardon and his scooter.

They cycled off and soon were laughing and imitating Lardon.

"Holy moly, guacamole!" mocked Thomas.

"You no account Injun!" sneered Cassie.

"You're mean!" scolded Nancy.

"I don't know why you're defending him. He's our enemy. He thinks you're just a little Brussels-sprout-eating squirt," Thomas said viciously.

They arrived breathless at Áine's cottage.

Scáthach was already there, stripping branches to make staves – stout sticks to be used as weapons. She threw them one each before they had time to say good morning. She wore a short leather tunic decorated with knotted Celtic designs and fabulous beasts and she looked strong and terrifying.

"You're late. Don't let it happen again."

"As if we need any lectures from the Sean Gaels about turning up late," muttered Cassie.

Scáthach gave them a piercing look that brooked no discussion and brandished her stick like a weapon. "Now whose strength do you have when you fight?" she barked.

"Your own," said Cassie as if it was a stupid question.

Scáthach crossed sticks with her. "I want you to run at me with all your might. Don't be afraid to hit me as hard as you can, you boastful, self-satisfied stripling!"

Annoyed at being insulted, Cassie mustered all her energy and, raising the stave, charged at Scáthach, determined not to hold back. Fractions from her, Scáthach stepped nimbly aside. It was too late for

Cassie to stop and all her energy went into striking a tree. She hit it so hard the stave flew from her hands.

"Ow!" Cassie screamed, rubbing her smarting hands.

"Lesson One. If you are clever, you have not only your own strength but your opponent's," said Scáthach.

In a temper Cassie retrieved her stave and tried to hit Scáthach from behind.

But Scáthach turned in the blink of an eye and kicked it from her hand. "Lesson Two. Never take your eyes off your opponent," she said matter of factly.

Angrily Cassie turned her back and went to pick up her stave. As she bent down, Scáthach crept up behind her and nudged her on the bottom with her foot. Cassie sprawled forward on to the ground.

"Perhaps you didn't hear what I said about losing sight of your enemy," Scáthach mocked.

Furious, Cassie picked herself up and raised the stick. Scáthach calmly walked up and looked her hard in the eye. They stared at each other for a few seconds. Then Cassie lost her nerve, averted her eyes and dropped her hand.

"At least you seem to have a grasp of Lesson Three," Scáthach said evenly. "Pick your battles. Be careful when you take on a superior enemy."

Cassie gripped the stick tightly and looked at the ground.

"You have a temper, girl," said Scáthach. "You must learn to control it before it betrays you and becomes your opponent's best ally rather than your own."

Worse than any physical pain, Cassie felt herself thoroughly humiliated.

All morning Scáthach drilled the children in the use of the stave. It was hard work, harder than gym or football training. Time behaved strangely as they sweated and clashed staves. The clock appeared to stop. When Scáthach said they'd finished, they were surprised to discover that only a few hours had passed.

Áine brought them ointments to soothe their smarting hands and helped them apply it.

Then they went back to the cottage to eat.

Áine had roasted a whole pig on the barbecue, which seemed an enormous amount until they saw Scáthach devour half of it. She also ate hundreds of potatoes and a barrel of apples. The children weren't far behind. Everyone was so ravenously hungry there was no conversation. Straight after eating, Scáthach bid them practise with their staves and departed in the shape of a raven.

Sennan arrived soon after and he led them to a group of hawthorn trees.

"You will have to travel in dreams and in the Otherworld to find Finnen," said Áine. "But I will not be able to travel with you, because of the *geas* forbidding me to use my magical powers. So we have to share our knowledge with Sennan. He is a druid and very wise."

"Let us talk of what we know of the disappearance of your sister," he said to her.

So Áine recounted how, in the First Battle of the Skies between the Tuatha Dé Danann and the evil giants, the Formorians, Balor had managed to capture the Star Splinter. This was a sliver from a star that had the power to become a new sun at the time of a mysterious comet that visited the earth every five thousand years. Áine inflicted heavy wounds on Balor but he escaped to the healing waters of Glimmering Lake. Her sister Finnen, who was guarding the lake, tried to get the Star Splinter from him. In the ensuing battle, Finnen turned into a swan and disappeared to escape Balor's wrath.

"The only sight of her since then was Cassie's vision of her beyond the stars after we had defeated Balor," Áine concluded.

"And I've been having this dream of a woman imprisoned in glass who cries tears of blood. There is an explosion but all that is left is a swan's feather," said Cassie.

"And there have been no other signs, Cassie?" asked Sennan.

Cassie racked her brains but nothing came to mind. There was something in a corner of her memory that she'd seen on Glimmering Lake when they'd been cleansed in the burning fire, but she couldn't winkle it out.

"I gather from your last attempts that you are rusty at shapeshifting and other magical skills," said Sennan. "You will need to learn them again as well as some new ones, including the secrets of the Crane Bag."

He held out his hand and the bag of animal skin, the Crane Bag, appeared. He explained it would turn up when they needed it. He rummaged about in the bag and showed them a helmet belonging to the King of Lochlainn, which he explained was a kingdom in the north. Then he dug out the bones of the magical pigs of Assal, and a large smooth bone from the back of the great whale. He said he would explain their significance when the time came.

He fished out a tunic that was made of sea foam and breezes and frothy waves. Its magical cloth seemed to be like a screen showing the secrets of the sea. "This is the shirt of Manannán that ensures your safe return from the Otherworld," he said. "It will help you to refine your dream-walking."

The shirt twitched in his hand and darkened as if a heavy sky had rolled in over the sea. It showed a bird's-eye view of a long, narrow island beset by storms.

"We must join Lugh on Tory Island," Sennan said with urgency. "That is where our enemy Caitlín, his grandmother, was imprisoned in the glass tower and he wishes to speak to you about her. It's the one place we know she won't return to in person, though she may try to assail us with her ice magic."

Áine left them and Sennan traced a circle in the ground with his staff and divided it into four quarters. He instructed them to each sit down in a quarter.

He intoned:

"*Dark of the north,*
Warmth of the south,
Sunrise of the east,
Sunset of the west,
Carry our spirits in the brightness."

They fell into the drowsy half-sleep of meditation.

"Take the shape of water-birds," instructed Sennan, "and let us fly across the sea."

Cassie felt her senses pop and there was a sizzling sensation as if she was a corn kernel about to burst into popcorn. She took on the shape of a puffling, a baby puffin.

Thomas focused on trying to imagine the sensation of flight. He opened his arms and felt his spirits soar. A tingling feeling spread through his arms. He became a black cormorant streaking through the sky.

Nancy giggled to herself. The feeling of growing feathers made her feel ticklish. She became a gawky baby guillemot – a black seabird with a white breast and white patches on the wings.

Sennan was transformed into a seagull. Soon they took to the air and flew in their inner dream state towards Tory Island, north across the waves.

They hadn't travelled long before a cold, biting wind blew from the north and they were caught up in an ice storm. It pounced on them, like a cat on a mouse, and pawed them roughly. Fine needles of hail railed against their feathered wings and breasts. It was like flying into a hail of icy bullets.

They struggled on and in the darkened sky the rugged cliffs of Tory Island loomed ahead of them.

They glinted with a pinkish glow in the eerie light of the ice storm.

Just as they thought they were going to have to turn back, a yellow beam cut through the storm, creating a tunnel of light. Sennan swooped down and Thomas followed.

As they neared the land, they saw that the light was beaming out of Lugh's right hand. They reached the ground and took on their normal shapes. Lugh created a protective shield of light around them. The ice storm continued to rage around it.

They stood in a fortress with two ramparts and many stone huts. Shards of broken glass, as big as ice floes, lay scattered all around. The jagged stump of the glass tower that had shattered in two loomed out of the ground.

"This is where Caitlín broke free from the tower," said Lugh. "If she was strong enough to escape the tower, she is more powerful than we thought."

"And now she will do everything in her power to get revenge for Balor's defeat by the Chingles," said Sennan.

The children gasped.

"If she's anything like Balor, there's plenty to fear," Thomas trembled, remembering his wounds from the shapeshifting battle.

"She's worse," said Lugh. "She was clever enough to slay The Daghda at the Last Battle of Moytura. It took all our strength to revive him and it left us weakened for a long time."

"She is more crafty and subtle than Balor," explained Sennan. "She is a soul-splitter."

"A soul-splitter? What's that?" asked Cassie.

"She uses people against themselves," said Lugh. "You've already seen something of her power with the way she brought out the worst in you with your shapeshifting. If she gains control over you, she splits you into your good and bad self. But the good part of you is physically weak while the bad part has all your strength and guile. She knows just how to find your weak spot so you destroy yourself."

"What if you're perfect?" asked Cassie.

"That would be your weakness," smiled Sennan. "She'd play on your pride and get you to attempt something that was beyond your capabilities, so you'd destroy yourself in the process."

"I didn't mean me," said Cassie blushing.

"I know," smiled Sennan. "She will even use your strengths against you. If, for example, you loved someone very much, she'd get to you through them."

"She sounds horribly nasty," shuddered Thomas.

Then he screamed as beads of blood broke through the skin on his C-shaped scar.

Sennan waved over it and the pain and the blood disappeared. "That was her doing," he said.

"It is not just enough for her to defeat you. She has to torture and humiliate you as well," said Lugh. "I have seen men slit their own throats to escape her."

"How on earth do you defeat her?" asked an ashen-faced Cassie, all too conscious of her many weak spots.

"By self-mastery," said Lugh.

"And solidarity with others. Standing together against the common enemy," said Sennan.

"That sounds awfully vague if you don't mind me saying so," said Cassie.

"It's not vague, only difficult. And not just for the young and impetuous," said Sennan. "But there are also skills, like the battle craft that Scáthach is teaching you."

"And our magical arts," added Lugh.

There was a loud screeching noise, like nails on a blackboard, and each of them flinched as the needles of ice began to pierce the cocoon of light. Lugh raised his left hand and created another light defence around the first one.

"This is no ordinary ice storm. Caitlín, as you know,

has an affinity with the sharp and cutting: ice, glass, needles and knives. Right now she is gathering her power to take on human shape but she can work through these when she needs to," he said.

"Like Lardon," said Thomas vehemently. "She's working through him. I know she is!"

"Be careful," said Sennan. "Caitlín is very subtle. Don't make any rash moves. It can be an advantage to keep your enemy close so you can find *her* weak spot."

"Before Áine pulverised Balor, he said that he wanted Finnen to be his queen. I bet Caitlín will want to hurt Finnen too, and Áine, as it was she who finished Balor off," said Cassie thoughtfully.

The light defence buckled under a sudden attack of ice needles but still held.

Lugh looked absorbed in thought. "She is playing with us. She will want you to lead her to the Swan Maiden. Be careful when you search for Finnen."

"So now, not only do we have to search the whole of everywhere for a missing goddess but we've got a nasty old woman on our tail who wants to split us in two. And I'm freezing," Thomas groaned.

"Be careful. That is the kind of discontent Caitlín feeds on," said Lugh.

As if in confirmation, even bigger shards of ice

pierced through the outer shield of light. Lugh winced every time a jagged edge cut through.

"I must stay here to cleanse this place," he said. "You must return by sea. My brother and sister will protect you. They turned into seals when Balor cast them into the sea."

The childen and Sennan stepped forward and felt a sudden searing cold as they passed through the golden glow of Lugh's shield of light.

Poor Lugh, thought Thomas as they approached the cliff's edge, he really did have rotten grandparents.

They stood overlooking the water and Sennan bid them all hold hands. Below them was a sheer drop to waves crashing against the rocks like cymbals. Their faces felt raw and fear lurched in their stomachs.

"On my command you must turn into sea creatures," said Sennan. Suddenly a high-pitched laugh rang out, causing their nerve-ends to jangle. They leapt forward into the waves, a streak of screaming following in their wake.

Thomas cut through the water elegantly, as a dolphin. Cassie belly-flopped as a salmon and Nancy plunged in as a skittish baby seal, with white down and brown splodges. As they swam underwater two strong seals surged by their sides. One was brown and speckled, the other sleek and black. When the children saw their large, sad brown eyes they knew that they were Lugh's brother and sister.

The seals rose to the surface, beckoning to Nancy, who instantly followed them and began a series of honks with them.

"Big gathering on Tara," said the dark male, Rónán. "Merrows talk, talk."

"We saw that horrible woman with the crooked teeth," said Nancy.

The female seal, Tethra, barked loudly. "Evil one who got Balor to cast us into the sea, our grandmother! Dark Merrow Fand goes back to Balor's resting place. Evil grandmother will try to bring Balor back. Warn others!"

"We will keep watch," said Rónán.

"I'll try," said Nancy in perfect seal-speak, "but because I'm little they don't always pay attention."

The two seals and Nancy dived back down into the depths of the ocean to rejoin the others.

As the Chingles reached the shore, Áine guided them back to their own bodies and clapped her hands.

Back in Áine's garden, Sennan turned into a raven and flew off. The children lolled on the grass, drowsy from their adventure. But behind their tiredness, both Cassie and Thomas felt a creeping anxiety.

"There you are!" A familiar voice cut through their exhaustion like an unwelcome alarm clock. It was Aunty Angel.

Cassie opened her eyes first and saw Angel was wearing a pair of flowery wellingtons with her nanny's uniform.

Thomas gulped. They'd completely forgotten about Lardon. Oh dear, thought Thomas, I hope he's all right. If he's not, I'll get the blame.

Áine jumped up, flustered, but Aunty Angel bounded forward enthusiastically, holding out her hand.

Thomas's panic died down. Lardon must be okay if she was dropping by for a chat with Áine.

"Why, you must be Áine," she said. "No wonder Jarlath fell in love with you. You look more like a goddess than a herbalist."

Áine blushed.

"I'll get straight to the point. I don't know what your quarrel is over," continued Angel. "The usual lovers' tiff, no doubt. But it's no good. Jarlath is miserable and he's making everyone else so."

Áine's expression flitted between relief to hear that Jarlath was missing her and anguish that he was unhappy. "I wouldn't hurt Jarlath for the world," she replied. "It's just . . . complicated . . ." She trailed off.

"I hope we can be friends," said Angel kindly. "The children and Connle adore you and just because Jarlath's being an idiot doesn't mean I have to ignore you."

Áine's face lit up with pleasure. "I'd like that very much."

"Frankly we're just so relieved Jarlath managed to find a girlfriend," said Angel confidentially. "He can be so caught up in his inventions and maths that you might as well be from another planet."

Cassie shot Áine an alarmed look, as this wasn't so far from the truth.

But Áine was equally misty-eyed about Jarlath. "Oh, but he's so kind and clever," she said, going into a dream. Then she remembered herself and continued, "I hope you'll be happy for the children to continue to visit me. They like to . . . learn about my world."

"I didn't know they were interested in herbalism," said Angel. "How thrilling!"

"Oh, we just love it!" said Cassie, prodding Thomas.

"Yes, we love plants and leaves and stuff," he said, his voice heavy with sarcasm.

"I like daisies," said Nancy sweetly.

They set off back down the boreen, pushing their bikes, and as soon as they were out of earshot Aunty Angel turned on them.

"So how come you abandoned Lardon in the lake?" she asked in measured tones.

"Is he okay?" asked Thomas in a small voice.

"He's been home and had a shower and changed. We came back to pick up his scooter. He's waiting for us now at Tadgh's Tower. He said you broke his scooter and tried to feed him to a monster."

All Thomas's pity for Lardon evaporated. How dare he falsely accuse him of breaking the scooter!

"It was an accident!" said Thomas savagely. "I'm sick of having to put up with him. He's a scum-bucket sick-bag pillock!"

"Oh, children. Language!" said Angel. "I know he's got challenging behaviour. But he has such a hard life. Just try to be nice to him."

"Poor little rich kid," sneered Cassie. "He's really suffering – being stinking rich and a self-proclaimed child genius!"

"Well, people can be hurt on the inside," said Angel, "even though they appear to have everything. Besides, his father's studio is always on the brink of failure – they could lose everything overnight. Lardon's not that bad really. He's spoilt, yes. His parents give him everything except their time. And that is the most important thing of all."

"Hey, you shirking no-good Irish airhead!" called out Lardon to Angel as they neared Tadgh's Tower. "What took you so long? I'll have you arrested for abandoning me!"

Lardon was sprawled at the foot of the steps by his broken scooter, like a helpless baby.

"Couldn't I just give him one little Chinese burn?" whispered Thomas to Angel.

She suppressed a smile and playfully tweaked his ear. "The children have something to say to you, Lardon," she said.

They looked at her blankly.

"Apologise!" whispered Angel.

"We're sorry we left you in the boat," mumbled Cassie.

"We didn't want you to drown, really," said Thomas and then mumbled under his breath, "at least when we couldn't enjoy it."

"I forgive you," said Lardon loftily. "My psychiatrist said it was bad for me to carry any baggage around with me."

"But you had tons coming off the helicopter and what's that got to do with us leaving you in the boat?" said Thomas, bewildered.

"Not that kind of baggage. Emotional stuff. You wouldn't understand," sighed Lardon.

Angel smiled at him sympathetically but when she was out of earshot he leaned over to Thomas and whispered, "If you pull one more stunt like that I'm going to sue your auntie's ass."

"*Oink*, *oink*, little streak of bacon!" sneered Thomas.

"Loser!" replied Lardon, waving a hundred-dollar bill at him.

Since Lardon felt too weak to climb up the stepladder, Angel decided to take him home, with poor Derry the Donkey having to pull the scooter. She told them Jarlath was expecting them at his workshop later but Cassie insisted she wanted to see Tadgh first.

Tadgh ran the local library from his round tower but had previously been a professor and an explorer. He knew all about history and mythology and she wanted to consult him about Finnen.

Tadgh, a tall thin man, was delighted to see them and led them up to the main manuscript room. Cassie gazed at all the dusty volumes and wondered if they might contain vital information.

"Are you still interested in mythology?" asked Tadgh.

Thomas looked at him blankly.

"The ancient stories of gods and goddesses," Tadgh added helpfully.

"More so than ever," said Thomas enthusiastically. "We want to find out all we can about a goddess called Finnen who seems to have disappeared." They told him all they knew about her.

Tadgh scratched his head and began to take down several volumes. Little did he know that the children had to find Finnen for real. The Chingles' contact with the Otherworld was their secret, though at times Cassie felt that some of the islanders knew more than they let on.

The first clue Cassie thought worth pursuing was her own vision of Finnen beyond the stars. The image had been unclear but she wondered if the goddess had gone to another planet. And then that memory she'd been trying to retrieve since they'd been cleansed by the burning fire on Glimmering Lake came back to her: the image of a planet and a map showing the Northern Hemisphere. She had a sudden feeling that this might be the right track. She didn't want to reveal the full story to Tadgh but she risked a general enquiry.

"Are there any accounts of gods and goddesses in outer space?" she asked.

He took down a large volume, bound in red leather, and opened it on an illustration of the night sky. "Irish mythology isn't much obsessed by the heavens. But in Greek and Roman myths many of the gods and goddesses gave their names to stars and planets."

"Like Venus?" asked Cassie.

"That's right. And Mars the red planet, the God of War, and Jupiter the King of the Heavens, the largest planet in our solar system. There's Mercury the Messenger of the Gods, our fastest planet to go round the sun, and the blue planet Neptune named after the God of the Sea. Venus is of course the brightest and most beautiful planet and is named for the Goddess of Love. Did you know that astronomers have discovered a new object in our solar system?"

"Is it called Finnen?" asked Cassie excitedly.

"No, it's been named Sedna for the time being. They're not sure if it's a planet or a comet. Sedna appears to be half rock and half ice, so it might be something in between. Or even a minor planet known as a planetoid."

"Who is Sedna anyway?" asked Thomas.

"Sedna is Inuit – Eskimo – and is the Goddess of the Ocean," explained Tadgh. "You see, each culture has its own gods and goddesses. But they tend to represent the same elements and qualities."

"Are there any gods and goddesses in Ireland connected with the stars?" persisted Thomas.

Tadgh opened another page. "In Ireland we had sun gods and goddesses like Áine, and also in Wales, but few gods connected to the stars. But, you know, Celtic gods and goddesses were also venerated on the continent." He pointed to places in France and Germany. "This map shows ancient settlements of Celtic tribes throughout Europe. There were lots of Celtic sites of worship of gods and goddesses from Hungary to Brittany. They may have had a star god or goddess. I'll have a look to see what more I can dig up if you like."

Cassie and Thomas perked up. Any lead at all was helpful.

"And they are always discovering new planets and stars," added Tadgh. "So you never know, they could name one Finnen."

"Some of those gods and goddesses sure get around," said Thomas.

"The Hams' tour," Nancy suddenly piped up, tugging Cassie's jumper. "It made my tummy tingle."

"Does she mean those Ham Players that Angel's usually with – the world's worst actors?" asked Thomas.

"The Hams," said Nancy brightly.

"Shut up," said Cassie, giving her a pencil and paper to amuse herself while she concentrated on the task of getting information.

Tadgh was thumbing through a dusty manuscript.

"So what do you know about Finnen?" Cassie asked him.

"She's the sister of the sun goddess Áine. Or more correctly half-sister. I myself think she was related to Caer Ibromaith – the name means Yewberry – of the Legend of Aengus Óg. They are, I think, both Swan Maidens. And Áine is linked to the yew. Sometimes Finnen is seen as a moon goddess."

"Do you know where Finnen is?" said Nancy.

"I'm afraid not," said Tadgh laughing, apparently humouring Nancy.

"We have to find her!" said Nancy.

Cassie looked with exasperation at her little sister for giving away too much information.

But Tadgh seemed really interested. "Maybe she went to live abroad," he continued. "Did you know that gods and goddesses often move around from mythology to mythology? As the Celts on the continent shared some gods with us and even the Romans, she'd have plenty of places to go."

Thomas looked at his watch. "We'd better run. We have to meet Jarlath at the beach."

Outside, Cassie told Thomas about the map of the Northern Hemisphere and the red planet in her vision on Glimmering Lake.

He scratched his head, puzzled. "It's a bit vague but it's a start."

"It's the best lead we have so far," said Cassie as she mounted her bike. "You know, I think we should set up an Incident Room, like you see on detective dramas."

"That would be cool," said Thomas.

At the crossroads to the beach, they bumped into Stephen Guilfoyle who was returning from their house where he'd delivered several hundred kilograms of Brussels sprouts. They also met Jarlath who was pulling a cart covered with tarpaulin. He was glad of Stephen's offer to help with the load.

But when the farmer left them at the beach, Jarlath suddenly became preoccupied and looked slightly scared.

"I know it's silly but I have this dream – over and over again – where I'm drowning and these strange creatures with fishes' tails capture me and then –" He drifted off, staring into space.

"Oh, it's the Merrows," said Nancy. "They want you back."

"You must have eaten fish that's gone off," said Cassie.

Jarlath looked grim and pushed with all his might to get the cart onto the beach. The sand was pockmarked with raindrops from a recent shower and the wind off the sea felt like warm air from a hair dryer.

Jarlath cheered up when he pulled the tarpaulin off the cart.

"I have pleasure in introducing you to the next stage of the Flying Marine!" he announced with a flourish, his earlier worry about the Merrows temporarily forgotten. The machine appeared to have a few more bits and pieces on it – though there was no disguising the fact that it still looked like a large rubber wheel with a clunky metal frame on top.

"I've now fitted the propellers under the platform," explained Jarlath. "They are geared to one hundred horsepower engines. This will produce the air stream for thrusting. Now do I have a volunteer to have a closer look?"

Cassie stepped up onto the pilot's cage on the platform. With its metal frame balanced on a huge rubber ring, the invention looked ridiculous and utterly impractical.

"Will it float if it falls back in the water?" asked Cassie.

"Better than that – it sails!" said Jarlath proudly.

"But how does it do that?" asked Thomas.

Jarlath pointed to a control panel on the steel cage. There was a dial marked "*sails*". The children edged closer to the panel.

"Don't touch it!" Jarlath leapt forward. "That button releases a sail from the back platform but I'm still ironing out the details."

Thomas joined Cassie on the platform.

"How do you make it stop?" she asked.

"At the moment you just turn the engine off," said Jarlath. "It's still a test model."

Jarlath went back to the cart and returned wearing a helmet with donkey's ears on the side, goggles and a life jacket that made him look like he had a hump on his back.

"This is another invention," he beamed. "A life jacket that is also a parachute – a 'life-a-chute'. But what is really clever about it is that it senses which you need according to air pressure. It's fuelled mostly on fresh air alone."

"So let me get this right. The Flying Marine runs on fresh air and nothing else?" Thomas enquired. "So you don't need fuel?"

"You just need a little bit to get the engine started

and up in the air," said Jarlath. "Until I've perfected the model."

Thomas and Cassie just nodded sagely.

Nancy had abandoned all pretence at being interested and was building a sandcastle. "The seals said the Merrows were looking at the wreck of Balor for something," she said suddenly, pointing out to sea. But the others ignored her as usual.

Cassie and Thomas jumped down from the platform and changed places with Jarlath, but just as he was about to press a button a strange expression came over his face. He stared out to a fixed point at sea. Cassie thought she caught the flick of a large fish's tail but couldn't be sure.

But Nancy was. "See, I told you! It's those Merrows!" she said. But again nobody paid her any attention.

Jarlath hesitated and looked as if he might keel over. "I can't," he said, trembling. He got down from the platform, his whole body heavy with disappointment. Slowly he removed his goggles, helmet and "life-a-chute". He stumbled on the wet sand and went to be sick behind a rock.

"Jarlath is a nervous wreck," said Thomas, going to see how his uncle was, followed by Nancy.

"Seems a shame to waste the chance," said Cassie,

idly picking up the helmet. Before she knew it, she'd donned the helmet and goggles and found herself standing in the strange cockpit, shaped like the Zimmer frame her English nan's friend Gladys used to help her walk. In a split second she pressed the button and the Flying Marine juddered into life.

"What the hell!" cried Jarlath as the machine rose and vaulted straight into the air over the sea.

Cassie felt like a rocket that had been launched into space.

"Look out!" shrieked Thomas.

"Push back on your heels to turn round," shouted Jarlath but his words were eaten by the wind and Cassie heard nothing except indistinct muffles and cries.

It was alarming to be carried on a flying platform but Cassie soon remembered the weight and ankle action she'd learned on the ball in Jarlath's workshop. She surveyed the earth from the air. She was flying over the ocean in her own personal flying craft! She really was! She stared at the distant horizon and headed further out to sea.

"*Ah ha! Hooray! Fantastic!*" she shouted to herself and then screamed in pleasure. As soon as she got the hang of it, she began to experiment, flying figures of eight and turning in circles. The velocity of the wind beat against her body and she tasted the salty tang of the sea. When she looked down there was only air between her and the waves.

She turned the Flying Marine back towards the shore where Jarlath was waving his hands like a human windmill. Nancy and Thomas looked like toy soldiers or pieces on a chessboard. Below her the sea rolled and she could see all the way to Tadgh's Tower and Áine's house. Smoke circled out of the chimney at Stag's Cliff and she saw the ferry heading back to the mainland. It was an extraordinary sensation – like riding a lawnmower inside a huge tumble-drier. She felt more and more daring. About half a kilometre from the shore, she decided to try out the sailing mechanism. Jarlath will be pleased if I show him it works, she thought to herself. She pressed a button and there was a weird noise of gas escaping.

In a millisecond she dropped like a stone. She felt her chin pushed up to her cheeks and nearly bit her tongue. But the machine's ducts caught a current of air and it slowed, landing on the waves in a bumpy motion. Almost at once a panel opened at the back of the platform. There was a flapping sound and behind her a balloon sail billowed into life. The craft became unstable as the sail tugged the floating platform and Cassie was pitched and tossed on the waves. She began frantically pressing buttons, hoping that one would stall the balloon sail but she could hardly see as her goggles became speckled with seawater. Then a change of wind pitched the sail in the opposite direction, spinning the platform on its side and tossing Cassie into the sea.

She struggled to stay afloat and coughed and spluttered as she swallowed great mouthfuls of seawater. She had forgotten to put on the life-a-chute. Suddenly a current dragged her under the waves.

She plummeted noiselessly and panicked when she saw that she had been pulled under right by the wreck of *The Ocean Beast* where Balor had come to grief. The wreck had burned solidly for hours and the blackened steel hull looked like the skeleton of a whale.

She began to black out. Then she gave a start when she thought she saw the flick of a tail, a red cap and long flowing hair. A Merrow was searching for something among the waves. An icy current tugged at her feet, pulling her further down. She felt she was about to explode as her lungs contracted with the lack of air. She struggled, afraid she was drowning.

But, just as she thought she'd met her end,

something rising from the sea floor hit her and propelled her towards the water's surface. She burst through the waves and gasped for air, spluttering in the daylight world. Something soft and sleek was supporting her in the water. She put out her hand to touch it, thinking it was the rubber doughnut of the Flying Marine.

It was the silky skin of a seal – Lugh's brother Rónán. He gently carried her towards the shore. As he did so, he honked and barked intensely, trying to communicate something urgent to her. She wished she had Nancy's ability to communicate with animals. And then she dimly remembered Nancy's warning that the Merrows were searching the wreck of Balor's boat.

As she neared the shore, Jarlath plunged into the water.

"Keep paddling, Cassie, I'm coming," he called out breathlessly.

The seal left her and pushed the Flying Marine towards them before diving beneath the waves. Cassie managed to grab hold of it as Jarlath neared her and together they paddled it in to the shore.

Nancy and Thomas cried with joy to see her safe. An anguished Jarlath hugged her tight.

"God forgive me, Cassie, I'm such a fool," he said.

"Never do anything like that again. Oh, you put the heart crossways in me! But you're safe. And the Flying Marine worked. Oh, what a brave girl you are! I mean a foolish girl. Oh, just give me a hug!"

Cassie sobbed in relief but something disturbed her about her time under the waves. Something about that flicking tail near the wreck of Balor wasn't quite right.

Jarlath and Cassie were soaked through, but luckily it wasn't far to Jarlath's workshop where they changed into some old overalls and Thomas made them some hot chocolate.

Despite his guilt, Jarlath couldn't help asking questions about the Flying Marine.

"It was absolutely brilliant," Cassie replied. "I mean the flying bit not the drowning bit. It just got unstable when I tried to release the sail and when the wind changed."

"That's a wrinkle I need to iron out," pondered Jarlath, reaching for his graph paper and pencils. "I need to build in a feature so that you can't release the sail until you are stable on the water. But, no, enough of this! Time to get you home."

As they neared the house, Jarlath whispered to them

that it was perhaps better if they didn't go into too much detail with Aunty Angel.

They were surprised to see Lardon standing at the gate holding three lollipops. He was wearing black binliners over his trainers to keep them clean.

"Well, if it ain't my little old buddies," he said chummily, handing them each a lollipop. "Why, Cassie, you look fabulous in that boiler suit." Nancy eagerly licked her lollipop but Cassie and Thomas regarded theirs with suspicion, expecting them to be laced with arsenic. As they trudged up the path, they soon saw why Lardon was currying favour. A huge mound of Brussels sprouts blocked the back door where Angel stood with her arms folded and a face like thunder.

"Well, children, now's your chance to make it up to Lardon over breaking his scooter. I want all these Brussels sprouts in the old shed before dinner."

"I didn't break his scooter," insisted Thomas. "It was an accident."

"I'm tired," yawned Cassie. "After all I've been through, nearly drowning and everything over Jarlath's –"

Thomas and Jarlath shot her a stricken look as Angel regarded her intently.

"I meant nearly drowning myself by spilling a cup of

water over Jarlath's papers," Cassie corrected herself quickly.

"Is that why you're wearing those horrible overalls?" Angel's eyes narrowed.

"They're all the rage in East Croydon," Cassie bluffed.

"Just get carrying," said Angel with menace.

Reluctantly, Cassie and Thomas began the task of clearing out the old shed that was a jumble of old tyres, rusty pots and pans and other unidentifiable mangled objects. This took them the best part of an hour while Lardon did stretching exercises saying his back hurt. Mostly it looked like he was scratching his bottom. Then Cassie and Thomas fetched a wheelbarrow and began the task of ferrying thousands of Brussels sprouts into the shed. Finally they goaded him into action and Lardon managed to carry one small basketful of sprouts with frequent rests as he staggered down the garden.

It was Nancy who had the bright idea of storing them in the hessian sacks that lay unused in the corner of the shed.

"It's not even as if we are getting a share of the profits," muttered Cassie.

"I don't even like Brussels sprouts," Thomas complained.

When they finished and went into the house they

were dismayed to discover that their hard labour hadn't finished. Angel presented them with three aprons. Lardon was seated at the table with a bib on.

"I've decided, children, that since you have shown such talent and would like to be actors, you'd better all learn how to wait tables."

"We never said that," said Thomas hotly.

"We let her believe it," Cassie muttered to him. "Remember, in our animal phase."

"You'll have to work in restaurants while you wait for your break. Unless you want to work as a nanny," said Angel in a warning tone.

Lardon gloated at them.

"Why doesn't he have to learn? Oh, I forgot, his dad owns the studio," said Cassie resentfully.

"I have another lesson in mind for Lardon since he's got such fabulous taste buds," said Angel, ladling up the first dish and handing the bowl to Cassie.

It was Brussels sprouts soup. Followed by fried Brussels sprouts, steamed Brussels sprouts, boiled Brussels sprouts, baked Brussels sprouts, poached Brussels sprouts and Brussels sprouts salad. Aunty Angel stood over Lardon and made him taste every dish. He grimaced and moaned but he still did as he was told.

"I thought you'd like to sample what you want to

give the Japanese," said Angel with a glint in her eye as she handed him a dessert of Brussels sprouts and custard.

Lardon gagged as he tasted it. "I never want to set eyes on a Brussels sprout again!" he wailed.

"And don't forget, children," Angel said to Cassie and Thomas who were banging the dishes about as they removed them from the table with scowling faces, "if you give good service, you get a tip."

"My tip to you deadbeats is don't expect a free lunch," tittered Lardon.

"Maybe we should be learning how to fold clothes so we can get a boring job in a shop while we wait for our acting careers to take off," muttered Thomas.

"That's a brilliant idea," said Angel. "It's good to be able to do all kinds of jobs, so you can earn your own living. We'll fold clothes tomorrow. Now get out of my sight."

Thomas wished he'd kept his mouth shut.

A loud rumbling sound rent the air as Lardon let out a giant fart, followed soon by another one. He farted so much it sounded like a steam train. The children, gasping with laughter and for air, had to leave the room as Lardon retreated to his bedroom. But his farting attack gave Cassie an idea.

"I think you must have an allergy to Brussels sprouts," she called after him. "You must never set foot in the shed ever, for the sake of your health."

When Angel allowed them an hour's playtime before bed, Cassie dragged the others down to the old shed.

"I think this should be our Incident Room for Finnen," said Cassie. "It's perfect, the one place where Lardon is guaranteed to leave us alone." She tossed a Brussels sprout in the air with glee.

She got out Post-it Notes, sheets of paper and pens.

"So what do we know?" she began, in her best detective's voice. She called out her notes as she wrote them:

"*Missing: one goddess.*

Name: Finnen. Also known as: Caer Ibromaith – that means Yewberry.

Age: Immortal.

Hair colour: red but going white in my visions.

Distinguishing features: can turn into a swan.

Could be a Moon Goddess.

Likes to frequent: lakes, streams and stars.

Known associates: Swans."

"*Last seen at Glimmering Lake thousands of years ago,*" added Thomas, writing as he spoke, "*disguised as a swan after a battle with a deadly assailant, Balor.*

Last positive sighting: vision of Cassie seeing her beyond the stars.

New leads: recent dreams of her imprisoned under glass with tears of blood running down her face."

They surveyed their notes.

"*Possible whereabouts: another planet, somewhere in the Northern Hemisphere*," said Cassie.

"That sure narrows it down," sighed Thomas. "It's so much worse than finding a missing person in the real world where at least you know what dimension they're in."

"Yeah, we've got to search in dreams, the Otherworld, the past and maybe even outer space," said Cassie.

"I want my postcard," chimed Nancy. "From the Hams."

"Later," said Cassie distractedly. "Do you remember what Tadgh said about there being a new planet-like thing in the solar system? I was just wondering. I had my vision of Finnen beyond the stars after Áine cast the Star Splinter into space and said it was a new star in honour of her sister. And then I saw a planet, a red one, on the lake. Do you think there's some connection?"

"But Tadgh said it is called Sedna," said Thomas. "That's the Inuit Goddess of the Ocean. It must be something different."

"But no one is sure if it's a planetoid or something else being half rock and half ice. And the name might change anyway," added Cassie.

"True, and how is some scientist halfway round the world to know that Áine called it after Finnen?" asked Thomas.

"Finnen's always changing her name anyway," reasoned Cassie. "Oh dear, it really is like looking for a needle in a haystack."

While they'd been talking, Nancy had gone back into the house. She came running back with the postcard that Muiris had handed them when they were in their animal states. Cassie had hidden it in a bedroom drawer with the letter addressed to Jarlath and then forgotten about it.

Nancy held up her postcard. "Can we put it up now? I told them to go there!"

Cassie took it up absent-mindedly. It was to Angel and Nancy from the Ham Players. They had sent it from a place called Pech-Merle in the south of France. It depicted drawings made by cave dwellers back in the Ice Age.

"*Dear Angel and Nancy*," Cassie read, "*This is Pech-Merle, near Cahors, the Sistine Chapel of cave paintings. These drawings were done over fifteen thousand years ago.*

What a fabulous location for us to put on a play and begin our tour!

Love THE HAM PLAYERS."

"It makes my tummy tingle," said Nancy. "Like when I swallowed the Star Splinter. It's to do with her, Finnen."

"Stop talking nonsense, Nancy. We need to concentrate," said Cassie irritably.

"But it's a glue," insisted Nancy.

"Oh shut up," snapped Cassie. "And the word's 'clue'."

She threw the card on a pile of Brussels sprouts but Nancy, in tears, picked it up and put it in her pocket.

A sudden scratching sound made Cassie look to the window. Then a loud thud and a farting noise came from outside. Cassie ran to the door in time to see Lardon scuttle back into the house.

"You've been spying on us," she shouted after him. "I'll get you for that!"

That night before bed, Cassie thought they should have a go travelling in dreams to see if they could find anything out.

Thomas was dubious. "It's not like we have a plan,"

he yawned. "Any journey we make now would be just messing around."

"Please take the postcard, Thomas," said Nancy. "Not Cassie because she made me cry."

"I'm sorry for snapping at you," said Cassie. "It's just this Finnen business is getting on top of me. I feel totally at sea." She gave her little sister a hug.

Timidly, Nancy took the postcard from her pyjama pocket.

"It makes my tummy tingle," she insisted. "It's from Finnen. We have to go there."

"Remember last year when Nancy swallowed the Star Splinter," said Thomas thoughtfully. "The last person who had it before her was Finnen. Maybe Nancy does have some strange link with Finnen? A link through the postcard?"

"And you think somehow Finnen is controlling the Ham Players and sending us a message? A message that doesn't make any sense," said Cassie. "It's a mad idea."

"If you're a goddess on the run, you might choose some strange ways of sending information," argued Thomas. "Why not through a postcard from a bunch of really bad actors? It's not going to raise suspicions."

Nancy pointed at the card. "We have to go there *now*," she insisted.

Thomas shone the torch on it. It showed an underground cave with stalagmites and stalactites and sketchy cave paintings.

Cassie yawned. "Well, let's give it a whirl."

They lay down together on the double bed, Nancy in the middle. Then they drifted off to sleep, Cassie and Thomas with their fingers touching the postcard balanced on Nancy's tummy.

They came to a dream landscape, a rocky mountain area where the earth was covered by thick ice and snow. The freezing air sliced through their lungs as the snow swirled about them and large drifts formed against jagged outcrops of rocks. They shivered in their pyjamas. An icy wind whipped their faces and they were pelted with frozen balls of snow as big as Brussels sprouts. Thomas looked skyward. The clouds took the shape of a giant mouth with ragged broken teeth. *Caitlín*, he thought. Desperately he cast around for a hiding place and saw a gap in the rock face like the entrance to a cave. He grabbed Cassie and Nancy by their pyjamas and pulled them through the ice storm. The cave was warm and dry and to their surprise lined with animal pelts. They discovered tinder for firewood in one corner, a pile of rough-hewn logs and the ashes remaining from a fire. Dried carcasses of dead animals hung from the cave wall.

"It's the home of a cave man!" said Thomas.

Towards the back of the cave they saw that the light source was a lighted taper in a holder. It was a primitive candle made out of a big lump of animal fat with a wick of animal sinews. Cassie picked it up and shone it towards the back of the cave. It revealed a narrow opening, wide enough for them to squeeze through.

On the other side, the candle illuminated a rough stairway of stones. It tapered into a tunnel below that glinted with a silvery stone. They descended carefully, their footfalls echoing eerily in the vast cavern beneath.

At the bottom, the underground cave took their breath away. Stalagmites and stalactites shimmered in the candlelight like a vast, scrumptious cake of icing and whipped cream.

"The ones coming down from the ceiling are stalactites. See, they hang down, like tights, and the ones coming up are stalagmites," explained Cassie as they glowed in the light of the taper.

Drops of water glistened at the ends of the rocks and, falling to the floor, punctured the silence.

"That's how the rocks were formed," Cassie explained. "The drops have little bits of chemicals in them and over millions of years they harden and become rock formations."

Cassie shone the taper around the interior. Her attention was snagged by scratch marks in the side of the porous rock, just above a natural hollow in the bedrock. She brought the light into the hollow and noticed bones and animal carcasses.

"Look!" exclaimed Nancy, pointing towards a large soft animal skin. She reached to stroke it but instinctively Cassie pulled her back.

There was a low growl. It took Cassie a second to take in the fact that it was a live bear. A live hibernating bear that they'd just woken from sleep! They backed off as the bear crawled out of the cave and stood up on its hind legs. It raised its front legs and let out a roar.

The bear was huge, much bigger than the ones they'd seen in the zoo. In the flickering light they saw its savage canine teeth loom towards them in its pig-like, snouty face. As its growl echoed around the chamber, its sharp bear claws slashed at them. Cassie dropped the taper in fear and, pushing Nancy and Thomas behind a rock, crouched into a ball. They were alone in the darkness, the smell of their damp fear betraying their position, moments from being killed.

"*Whoo, woo!*" Suddenly a cry rang out and a lighted taper cut through the air.

For a moment Cassie thought the bear had picked up the taper but then she realised there were two sources of light. Huge frightening shadows loomed on the cave wall. The two tapers were thrust towards the bear and it seemed that a giant was challenging him. There was a smell of singed fur. The bear let out a roar and retreated into the darkness.

Cassie squinted in the dark in amazement. Before her stood a teenage boy, holding two lighted tapers. He had broad features and shaggy brown hair and was wearing a garment made of animal skin. Around his waist he wore a belt plaited from animal gut on which hung a crude knife, a flint and a skin pouch. He had a large scar in the shape of a crescent on his right cheekbone.

He placed the lighted tapers in crevices in the rocks and helped Cassie to her feet. His hands were rough and leathery and spattered with blood. He pointed to his scar and then in the direction the bear had disappeared.

"He did that to you," said Cassie, feeling the scar.

The boy looked intently into her eyes and then with wonder at her mouth. He pointed at his own mouth and grunted.

"What's so strange?" said Cassie.

The boy reached out his hand and traced the shape of her lips. It was a gentle gesture, as if he was patting a strange animal. Then he leaned closer, pushed his fingers into her mouth and tried to peer in. Cassie gave him a sharp push.

"Steady on! I know you've saved my life but anyone would think you've never heard someone talking!"

Thomas and Nancy stole out from their hiding places.

"Perhaps he hasn't – at least not talking English!" Thomas said, offering his hand to the boy.

The boy just looked at it, then he noticed the C-shaped scar on Thomas's arm and made a sad face, pointing at his own. Thomas smiled in recognition. Then the boy's attention turned to their clothing. He fingered their pyjamas and his eyes filled with wonder. He held their hands to his animal skin. The coarse hairs were like wire wool. He mimed something coming out of his forehead and, falling to all fours, made lumbering movements.

"*Ah-oh*," he said. They looked at him in bewilderment. He snatched the knife that was hanging from his belt and they all recoiled but he made strokes on the cave wall, swiftly sketching an animal. It was a hulking shape with a tusk coming out of its forehead and he drew in short dashes to indicate hair.

"It's a woolly mammoth. They're like big hairy elephants," exclaimed Thomas. "I remember it from my Ice Age book."

The boy continued to point from his clothing to the drawing and saying, "*Ah-oh.*"

"I think he's trying to say that he's wearing woolly mammoth's skin," Cassie said.

"Are we in the Ice Age?" Thomas wondered. "Me Thomas," he said to the boy, thumping his chest, and then he pointed to his sisters, "Cassie, Nancy."

The boy smiled and thumped his chest. "*Kapo*," he beamed. Then turning to Thomas he punched him gently and said, "Me Thomas," and "Cassie" and "Nancy" in turn to the girls.

"It's just Thomas," Thomas began. "Oh, never mind!"

Kapo pointed with his knife to the drawing of the woolly mammoth.

"*Kapo ke tu ah-oh*," he said slowly, slashing the drawing with his knife. Thomas smiled in acknowledgement. "Kapo killed the mammoth. *Kapo ke tu ah-oh*."

"Thomas," said Cassie urgently, "we have to try to explain to him about Finnen."

"*Finna!*" Kapo exclaimed.

He picked up the lighted tapers, thrusting one into Thomas's hand, and signalled that they follow him.

He led them on to another magnificent chamber with rock formations like crystals. The area blazed with light from a large fire and lighted tapers. A cleft in the rock formed a natural chimney. Along one side of the chamber was a flat wall of rock decorated with wonderful paintings of woolly mammoths, cattle with lyre-shaped horns, horned goats and other strange beasts.

What looked like artist's materials were assembled on a slab of rock at waist height that served as a table. There were several brushes made with animal bone and stiff animal hair. There was a stone with a natural hollow containing black paint, one with red and another with orange paint. They realised it was red paint on Kapo's hands, not blood. He smiled broadly, revealing a broken tooth, then pointed to the paintings and then to himself. Clearly Kapo was a cave painter.

On the right-hand side of the rock face was a natural indentation like the long nose of a horse. Kapo had already traced half the outline of the rest of the horse around it, in black paint. Their cries must have disturbed him in his work. He led them to a deep curve in the rock and pointed to a pile of bones that was set into the floor. It was some kind of primitive altar. Around it were burning plugs of animal fat on stones.

Beside each was what was unmistakably a swan's feather.

"Finnen!" exclaimed Thomas and Cassie in unison.

"She's been here, I know she has!" said Cassie.

"*Finna*," said Kapo who stood behind them. He shone his taper onto the roof of the altar area. On the ceiling was the outline of a woman with large wings like an angel's.

"That could be an angel," said Thomas.

"Or a Swan Maiden!" exclaimed Cassie.

"Swa," repeated Kapo. He pointed to other shapes etched into the ceiling and then to the children. There were three figures, two roughly the same size and one smaller. The proportions echoed theirs.

"It's almost as if he was expecting us," said Cassie.

Then he led them back to the altar and bent down, pointing with insistence. Thomas peered at the bones.

On closer inspection they formed a pattern – a central column with five bars cutting across it.

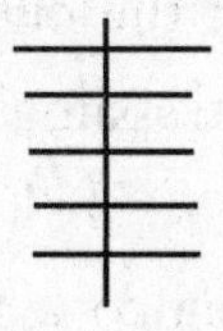

Kapo pointed to the feathers. Thomas drew nearer with a lighted taper.

He counted nine. Then Kapo pointed to the ceiling. The same symbol was drawn there with two feather shapes circling it.

"It's like some kind of clue," said Cassie memorising the shape and number of feathers. "The same symbol twice, first with nine feathers and then with two feathers.

"Finnen has left it for us," said Nancy with certainty.

A trail of sunken lights, small pits plugged with animal fat, led to a deeper part of the cave. They followed the route and came to a part of the cave where the rock formations were like giant columns bursting into mushroom and cauliflower shapes. They heard the whisper of a soft gurgling noise.

"It's a spring," said Thomas, coming to the lip of a rock ledge. "I wonder if this is part of the message too?"

"A bubbling spring, a swan's feather and the drawing of Finnen. What does it mean?" mused Cassie. "If only we could ask Kapo!"

"Didn't Oghma give us the gift of understanding strange languages?" said Thomas

"You're right," said Cassie, frowning. "I forgot. He did say that but –"

A deep rumbling sound stopped their speculation. Kapo tensed and reached for the knife hanging from his belt.

"The bear!" said Nancy, terror-struck.

Vast shadows loomed from the darkness. But they weren't bear-shaped. It was some massive creature with spikes on its back. A sudden shattering sound like thousands of windows breaking made their blood run cold. Heaving, splintering sounds rent the air. Around them the stalagmites and stalactites were crashing to the ground.

In a heartbeat, Kapo illuminated a narrow crevasse in the rock face and pushed them through. Thomas looked back briefly and glimpsed a herd of rumbling creatures like misshapen mammoths with spikes on their backs. Kapo led the Chingles through a natural stairway in the rock where the creatures couldn't follow them.

As they rose, the air grew more ragged and cold in their lungs, rasping their throats. Soon they were back in the cave where they'd first entered. It was dark now outside.

Kapo went to the mouth of the cave and looked up at the sky.

"*Finna*," he said, pointing to a star.

The children shivered in the cold. They had begun to feel weak and light-headed.

"We must get back," said Cassie. "I feel our powers

are fading. I think we can only stay a short while out of our bodies when we travel in dreams and vision quests."

Then Kapo went to a corner of the cave and donned an animal skin. It was the pelt of an elk, with huge antlers on either side of its head. He began to hum a low repetitive chant. He traced a circle in the snow around the children with a stave carved with elaborate swirling designs and continued to hum.

The children held hands. They closed their eyes. All was silence. All was blackness.

They awoke the next morning in a tangle of sheets and duvet in the double bed. Nancy was still clutching the postcard.

"Nancy was right," said Thomas.

Nancy jumped on the bed and rubbed her tummy. They smiled in unison and felt lit from within. They had finally had a breakthrough in their search for Finnen.

CHAPTER 6

Next morning they decided to use up one of their consultations with Sennan. Cassie blew into Oghma's ring and to their surprise Sennan's face appeared on the flickering rainbow stone. He asked them to meet him in the castle grounds in a bank of trees near where the Sacred Grove used to grow. They hurried there and found Sennan awaiting them.

Thomas excitedly told him about the postcard of the Ham Players and their dreamtime travel to the Ice Age. He was surprised that an ancient druid seemed to understand what postcards were.

Sennan was equally excited. "Finnen communicated with this Kapo in that other time and prepared him for your visit. He is, I think, a shaman – a person who is in touch with the spirit world. "

"Nancy said the postcard made her tummy tingle. We think it's something to do with her swallowing the Star Splinter last year," said Thomas. "The last person to have it before Nancy was Finnen."

"The Star Splinter records all around it that comes to pass," mused Sennan. "But it is a mysterious stone. Yes, they may have a link." He placed his hands on Nancy's head and recoiled as if he'd been burnt. "Nancy is your link to Finnen," he pronounced to Cassie and Thomas.

He beamed at them, his white beard shaking with mirth. "Your little sister is your dream-walker. She can lead you through your dreamscapes. Finnen must have something she wants to reveal to you."

Thomas jiggled up and down, fit to burst with excitement. "Kapo showed us a symbol with feathers. Could that be some sort of clue?" he asked. He sketched the symbol in the ground for Sennan, a straight line with five crossed lines.

Sennan's eyes popped open with delight. "I can help you with the symbol," he said. "That is the letter 'I' – or it could also be 'Y' or 'J' – the sounds were similar – in the secret Druid's code, the Ogham alphabet."

"A code!" said Thomas with delight.

Cassie looked sceptical. "I'd never say 'Y yump with ioj' for 'I jump with joy'," she said.

"But once you realise it's a code you could figure it out," said Sennan.

She realised this was true.

Sennan raised his hand and the Crane Bag appeared. He asked Nancy to pick something from it. She drew out a bone of the magical pigs of Assal. It was inscribed with a straight line crossed with five horizontal lines and on the other side it bore nine carvings of feathers. Just like the symbol in Kapo's cave. This had to be more than a coincidence. Sennan looked at the children, the light of understanding dawning in his eyes.

A thought struck Cassie. "We saw the symbol twice," she noted.

So Sennan told Nancy to reach back inside the Crane Bag and pull out another bone. It had the same Ogham symbol, this time with a carving of two feathers. Another "I", "Y" or "J".

Sennan held the bones in his hand and seemed to go into a trance.

"The bones confirm it. You will be summoned to different places and in each one you will find an Ogham clue left by Finnen," Sennan explained. "When you have them all, her hiding place will be revealed."

"But we don't know what the symbols mean," sighed Cassie.

"So you must learn the Ogham alphabet," said Sennan.

"This is so exciting!" said Thomas. "I love puzzles and secret codes."

They sat down on a mossy bank surrounded by trees swaying in the breeze that seemed to edge closer as Sennan spoke.

"Long ago in the mist of time, Oghma invented a secret code for writing the Old Irish language," explained Sennan. "Each letter is depicted as a series of lines and crosses. They roughly correspond to letters in your ABC alphabet."

"So each symbol is a letter," said Thomas.

"Exactly," said Sennan. "You have to remember which symbol corresponds to each letter. There are twenty letters in the alphabet. As I said, some symbols stand for more than one letter – when sounds are alike – for instance, the one you have found: 'I', 'Y' or 'J'."

"That isn't simple at all," worried Cassie. "How will we remember them? Is there a guide?"

"It is straightforward enough and I will be your guide," said Sennan. "The letters are organised into different groups. So the vowels are all written with short lines across a central stem. 'A' is one line, 'O' is two , 'U' is three , 'E' is four and 'I' is five ."

He etched them into the ground.

"Other groups of letters are written with lines to the right and to the left and some are slanted across the stem," he continued.

"That's hard to remember," said Cassie, squinting at the symbols that looked like bird prints in the ground.

"Well, I'll let you in on a secret. Each letter was called after a tree by the druids, so Ogham is also known as the Tree Alphabet," said Sennan. "The first letter of the tree's name in Old Irish corresponds to the Ogham letter. For example, you already know the name of the letter 'D' quite well – from the Sacred Grove."

"Dair!" Thomas blurted out. "D for Dair the Oak Tree!"

"Yes, indeed." He wrote the word "*Dair*" on the ground next to the D symbol. Then he added the word "*Íodha*" after the "I", "Y" or "J" symbol, saying, "And the symbol you have already found is called Íodha after the Old Irish name for the Yew Tree."

Considering the complicated spelling, the Chingles were surprised to find that "Íodha" sounded a little bit like the English word "yew".

Sennan smiled at their anxious faces. "Now that is

more than enough for one day. My allotted time with you is drawing to a close. I can help you with the Ogham as you find more clues."

"What about the feathers?" asked Cassie hurriedly. "Are they also some kind of code or just Finnen's signature?"

"I do not know yet – until you find more clues," said Sennan.

"The only problem is Caitlín seems to be on our tail," said Thomas. He told him about the stone monsters and the hailstorm with the ragged mouth in the sky.

"Caitlín was tracking your journey," said Sennan. "She cannot find Finnen without you. So she won't try to kill you yet. Just wound or maim you. She needs you too much."

"How reassuring – not!" said Thomas.

"When you get really good at Ogham, you'll be able to do hand signals." Sennan moved his fingers in a series of gestures.

"What's that?" asked Cassie.

"Goodbye," Sennan said.

"Wait! One last thing!" said Thomas. "We could barely understand what Kapo was trying to tell us. Didn't Oghma say we would be able to understand other tongues?"

"Did you blow on the ring he gave you?" asked Sennan.

"No!" said Cassie. "We forgot that! We only remembered it was for summoning you!"

"Remember next time." With that, he disappeared.

"I hate it when they do that," harrumphed Cassie. "I wish they'd spell it out a bit more."

"You forgot to tell him about your vision of the planet and the map of the Northern Hemisphere on Glimmering Lake," said Thomas.

"It will just have to wait for another day," said Cassie gloomily. "There's enough to do mastering Ogham."

As soon as they got home, they immediately went to the shed and Thomas wrote down the Ogham symbol they had seen and beside it "*I, Y or J*" and in brackets "*Íodha the Yew*". He noted that they'd seen it twice. Then he took a note of the number of feathers: "*9 and 2*". "If Finnen is leaving us a puzzle, it will have to be more complicated than just a few letters," he insisted. "It will have to be encrypted like a code in case it falls into the wrong hands."

"But knowing exactly where to find the clues is still a problem," said Cassie. "We know Nancy is the dream-walker and we have to look for Ogham letters. But how exactly will we know where and when to go?"

"The postcard from the Ham Players," insisted Nancy.

"But we can't rely on postcards arriving out of the blue," argued Cassie.

"I accept that Nancy has some sort of telepathy with Finnen through the Star Splinter and that Finnen has to be very careful about the information in case it falls into the wrong hands. But what I don't understand is how the Ham Players are going to know where the clues are, to send back the postcards."

"I told them," said Nancy stubbornly.

"You're a pretty smart kid, Nancy," smiled Thomas, "but you must be the youngest theatrical tour director ever."

"I am!" she insisted.

Later that afternoon, they learned she was right. After lunch, Muiris arrived with the post and handed a postcard to Nancy.

"It makes my tummy tingle," she said.

"Funny, that's what she said when we were arranging the tour," commented Angel, idly turning it over.

Cassie snapped to attention. "What do you mean?" she asked.

"Well, when I was organising the tour, I wasn't sure

where to go. Then Nancy closed her eyes and started to point to places on a map of Europe. She said they made her tummy tingle. Now I'm a great believer in intuition, so I organised the tour along Nancy's guidance. I then got the call to go to America and I had to miss the tour but the Ham Players promised to send back postcards to Nancy and me from each location. Nancy was most insistent that they did so."

"She really is the world's youngest theatre tour director!" laughed Thomas.

Nancy beamed with pride.

Cassie tried not to show too much excitement when she looked at the postcard. It was from Cahors in France and featured a picture of a spring. The caption on the back said: "*The Sacred Spring of the Goddess Divona which still provides water for the town of Cahors*." Cassie looked at Thomas in amazement. The link with a goddess was more than a coincidence.

Cassie quizzed Angel about the other locations but neither she nor Nancy could remember the precise details of the tour.

"We will just have to wait and see what the post brings," said Angel.

The Chingles set off on their bikes to Áine's with the postcard in a state of great anticipation.

"No wonder Nancy kept going on about postcards," said Cassie.

"It's quite ingenious really," said Thomas. "Anyone else looking for Finnen would never guess a group of scruffy actors were following her route."

"I told you so," said Nancy happily in a singsong voice.

"I apologise for doubting you," Cassie said to her. "I'm convinced now the postcards hold the key."

"When we have all the clues, we will know where to find her," said Thomas. "Now all we have to do is crack the code! And fight off Caitlín and her evil henchman Lardon. Oh and any other monsters we run into!"

When they got to Áine's house they dumped their bikes and raced up the path but Scáthach blocked the way.

"Please, we must see Sennan urgently. We've had another breakthrough," Cassie said self-importantly.

"I am here to teach you battle craft and everything else will have to wait. Warriors need to know their priorities," said Scáthach sternly. Áine's garden had been transformed into a training ground.

Cassie looked daggers at her and turned away resentfully, cuffing her spitefully as she turned. Scáthach gave her a hard glance, picked her up by the scruff of her neck and tossed her into a bramble bush.

Cassie tried to fight her way out of the brambles, squealing from the thorns. Her skin was scratched and her clothes torn.

"It's not fair," she cried, fighting back the tears. "You're bigger than me!"

Scáthach came and gave her a hand to escape the thorn's prickly embrace.

"Let that be a lesson to you, Angry One. Pick your battles. It is a better strategy to hold your tongue until you can win a fight."

"But it's still cheating," said Cassie, like a dog with a bone.

Scáthach let go of her and Cassie tumbled back into the wreck of the bush.

"I fear your worst enemy is yourself," Scáthach said pityingly. "And that is the worst enemy of all."

Thomas and Nancy glared at Scáthach in solidarity with their sister, then lowered their eyes when she glared back at them. Her glances were more bruising than a blow.

"My quarrel with Cassie is no concern of yours. Loyalty has its place but shouldn't be blind. It is more loyal to help your sister correct the error of her ways."

Cassie winced as she extricated herself from the bush but her pride hurt more than the sting of the thorns.

"We are going to learn the Breath Feat, the Fine Dart Feat and the Rope Feat," said Scáthach. "Then, if we have time, we will master the gae bolga. But first, the Breath Feat."

She breathed in and exhaled through her teeth. They felt their hair ruffle in the breeze. The children did the same back to her. She smiled at them. Then she breathed in again. The smoke in the chimney changed direction. Cassie and Thomas huffed and puffed but Nancy managed it quite easily. Then Scáthach turned her attention to the trees. She inhaled a deep gulp of air, then puffed out her cheeks and blew with all her might. The gust she created was so strong that leaves were blown from the trees. While none of the children managed this, they created steady streams of air.

"Your breath control is good," she said, impressed. "But to move on to the next level you must imagine that you are vessels of the wind and your whole body is a bellows. You are the pump for an infinite circle of air."

They tried their best but it was exhausting. They

ended up red-faced and panting. But just as they thought they couldn't do it, Nancy gave one last gulp and managed to ruffle the top of the branches.

Without giving them the chance to catch their breaths, Scáthach produced three lengths of rope. They had to lasso staves that she threw at them. They ended up with rope burns on their hands. After a while Cassie mastered it but Thomas tied himself into knots.

Barely had they caught their breath when Scáthach took out a bundle of needles from a basket.

"I am going to demonstrate the Fine Dart Feat," she said. She hurled the needles into the air and, to their amazement, they formed into a long string, each one with its point in the eye of the previous needle.

"Gosh, how did you do that?" exclaimed Cassie.

"I concentrated my attention into a point," she said.

"We can't do stuff like that," said Thomas.

"Every time you travel in dreams you use these skills. I am just showing you that talents you have developed in one area can be applied in another."

Scáthach tossed the needles towards them. Thomas and Cassie made a run for it but Nancy glared at the needles. To her amazement they stopped midair and clattered to the ground as if drawn by a magnetic force. Scáthach picked them up again and flung them back at

Nancy. This time they were pulled together like mesh and fell to the ground.

"Good," said Scáthach. "Now I am going to demonstrate for you the gae bolga."

"Excuse me," said Cassie, putting up her hand.

Scáthach regarded her as if she was an irritating fly she'd like to brush aside but Cassie persisted.

"How are we ever going to learn anything if you just keep rushing us on to the next skill before we've mastered the previous one."

"A good question," conceded Scáthach. "I can only refine the talents you already have. First, I need to know what these talents are. But also we don't have much time."

"Will they help us beat Caitlín?" asked Thomas.

"Time will tell if you are truly warriors," said Scáthach gravely. "It is not just physical skill that is needed but strength of mind. It is not just strength but consistency. We shall see. Nancy has promise. She is young enough to learn new things. She has been gifted by the Star Splinter. Now enough time-wasting. I want to demonstrate the gae bolga."

"But I defeated Balor through shapeshifting and Cassie beat the Corra," insisted Thomas.

"Ah, but it is true what the Merrows said. You were

aided by the magic of the Sacred Grove. Maybe that was a fluke. You face a bigger test this time."

"Well, if we don't have any natural ability, perhaps we shouldn't waste your time," said Cassie, flouncing off in a strop.

Nancy and Thomas ran to stop her but Scáthach leapt forward and barred their way with a stave.

"Let her go," she said. "She has deliberately misunderstood what I meant. Some warriors are born and some are made. You work with whatever ability you have. True warriors stay to fight whatever the odds." She held up a fearsome weapon. It was a lance of driftwood in the shape of forked lightning with a bulging tip like a miniature harpoon. As she tossed it into the air, it developed several forked barbs. She caught it and launched it in the direction of Cassie. Nancy let out a scream but Cassie turned nimbly on her heels and caught it. She examined it closely and her face lit up in recognition as it returned to its driftwood shape.

"It's the piece of driftwood I used to whack Balor when he was in his wasp shape and then I chucked it out to sea!" she exclaimed.

Cassie pitched it back forcefully at Scáthach. It shot out of her hand like a bolt of lightning. In midair the barbs came out. Scáthach caught it nimbly at the handle end. They noticed it was deeply notched.

"The gae bolga enters the victim at one point but makes many barbed wounds within," Scáthach explained. "It was forged in the Otherworld from the bones of a sea monster in a bolt of lightning."

Cassie crept back to join the others.

"To truly master the gae bolga," Scáthach continued, "you have to cast it from the fork of your foot." She placed the weapon between her big and second toe. Her toes all worked independently, like fingers. She raised her leg and tossed it in the air. It rose like a firework and, arching like an arrow shot from a bow, it pulverised a wooden post to splinters. Cassie ran to retrieve it. She managed to grip it in her toes and toss it towards a bush; it shuddered towards the target and just glanced it. Scáthach took the gae bolga and placed it back in the cache of weapons and handed them each a replica instead.

"You show a certain aptitude," she said to Cassie. "Now you must practise to refine it."

Despite herself, Cassie couldn't suppress her pleasure at the compliment. But then Scáthach made her practise it blindfolded. It was hopeless.

Nancy was too little to grip the weapon in her foot

so Scáthach gave her a slingshot to play with. This she mastered instantly and had great fun pinging stones at tin cans. But Thomas could barely grip the gae bolga. Scáthach gave him exercises to improve his flexibility and grip.

She proved a patient and diligent teacher, correcting them like a potter does a bowl on the wheel, just a touch here, a steadying hand there. By the end of the morning each of them had improved. Cassie was easily the best with the gae bolga but Thomas had just managed to pick up the weapon in his foot and toss it limply in the right direction. His skill with the rope trick had also improved but no matter how hard he practised he was still not as good as Cassie. It was beginning to get him down. Nancy proved a natural with the slingshot. After she whacked Scáthach on the head with a stone, she made her use bits of twigs instead.

"Who do you think performed best with the gae bolga and rope trick this morning?" Scáthach asked as she gathered up the weapons.

"Cassie," Thomas said glumly.

"If I didn't have to wear a blindfold," his sister complained.

"Cassie has natural ability and has merely refined it.

Likewise Nancy is dextrous with the slingshot and needs only to acquire skill. But you, Thomas, have no natural ability for these at all," Scáthach said.

"I know," he said despondently. "I don't think I am a warrior after all."

"And yet you have made the greatest progress because you have been stubborn and persistent. Warriors don't always win but they always stay to fight. That is the way towards mastery. Remember no baby learns to walk without constantly falling down." And with that she lifted up her cloak and took to the sky as a raven.

"She really does go on a bit," muttered Cassie as she watched her fly off. "All those wise words and sayings. She's like those fortune cookies you get in Chinese restaurants."

"You're just jealous because she said I was the best," said Thomas.

They were so tired after their morning's exertions that they fell asleep after lunch and were startled when Sennan gently shook them awake.

"Scáthach tells me you wished to speak with me urgently," he said.

They looked at him blankly. Then Cassie came to

her senses. The events of the night before! Funny how the training had made them flee her mind.

"We've established a definite trail through the link between Nancy and Finnen," Cassie said. "We've found out that Nancy did pick the locations for the Ham Players tour by sticking a pin in a map of Europe. You were right. They are linked through the Star Splinter."

Cassie then remembered to tell Sennan about her vision of the map of the Northern Hemisphere and the planet.

"That may be a clue to the locations," said Sennan.

"And what about the Ice Age man Kapo?" asked Thomas. "Will there be other guides?"

"Finnen may also have made contact with other helpers like the shaman last night," said Sennan. "Keep an eye out for them. They may not all be human."

"I'll remember to blow on Oghma's ring next time so we can talk to them," said Cassie. "Nancy can interpret the animals."

Nancy smiled happily and nodded her head.

"I love this puzzle," Thomas said eagerly. "And will the bones of Assal in the crane bag always confirm what we find?"

"That may be right. You must travel to each destination and search for a sign as soon as you can,"

Sennan pronounced. "Be vigilant. Remember, Caitlín is also searching for her. When you have all the clues, consult the bones of Assal's pigs at high tide." With that Sennan disappeared.

"Do you remember what Tadgh said before about gods and goddesses moving about between different tribes and mythologies?" said Cassie. "If we know a bit more, maybe we can recognise a pattern."

"We'll follow every lead we can," said Thomas. "But I wonder how we'll know we have all the clues?"

They made their way to Tadgh's on foot, practising their fighting skills as they went. When they arrived he was in the middle of cataloguing a big pile of dusty books.

He led them into the manuscript room. The books they'd consulted the day before were still out on the table with a few more ancient volumes.

"I chased down some goddesses for you in continental Europe and I thought you might be interested in these," he said. He showed them a picture of a sacred spring in a town called Cahors in France – the exact same place as their postcard!

Cassie read out the passage: "*Divona founded the sacred spring of Cahors in the South of France that still provides water for the town. She appears to be the same as the Gaulish goddess called Sirona – whose name means 'divine star'. Her cult has been recorded on sites from Brittany to Hungary. Sirona was a goddess of healing springs – a fertility and healing goddess.*"

Cassie could hardly keep from exclaiming her delight. She signalled to her brother and sister to get going.

"We have to travel as soon as we can," she whispered.

"We have to go now," piped up Thomas in one gulp.

"If you like I can try to dig out an illustration and a bit more about Sirona," said Tadgh, already foraging among his books.

"Later," said Cassie, making a great fuss of looking at her watch.

They rushed out of the tower in a flurry.

"That's a definite link between sacred springs and divine stars. Divona must be an alias Finnen adopted in Cahors," said Cassie as they pelted down the spiral staircase. "There's no time to waste!"

They decided to travel in dreams at Glimmering Lake because of its link with Finnen so they tore off there as fast as they could.

On arrival they made themselves comfortable at the Standing Stones.

"Don't you think it's a bit risky to be out of our bodies in this open place?" worried Thomas.

"Nobody really comes here except us. It's a risk we have to take – there's no time to lose," said Cassie decisively. "If we crouch down behind the Standing Stones no one will see us."

Nancy took the card from Cahors from her pocket. Thomas said no more. The three children laid their hands on the postcard and began to intone.

"*As the sky meets the earth,*

So we travel beyond and between,

In our mind's eye."

They fell into a deep trance and found themselves pulled downstream in a crystal boat on a river. It passed under a bridge with three towers that had also been depicted on the postcard. The boat drew up alongside a quay and they disembarked. They walked a little way along the riverbank. They followed a channel of flowing water that joined the river and a little way from the riverbank they discovered it came from a deep ravine of about forty metres from which water gushed.

"This must be Divona's spring," said Cassie.

The beating of powerful wings disturbed them and a swan swooped down towards them.

"Maybe it's Finnen!" cried Thomas excitedly.

Nancy immediately started to talk to the beautiful bird.

"He's not Finnen but he said to follow him," Nancy said.

In a heartbeat Thomas and Nancy changed shape into young swans but Cassie had to make do with being a mallard duck. She struggled to keep up as the others soared in flight.

They rose over the three towers of the bridge. Cassie wasn't able to rise as high and her flapping wings passed close by one of the towers. Just as she thought she'd cleared it she plummeted in a squall of feathers but managed to correct herself mid-flight. As she rose again, she realised the carved devil on the middle tower of the bridge had come to life and was trying to swipe at her!

The devil took to the air on his little stone wings, like a bat's, and chased her. She dropped lower and then rose in the air behind him. She saw another demon's head peeping out of his backside. Her cries alerted the others and the large swan returned and swooped towards the stone demon, distracting his attention. But the bird was beaten back and, exhausted, had to retreat behind the bridge to recover as the demon's two malevolent heads spat and grimaced. But this gave Cassie enough time to land by the boat and resume her own shape. She picked up a rope.

The stone demon went in pursuit of Nancy in her swan shape. He screamed and hissed and spat ice from his two stone mouths. Cassie leapt to the top of the tower and swung the rope. She lassoed him and caught him by the left leg, then swung him in loops over her head. He whirled around, spitting ice and striking out in all directions. She dashed him against the stone tower with such force the rope flew from her hands. But the stone demon didn't break. Immediately, she drew in her breath and released a stream of air at the demon, forcing him back into the tower so that only his head peeked out from the stone. But then the demon hissed and let out an icy breath full force in her face, nearly blinding her. Cassie retaliated by using all her strength to perform the Breath Feat. He stopped moving, once more becoming a mute piece of sculpture.

The swan returned, beat his wings and let out a cry.

"He said to go on his back," Nancy instructed Cassie.

They flew along the river and descended at a bend where a small village clung to the limestone outcrop. They found themselves in a grove of trees. The swan slid Cassie gently to the ground then, letting out a cry, flew off. Thomas and Nancy resumed their own shapes.

In the centre was a clearing with two shapes covered in ivy. Cassie and Thomas pulled off the foliage and saw they were standing stones. They bore identical markings: an upright line with two slanted slashes across it going downwards left to right.

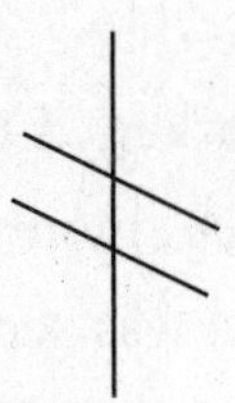

"It's another Ogham letter," said Thomas in great excitement. "Let's memorise it and check with Sennan."

"I can't see any feathers," said Cassie.

They examined the stone in detail.

"They're around the edge," said Thomas, feeling the grooves cut into the rock.

Cassie looked at the carefully carved feathers curling up around the edge of the rock.

"I think they call standing stones 'menhirs' in France," said Thomas as he felt his way around one stone and Cassie the other. "This one has seven feathers."

"This one has eight," said Cassie.

"What do they mean?" said Thomas.

"Maybe they are just her sign after all?" suggested Cassie.

Thomas shook his head. "No, I don't think so. Then she would just leave one feather in each location. Right?"

"We'll just have to wait and see if a pattern emerges," said Cassie. "We're wasting time – we'd better get back."

Suddenly the sky darkened to pewter and they saw the stone demon once more descending from the clouds. But this time he was accompanied by hundreds of other flying stone demons. They had demons' heads protruding from their bellies and backsides as well as their necks. Their hisses rent the air and almost made the children's ears bleed. The demons spat arrows of ice at them, just falling short of hitting them. Then they fanned out into a circle around the menhirs and began to close in on the children.

"What shall we do?" said Cassie. "Since that demon spat at me I feel terribly weak. I don't have the strength to fight them."

Thomas grabbed his sisters and they crouched down by one of the menhirs. They froze in terror.

They could see the snarling faces, the evil eyes, the icy breath.

Panicking, Cassie blew on Oghma's ring.

Suddenly a raven flew out from a copse of bushes

a little way off from the menhirs. In a split second it changed into Sennan who covered them with his cloak.

They found themselves back, shivering, at the Standing Stones by Glimmering Lake, with Sennan by their side. Cassie could barely see and there was a faint wound on her left cheek where the demon had breathed on her. It was in the shape of a C.

"I am glad you summoned me," said Sennan. "It was risky of you to travel in the Otherworld in such an exposed place. You sapped your strength because part of your concentration was back here on the island."

"I told Cassie it was a bad idea," said Thomas.

"It was my fault for telling you to travel as soon as you could," said Sennan. "You are still learning how to travel in the Otherworld – you must be careful."

"Caitlín is growing stronger," said Thomas.

"But she is unstable," said Sennan. "Those stone demons she worked through had evil of their own and she wasn't fully in control. They would have killed you but Caitlín needs you alive to find all the clues. She seeks vengeance on Finnen."

"Thank you for saving us even though you're only

supposed to teach us," said Cassie. "Will the Tuatha Dé Danann punish you for breaking the agreement?"

"Consider it a debt paid," smiled Sennan. "I don't care about the petty rules imposed by the gods. Now about that Ogham symbol. Let's see what Nancy fishes out."

Suddenly the Crane Bag was there in his hand. Nancy reached into it and pulled out two linked bones of Assal. They now bore the Ogham symbol of a straight line with two downward slashes, left to right, with seven feathers on one and eight on the other, confirming they were indeed messages from Finnen.

"That's 'G'," said Sennan. "Its name is Gort for Ivy in the Druid's tree alphabet."

"The menhirs had ivy growing all over them," noted Thomas.

"So this location also led to two letters – two 'G's," Cassie said, wincing. The wound on her face hurt when she talked.

"Speak softly. You must keep these letters secret," Sennan whispered.

But immediately a mist rose from the lake and formed into the shape of Fand the Merrow.

"You have broken the terms of your *geas* by saving them from the stone monsters of Caitlín," she screeched at Sennan.

"But you would not have them killed!" Sennan replied furiously.

"I didn't make the rules!" Fand said smugly. "And there's no way you'll be allowed to tell them Chingles any more about that stupid old druid's alphabet!"

"It's not fair!" Thomas shouted. "It was agreed Sennan could help us on so many occasions and we could summon the Sean Gaels by blowing on the Ogham ring in an emergency!"

"I might have known you shower of chancers would have to cheat!" mocked Fand. "You just wait until I tell Manannán and the gods! Then you'll lose old beardy Sennan and the little Chingles won't have anyone to go running to for help. *Boo, hoo!*"

"That's just so petty of you," fumed Cassie.

"We have to obey for now," said Sennan, then added under his breath, "until I find a way around it." Thomas smiled when he caught the gleam in crafty Sennan's eye.

"You will have to find the remaining Ogham symbols without my guidance. But remember Oghma's ring can decipher strange languages. I shall leave you the Crane Bag. It will appear when you need it. Good luck."

With that Sennan took to the skies.

Fand smirked, then was covered in mist and disappeared.

"I hate that Fand!" shouted Cassie.

It began to rain softly so they headed back to the house.

As they took the fork in the road by some blackthorn trees, Nancy suddenly cried out. She held up her arm. It was pierced with fine needles and looked like a porcupine's back. The needles left pinpricks of blood on her arm when Cassie extracted them. Thomas also cried out and his hand flew to his cheekbone. Cassie pulled out several fine needles. They looked around, bewildered. The rain got slightly heavier. Each of them felt tiny pricks on their exposed flesh.

"It's raining needles!" Cassie cried. They ran for cover and found shelter under a large rock. Most of the needles had lodged in their clothing, so carefully they helped each other to extract them.

The needles fell thick and fast on the ground, clanking with a screechy metallic sound on rocks and stones.

"The Fine Dart Feat," said Thomas. "It's our only chance! Nancy, see if you can do it."

Nancy concentrated with all her might, scrunching up her eyes. She whispered quietly to herself. Next thing the needles froze in midair. Then the tip of each one went into the eye of the other. They formed into long spiralling shapes.

"Use our breaths, Thomas," urged Cassie. Together Cassie and Thomas sucked in air until it curled their toes. But the needles began to travel towards them in the air current, so quickly they expelled their breath. The force of their combined breath was enough to make the columns of fine needles shift over the bog. They blew again and hammered the needles into the bog. They heard a satisfying suck as the earth swallowed them.

Without delay, they ran home and dived straight into the shed, where they set about covering up the windows with "Keep Out" signs of skull and crossbones with a border of Brussels sprouts so Lardon couldn't spy on them.

Then they added the latest clue to their crime-scene charts – two letter Gs.

"Two Is and two Gs: 'Gigi'. Doesn't make much sense." Thomas scratched his head. "Don't forget to make a note of the feathers. They may unlock the code."

So Cassie listed the number of feathers against each letter.

"Caitlín's really on our case now," she said. "Just when we thought we were on Finnen's trail."

At that moment they heard someone blundering about outside. They knew it was Lardon.

He sidled up to them as they went back to the house and held out huge chocolate bars.

"We don't accept bribes," sniffed Thomas.

"Who's Finnen?" Lardon asked slyly.

"She's a goddess we're trying to find," said Nancy, reaching out for a chocolate bar.

"Oh, don't you know that already?" Cassie asked Lardon, eyes narrowed. "Hasn't your friend in the mirror that you're always talking to filled you in? The one with the diamond tooth?"

Lardon looked mystified then somewhat ashamed.

"Sod off, you copper-nosed sad-sack scum-heap!" Thomas shouted at him. Then turning to his sisters, he said, "I told you he was our enemy."

Lardon looked at them with hurt in his eyes.

Nancy held up her hand. "I'll play with you," she said kindly.

Lardon swatted her away. "You're just a kid," he said gruffly as he walked off in a huff. "I'm going to show you all some day."

Cassie and Thomas felt a bit mean.

"Maybe we shouldn't be so hard on him," Thomas began.

"It's too dangerous to be friendly," Cassie said decisively.

They went into the house.

"Another postcard arrived in the mid-morning post," Angel told them. "Muiris and Róisín are run ragged keeping up with the deliveries. They think the Ham Players are rushing around Europe as if on some mission."

The children grabbed it eagerly. It was from a place called Hochscheid in Germany in the Rhine Valley. The greeting was very terse. "*Show a triumph, kiss, kiss, Ham Players.*"

"Can I have it?" Nancy asked Angel sweetly.

Angel looked at her with affection and immediately handed over the postcard. "You are such a funny little thing, Nancy, but I remember I used to get collection passions like that when I was your age."

They took the postcard down to the Finnen Incident Room in the shed. It showed a statue of a woman with a dog on her lap and a snake coiled around her arm, its head pointing towards three eggs.

"I wonder who she is?" said a puzzled Cassie. "Do you remember Tadgh saying something about trying to find an illustration of Sirona, the goddess whose name means 'Divine Star'? The one who may be the same as Divona from Cahors? I wonder if it could possibly be her?"

"Let's go and ask him," said Thomas.

They cycled like maniacs down the boreen, startling sheep and birds, so they would be back in time for supper.

Tadgh wasn't at home but they thought he wouldn't mind if they went into the tower on their own. Thomas retrieved the key behind the secret trick stone and climbed up to the door that was several metres from the ground. He then let down the stepladder for his sisters.

Tadgh was as good as his word and had pulled out several books with "mythology" in the title. Cassie leafed through a volume foxed with old-age marks, careful not to tear the pages. It was so full of dust they all burst into sneezing fits. She opened a page on an old-fashioned drawing of a goddess with a dog resting in her lap. On her head was a crown. She held three eggs in her hand and there was a snake coiled around her arm, its head pointing towards the eggs. It was exactly like the latest postcard. The caption said it was Sirona, the Gaulish goddess whose name meant Divine Star!

"It says here that Sirona was a fertility and healing goddess from pre-Roman times and her most important shrine was in Hochscheid in Germany," said Cassie.

"That's exactly like our postcard! '*Sirona appears to be identical to the goddess known elsewhere as Divona. She seems to have moved from Celtic tribe to tribe, changing her identity and name slightly each time*'!"

Impatiently, Thomas flicked through an *Encyclopaedia of Mythology* for information.

"*She was often paired with another god called Apollo Granus,*" Thomas read, "*and she may have had a son called Boro or Borvo who was associated with boiling springs. He took over her duties – when she disappeared!*"

"This is definitely the Case of the Disappearing Goddess," said Cassie as they flew headlong down the stairs so they wouldn't be late for supper.

Once they'd eaten their supper they were eager to go to bed early, much to Angel's surprise.

Lardon said he was going to his room to write his autobiography, which Cassie explained to Nancy was a book about your life.

"Aren't you a bit young to be writing your life story?" asked Thomas. "I mean you're just a kid."

"You'll see, suckers," said Lardon defiantly. "I've got real estate, bank accounts, talent and someday I'm going to inherit a fortune."

"We have things you'll never have and no amount of money can buy," said Cassie. "Each other."

"Some loss," said Lardon, a sneer on his lips. He disappeared into his bedroom and slammed the door.

Cassie, Thomas and Nancy went up the stairs to their attic bedrooms.

Both Cassie and Thomas felt exhausted from the day's adventures. But Nancy looked feverish.

"I'm all hot," she moaned. "And I have a pain." She pointed to her left ear.

"Should we tell Angel she's not feeling well?" Cassie wondered.

"Maybe it's one of those needles," said Thomas.

He applied a salve that Áine had given them and it seemed to soothe Nancy.

"Maybe we shouldn't travel to the Otherworld tonight," Cassie said.

"We must!" insisted Nancy. "My tummy is fizzy. I feel better now."

As soon as they heard snores coming from Lardon's room, the children lay down together, Nancy clutching the postcard, ready for their next journey to find Finnen. But this time they were both terrified and exhilarated about what they might find.

CHAPTER 7

They found themselves in a dream landscape of a lush valley. Vineyards lined the hills that sloped gently down to a softly flowing river. The air was warm and soothed them.

"I think this is that place Hochscheid on the postcard," said Cassie. Inside some stone ruins there was a bubbling spring. A tall imposing man sat by it on a stone throne. A snake curled round his right hand and in his left he held three eggs. The man spoke in a strange language.

Cassie blew on Oghma's ring.

"I am Apollo Grannus," he said, "God of Fertility and Plenty."

"Do you know a Finnen, or she may be called Sirona or Divona?" asked Cassie, rubbing Oghma's ring.

"Sirona was my fellow guardian," he said, "but she has gone."

"Do you know where?" Thomas asked.

"I know not. Boro, her foster son, and his wife, Damona, have taken over her duties. He is the God of Bubbling Springs."

At that, Apollo Grannus turned to stone and crumbled.

They heard the boil and hiss of water and saw that behind a rocky outcrop was the source of the bubbling spring. On its surface a fat jolly face appeared.

"You seek my foster mother," he said. "Under the rowan leaves." He disappeared.

They headed for a nearby grove of trees and looked around. Finally, Thomas came upon a large stone covered in undergrowth and decaying leaves. They pulled back the greenery and discovered another statue, this time of a woman.

She wore robes like a Roman noblewoman and a small dog sat in her lap. A snake coiled around her left arm and its head pointed to three moonstone eggs that she held in her hand. She wore a tiara in the shape of a star.

"It's a statue of Sirona, just like the ones in the books," said Cassie. "Let's see if we can find an Ogham symbol." They walked around the statue and examined it minutely but could see no trace of an Ogham letter.

Baffled, they explored the grove of trees. Cassie picked a leaf with many short leaves along a central stem. She noticed some of the trees had bright red berries. They were rowan trees, she recognised them now, rustling in the wind, just like the ones growing along the bog.

Nancy went back to the statue and began to pat the stone dog.

"Do you have a message for us?" she asked in dog language. A gunfire of barks came from the stone dog and he jerked his head towards the trees.

"He said the answer was growing in the ground," said Nancy, "but watch out for the snakes in the grass."

A low hiss shattered the air. They froze. Thomas moved his head a fraction and saw that the snake that had been around the statue's arm had come to life. It was growing and strangling the stone dog and the statue of Sirona. It hissed and uncoiled towards the ground.

The stone snake had a triangular head like an adder's. As it slithered along the ground, its forked stone tongue shot out. The children ran and Thomas and Nancy climbed into the trees but Cassie stumbled and lay splayed on the ground.

"Hurry!" they shouted at her.

But in seconds the stone snake had coiled round Cassie.

"I'm going back for her!" Thomas told Nancy.

He decided to try to leap. He rose in the air in an arc through the trees and felt his body change into the sleek form of a salmon – but almost as soon he forced himself back into his own body. In terror he saw the ground rise before him and landed with a thwack flat on his belly. He felt shaken but there were no bones broken. He grabbed a stick. He heard Nancy's cries. The snake seemed to be growing and was now also coiling around the trunk of the tree where Nancy was sheltering.

"Try your Breath Feat!" he called out to her.

Nancy blew with all her might. The snake recoiled but instantly shot back at her, its forked tongue centimetres from her face. She blew again, the snake withdrew and she immediately shimmied down the tree trunk. She darted through the trees to her brother's side. Thomas was striking the stone tail of the snake but worryingly Cassie and the stone dog had stopped crying out. The snake began to coil back on itself in their direction.

"We'll have to distract it," said Thomas, picking up

a stick. "I'll make the snake follow me and I'll try to push the stick down its throat."

But Nancy ignored him and walked towards the head of the dangerous snake, as if mesmerised. Thomas held his breath as she drew closer to the hideous stone reptile. In a matter of moments the snake would strike her with its forked tongue unless Thomas thought of something.

"Leap as a salmon and land as yourself!" he shouted with sudden inspiration. He was so terrified for his little sister he could hardly bear to watch.

But, to his amazement, Nancy did just that.

The stone dog suddenly barked before falling once more back to mute stone.

Nancy landed behind the coiled snake who hissed and turned his head towards her. Just as the snake was about to strike her, Thomas took aim and hurled the stick through the air, narrowly grazing the snake's puffy cheek. The enraged snake uncoiled and whipped towards Thomas in an instant. He saw its fearful fangs ready to bite him, its evil narrow tongue, its stone-cold dead eye.

Another chilling hiss rent the air. The snake whipped around. For a dreadful moment Thomas thought there was another snake. But then a stick came sailing back through the air and pierced the snake's eye. Thomas glanced over by the trees. His little sister waved at him and let out another hiss. He laughed. Nancy had not only mastered snake speak but she'd hit the target.

Immediately the snake froze and crumbled to the ground. Cassie was released from its stony grasp and staggered to her brother and sister.

"The dog told me to aim at its eye," Nancy said, pointing at the stone statue. "And he told me to look at the eggs."

They rushed over as the statue was beginning to crumble. They were just in time to see that one moonstone egg had a feather carved on it.

"We'd better search quickly for the Ogham letter before everything disappears!" shouted Thomas. But the ground around the statue began to heave and splinter, like an earthquake.

All three of them took to the air as swans. As they flew over the rowan trees with their bright red berries, something about the planting snagged Cassie's attention. She flew back over and saw that the rowan trees in the grove were planted in an unusual formation. They made a shape – a vertical line with two lines on the right side. She carefully memorised it.

"Those were rowan trees," said Cassie when they awoke the next morning. "I remember them from a school nature trip. Didn't Sennan say that each of the Ogham symbols was given the name of a tree in Old Irish? And the first letter of the tree is what the symbol stands for? So if we knew the name for 'rowan' in Old Irish, we'd have the letter."

A thought struck Thomas. "What about blowing on Oghma's ring? He invented Ogham and the ring deciphers languages. Maybe it can decipher it when we say the word."

So Cassie blew on the ring as Thomas asked, "What's the Old Irish word for 'rowan'?"

Then suddenly they knew! The knowledge just popped into their heads.

"It's Luis, the letter 'L'!" said Cassie.

"Great! But I'm still puzzled by those feathers," said Thomas. "We've jumped from high numbers to one. There was just one carved on the egg last night. I can't figure it out."

After breakfast, they were none too pleased when Angel told them they had to play with Lardon.

"But we have to go to Áine's," complained Cassie.

"It wouldn't be good for his allergies what with all those flowers and plants," said Thomas slyly.

Lardon began to sneeze violently at the very thought of it. "I'm too tired," he moaned. "My scooter's broken. It rains all the time and there's lots of dangerous creepy crawlies. And why don't they just cement over the whole damn place to get rid of all that dirt!"

Angel insisted that Lardon had to get some fresh air. If he wouldn't walk, he had to ride the donkey as far as the crossroads with the children.

"But he smells," complained Lardon. "And so do those kids."

"It's that or walk," threatened Angel.

So they set out. Lardon kept panicking and shouting out that Derry was going to throw him but Cassie and Thomas pretended not to hear. Nancy kindly went back and held Derry by the reins, chattering to him in brays and hee-haws.

At the fork in the road, they saw Muiris cycling up on his bike. Thomas raced ahead.

"Your friends go to some places!" said Muiris, handing him a postcard and dashing off.

It was a picture of an observatory station and a red planet, but Thomas didn't get to read it because Lardon drew up on the donkey.

"Did Muiris give you a letter or something?" he asked.

"None of your business," retorted Thomas. "Look, we only let you be with us because Angel forces us."

"I wouldn't hang around with you deadbeats if you were the last children on earth!" retorted Lardon as they continued down the boreen.

"Shut up, pus-face!" shot back Thomas.

"Stop fighting," pleaded Nancy.

"You think you're so special, you Shingles. What are you? Some kind of skin disease?" taunted Lardon.

"It's Chingles," said Cassie.

"How do you know our nickname?" said Thomas.

"So East Croydon, is that the dullest no-account place on Planet Earth?" sneered Lardon, ignoring the question. "Oh no, that would be Inishawful, the soggiest god-forsaken hellhole this side of Death Valley!"

Both Cassie and Thomas attempted to pull Lardon off the donkey. But Nancy gave a signal to Derry and Lardon shot off down the road just where the road forked.

"Why did you let him escape?" fumed an exasperated Cassie.

"You're not supposed to fight," said Nancy firmly.

Cassie bent down towards her menacingly. "Just don't get us into any trouble, you silly little fool!"

Nancy looked at her defiantly but her bottom lip trembled.

"Stop picking on her!" Thomas got in between them. "If it wasn't for her last night you mightn't be here. Remember what Scáthach said about knowing your enemies? Nancy is one of us."

"Oh, 'remember what Scáthach said'," Cassie mimicked cruelly. "You were slagging her off yourself recently enough."

A raven swooped just in front of her left ear and alighted on the path ahead of them. In the blink of an eye it changed into Scáthach.

"Who has been taking my name?" she said crossly, her cloak of ravens' feathers billowing in the wind. "Vigilance at all times. You never know when your enemy may appear." She tossed them three staves and bade them pass her on the road.

In the blink of an eye, Nancy rose in the air and transformed into a salmon as she sailed over Scáthach's head. She landed as herself. Thomas followed suit.

"I haven't even taught you that," said Scáthach approvingly, as she engaged Cassie in combat.

Thomas came from behind Scáthach and held the stave up to her throat.

"Let Cassie pass," he said.

Scáthach put down her stave. "Well done! You have used skill and cunning."

"I want to fight," Cassie said stubbornly.

"Have the grace to accept help," Scáthach scolded her. "Don't let your pride jeopardise your safety or theirs."

Cassie fumed inwardly but held her tongue. She was angry that not only had her younger brother and sister saved her last night but they were now lording it over her in front of Scáthach.

"Where did you learn the salmon leap?" Scáthach asked.

"I worked it out last night when we were travelling in dreams," said Thomas. "It just came to me to use a salmon's ability to leap to improve a jump."

"Clever," said Scáthach. "You have discovered one of the secrets of our warrior prowess."

As they walked towards Áine's house, they told Scáthach about their adventures of last night and the earlier hail of needles.

"I still have a pain in my ear," Nancy complained, pointing to the spot. When they got to her house, Áine applied ointments and herbs to the sore point. Then Scáthach pinched the skin and pulled out a fine transparent needle made of crystal.

"Caitlín is using her stone magic to track you," said Scáthach, crushing the needle to smithereens between her forefinger and thumb. "But she won't kill you yet – she needs you to lead her to the clues."

"But she will hurt you when she can," added Áine from the threshold as the children followed Scá11

thach outside. "Be careful!"

The children shuddered but Scáthach got down to business. She distributed lances among them – each with a pointed tip of metal nearly a metre long.

"Today it's time to move on to the lance. First, it's the Edge Feat," she said briskly, "the art of running up lances. This feat requires lightning precision and concentration."

They looked at her with incredulity. They were struggling to even hold the lances up.

She then instructed Cassie to strike her in the breast, which she tried to do with vehemence. To their astonishment, Scáthach leapt into the air and landed on her left foot on the tip of the lance. She balanced for a moment and then jumped down. The lance flew out of Cassie's hand and clattered to the ground.

Scáthach picked up the lance and held a shield on top of it.

"This is the Lance and Shield Feat. Now I want Nancy to try. She shows promise, to perform the salmon leap so young. Younger than Cúchulainn who also excelled at the slingshot."

"Who's he?" asked Thomas.

"One of my best pupils," said Scáthach. "A hero of Ulster but he was also a vain, boastful fellow, too fond of his own powers. But enough talking."

Nancy took a leap and landed nimbly on the shield. Then it was Thomas's turn. But he'd lost the knack which had come to him so naturally before. He tried jumping in his own shape but couldn't rise high enough, so mid-jump he changed himself into a bird and perched on the shield.

Scáthach viewed him with amusement.

"Ingenious solution," she said. "But the salmon leap requires that you turn into a salmon. It is more effective than the flight of a bird. You've done it before."

Thomas tried again to shapeshift into a salmon in mid-jump. But he panicked and narrowly missed the shield, falling to the ground in a flurry of limbs. He immediately picked himself up and tried again. This time he made contact with the shield for a brief instant before falling to the ground once more. It really bothered him. He was an excellent shapeshifter and seemed to be losing his ability.

"You just have to relax and stop trying too hard," Scáthach reassured him. "It will come."

Then it was Cassie's turn. She easily vaulted up the stave of the lance and landed on the shield. So, to her annoyance, Scáthach made her practise it blindfolded.

Scáthach kept them at it all morning. She sank lances into the ground and placed shields on them and they had to jump from one to the other. Then she spun the shield on a lance, making it more difficult. Nancy was easily the best.

Thomas tried to ignore what his sisters were doing and concentrated on his own jumping. He told himself it was just a game and it didn't matter if he wasn't the best. It worked and he soon improved and regained his old confidence and skill. Now that he was relaxing, he was able and fast. Soon he was jumping better than Cassie. Thomas became so good, Scáthach made him practise it on one leg but he was hopeless at this and just ended up bruised and sore.

Thomas may have been better at the salmon leap but Cassie excelled at staying on the spinning shield. She was made to practise that blindfolded also. As she plunged to the ground in a jumble of limbs, Nancy laughed.

"It's not that funny," fumed Cassie.

Scáthach plunged staves into a tree trunk, creating a ladder, and as Nancy began to climb, Cassie spitefully tripped her little sister up. Nancy looked shocked but said nothing. But Scáthach observed the foul.

Then it was Cassie's turn to climb up the lances but every time she thought she had ascended to the top of the ladder another lance appeared. Soon there was a line of lances reaching up to the sky, beyond the treetops. Cassie regarded them with dismay.

"I'll never climb all those," she cried. "It's not fair!"

Scáthach ignored her as she continued to instruct the others. A furious Cassie teetered above their heads. Then, each time she raised her foot on to the next lance it disappeared. She slipped down several lances, clinging to them to stop herself falling off. She couldn't move in either direction without losing her footing and stumbling.

She was stuck, unable to join the others for lunch, and watched in frustration as they tucked into a feast.

Nancy tried to throw her an apple but Scáthach stopped her.

"She cannot come down until she realises what is tripping her up," said Scáthach.

Cassie hung there fuming for most of lunch but finally gave in. "I'm being punished for being mean to Nancy," she said in a small voice.

"By tripping Nancy up, not only are you cheating but you are wasting energy tripping a rival when you should be concentrating on learning for yourself. What profits you to make an enemy of Nancy? It doesn't improve your own talent. Respect your comrades, Cassie. Some day your life might depend on their skill. Concentrate on fighting your enemies, not your allies."

Cassie felt her cheeks burning. She remembered Nancy's bravery the night before when she had saved her from the stone snake. She felt guilty. She'd been behaving just like the most despicable bully. Even Lardon wasn't cruel enough to pick on a kid.

"I apologise, Nancy, for being a jerk," she called down. As soon as she said it the lances above her head disappeared and she was able to descend to the ground.

They spent all afternoon practising their new skills. Then suddenly Scáthach disappeared in the blink of an eye.

"Oh, I hate it when she does that!" Cassie muttered.

Almost immediately, they remembered the postcard. It was funny how training with Scáthach drove everything else from their minds.

Thomas produced the postcard. It read: "*We stopped off at this great observatory to take a look at the solar system. We saw the new discovery – Sedna! Quite exciting! Ham Players.*"

"That's Sedna, the newest planetoid! It's an odd clue but still associated with stars," exclaimed Cassie. "And I saw a planet on the lake. The trail is red hot!"

Thomas suddenly felt a compulsion to use the Crane Bag. "Let's see if the old bag of bones can give us another clue," he said as he reached into thin air for it. It was immediately in his hand. "Reach in, Nancy."

Nancy pulled out an egg-shaped moonstone that looked like the one held by the Goddess Sirona.

"Strange," said Thomas. "What does it mean? I wish Sennan was here to advise us."

To their surprise Sennan's face appeared on the moonstone. "Fand the Merrow has complained to the gods and I have been forbidden to continue your instruction in person. But no one has said I can't communicate with you in spirit," the druid said cannily, his green eyes twinkling.

"I bet the Merrows will make sure they close any loophole," said Cassie.

"Well, until they do, let's get on with it," said Sennan. "Now each of you, reach into the Crane Bag."

Nancy and Cassie both pulled out an egg-shaped moonstone identical to Thomas's.

"I believe Finnen wanted you to have them so you can master moving through time," said Sennan. "You are skilful dream-walkers. But for this clue you also need to be able to time-travel when you get to your dream landscape. This will help you accelerate back and forth in time." He instructed them to roll the eggs around their hands.

They slipped into a trance and found themselves hurtling through space, icicles forming on their eyelids as they were thrust beyond the stars through infinite blackness. They looked down and saw Áine in the past thrust the Star Splinter into the heavens. It rose past the Milky Way and then it anchored on the edge of the universe. They realised they were watching the birth of a planet. Gas and fire burned and the planet was a fiery red. The moonstones tugged in their hands like magnets and pulled them to hover over the planet, in front of a volcano. There was a burst of fire and lava spurted from the mouth of the volcano. It rolled downhill in an angry spume and ran into a glacier where it froze into the shape of a tree covered with masses of flat-topped flowers. It looked beautiful, like an etching. On its bark it bore a straight line with five slashes leaning downward to the right.

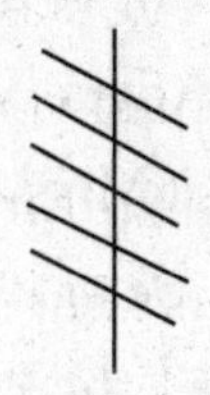

Then the volcano belched. They saw smoke rise and form into the shape of a feather. This happened five times.

"Five feathers this time," noted Thomas.

"Finnen spread those clues over millennia," said Cassie. "It's really quite clever because unless we had the moonstone egg to help us speed through time, the clues would just have been so much smoke."

They plunged back through the galaxy and were then back in the clearing near Áine's house.

Eagerly they reached for the Crane Bag. The bone Thomas pulled out bore the Ogham symbol and the five feathers.

Cassie noticed that a tree outside Áine's house ressembled the one they had seen etched on the glacier. She ran to the house and asked Áine its name in Irish.

"It's Ruis the Elder," Cassie told the others excitedly. "The letter 'R'."

They rushed home, hoping there might be a new postcard signalling their next destination but all they found was a note from Angel beside covered dishes of food. It said: "*Gone to visit Mrs Moriarty. Help yourself to food. Lardon is in charge. Be nice!!! Love, Aunty Angel.*"

When they they lifted the covers, there were only crumbs left on the plates.

"Lardon!" fumed Cassie.

Lardon ambled into the kitchen and burped loudly. He made chicken noises and flapped his hands. "Ah, it's the poor Shingles! Named after a form of chickenpox."

"You haven't seen a postcard, have you?" Thomas asked casually.

"I might have. What's the big deal with the postcards?" Lardon said suspiciously.

"They are private property," said Cassie.

"I'm the one in charge here," crowed Lardon.

"We'll do something for you if you let us see the card," Thomas wheedled.

"Wanna do a deal, huh? Sit down!" Lardon commanded as if he was a police chief. Lardon always seemed to be acting in some private TV drama in his head.

They ignored him.

"What's going on in the shed, spawns of Satan?" he demanded.

They said nothing.

"Tell me who this broad Finnen is. Is she a witch? A crime boss? Is this line of questioning *alien* to you?" Lardon demanded.

"What planet are you on?" sighed Thomas.

"Planet Earth," croaked Lardon. "What is yours?"

"Know any old hags with hideous crooked teeth and one diamond one and a liking for needles and sharp objects?" hissed Thomas.

"Your adored Aunty Angel," said Lardon spitefully.

Cassie picked up a sweeping brush but Thomas restrained her and whispered: "Remember what Scáthach said about not losing your temper."

Reluctantly Cassie put the brush down. Struggling to control her temper, she looked around the room and her eyes rested on Aunty Angel's sewing box. She flipped the lid and saw a pincushion full of needles like a porcupine. Before she knew what she was doing she'd blown them all up in the air and made them hover above Lardon's head.

"No, Cassie!" shouted Nancy.

Lardon looked up in horror and shielded his head with his hands. "They'll prick me!" he yelled, running around the kitchen. But every time he moved, the needles just followed.

"What will prick you?" goaded Cassie. "Your conscience?"

"Those needles!" yelled Lardon. He flung open the back door and, seeing how muddy it was, hesitated before running out. But Cassie blew the needles outside and soon they were back over his head. Lardon flung himself into the ditch, roaring as the murky water soaked him through. He gazed in despair at his dirty trainers and tracksuit and ran back into the kitchen.

"Help me! " he wailed.

"Stop it!" shouted Nancy.

"It's wrong to misuse your powers," warned Thomas.

Guiltily Cassie blew the needles back into the sewing basket.

"You kids have me weirded out!" Lardon squealed. "You were trying to needle me!"

"I didn't see any needles," said Cassie innocently.

"Can we have the postcard, please?" said Thomas sweetly. "And we promise we won't stitch you up."

"My tracksuit is filthy – I'll have to change first!" Lardon moaned.

"You're not going anywhere until you tell us about the postcard," insisted Thomas.

"I tore it up and fed it to the donkey," Lardon croaked.

The children raced outside, leaving Lardon screaming for mercy.

Derry was grazing in the bottom field and reared back to see the children thundering towards him. The donkey brayed out in alarm and pointed his nose towards the half-chewed remains of a card.

"He says he's sorry," Nancy translated.

Cassie held up the remains of the soggy card. It was all mangled and squidgy but they could see there was a picture of a modern seaside resort on one half of the card and mountains and a palace on the other. There was a hole in the middle.

"Here's another bit of it," said Thomas, and he covered the hole with the missing piece.

They could now see there were two strange conical chimneys in a circle in the middle of the card.

Cassie turned it over. It was almost impossible to read anything on the back. She made out the words "*two chimneys*," "*Sin*" and "*ugal*".

"At least we'll still be able to use it to guide us," said Thomas hopefully.

They trooped back into the kitchen to see a purple-faced Aunty Angel with a ruffled Lardon.

"I can explain," began Cassie.

"Straight to your rooms," said Angel tersely. "Nancy, were you involved?" Nancy looked guiltily at her brother and sister.

"He got Derry into trouble," she said.

"That's like so totally untrue!" wailed Lardon.

"He threw away my postcard," Nancy said.

"It blew away," insisted Lardon.

"Hand it over. The postcards are not yours, Nancy," said Angel. "They are addressed to both of us."

Reluctantly Cassie handed over the card.

"My goodness!" said Angel. "It's in bits!"

Then surprisingly Nancy threw a tantrum and started kicking Angel. Even Cassie and Thomas were astonished.

"You children are a disgrace," Angel said, restraining Nancy. "I'm ashamed of you. You've turned into surly, cruel bullies!" She ordered them to their rooms.

They trooped up the stairs, their heads hung low, to the sound of Lardon's sniggers. Forlornly they changed into their pyjamas. Just as they were about to get into bed, Angel knocked on the door.

"I want Nancy to sleep in my room tonight," she said. "You two are a bad influence on her."

"But she can't!" protested Cassie.

But Angel looked stern and Nancy did as she was told.

"I'll sneak back," she whispered to Thomas as she nipped back in to pick up Dog the Teddy.

"What are we going to do?" sighed Thomas. "No postcard, no Nancy." From her pocket, Cassie took out the piece of card showing the two chimneys. "Let's hope this is enough!"

"Oh, you didn't hand that piece over! Quick thinking!" said Thomas.

"And remember the words we read: '*Sin*' and '*ugal*' ". As quietly as she could, she pulled down a dusty old school's atlas from a bookshelf.

"The Ham Players are doing a European tour and in my vision at the lake I saw a map of the Northern Hemisphere with Europe in the centre," she whispered. "There were some places lit up on it – maybe the Ham Players' destinations?"

They opened on the map of Europe. Cassie surveyed Eastern Europe on the right-hand page and Thomas looked over Western Europe on the left.

They tried putting their fingers over the front of country's names. It was a laborious process but they persisted. Through Scandinavia, Eastern Europe, the Mediterranean.

Then Thomas saw it.

"Look," he whispered excitedly, "why didn't we think of it? It's *Portugal* of course – and there's a place here off the coast called Sintra!"

It was several miles from the coast, going north from a place called Boca do Inferno, which was translated as the "mouth of hell".

Cassie pulled an old guide to Europe from the shelf. It was from the 1980s when their mother toured the world. She looked up Sintra and could hardly contain her excitement.

"*Named after a Celtic goddess of the moon,*" Cassie's eyes lit up as she read, "*Sintra is a mystical landscape steeped in mythology and famous for its number of palaces and castles. Visit the National Palace full of Arab mysticism and the ghostly Gothic castle and grounds of the Quinta da Regaleira whose stunning tower reeks of alchemy and mythology.*"

Thomas punched the air in a victory salute but then he dropped his fist dejectedly. "But can we even travel without Nancy and the rest of the card?"

They heard Lardon snoring. Jarlath had taken to sleeping in his barn and Angel had long gone to bed.

"We'll just have to try," said Cassie.

They both touched the piece of postcard and intoned the words:

"*Power of the stag be mine,*

Strength of the eagle be mine.

Change, Chingles, change!"

To their surprise, it worked. They found themselves sinking fast through deep water, then plunging in free fall as if from a very high cliff. Cassie landed badly on a jagged rock. She was narrowly perched on a rocky outcrop. The noise was deafening as the waves lashed it. She guessed it was the "mouth of hell". She was terrified of being swept off her narrow sanctuary. But where was Thomas? The light was blue-black and sea spray washed over her body, whipping her like a lash. Her pyjamas were drenched through.

"*Help!*" She heard her brother's voice. Above them, noisy seabirds cawed and roared. Her eyes adjusted to the poor light. Thomas was clinging to a nearby rock.

"*Change!*" she called out.

Immediately both of them turned into falcons and rose above the boiling waters. They landed on the cliff edge and changed into their normal shapes. Below them, waves crashed thunderously against a gaping cavern that had been gouged out of the rock over time.

Their eyes adjusted to the half-light and they looked around on a barren landscape of blasted rock and baked earth.

"There's something bothering me about that card," said Cassie. "I think it contained several clues because it showed different landscapes."

"Perhaps we should change back into falcons and survey the countryside," suggested Thomas.

So they shapeshifted back into falcons, magnificent birds of prey with keen eyesight that could scan the horizon with radar vision. They flew off side by side. As they hovered over a sea wall, trying to get their bearings, they were surprised to hear a familiar voice.

It was their little sister Nancy.

"I found you," she said pleasantly. "All by myself. I stoled the card from Angel and here I am."

They were happy to see her. Nancy concentrated and changed into a baby falcon with tufted feathers and fluffy plumage.

"Follow me," she said, taking wing.

The landscape swirled with fog but out of the mist they saw the jagged outlines of a castle ruin. Nancy swooped into a window that led into a library where ancient books crumbled on the shelves. She seemed to know what she was looking for. She plucked out a grey pamphlet in her beak. Then the children changed back into their human shapes.

Cassie thumbed through the pamphlet. It was called *The Thermal Springs and the Climate of Estoril in Chronic Rheumatism and Gout during Winter* by Dr D G Dalgado. It was published in Paris in 1910 and the price was two shillings.

Cassie scanned the pages. She read that Estoril meant "place of the falcons" and was the site of three springs with legendary healing properties. Then there was lots of boring stuff about the gouty being irritable invalids and big words like "scrofulous" and "homologous".

Thomas flicked through the pages and came to a foldout map of the coast and the Sintra area. He pulled out the map. A place called Alvide north of the rocky cove named Boca do Inferno was marked with two stars.

Nancy pointed. "This bit makes my tummy tingle," she said, pointing to Alvide.

"Stars, the sign of Finnen." Cassie smiled. "We have to find this place."

They changed back into falcons and flew for miles over pine forests and hills covered with low scrubby bushes and pretty blue, yellow and white flowers.

They descended in a shady part of the forest where there was a deep dark pool filled by a cascading waterfall. Then they changed back into human shape and discovered a cave nearby.

"This is it," said Nancy, patting her tummy.

"What do we do now, Nancy?" asked Thomas.

Nancy wandered round and stopped at a spot by the cave. "There is something here that makes me tingle," she said, rubbing her tummy.

But all they could see was the bare ground.

"Maybe it's buried, whatever it is," reasoned Thomas.

So they started to dig with their bare hands. About half a metre down, Cassie felt something solid in the soil.

"I've found something made of wood!" she called excitedly.

Thomas picked up a stick and used it to lever Cassie's find out. They pulled out a wooden box about the size of a jewellery box, with a curved handle of ivory. Cassie cleared off the soil and saw that it was covered in intricate carvings.

"I guess we better see what's inside," Thomas said.

With trepidation Cassie raised the lid on its rusty hinges and was flabbergasted when a white shape sprang out.

Before them stood a funny little ghost of a man wearing a neckerchief, a linen suit and a panama hat.

He had a pointy clipped white beard and round spectacles perched on a thin beaky nose. Despite having been shut away in a box, he looked freshly laundered and pressed. He bowed in their direction.

"Dr Dalgado of the Royal Academy of Sciences of Lisbon at your service." He spoke very precise English in a high-pitched voice with the trace of an accent.

"We are sorry to disturb you," said Cassie politely, "but we are searching for the Goddess Finnen and wonder if you know anything about a clue with swan's feathers and an Ogham symbol."

But Dr Dalgado wasn't really taking any of it in. In a flurry, he ran under the waterfall. The water just passed through him because he was a ghost.

"Chloride of two point eight seven grams, traces of sodium barite. How I've missed the revivifying waters!" he cried.

"If I could just be so bold as to ask you," Cassie tried again, "do you know anything of the whereabouts of a Goddess Finnen, a Swan Maiden also known as Divona and Sirona?"

"Swan, you say?" he pondered. "Just before my death, I started to have dreams where I was visited by a woman with swan's wings. Having been a man of science, I began late in life to train as a shaman. I wasn't very good. But in my last illness I had a dream of a Swan Maiden that told me she had founded the springs and I was so taken by this that I asked for my remains to be stored in a carved box decorated with swans' feathers. She told me that one day I would be visited and released by three 'Chingles from the East'. Most peculiar for a man of science." He shook his head. "There was another message, something about trees. I'll try to remember."

They examined the box. Thomas counted the feathers. There were six. Cassie looked at the underside of the box. It showed a carved leaf that they recognised immediately. It was oak and they realised they were standing in an oak forest. There was also an inlaid mother-of-pearl symbol on the inside of the box – a straight line with two horizontal lines on the left-hand side.

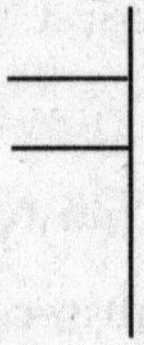

"Well, we know this one!" grinned Thomas. "Dair the Oak!"

The children smiled at each other. They'd found another Ogham letter.

Cassie placed the box beside the pool.

Thomas looked thoughtful. "But I think you were

right about there being more than one clue here because of the number of pictures on the postcard," he said. He turned to Dr Dalgado. "This is Alvide?"

Dr Dalgado nodded. "The sacred pool here is renowned for its healing qualities," he added.

"Do you know if Sintra has any connection with swans?"

"Sintra was a Celtic moon goddess," he said in a lecturing voice, "though some say she was named for Cynthia, another name for the Greek moon goddess. And swans were the favourite symbols of the Kings of Portugal who lived here. Perhaps you should visit the National Palace. Look out for the two tall chimneys. There must be some reason I was visited by a swan lady! Gosh, I really wish I'd starting becoming a shaman earlier. It's really most interesting."

"And what will you do now?" they asked.

"Come with you if I may." He bowed low. "You know, there are several mysterious palaces and castles in Sintra. Perhaps I can be your guide."

The children nodded enthusiastically.

"And perhaps you could fill the box with the healing waters," he requested. "I'd like to have it for sentimental reasons."

They happily did as they were asked.

Then the children rose in the air as falcons. Thomas dipped back down to sweep up the ivory handle of the jewellery box in his beak. Dr Dalgado floated alongside them as they headed towards Sintra over pine-covered hills.

Soon they saw the bulky outline of what looked like a Gothic castle in a clearing in the forest. They landed on an outcrop of rock that overlooked it. Swiftly, they changed back into their normal selves and gazed down at the extraordinary scene below them – a fairytale creation of turrets, elaborate gardens and an artificial lake surrounded by the pine forest. At the heart of the fanciful creation was a roofless tall tower.

There was something threatening and mysterious about the whole place.

"That must be the 'stunning tower' that was mentioned in the guide book!" said Cassie, gazing at the tall tower that sprang upwards like an exclamation mark.

"We need to go there," Nancy said to Dr Dalgado, pointing at the tower. "Ah, the mysterious tower of the Quinta da Regaleira!" sighed Dr Dalgado. "The castle was build by Baroness Emelinda whose family were originally Irish, I believe, and hailed from the Bog of Allen. It is full of supernatural revelations and legend has it that the tower hides a secret. Become falcons again and follow me!"

But Cassie hesitated. She'd spied some stone gargoyles leering at her from the masonry. She suddenly felt Caitlín's presence.

"No! It's too dangerous!" she cried. "We can't fly here! Those stone demons are like the ones that attacked us at Cahors. We must find another way!"

"We can enter the maze of tunnels but they are most confusing," said a perplexed Dr Dalgado.

"My tummy's tingling! I know the way!" proclaimed Nancy trotting off towards the tower.

"We should trust the dear child," said Dr Dalgado, following in her wake.

They plunged on foot towards their destination with Nancy leading the way down the steep hill.

Soon they reached the castle gardens, which were surrounded by a low stone wall. They scrambled over it but it was by no means clear how they were going to reach the tower. The whole place was a labyrinth of mysterious arches and pathways. Cassie spotted brooding stone statues wherever she turned her gaze.

"We can't go through here!" she insisted again, fearfully. "I feel as if Caitlín is lurking in those statues!"

"It's OK, Cassie," said Nancy, taking her hand. "I know another way."

She led them towards a small artificial lake that was covered in vile, slithery green algae.

"I'm getting that tummy tingle again!" she said excitedly, pointing to an unexpected doorway in a cave by the lake.

It led to a passageway that to their astonishment went under the waterfall that flowed into the lake.

"This place is like an underground maze!" exclaimed Thomas.

They progressed carefully on the slippery stones, both enthralled and bewildered by the bizarre tunnels and passages. Under the waterfall, they discovered a stairway to a tunnel that seemed to spiral under the lake.

"This seems to be the way!" said Dr Dalgado, merrily glancing at Nancy. "Follow me!"

Cassie and Thomas looked at each other, suddenly wondering if they would ever find their way to the tower. It was so weird to be walking in tunnels that went under a lake and a waterfall!

"Come on!" said Nancy with confidence as she patted her belly.

They started down the tunnel. It was narrow and so low they had to stoop as they walked. The air was musty and damp, water dripped from the walls and the rocky floor was slippery and treacherous underfoot.

Here and there small skylights were bored in the tunnel roof overhead, letting in just enough light for them to make their way.

Then they came to a fork in the tunnel. Nancy insisted they follow the right-hand passage.

They reached a dark, waterlogged tunnel. Thomas felt doubtful about going on. He leaned against the wall and felt smooth rounded stones like large cobbles. But he recoiled immediately. Something had tried to bite him.

Cassie peered at the stones. "They're skulls," she said.

Instantly, they all shrank back and Cassie was nipped by something on the opposite wall. The air was filled with chattering noises. The walls were completely lined with skulls gnashing their teeth. Dr Dalgado tried to frighten the skulls but he wasn't very convincing. The skulls let out a gruesome laugh.

"We must go back to the fork!" said Thomas.

"No," said Nancy. "This is the way."

"Come on, children!" called Dr Dalgado, who seemed to have great faith in Nancy.

But could they avoid touching the walls? Their only chance was to slither along the ground where the tunnel was widest and hope they didn't touch the sides.

They dropped down into the squelchy mud and dragged themselves carefully through on their hands and knees. Thomas tried to crawl on his elbows as he balanced the box in his hands above the mud but he kept slipping.

"Almost there," encouraged Dr Dalgado.

Thomas risked raising himself slightly, checking for the light. But he miscalculated.

"I'm caught!" he yelled as a skull caught his pyjama top in its chattering teeth. He had to wriggle out of his pyjama top but managed to hold on to the box.

"Do be careful, Nancy!" he cried.

"I'm OK," said Nancy. "I'm too small. They can't reach me with their nasty teeth."

As they journeyed on the tunnel widened and Cassie, stiff from crawling, raised herself on her arms. But she misjudged the height and her shoulder grazed the ceiling. She screamed as a pair of stone teeth nipped into her flesh. She flung herself down low as the stone skulls hissed in her ears.

"Are you alright?" called Thomas.

She assured him she was fine as they crawled on through the mud.

They were glad to reach a patch where the light

streamed through and the ground became drier. They came out above ground and breathed the fragrant air heavy with the scent of pine trees into their lungs. A soft breeze kissed the napes of their necks.

Before them was the roofless tower surrounded by pines that they'd spied from the rocky outcrop.

But Cassie's wound was worse than she thought and she was bleeding badly.

"Can you go on, Cassie?" Thomas enquired anxiously. "Maybe we should go back. None of us has ever been so badly injured in a dream state before."

"No," said Cassie in a small voice. "We're too close."

"Are you real children?" asked Dr Dalgado. "I had assumed, when you turned into falcons, you were some sort of spirit shapes."

"It is hard to explain," said Thomas. "We are human children travelling from another dimension. And we are shapeshifters. Our real bodies are back home in bed. But our spirit bodies are solid too. We know not to drink or eat in the Otherworld when we travel in dreams but we're just learning about injuries. We can be injured in our dream state and those injuries may turn up on our real bodies."

"Well, I'm new to spirit practice but perhaps the healing waters might help," said Dr Dalgado.

Thomas applied the water, which smelled of rotten eggs, to Cassie's wound and she rallied a little.

They approached the tower and entered it. To their astonishment they found that it descended underground. A seemingly endless staircase spiralled inside its round stone walls that were built into the bowels of the earth. They walked carefully down all the stairs, journeying deeper underground. Thomas counted at least nine stairwells. Finally, they reached the bottom, just visible in the patch of light that penetrated the roofless tower. There they discovered a metal eight-pointed star set into the ground and partially hidden by soil.

"A star is an emblem of Finnen," said Cassie, determined to be positive.

"There's no sign of an Ogham letter," said Thomas, disappointed.

But Nancy scratched at the soil like a dog trying to unearth a bone. Thomas joined her. They cleared away the earth and uncovered an Ogham symbol set in the star's centre. It was shaped like a cross.

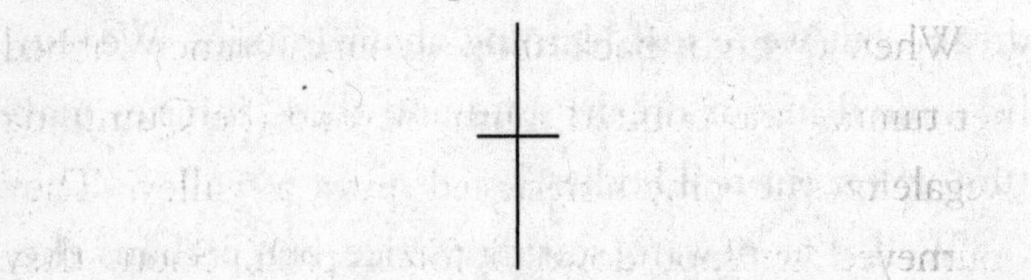

Thomas beamed at his little sister. "You're a right

little detective, you are," he said with pride. "Now all we need is to decode the symbol."

Cassie remembered the forest surrounding them. "Dr Dalgado, are they definitely pine trees growing all around?"

When the doctor confirmed that they were, Cassie blew on the ring while Thomas requested the Old Irish word for pine. It popped into their heads.

"Ailm," confirmed Thomas. "The letter 'A'."

They searched around for a sign of swan feathers.

Suddenly overcome with exhaustion Cassie slumped down by the metal star, not caring that the newly disturbed earth clung to her pyjamas. Then something caught her eye, something that they'd missed. Etched into the metal around the star were four feather engravings. She felt their raised surface under her fingers.

"Bingo!" she said. "But we're not finished yet. If my hunch is correct, three pictures on the postcard means three clues."

When they got back above ground, Nancy rubbed her tummy and pointed south. Beyond the Quinta da Regaleira the pine forest led into a valley. They journeyed on foot down a forest path. Soon, they noticed the tops of two conical structures that poked up over the treetops. They looked like giant twin dunce's caps. Nancy marched resolutely on.

"Ah, the two chimneys of the National Palace that I said we should visit!" exclaimed Dr Dalgado. "The home of the Kings of Portugal and full of swan imagery."

"The chimneys on the postcard!" said Thomas.

They journeyed on down the hill to the National Palace. But Cassie was so weak she had to lean on her brother and sister for support like an old lady.

The light turned to blue dusk and a sliver of pale new moon came into the sky. Ahead of them lay the palace, eerily quiet like a stage set, its extraordinary conical chimneys looming over it.

The rest of the building was a hotchpotch of different styles built over many centuries, as if the Kings of Portugal were always putting up extensions. Cassie was too weak to go any further so they left her in the care of Dr Dalgado.

Thomas and Nancy surveyed the building. The main door was large and heavy.

"Let's go in through the chimneys," said Thomas.

They changed into blackbirds with bright yellow beaks and flew towards the chimneys that poked up from the rest of the palace. Each of them chose a chimney and spiralled down inside its immense whiteness.

Soon they were inside the vast expanse of the kitchen decked out with gleaming pots and pans, with giant fireplaces set into the walls.

Inside the palace every surface was decorated with ornate tiles. They crossed a patio in an internal courtyard where there was a rectangular pool of water fed by a fountain. Gargoyles on the wall spat water. Nancy flew around and alighted on a tree. It was a willow.

Thomas remembered their friend Saille the Willow. "This clue will be an 'S'!" he said, turning back into his own shape. "Let's look for the Ogham symbol."

He searched the courtyard. He looked under the gargoyles and examined the stone sculptures with no luck. Nancy flew around the patio and settled on a highly ornate flagstone with a diamond design in bright blue. Thomas examined the flagstone. It was smooth but then he noticed the grouting around it was loose. He turned it over. The back of the tile was also decorated with an ornate pattern etched out in bright blue. It was a symbol of one straight line with four horizontal lines on the left-hand side.

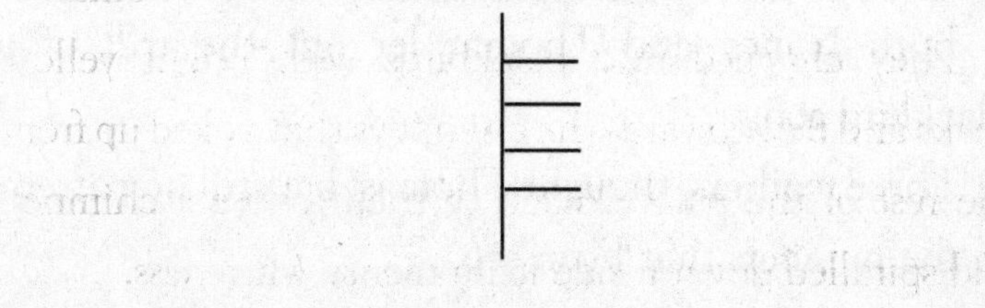

"We've found it!" Thomas cried triumphantly. "And I bet this will be an 'S' for Saille the Willow!"

But almost immediately the stone gargoyles began to spout ice as sharp as glass. Thomas immediately turned back into a blackbird and followed Nancy as she flew through a window.

It opened into a large room that appeared to be a ballroom. The walls were lined with chequered tiles. Nancy flew up towards the ceiling, which was hung with huge chandeliers and decorated with a beautiful fresco depicting swans. Thomas counted at least twenty-six. There was bound to be a feather clue among this lot, he thought. Then he felt overwhelmed, wondering if they had to count *all* the feathers on all twenty-six painted birds. That would be almost impossible. He felt suddenly tired at the thought.

They perched on the chandeliers.

Then something strange happened. The swans in the central panel flickered into life for a moment and three feathers fluttered to the floor.

Both Nancy and Thomas let out the trill of a blackbird song.

Three feathers, thought Thomas, but still no pattern to the numbers that I can see.

Just then they were startled by a loud bang as the window slammed shut.

They flew wildly around the room, looking for an exit. To their relief the door at one end of the long gallery was slightly ajar, just about large enough for a small bird.

On the other side was an ornately furnished throne room. And then they heard it – a horrible cawing sound. Thomas looked up. On the ceiling was a painting of hundreds of magpies carrying ribbons in their beaks.

He and Nancy hovered on the wing, not sure what to do. But when Thomas looked up again, he saw the ceiling was a heaving mass of black and white feathers. One magpie, then a second, closely followed by a third, came alive, dropped their ribbons and dived towards the children with an evil cry. In their bird shapes, Thomas and Nancy dropped low to the floor and tried to fly back towards the door but the way was blocked by scores of angry, screeching magpies furiously beating their black wings.

At the other end of the room, Thomas scoped another door. The best hope was to change and go for it. He had an inspiration and changed into a magpie. Nancy saw what he was doing and did likewise. She flew behind him as he headed for the other end of the gallery.

I hope we don't lose sight of each other, he thought. But it was impossible to stay together among the angry magpies who flew around in a noisy flurry, angry as fishwives. The birds started to attack and fight each other.

Thomas ducked past several, beating a steady path to the door. He hoped that Nancy was on his tail.

He cast around the room trying to spot her. But it was pointless. The room was filled with identical birds savagely attacking each other. Maybe turning into a magpie hadn't been such a good idea after all. Even if Nancy could cry out, there was no way he'd hear her above the racket. Then one bird came towards him with three on its tail.

Thomas quickly changed into himself. One of the birds immediately attacked him, aiming at his eyes. He put up his arms to defend himself and received a nasty gash on his hand. The aggressive magpie squawked and flew into the air. He crouched down and quickly opened the door a little. The magpie circled back ready to attack again but another smaller magpie immediately flew at the attacker, distracting the vicious bird. Thomas guessed it was Nancy. Thomas changed into a falcon and Nancy did the same. The angry magpie backed off. They flew through the opened door and took on their human shapes once more, slumping against the door to shut it tight.

"Caitlín has enchanted this place," Thomas panted. He looked at his hand. It was bleeding. "We'd better get out quick."

They spied a window that led back on to the patio with the willow tree. It was open just a crack. They'd have to find a way of braving the showers of glass.

Thomas felt tired and frustrated, his brain working slowly. "We'll have to become something small and quick." He could hardly speak with exhaustion and the thought of changing in his weakened state daunted him.

"Hummingbirds!" exclaimed Nancy.

So in the blink of an eye they became hummingbirds, one of the smallest birds. They flew towards the narrow gap in the open window.

The courtyard rang with the sound of breaking glass as the gargoyles vomited up a steady stream. Shards ricocheted all over the courtyard. It was like the scene of a continuous bomb explosion.

The two tiny hummingbirds flapped their little wings almost fifty times a second, relying on their instinct to give them safe passage. As they zoomed past the large gallery in a blur, they got a shock when all the magpies hurled themselves against the glass windows in a mass. Several managed to fly through the windows but were cut to shreds by the glass. Their bodies disappeared as soon as they were felled.

But the valiant little hummingbirds made it. Soon they had flown up the chimney and were back outside.

They flew in a whirr past Dr Dalgado's face, startling him. In a twinkling, they changed back into their normal shapes and embraced Cassie.

"That was a close thing," Thomas gasped. He quickly related what had happened and told Cassie he was sure the Ogham symbol was "S".

"We really must get back," said Cassie. "Look at your hand, Thomas."

He was bleeding badly. Dr Dalgado shook the remains of the healing water on the wound.

"Before you go," said Dr Dalgado, "I must tell you something. I've remembered one other thing. In my dream, Finnen gave me a strange message. She said '*Nine letters for an Ogham key to another tree, reversed*', if I remember correctly. She repeated it several times and was most insistent about the number nine."

"Why nine?" pondered Thomas. And then it

dawned on him. "It must mean there are nine letters in the clue! How many letters have we collected so far?"

Cassie counted on her fingers all the letters they'd found on their dream journeys to the Otherworld. "We have all nine letters now! We've found all the clues!" She and Thomas gave each other a brief hug. "But whatever did Finnen mean about 'reversed'?"

"I don't know – but we'll have to figure it out later," said Thomas. He turned to Dr Dalgado. "What shall we do with your box?"

"I think I will take up residence at the various springs but it would be nice to keep it for sentimental reasons."

So Thomas hid it behind a stone in the wall.

The children bade goodbye to the doctor. He rose in the air as a falcon. Then they joined hands and concentrated their attention. They felt themselves hurtling through space as if tossed into an abyss.

They awoke to realise they were back in their beds in Inish Álainn. Thomas had a nasty C-shaped scar on his hand and Cassie was very poorly, shivering and sweating by turns. Nancy came tip-toeing in from Angel's room.

All their pyjamas were cut to ribbons. Thomas's

pyjama top was gone. They were going to have some explaining to do. But they now had all the pieces in the puzzle according to Finnen's message to Dr Dalgado and were getting closer to her hiding place.

If only they could crack the code.

CHAPTER 8

Next morning, they hid the tattered pyjamas in the Incident Room under the Brussels sprouts, then checked their Ogham list and verified that the new letter was "S" by blowing on Oghma's ring.

Then, because she was so weak, Cassie travelled on Derry the Donkey to Áine's cottage while Thomas cycled alongside, Nancy on his crossbar.

Áine was very concerned when she saw Cassie and immediately made her lie down on the crystal bed. She was also worried by the gash on Thomas's hand.

"An injury to your spirit body in the Otherworld requires magic remedies. Caitlín is trying to weaken you," she explained as she lit a fire and sprinkled many herbs on to the flames. Then she fanned the smoke over Cassie. She held up a pyramid of crystal and looked through it with her eyes blazing, sending a prism of many-coloured light around Cassie's body.

Cassie stopped shivering and rose from the bed and yawned. Thomas's hand was given the same treatment. Both of them felt charged with energy.

Cassie told Áine that they now had all the clues left by Finnen and needed to get on with deciphering the Ogham message. Áine's face lit up.

"That is good news," she said. "But you must wait until after your lesson with Scáthach."

Cassie said nothing but was determined to push on with solving the Ogham puzzle.

But when they went outside, one look at their teacher's face banished all thoughts of raising any issue. Scáthach looked as if she was about to explode.

"Today I want to tell you about the Warp Spasm, the gift of Battle Fury," Scatchach barked, taking up the gae bolga, the lance and a fearsome sword. "Truly this cannot be taught and will only come upon you in the heat of battle, if at all. It is a gift of The Morrigan. But I want you to recognise it so you will know how to use it if it happens."

Scáthach lifted up her arms above her head and shook like a reed in a fast-flowing river. The muscles and sinews in her arms stretched and bunched. Her face distorted into a mad-eyed expression, her eyes standing out on stalks and her lips peeled back in a grimace. It was almost as if fire flecked from her mouth. Her hair stood out as if every hair was a steel nail hammered into her head. A trick of the light made it seem as if streams of blood rose out of the top of her head and then turned to dark smoke. She seemed to expand to at least three times her size and was truly terrible to behold. She brandished her weapons at the children and they screamed and ran behind a bush.

Scáthach leapt over them and hacked the bush to pieces, turning it to splinters within a matter of seconds. Then she flamed her attention to the rotting ash tree they used as target practice and hacked it to the ground with such ferocity that splinters kindled and burst into fire. She leapt at the fire, rising two metres in the air and letting out a blood-curdling yell, then stamped it out with her feet. The children cowered and held on to each other.

"You can come out now," said a breathless Scáthach. She was drenched in sweat and her face was red with exertion. They peeked out. She had returned to her averagely terrifying self. She flicked her hair back as if nothing had happened.

"Now you try," she said, throwing them swords.

"Think your angriest thoughts. Whip yourself into a fury. Imagine the face of your worst enemy – imagine Caitlín."

The children just succeeded in looking very hot and bothered, even Cassie who was no stranger to towering rages. She just couldn't transform herself despite imagining Balor, Caitlín and even throwing in Lardon for good measure. But she did have a curious sensation of her skeleton being rearranged and her hair shooting up when she thought about how Scáthach had humiliated her on occasions. Thomas felt inflamed and his cheeks went as red as if he was on fire but he felt rather silly prancing about. Nancy just kept giggling.

"No matter," said Scáthach. "It will only truly come upon you in the heat of battle when you are truly beside yourself with rage. Now let us practise our Battle Cry."

She rose in the air as a raven and the children followed. They passed Tadgh's tower and saw Angel hanging out the washing at their own house. Thomas couldn't resist crapping on Lardon who was sunning himself in the garden.

They headed to Poolbeg Rocks on the north-east of the island where the waves muffled every sound. They alighted on the rocks and changed into their normal shapes and spent an agreeable hour shouting into the wind.

"The trick is not to scream from your throat but to push the air out from your toes," Scáthach instructed.

Thomas and Cassie managed well enough but Nancy's scream sounded penetrating enough to shatter glass.

While they shouted and roared, Nancy could have sworn she saw the Merrows diving by the spot where Balor's boat lay. She tried to tell the others but they were so busy shouting they paid her no heed. Then she forgot all about it.

They returned to Áine's for lunch where they tucked into roast pig. All the screaming had given them an appetite.

"This may be our last meeting for some time," Scáthach said when they had finished eating.

To their surprise the children felt sad, particularly Cassie who often felt she hated their teacher.

Scáthach stood up to take her leave.

"Caitlín's power is growing and I see you lost in the Land of Fire and Ice. But I see you learning your power animals there. The stars are not what they seem." She paused, as if in a trance, then collecting herself she continued: "But remember the lessons I have taught you. To be a successful warrior the first enemy you must defeat is yourself. When you have mastered your own weaknesses and become whole then you can use all your qualities against the foe. And remember: do not rely only on the skills that you excel in." She turned to go.

"Wait!" cried Cassie. "We have all the clues about where Finnen is. We need to know what to do next."

"What do the feathers mean?" asked Thomas.

Scáthach hesitated for a moment and for the first time a look of uncertainty came into her strong face. "I cannot help you with signs. That is Sennan's gift."

"But Sennan can't help us," said Cassie ruefully.

She paused and looked almost kindly at them. "Consult the bones at high tide," she said finally.

With that, she rose into the sky as a raven and was gone.

"We're going to have to manage on our own now," said Cassie sadly. "We've lost our teachers."

"They are always giving us strange messages," said Thomas. "I wish sometimes they'd just speak plainly."

"What did she mean about consulting the bones at high tide?" puzzled Cassie and then she looked at Thomas, the flutter of a memory inspiring her thoughts. "I remember Sennan saying something similar after we found the second clue."

Thomas's eyes sparkled. "Let's go down to Boogan Beach. It must be nearly high tide now."

They went back to the shed to collect their bicycles. Then, checking no one was around, they set off for Boogan Beach.

They pulled up by the shoreline, near the Boogan's cave. They heard the friendly creature of seaweed moving within his home. They greeted him and he called out, promising to keep a lookout for them so they wouldn't be disturbed.

The tide was still going out. Thomas reached into the air for the Crane Bag and pulled out all of the bones of the magical pigs of Assal, which bore the Ogham letters and the shapes of feathers on them.

"I say we lay them on the sand in the order we found them," said Cassie getting all bossy.

Out at sea the tide turned and at that exact moment, the Ogham symbols on the bones transformed into the familiar letters of the ABC alphabet. "The Ogham symbols translate into I, Y, G, G, L, R, D, A, S – Iygglrdas," pronounced Cassie, surveying the bones. "Is that even a word? It doesn't seem to be the key to a tree."

"What if it's like one of those crossword puzzles where all the letters are out of place?" wondered Thomas.

They mixed up the bones with the letters on them a few times but just kept coming up with nonsense words.

"I still think the feathers hold the key," said Thomas. He walked up and down the sand, churning it with his feet. He gazed out to sea. The tide was coming in fast and if they didn't have a brainwave they would lose the moment to solve the mystery.

Then Thomas felt the glimmer of an idea. "Let's try rearranging the letters according to the number of feathers. And let's do them as a column like a down crossword clue. I don't know why but I feel that's important."

They reassembled the bones with the letters according to the order of the feathers, one to nine.

With the tide just metres from it, they surveyed the column of bones in the sand.

L
I
S
A
R
D
G
G
Y

"LISARDGGY," Thomas read from top to bottom as if it was a crossword clue.

They gazed at the bones, perplexed.

The tide was drawing closer and would soon cover the bones.

They looked at Nancy for inspiration.

"Is that word right, Nancy?" asked Cassie. "Does it make your tummy tingle?"

For answer, Nancy dipped into the Crane Bag. She took out a moonstone egg and rubbed it. The image of Sennan appeared on its smooth surface. His eyes glinted when he saw the bones.

"Clever Finnen!" he said. But then the image clouded over in a spume of sea spray and Fand appeared out of the waters on to the beach.

"You aren't allowed to help them," she scolded. "Or you will be turned into a stone!"

"How funny if I was an Ogham stone, that you read from the bottom up, like in the old days," Sennan said gravely.

"Less of your stupid blather, you white-haired old fool!" exclaimed Fand covering them in sea spray as Sennan disappeared. She turned for a moment to stick her tongue out at the children and was gone.

The waves began to lick at the bones. But just as the

tide began to turn, Thomas realised what Sennan meant and clapped his hands. "We read it from the bottom up! Crafty old Sennan gave us a clue without Fand finding out. It's upside down!"

Cassie stared at the letter sticking up on the bones out of the sand. "Y, G, G, D, R, A, S, I, L," she read. "Yggdrasil. At least it looks like more of a word."

"Remember Doctor Dalgado's message: '*An Ogham key to another tree, reversed*'!" It must mean the letters spelt backwards – or upwards in this case – mean another tree," Thomas concluded.

"It may be that Finnen is hiding in another tree, called 'Yggdrasil'," said Cassie. She said the word and blew on Oghma's ring. The answer came into their heads.

"The World Tree!" the Chingles exclaimed in unison.

"But whatever does it mean?" puzzled Cassie.

They felt they were tantalisingly close.

"Let's go to Tadgh's," Thomas suggested.

They thought about making a salmon leap but judged it too dangerous, so they set off on their bikes.

As they gained the crossroads that forked to their house, no one noticed Lardon on Derry the Donkey hiding behind a hedge. They were in such a hurry that they didn't hear the donkey's warning bray behind them as they raced on their bicycles down the boreen to Tadgh's.

Tadgh led them to the room in the middle of the tower. They set down their bones to spell out "Yggdrasil".

Tadgh was fascinated. "How interesting to see Ogham letters on bones."

"We did it for a school project," bluffed Thomas quickly.

"Yggdrasil – is that an Ogham word?" asked Cassie, impatiently. "Is it the name of a special tree?"

"Well, Ogham was a mysterious alphabet often used for codes," said Tadgh. "But the word it is spelling out is not Irish but Norse." He took down a large volume in a strange language. "Norse mythology had its own system of magic and divination called the rune stones. See here," he pointed. "This is Yggdrasil, the World Tree, in Norse."

Nancy clapped her hands.

"The World Tree!" said Cassie with delight.

"So the Ogham clues mean the Norse World Tree," Thomas repeated, absorbing the information. "Is it some kind of big tree?"

"Yes, it's the Norse World Tree, the Tree of Knowledge," said Tadgh.

Cassie had to resist the temptation to squeal with excitement.

"'*An Ogham key to another tree*'," repeated Thomas.

"Some say that Yggdrasil, the World Tree, is an ash-tree but others that it means 'yew pillar'," continued Tadgh, gazing down his spectacles and flicking through his book.

"Finnen's other name is Yewberry," whispered Cassie excitedly to Thomas.

"For the Norse who are also known as the Vikings," Tadgh went on, "it was not only the Tree of Knowledge but the tree in the centre of all the worlds. Each of its roots extends into nine different worlds. On its highest branches sits an eagle and twisted round its roots lies a snake-dragon gnawing at its roots. A mischievous squirrel runs up and down the tree telling tales about what each of them is saying."

"Is there a link between Celtic mythology and Norse mythology?" asked Cassie excitedly.

"A good question," said Tadgh. "Scholars believe there may be one but no one has ever been able to establish a direct link. But there are several similar characteristics. For example both mythologies contain Swan Maidens. And the Crane Bag holds the King of Lochlainn's helmet, which is commonly understood to mean

Scandinavia. 'Lochlainn' means 'the place of lakes' in Irish."

"Do any swans or Swan Maidens live in the tree?" asked Thomas, barely able to contain his eagerness.

"Oh yes," said Tadgh, flicking through the pages. "Norse mythology is full of Swan Maidens." He showed them a diagram of the Yggdrasil. "The Norse believed the world was divided into different spheres, those of giants, gods, humans and the underworld. Nine different worlds. At the roots of the tree that lead up to Asgard, the dwelling place of the gods, is the Well of Urda. It is guarded over by the three Norns, three sisters who represent the past, present and future."

"We want to go there," Nancy said suddenly.

Cassie and Thomas's hearts leapt to their mouths, worried at Nancy's directness.

"Where is it?" Cassie said quickly.

"Legend has it that it's somewhere in the Realm of Fire and Ice," Tadgh said. "In the vast northern wastes of Scandinavia or Iceland where the Norse people also lived."

Thomas gave a start. Scáthach had mentioned something about the Land of Fire and Ice.

"The old stories say that the gods of the World Tree built a rainbow bridge from earth to heaven," Tadgh continued. "The rainbow's name is Bifröst, which may mean 'shining path' in Old Norse. So maybe you have to follow the rainbow!" he joked.

Follow the rainbow! Cassie could barely breathe.

"We're going to find Finnen there," said Nancy. "She's hiding from the bad queen with the buck teeth."

Cassie and Thomas shot each other a look of horror.

"I'm not sure you'll find Finnen there," said Tadgh, taking her seriously. "She's an Irish Swan Maiden. Mind you, scholars have often tried to find a link between Ogham and the Norse runes. And why not! Celts and Vikings have always been close. The Vikings founded most of our cities. In fact, many people think that all mythologies are linked since we all share common ancestors. Each tribe or region just gives different names to different aspects or qualities."

Tadgh opened a drawer and produced a set of counters with different symbols on them.

"These are the Norse runes," he said. The symbols looked a bit like Ogham but with more lines and crosses. Then he winked at Nancy. "Who knows, you may come across them on your quest. The runes can also be used to tell your fortune."

There was a sudden racket of braying and cursing. The children ran to the window to see Lardon clambering onto Derry the Donkey's back and making off up the boreen. Despite Derry's best efforts to throw him, Lardon managed to cling on.

"Stop that, you creep!" shouted Cassie from the window. But the noise panicked Derry and he bolted.

The children sped off in pursuit on their bicycles. At the crossroads, they scanned the roadways. Then Thomas saw Derry coming back down a track from the north of the island.

"Derry must have thrown Lardon, so he can't be far," said Cassie.

Then further up the track, they saw a white tracksuit-clad shape rise like a ghost from behind a bush – another figure by his side. It was Lardon, deep in conversation with an old woman with a crooked back that they'd never seen before.

And they were bizarrely hovering in the air!

The children got off their bicycles.

"We've got to do the salmon leap," said Cassie.

"It's too risky," said Thomas.

But Nancy was already gone, rising in the air as a salmon and landing as herself. In a heartbeat, Thomas and Cassie followed her.

"It's her!" exclaimed Nancy, clutching her stomach.

The old woman looked down at them and grimaced.

They saw she had ugly, crooked teeth, a cavernous mouth and a forked black tongue.

With one voice, the children erupted into a Battle Cry and charged, ready to leap up at her.

Lardon, suddenly realising he was floating in mid-air, screamed in fright and fell to the ground. There was a sudden blast of icy mist and a high-pitched mocking laugh. The old woman disappeared.

Furious, Cassie turned on Lardon who lay sprawled on the ground. "What were you talking about to her?" she demanded. She felt a rage invade her bloodstream. Her hair shot up on her head and her muscles and sinews bunched and expanded. Fury shone in her eyes. Lardon quaked and fainted.

"You're going into Warp Spasm, Cassie! We mustn't reveal our power!" cautioned Thomas. He glared at Lardon who lay in a daze. "What did that old woman ask you?" he demanded.

"Wh-what old woman?" stuttered Lardon, coming round. "Don't hurt me – I'll give you this." He held up a diamond ring. "She gave it to me!"

Cassie threw it back in contempt.

Lardon looked stupefied. "I–I don't know what happened. Don't let her come near me," he pointed at Cassie. "Please! I'll give you anything!"

"Just tell us what you told the old woman," demanded Thomas.

"I followed you to the tower and heard you talking to that old guy about Iggdra or something like that," quaked Lardon. "Then the ugly old broad offered me a diamond ring to tell her what I'd heard. I didn't mean –"

"Shut up!" snapped Cassie. "Just get out of our sight!"

"He's telling the truth," intervened Nancy. "I feel it in my tummy."

Lardon tried to climb on Derry's back but he was too weak. So Thomas and Cassie reluctantly gave him a leg-up. Cassie slapped the donkey's rump but he didn't move until Nancy brayed to him in donkey language to take Lardon home. The donkey brayed back.

"Derry says sorry," Nancy translated. "He doesn't mean to get us into trouble."

"It's not Derry's fault," said Thomas kindly. "He has to do what humans tell him."

"That was Caitlín," Cassie said with urgency. "Even though we managed to defeat her evil forces at every location and stop any clues falling into her hands, she's now got the information from Lardon about where to find Finnen."

"We'd better hurry. She's now one step ahead of us," agreed Thomas.

The Crane Bag suddenly appeared and he pulled out a helmet of beaten silver with brass horns on either side, like an old Viking helmet.

"The King of Lochlainn's helmet!" he exclaimed. He put it on and an instruction came into his head: "*Travel to Yggdrasil by the shining path where Finnen's powers were greatest. Consult the three wise women known as the Norns at the Well of Urda*."

"Finnen's powers were greatest at Glimmering Lake!" Cassie shouted. "If only Caitlín wasn't ahead of us!"

Thomas thrust the helmet back into the Crane Bag, which then disappeared.

The three of them held hands and made a salmon's leap to the lakeside.

CHAPTER 9

A beautiful rainbow appeared and vaulted over the lake, shimmering with light into the clouds.

"It's the shining path!" yelled Thomas. The three children held hands and ran towards its foot. They began to climb. Each step looked misty and they feared falling through air but it held solid as if they were walking on a glass floor. Beneath them, the colours of the rainbow merged into a thousand shades and swirled with the symbols of the Norse runes that Tadgh had shown them. Halfway up they left the sight of Inish Álainn behind and passed through cloud. They walked along a flat stretch that appeared to be licked with red flames of fire. But the children walked through unscathed and they emerged into brilliant light. They felt they'd passed through to the other side of the world.

It took a few moments for their eyes to adjust to the blinding light.

Before them lay a land of fire and ice. Fiery volcanoes belched smoke that turned to snow. Huge bubbling pools and geysers dotted the landscape. Waterfalls froze in mid-flow and hardened into icicles that fell into burning pools of boiling waters. Steam swirled from the waters and softened the savage white of the snow. The air was crisp and clean and extraordinarily refreshing as they descended the rainbow into the land of burning ice.

They were surprised to see a pleasant young man standing close by. Cassie held up Oghma's ring and blew on it so that even if he spoke in a foreign language they would understand him.

"Greetings! I am Heimdall, the Guardian of the Rainbow!" His voice rang out loud and resonant. "What is your purpose?"

They explained to him about their quest for Finnen.

"You must speak to the swans of the Well of the World Tree," he said smiling. "You will have to journey to the place of mists that we call Niflheim."

"I don't remember Tadgh saying it was there," said a puzzled Cassie.

Then they noticed he had a scar on his forehead that was bleeding.

"Sir, are you hurt?" asked Thomas.

The young man wiped his brow. "Oh, that is of no account," he said. Then his expression darkened. "I do not let all those who ask pass. Do you wish to pass or not?"

The children nodded their assent.

"You will find the swans at a well called Hvergelmir – the Roaring Kettle. The Guardian there is a most unusual swan called Nidhögg – Dread Biter."

Cassie was about to say that they had been advised by Lochlainn's helmet to go to the Well of Urda and consult the Norns but there was something unsettling about the young man that put her on her guard. He directed them to a great chasm that was fashioned out of wood so hard and polished it had the sheen of diamonds.

"That will take you to the roots of Yggdrasil – the World Tree," he said and was gone.

The journey down the chasm was utterly disorienting and baffling. The scale was so vast they couldn't get a sense of it at all. Above them was a canopy of green woven between vast wooden rafters. There was the odd patch of dappled light that suggested they were walking under leaves and branches so vast they blotted out the sky. Before them lay a surface of bark so extensive it was like a mountain ridge made out of wood. It was huge and impenetrable and stretched in every direction. And yet underfoot the earth was also made of wood, hard and grained like a giant tree.

"Nancy, what direction should we take?" asked Thomas.

She patted her tummy. "I don't feel anything," she said.

They stood, perplexed.

"You're not going to get very far by standing still," a chirpy voice rang out. They jumped out of their standing. Scurrying down a branch came a red squirrel.

"Greetings, strange folk," he chirped. "My name is Ratatösk, which means Swift Teeth. I travel between the worlds of Yggdrasil – the World Tree. What brings you here?"

They told him of their quest for the Goddess Finnen and their meeting with the Guardian of the Rainbow who directed them to Niflheim, the place of mists, to question the swan called "Dread Biter" there.

The squirrel burst out laughing, baring its sharp little teeth. "And this guardian, did he have gold teeth and such amazing eyesight he saw you coming before you appeared?" he asked between guffaws. "Was his hearing so sharp he could hear the grass grow?"

"No. He was quite pleasant-looking except he had a bleeding scar," said Cassie.

The squirrel's little eyes nearly popped out of his head but all he did was chuckle. "He's sending you to the Roaring Kettle, is he? Ha, Ha! And the Guardian of the Well is a swan called Dread Biter?"

"I don't know what's so funny," said Cassie irritably. "Although it is an odd name for a swan."

"You'll soon find out," he laughed, his fat little belly wobbling. "But let me give you one piece of advice. Don't pass the Howling River that we call Gjoll."

"Look, could you just tell us how to get there," said Thomas.

"It takes nine days through great forests, deep valleys, high mountains and a dark cave," he said.

The children groaned.

"But I've got something *squirreled* away that will speed the journey," he winked. He beckoned them to follow him.

Cassie hesitated. "Can we trust him?"

"No," said Nancy firmly.

"But it's not like we have a lot of choice," Thomas sighed.

The squirrel scurried to the left in the unvarying landscape of wood and entered a whorl in the bark of the tree. He emerged with a long silken rope as fragile as a spider's thread, almost invisible to the naked eye.

"This here is a very special rope," boasted the squirrel, holding it out of their reach. "It's made from the noise from the footfall of cats, the beards of women, the roots of stones, the breath of fishes, the sinews of bears and the spittle of birds."

"What an unbelievable list of ingredients!" said Thomas.

"Why do you think women don't have beards and you never hear a cat coming?" sniffed the squirrel.

"But is it going to be a whole lot of use?" quizzed Cassie.

"I won't bother to give it to you then," said the squirrel querulously.

"I didn't mean to offend you," cut in Cassie. "It's just the rope doesn't sound very robust."

"How would a silly ignorant child like you appreciate Gleipner the Binder? This rope was made to tame a wild wolf. Not for stupid children."

"So, apart from wolf-taming, what is its purpose, wise squirrel?" asked Thomas in a way he would normally have thought of as creepy but it seemed to do the trick in pleasing the squirrel.

"Oh, it takes a squirrel to know potential," he winked. "It's actually a climbing rope that will stretch to infinity to bring you to where you want to go."

Swift Teeth helped them tie it to a knot in the wood near the whorled hiding-hole.

"It's a good sign if he wants the rope back," whispered Thomas as he clutched it. It felt strong to the touch despite its airy, non-existent elements.

They began to abseil down the crevasse, levering on the rope and kicking off with their legs.

As they moved away from the squirrel he called out, "Can't wait to see if it actually works! I'll meet you down there. Just have to see someone first. Such news to tell of little children visiting Dread Biter the Swan. Ha, Ha!"

"He's using us as an experiment," cried Cassie. But it was too late. They were already plunging down the bark of the tree at an alarming rate as if they were in a broken elevator. The rope was as light as gossamer, as spider's webs or the beat of a butterfly's wings and really did seem to extend to the bowels of the earth. As they descended they passed through a kaleidoscope of images: a startled dwarf, a village in mourning, a god in battle, winged women scouring a battlefield. All these pictures became jumbled in their heads. But soon, they descended into darkness.

They landed in a heap on top of each other in a gaggle of arms and legs. The earth beneath them was muddy and cold, sticky to the touch and a peculiar rust colour like congealed blood. They could barely see through a murky mist. But worst of all was the stench. It was like babies' dirty nappies, rotting fish, stink bombs, cat pee, sewers, rotten eggs and manure all at once. They gagged and lifted their tops to cover their mouths.

The light was dim but a flapping noise and a sudden gust made them jump. Cassie's eyes adjusted to the dimness and out of the corner of her eye she saw a giant eagle feasting on a pile of fresh bones. She wanted to throw up as wracking waves of nausea heaved up from her stomach. Then the roar of water in the distance hummed in their ears, commingled with wails and agonised cries.

"Look, that must be the Howling River that the squirrel mentioned we shouldn't pass," said Thomas.

Its waters looked blood red.

They became aware of shuffling noises and noticed other shapes and forms moving around in the gloom.

The skeletal form of an old lady bumped into Thomas.

"Beg pardon," she said meekly. Then she moved nearer to him to have a closer look.

Thomas flinched as her hollow face moved towards him.

She smiled sadly. "Are you sure you are in the right place?" Her thin bony hand reached out to caress his cheek.

He recoiled in fright. The old lady's hand was covered in boils and lacerating sores.

Another shape came forward from the murky mist. "They look too healthy to be here," growled a low voice.

It was a man who, they were distressed to see, had an axe in his head. His hair was clotted with dried blood and brains, although he didn't seem too bothered about it.

"Perhaps they did something dishonourable," he muttered in a guttural voice, leaning in to eyeball Nancy who spat at him. Cassie threw her arms around her brother and sister and backed away.

"Stay away from us, you monsters!" she yelled. She felt a bony elbow in her back. The three children screamed as numberless maimed shapes pressed in on them.

"Give them space," shouted the man with the axe in his head. The shapes backed off and formed a circle around them. Through the gloom the children saw they looked like the living dead, as if the graves had yielded up their rotting corpses.

"We won't hurt you," said a young woman in a tremulous voice. Her face was blue and her eyes popped out of her head. She had a rope around her neck and a deep red scar in her throat going green around the edges.

Cassie could barely breathe from the smell but she felt a peculiar compassion for these wraiths.

"We are the diseased and the dishonourable dead," the woman with the rope around her neck explained. "I am dishonourable. I was hanged for stealing a baby after my own died in childbirth."

"That sounds tragic rather than dishonourable," said Cassie.

"They're very strict here," sighed the woman.

"I was killed in a fight with my brother when he accused me of cheating him out of the farm. I too am dishonourable," said the man with the axe in his head.

"And I died of suppurating boils brought on from eating poisoned meat that I stole because I was starving," said the sad old lady. "So I'm both diseased and dishonourable."

"That really does seem very harsh," said Thomas sympathetically. "It stands to reason that lots of dead people must be diseased. And if times are hard, it's understandable that you have to steal to eat."

The dead people murmured in agreement.

"But we're not dead at all," said Cassie desperately. "We're from another world and we've been tricked by the Guardian of the Rainbow called Heimdall and a nasty little squirrel."

The wraiths backed off and muttered sympathetically.

"Heimdall, you say? Not like him to play tricks. He always tells the truth," said the old lady.

The children described him, including the scar on his face.

"Maybe it's Loki the Trickster," said the mournful axe victim. "There's a great upheaval in the heavens. Loki the Bad One has escaped. He's a shapeshifter but his powers must be weakened. He must have pretended to be Heimdall to play a trick on you."

"And Loki has a terrible scar," said the old lady. "He is normally imprisoned in a cavern. He is punished by a snake that drops deadly venom on his head every day, torturing him drop by drop."

"You certainly go in for harsh punishments here," shuddered Cassie.

"And what about the squirrel?" said a guilty Thomas, as he was the one who'd urged trusting him.

"That's Swift Teeth," said the hanged woman. "He's a terrible gossip and full of mischief too. He'd send you down here for the sport."

"I'll wring his neck when I see him," said Cassie spiritedly.

"Then you'll end up here," said the old woman sadly.

"It's just a figure of speech," said Cassie quickly.

Nancy began to cry softly.

"Don't cry, little one," said the old woman. She held out her bony, boil-covered hand and passed her a piece of bread. "This is Hel cake. If you give some to Garm, the Hell Hound, he may be able to help you."

Nancy smiled at her and touched her hand.

"Thank you, child," said the old lady, her eyes filling with tears.

The children pushed forward towards the river's edge and the wraiths of the dead parted to let them through. A ragged group followed at a distance.

At the water's edge they watched as a giant hound swam across to meet them. He emerged from the water and shook drops off in a fury. The children recoiled. He was truly ugly. He had a huge misshapen head with four eyes, a mouth of sharp pointed teeth and the mangy fur on his chest was the colour of dried blood. Nancy threw him a crumb of Hel cake. Even though it was only a speck, he fell on it greedily and devoured it in his massive, slavering jaws. He towered over them and barked.

"He said his name is Garm. We have to speak to his mistress Hel across the river," interpreted Nancy.

"But Swift Teeth told us not to cross the river," said Thomas, gagging into a hankie.

"Maybe if you don't actually touch the water, you can still leave these lower depths," advised a voice from the crowd. It belonged to a young man whose skin was rotting and green and whose hair had fallen out. "I was a magician's apprentice and was taught that if you come here alive and don't enter the river, you might escape. It's too late for me," he said bitterly.

"We'll have to risk it," said Cassie.

They forced themselves to look into the stinking river. It was a vile stew of vomit, rotting skin, bones, skulls and unidentified body parts that could have been kidneys, brains or stomachs. The water ran red with blood.

The children held hands and slowed their breathing. Then with one salmon leap the three of them rose in the air and vaulted safely over the vile waters.

Cassie looked back as they landed but already the other bank was obscured in mists. "I don't like this Norse hell. It seems a bit unfair to lump in the diseased with the dishonourable. And what they consider dishonourable seems sad and tragic to me," she said.

They ventured forward into the inky fog. The ground beneath them was hard and their footfall echoed into a funereal silence. It was eerily quiet in contrast to the chaos and turmoil on the other side. But the stillness frightened them even more. They trudged on. In the dim light, they made out a building that gleamed white through the smoky fog.

As they drew closer, they saw it resembled the banqueting hall in Tara. But on closer inspection, instead of being constructed out of wood, it was made of the interlocking bleached bones of skeletons. Here and there, they could make out a hand, a shinbone, thighs and ribs all ingeniously woven together. Thomas shuddered and held on tightly to his two sisters.

The front of the skeletal hall was open and through the gloom they saw two statues guarding an inner chamber hung with tapestries.

The children squeezed each other's hands as they cautiously approached. Closer in, they realised the statues weren't statues at all but an ancient old man and woman with matted hair wearing shabby sackcloth, moving very, very slowly.

"If you please, sir," said Thomas addressing the old man. It was all he could do not to pinch him. "We seek a woman called Hel who might be able to help us in a quest for a Swan Maiden."

The old man opened his mouth but all that came out were slow-motion grunts. Then the old woman's slack lips fell open and she too started to grunt. It was like listening to a tape recording that had been slowed down so much it made the words unintelligible.

In the smoky light, Cassie fixed her gaze on the curtains, which were woven from very fine threads in colours ranging from grey to black, red and brown. As she peered, she saw a curtain rustle and then in one swift movement it drew back. This startled the children, who had become numbed by the noises of the slow people.

A woman appeared through the curtains. She stood in profile so they could only see half her face. She was pretty with a pink-skinned complexion and blonde, lustrous hair. She looked completely out of place.

"You are wasting your time listening to Tardy and Delay," she gestured with impatience towards the old people. "Their names don't mean slow for nothing! They are my servants here at my palace, Sleet Cold, and they are still going on an errand I sent them on five hundred years ago. But come, please!" She seemed exasperated and nervous at the same time and walked with a limp. They followed her to a central chamber filled with white, strangely shaped furniture that she kept stroking and fussing over.

"I am Hel, mistress of this place. Daughter of Loki and the giantess Angrboda."

"We are Cassie, Thomas and Nancy," said Thomas, "and we have been the victims of a trick played by your father and that interfering squirrel. We seek the Swan Maiden, Finnen. We have been told to consult an unusual swan but we fear we have come to the wrong place."

Hel gave a snort of derision at the mention of her father. "I have no love for my father or my mother," she sniffed. "They gave me a mixed view of the world you might say." She turned around sharply and the children drew back in horror. For half of her was as ugly as the other half was beautiful. The other side of her face was deformed and misshapen, as if all the features had been burned in a fire. The skin that still clung to her bones was black and rotting.

"I also take after my mother's side," she laughed bitterly. But then, recollecting her manners, she coughed and smoothed down her dress, which appeared to be made from patches of very fine leather.

Probably dead human skins, Cassie thought with repugnance.

"But welcome to my Hall of Misery," Hel continued. "You have no idea how hard it is to keep a respectable house down here!" She gestured around the inner room with a mixture of pride and frustration. There were more weird tapestries and a bed that looked very crumpled and was surrounded by wall hangings in a softer fabric.

"Ah, you are admiring my sickbed," she said brightly. "I wove the hangings from the soft hair of unborn babies myself." The hangings glinted and shimmered. "I call them Glimmering Misfortune," she said sadly, fingering Nancy's hair.

The children immediately gripped hold of each other and Nancy jumped into Cassie's arms. Those other curtains that Hel had first appeared behind, Cassie realised with a shudder, must also have been made out of human hair.

"Ah, but perhaps you are not tired and would like to

eat," said Hel. She guided them to a table and chairs. They were made out of white bone, which Thomas recognised as human bones. The table was laid with a bowl that looked like the inverted top of a skull decorated with human teeth, a knife like a carved shinbone and a spoon that seemed to be made from a small kneecap and a bony-looking fork. The children felt almost numb with the gruesomeness of it all.

"You are admiring my dinner service," she said. "I call it 'Hunger'. I'm particularly proud of the forks. I fashioned them from quads that died young. That's how I got a matching service of eight."

The children turned white. Cassie suddenly thought of their own little twin brother and sister and how close they had been to death and tears came into her eyes.

"We really must find Finnen," Thomas said with urgency. He felt he would suffocate if he spent another minute in this chamber of horrors. "We were told to seek Nidhögg the Dread Biter at a well called Roaring Kettle."

Peals of bitter laughter came from Hel's twisted mouth. She turned her ugly misshapen side with the black matted hair towards them. "Hah, I didn't expect a social visit! No one ever comes to see me just because

I don't have nice things." Without warning she sprang towards them and seized Cassie and Thomas's free hands.

Thomas nearly died with fright as her black, rotting fist encircled his own. She was probably sizing them up as serving implements and he didn't want to end up as cutlery.

"Perhaps you should stay here with me," she breathed down on top of them.

Cassie's legs buckled beneath her and Thomas broke into a cold, clammy sweat. Nancy clung to her big sister and buried her head in her shoulder.

"B–But that's just what your father wants," stuttered Thomas, his hand going numb in the vice-like hold of her decayed hand. "You don't want our clumsy hands – I mean you'll be playing into his hands!" He looked with desperation at Cassie.

"Thomas is right," Cassie improvised frantically. "Don't you see the reason why no one ever comes to see you is the fear that they won't come back? Now if we do, we'll be able to tell everyone what a great time we've had."

Hel relaxed her grasp and let go of the children. Nancy peeped at her from between her curls. Hel put out her good hand to stroke her hair.

"Maybe I can just keep the little one. She has such pretty hair."

"Take it!" Cassie blurted out. "You don't need the whole of Nancy – just her hair. In fact, we can all give you a lock."

Thomas nodded his head vigorously and tugged at his own hair.

In a twinkling Hel seized the shinbone knife and greedily cut off a bunch of dark curls from Nancy, a handful of Cassie's nut-brown locks and a big tuft of Thomas's short blond hair. She fingered them as if they were threads of real silver and gold. Then she wove them around a spool that was a bleached rib.

"Is Finnen here?" asked a trembling Thomas.

Hel said nothing and led them out of the hall over bleak mudflats through shifting mists and swirling fog.

"We have passed through into Niflheim now," said Hel. "The land of icy mists."

Soon they came to a pool surrounded by small hummocks of caked mud. Blackened steam rose ferociously from the boiling pool as if from a giant kettle.

The heat was intense. They seemed to be gazing into the top of a volcano. As the steam rose it turned to snow that ran into eleven channels forming streams.

Thomas wondered where the streams led to and if it was possible to escape down them. It was a place where molten earth and frozen water met. Above, a huge straggly root of the Great Tree, its surface blackened from the steam, formed an arch.

As they drew closer to the pool, the ground beneath their feet began to shift. Their feet banged into sharp objects that they saw were the shards of discarded bones cleaned of flesh. They looked down into the fathomless blackened waters of the pool and saw a mass of writhing serpents squirming among bones and corpses. Among them, Thomas spied the curved shape of one serpent that seemed bigger than all the rest.

"Here is your swan!" cried Hel with derision.

The ground beneath their feet started to give way and they sank into a mire of rotten mud and crushed bones. They had been walking over a carpet of corpses. Despite their horror, they took a step forward. All at once they rose again and realised they were standing on a spiny ridge that moved in the black mire. They tried to keep their footing as they watched the monstrous serpent in the water.

The large head of a beast rose out of the spitting steam from among the writhing serpents. It had a round snout like a dragon on the long neck of a serpent. Its vast teeth chewed on a bone and, when it dropped it, fire breathed from its mouth. As the neck undulated, they realised it was attached to the spiny ridge that they were standing on. The spiny ridge was its body! So the dragon-serpent was Dread Biter! Its vast mouth with the bloodstained teeth sprang towards them. The corrosive smell of death overwhelmed them and they gagged and spluttered with nausea, their stomachs heaving.

"Stop!" Hel commanded the dragon-serpent. "Your enemy Swift Teeth, the squirrel, has sent them here."

They smelt the acrid breath of the dragon-serpent, but his head came no closer.

"We seek the Swan Maiden, Finnen," said Cassie in a quivering voice, her knees buckling under her. "We have been told to consult the Norns."

The dragon-serpent shook and they nearly fell off his back. He raised his vast head, which looked too heavy for his writhing neck, and gnawed on the root above his head.

"Dread Biter gnaws on the root of the sacred tree Yggdrasil and when he succeeds in destroying it, it will be the end of the world," said Hel. "And, as he gnaws, he can pick up messages from other parts of the tree."

Nancy found some of the crumbs of Hel cake in her

pocket and tossed them to the dragon-serpent. He caught them on his tongue of fire and let out a roar.

"He has heard of a Swan Maiden," said Nancy.

"The Swan of Urda's Well speaks of a maiden newly come. She hides in icy fire. Or hid," interpreted Hel.

"Can we trust him?" asked Cassie.

"Dread Biter is not a trickster like my father Loki," said Hel. "Go to Urda's Well. It is in another part of the World Tree. Go back to the main trunk by the means that you came here and descend by a different root."

They thanked Hel and with no time to waste made a great leap to the other side of the river. As they surged through the fetid masses of the dead, Cassie glanced back and saw Hel watching them from the other side. She looked anxious and fretful in her Kingdom of the Dead and Cassie felt a sudden stab of pity for her.

The rope was dangling back where they left it. Cassie and Thomas helped Nancy scramble on to it and followed her back up through the veil of mist.

Soon they were back in the world of dappled daylight and climbing up the wooden bark of the main trunk. Truly, they felt happy to be alive. A gentle rain fell and washed them clean and then a soft breeze and golden sunshine warmed them. They hauled themselves up and eventually found themselves back at the whorl of the tree where Swift Teeth had first produced the rope.

Within seconds, his little squirrel head with the buckteeth popped out of his hidey-hole.

"So did you enjoy Hel's kingdom?" he laughed.

Thomas glared at him and raised his arm ready to thump him but Cassie stayed his hand.

"Actually, it was brilliant," she enthused. "You can't believe the improvements that Hel has made. She'd love you to go and see for yourself. Everyone was saying just how important you are."

The squirrel's button eyes opened with inquisitiveness and his chest puffed up with pride.

"Well, you missed all the excitement up here." He leaned towards them confidentially. "The gods have been going wild trying to recapture Loki."

"Oh, and Dread Biter the dragon-serpent has a message for you," said Thomas. "He says if you pay him a visit he'll tell you something that will blow your mind."

The squirrel's eyes lit up with curiosity and he bustled off in a great hurry but then realised he'd forgotten something and backtracked for a moment.

"Give me back my rope," he demanded. But before

he could say anything more the noise of a horn shattered the air and a great shout erupted.

"*Seize him!*"

They saw a man with large flashing gold teeth running in their direction, pursued by someone who looked like his twin! Instantly, Thomas and Nancy leapt in opposite directions, pulling the near-invisible rope taut between them. The fleeing man rushed forward in a headlong manner, unaware of the rope at knee height. He soon went crashing to the ground and was joined by his pursuer. They got mixed up in a tangle of arms and legs. Thomas and Nancy whirled round them in opposite directions, holding the ends of Gleipner the Rope. The rope tugged them in a magical dance around their quarry and they leapt in the air with acrobatic skill. Soon the fleeing men were trussed up like mummies, one on each end of Gleipner.

It was impossible to tell them apart. Immediately they started shouting and accusing each other.

"I am the real Heimdall!" said the one on the left and the children realised the men were doubles, not twins. "I can help you find your goal!"

"You lying fiend! Now we will return you to the darkest pit where the serpent shall drop venom on your head for all eternity!" accused the one on the right.

The other just laughed in his face. "Children, believe me! I am the real Heimdall, the Guardian of the Rainbow that leads to the kingdom of the gods!"

"Children, I thank you for capturing Loki, the betrayer, the most spiteful of gods," avowed the one on the right.

The children looked at them, perplexed.

"How on earth can we know which is which?" said Thomas.

Cassie eyed them accusingly. "Tell us where we can find Finnen. Tell us the way to Urda's Well. One of you has lied to us already."

The man on the left blew out a steady stream of air to his left from his gold teeth.

It became a mist of light and sparked into fire. A flame ran along it and sparkled into a thousand colours. A rainbow was born and glowed indigo, green, red, yellow, blue, orange and misty pink.

"This is Bifröst, the Rainbow Route of the Gods. It will allow you to journey to your goal."

"Do not believe that liar! He has already sent you once to your doom," claimed the other. "It is only I who can set you on your route to Urda's Well."

He also breathed out a stream of air that became a rainbow to his right, identical to the first.

The children looked at the two rainbows going in different directions, utterly bewildered.

Suddenly Swift Teeth, who had been watching all this in great glee, burst into laughter.

"Ha, ha, here's sport!" he said. "One way leads to your doom, the other to your goal, but which is which?"

"Please help us," pleaded Cassie.

"Let me set you a riddle," said the mischievous squirrel. "One of these is an impostor and is really Loki who is a perpetual liar. The other is Heimdall who can only tell the truth. But you can find out the way you should go by asking one of them one question. What will it be?"

The children sighed with exasperation.

"Trust me," said the Heimdall on the left, flashing them a golden smile.

"Cast this evil liar into his pit of doom!" demanded the second man, bearing his glinting teeth.

Cassie and Thomas went into a huddle.

"What question could possibly tell us the way?" agonised Cassie. "We don't know who's the liar and who tells the truth!"

Thomas pondered for a while and then looked resolute. "It's a trick question. I think I know the answer."

He marched up to the man on the left. "Tell me, if we ask your enemy which is the way to Urda's Well, what way will he send us?" he asked in a clear voice.

"He is a liar so will send you to your doom. He will tell you to go left," he answered.

"So we will take the right," said Thomas decisively and, holding his sisters' hands, headed towards the right-hand rainbow.

Immediately, the Heimdall on the left turned back into Loki and the false rainbow dissipated into black smoke.

"Brilliant!" said Swift Teeth the squirrel appreciatively as he skipped along beside them.

"How did you figure it out?" said Cassie in amazement.

"Simple," said Thomas. "I worked out that they would both come up with the same answer and we had to do the opposite so it didn't matter who I asked. The liar would lie about what the truthful one would say. So the opposite would be true. And the truth-teller would tell the truth about what the liar would say, so we also had to do the opposite. It was the only question that guaranteed the same outcome."

"I'm glad now you waste so much time on puzzles,"

laughed Cassie. Thomas couldn't resist feeling proud.

They released the real Heimdall from the bonds and he held Loki at sword point.

"The child has snared you in your own lies," he said to Loki.

"You children think you are so clever," sneered Loki, "but I shall have the last laugh, for another has already beaten you!"

"Have you anything to do with Caitlín?" demanded Thomas, losing patience. "Did you send us in the wrong direction to give her a lead?"

"I make mischief for my own pleasure," said Loki contemptuously.

"Answer!" shouted the true Heimdall, tightening the knots of the rope. Loki fought for his breath. "She nears the goal," he gasped.

"Take him away," ordered Heimdall to two giants who now arrived on the scene, "for I hate to look at him." Then he turned to the children. "There are swans living at Urda's Well at the root of the World Tree. Perhaps the Swan Maiden that you seek has sought refuge there. But if you talk to the Weird Sisters, the Norns, be careful. They tell of past, present and future. The Past and Present sisters are friendly to humans but the Future sister is unpredictable."

Thomas bound up the rope Gleipner into a coil and wrapped it around his waist.

"I'm borrowing this, it might come in useful," he said to the squirrel. Swift Teeth glared at him but Heimdall nodded in approval.

"Just remember to throw it back into the sky when you're finished with it and I'll get it," the squirrel said grudgingly.

They said goodbye and set off across the rainbow. It glowed beneath their feet and swirled in multicoloured mist but it held fast. In places the swirls formed into the shapes of symbols like the Norse runes and they felt a powerful magic. Before they came to its end, they heard chanting in strong female voices.

"*In chaos, order,*

Darkness, light,

Death, life.

Same as it ever was.

Same as it ever is.

Same as it ever will be!"

Their voices mingled together, old, young and middle-aged. And in the background was the deep, sonorous note of a swan's cry, an ululating whoop. Then they heard eerie music, like a chorus of swans' singing.

As they came to the end of the rainbow, the magical

symbols became stronger and radiated with power. The mist cleared and all was illuminated.

Before them were three tall, striking women standing before a well. The one nearest the well was old and worn with long white hair, the second was young and confident in her movements and the third was veiled and stood further back from the others. They each held a pitcher that they lowered into the well where the water shone bright as silver. Close by, two swans rested on a bank. They realised that the swans made the strange sad music that made their hearts yearn.

The young woman raised her head and regarded them with an open friendly face. "I am Verdandi," she said, "and these are my sisters Urda," she gestured towards the old woman who turned round and bowed, "and Skuld." The veiled woman ignored them.

"Past and fate," said the old woman, gazing into the well as she dipped her pitcher.

"Present and becoming," said Verdandi, showing them her full pitcher.

"Future and necessity," said Skuld, throwing her water onto one of the roots of the great tree.

The children explained their quest for Finnen.

Urda and Verdandi listened attentively. Skuld had turned her back on them.

"Foolish children, wasting our time and their own," she muttered darkly. Cassie felt herself bristling but willed herself to be polite. There was something stately and commanding about the women that demanded respect. She gestured towards the swans. "Is one of them perhaps Finnen or do they know of her?" Her voice rose in hope.

The swans sang in their beautifully eerie voices and the music was so sweet it touched their hearts.

"Finnen came to them and they sent her to ice," translated Nancy.

Urda and Verdandi exchanged glances.

"The child deciphers animals' tongues," said Verdandi. "We must help them."

"I see from their faces they are brave and have performed noble deeds to be here," said Urda.

"We have work to do," said Skuld sternly, throwing water on the root.

"Come, come, sister, at least let them look in the water," urged Verdandi. Skuld made a gesture of indifference and Urda, the old woman, beckoned the children to the side of the well.

The children gathered around it and watched the water rise to the brim. Magical symbols rose from its depth, held for a moment on its surface and dissipated like ripples on a pool.

"These are the magical runes," said Verdandi. "See what you will learn."

Thomas gazed at his own reflection and watched as it flicked through different shapeshifting transformations from donkey to eagle to stag. It settled in the shape of a stag whose body rose out of the water like a silvery shadow. It held in the air for a second and was gone. Cassie's reflection hovered for a moment between salmon and bull then settled as a salmon. Its silvery form rose from the pool and disappeared. Nancy's reflection didn't waver. It became an eagle that took wing and vanished. The children regarded each other in wonder.

"These are your guardian spirits," said Verdandi. "When you are threatened, hide in them."

"These must be our power animals that Scáthach said would be revealed to us," said Cassie.

"But what about Finnen?" pressed Thomas. "We are not the only ones looking for her."

Verdandi and Urda looked to Skuld, hidden behind her black veil. Skuld turned towards Cassie and raised her veil for a moment. Cassie had the impression of gazing into a deep, unfathomable chasm. She felt sick as her stomach lurched towards her chest and her breath ran ragged in her lungs. Then images like in a half-remembered dream floated into her mind. She saw the seething cauldron of Dread Biter in the cold realm of mists, chunks of ice carried by a turbulent river. Then a shape of blackest evil hurrying ahead.

"You know already where to seek her next – the Chasm of Chaos," said Skuld.

"To the north of the Chasm of Chaos is Niflheim, the icy land of mists," explained Verdandi. "To the south is the Land of Fire. From Niflheim flow the eleven rivers that pour into the Chasm of Chaos and freeze there, slowly filling it with ice."

"We've seen the source of those rivers at the Roaring Kettle in Niflheim," said Thomas. "You mean if we'd continued further south from there we would have found her?"

"Yes, but it is very dangerous. From the land of fire come clouds of fire which melted the ice into a mist. It is the harshest place in the world and few come back alive," said Urda, the old woman.

"Through snow, through churning waters and into burning ice but only she with a heart of ice will reach her goal," intoned Skuld, pointing into the swirling waters of the well.

The children looked back into the well. They saw the water of the eleven streams that they'd seen born in Niflheim flowing into the void and turning into giant glaciers. And then moving between the ice floes, a dark, hooded figure.

"That's her, Caitlín!" shrieked Nancy.

"We must get there before her," Cassie said desperately.

"Surely we don't have to go all the way back to the land of mist and follow the rivers?" exclaimed Thomas. "There must be a shortcut."

Skuld nodded.

Cassie looked pleadingly at the sisters but then she knew.

"We can get there by plunging into the well, isn't that so?" she ventured. "You are brave," said Skuld. "You have seen the abyss yet go to meet your fate. Your path is strewn with peril and failure. Plunge if you dare."

Thomas had already begun to bind the rope Gleipner around his sisters. He tied it fast. Without a word they climbed onto the lip of the well's wall and, holding hands, plunged into the waters.

They felt like they were hurtled into the abyss, into infinity. The water caressed them like silk, like glitter, sluicing them through a tunnel. Then it gushed into a river and they were carried on top of its turbulent surface. Chunks of ice floated and crashed about but the magic rope held them firm together. Flecks of spray rose from the torrent and immediately turned into hard balls of ice that rained back down on them. The cold was excruciating but Cassie tried to will them to practise their breath discipline.

"*Focus on our breathing!*" she screamed through chattering teeth. "Turn the body first into water, then stone, then steel!"

But they were churned in the waters and risked being crushed between the ice chunks. With a supreme effort Cassie moved all her concentration into one point. She felt her skin grow silver in the silver waters and her belly extend into an elegant arch. She became a salmon and her fish instincts pulled a safe path through the seething river, guiding her brother and sister who also turned into salmon in her wake, all joined together by the magical rope.

They started to get a sense of their bearings. As the water hit the yawning gap in the Chasm of Chaos, it began to freeze. Soon the water no longer flowed and ice crashed into giant glaciers. Exhausted from her exertions, Cassie flopped and turned back into her normal shape. Thinking quickly, Thomas took on the shape of an eagle and Nancy followed suit. With superhuman effort they lifted Cassie, suspended in the magic rope, to the top of a vast glacier.

The light was a permanent dusk, hovering perpetually between cold brightness and dark. Nancy and Thomas resumed their human shapes and they rushed to each other, numb with cold. They bound the rope tighter around themselves and Cassie, so they were joined like mountain climbers in single file, and tried to get their bearings in the harsh landscape. A biting wind rose and lashed their faces, raising sheets of powdery snow to blind them. Thomas narrowed his eyes. A shining glacier with the sheen of glass glistened before him, almost blinding him.

"Look!" shouted Nancy, bending down. She picked up a white feather, gleaming purer white than the snow.

They walked on and found another feather, brittle with ice. They had stumbled upon a trail. Thomas felt a tiny fluttering of hope in his breast. They were in the right place.

"Let us turn into huskies," Cassie called out. So mustering all their strength they concentrated and transformed themselves into strong and powerful sled dogs. Suddenly they were quick and light on their feet and the going underfoot was no longer treacherous.

They surged forward like a sleigh team, tethered to each other in a snaking line, Cassie in the front, Thomas in the middle and Nancy bringing up the rear.

Before them was a dazzling edifice of ice that shone blue in the strange half-light of the Chasm of Chaos. The glare almost blinded their keen almond-shaped husky eyes but they realised they were nearly there. Their breath froze in a cloud of freezing fog as it came out of their mouths. The going was harder now but they pushed on.

But all at once there was a great splintering sound. Cassie, several footsteps ahead of Thomas, disappeared and he was pulled towards a yawning crevasse. With horror Cassie thought she saw licking flames of fire rising from the bowels of the earth.

Using all the strength he could muster in his powerful husky shoulders, Thomas managed to pull himself and Nancy back from the brink.

We are in great danger, he then thought, and I must take the shape of my power animal. So in a heartbeat he took the form of a stag. He reared up on his powerful hind haunches and, wrenching round, backed away from the yawning gap, pulling a terrified Cassie in the shape of the husky dog clear of the abyss.

Realising the danger of getting stuck in her animal

shape, Cassie willed herself to go back to her human form. She was blue in the face and half-frozen with the searing cold. Thomas breathed his hot stag's breath and Nancy her warm husky breath on her and she rallied. Nancy then changed and she and Cassie clambered onto Thomas's back. He was going to try and leap over the crevasse to reach their goal.

But the gap got wider and wider as the ice creaked and splintered. Curiously, scalding hot air rushed up from the widening fault line. It felt like an earthquake was taking place. Cassie remembered Skuld's words about burning ice and felt a fresh danger.

Shards of ice, sharp as glass, flew from the glacier on the opposite side. On its hard blue surface, Cassie saw their reflection – her and Nancy on Thomas's back in his stag shape. And then, narrowing her eyes, she saw beyond the surface into the heart of the glacier.

A dark hooded creature was tearing into the ice like a ravenous wolf and creating the ice shards. Frozen in the centre was a woman with swan's wings folded behind her. Cassie watched in horror as the hooded creature bit into the ice. It an instant she realised it was Caitlín. She saw now that Caitlín wasn't wearing a cloak but had black leathery wings like a prehistoric bird and a hideous woman's face with sharp fangs that bit into the ice. Her skin was coal back and hairless and her talons vicious. Caitlín had taken the shape of the Corra, the water monster. The stench of her evil made them gag.

Time seemed to slow down and Cassie found herself living her nightmare.

And the woman was Finnen, she was sure of it, in the heart of the glacier. But instead of them rescuing her, Caitlín was going to kill her. The crevasse ahead of them yawned and creaked wider. Cassie saw a claw scratch the woman's face and tears of blood course down her cheeks. It was her vision coming true and she felt sick to the stomach. For a moment Cassie's eyes lost focus and the reflection of the children in the glacier came back double. Then it was shattered in a splintering of ice.

"Stop, stop!" Cassie cried, her heart pounding against her ribs.

Then there was a sad, mournful singing, the most eerie, lost sound they'd ever heard. It was Finnen giving voice to her dismay and sorrow and it was enough to make the sternest heart melt. But in a moment it was drowned out by harsh, cacophonous laughter that bored into the children's heads with a spike of hatred.

Thomas as a stag ran towards the lip of the crevasse and hurled himself across the abyss. Nancy and Cassie clung to him, terrified of the cloud of fire rising from the lower depths. He jumped clear of the gap and landed heavily on the other side. Casssie and Nancy slid to the ground, shaking, and Thomas changed back into his own form.

Then Caitlín's monstrous form, half-Corra half-woman, rose from the depths of the ice. She carried a lifeless Finnen in her talons. Her cruel laughter rent the air as she bore down towards them.

"*Quick! Take the shape of your power animal!*" Cassie roared.

In the blink of an eye Nancy rose into the air as an eagle, wings outstretched.

Cassie and Thomas froze and concentrated. They both caught Caitlín's eye and nearly blacked out with the impact. Caitlín descended towards them, her baleful gaze trained on them, but just as she drew near Cassie flopped onto the ice as a salmon and Thomas resumed his stag shape.

Caitlín's monstrous figure sprang back as if repelled by a magical force field. She breathed frosted air and clouds of icy mist enveloped the children.

They were drowning in dry ice. Exhausted from the

constant shapeshifting, Thomas resumed his human shape.

"*Change back into yourselves!*" Thomas roared at his sisters. "Don't risk getting stuck in an animal form without the energy to shapeshift."

Nancy heard him and returned to her human shape.

Cassie hadn't heard him. Thomas tried to call out to her again but his words were drowned by an explosion. Chunks of ice and shards as sharp as daggers spewed out as the glacier erupted.

"*Cassie, change!*" shouted Thomas desperately. The salmon wriggled silver on the ice and once more became Cassie. The children huddled together, held fast by their magical rope. Cassie watched the glacier's destruction, transfixed. It was just like her nightmare except it was ice Finnen had been trapped behind, not glass as she had thought.

The ice explosion went on for what seemed like an eternity and then, as suddenly as it had erupted, it ceased. The glacier had been hacked to the core. Chunks of ice splinters lay all around, sharp as glass or steel. Cassie slumped onto the cold surface of the hardened snow.

"Only she with a heart of ice will reach her goal," she said bleakly, repeating Skuld's prophesy.

"Caitlín beat us," said Nancy tearfully.

Thomas's eyes filled with tears.

"Is she dead, Cassie?" said Nancy, sobbing. "Do we have to give Jarlath back to the Merrows?"

"I don't know. All I know is we have failed," said Cassie dully; she felt like all the energy had been drained from her body. "We'd better go back but I don't know how."

Thomas raised a frozen hand and the Crane Bag appeared. With fumbling fingers he grasped it and, reaching inside, pulled something out that shimmered like a piece of the sea, blue-green in the eerie Arctic light. "We have Manannán's shirt. Sennan said it could ensure safe return from journeys to the Otherworld."

They untied the rope Gleipner and cast it into the sky where it was caught by an invisible hand. They huddled together, tired and defeated, and Thomas unfurled the shirt and wrapped it around them. It enveloped them in salty sea spray and foam. They were hurled once more through infinite sea, tiny objects bounced around an eternal void, and then all went silent and dark.

CHAPTER 10

Cassie could barely stir and felt frozen to the bone in her bed. She opened her eyes and saw that she was covered in a thin layer of ice. As Nancy joined Thomas at the bedside, they seemed to sway and ripple and she felt as if she was looking at them from the bottom of a very deep pool.

"Breathe," Thomas instructed Nancy.

All at once Cassie was enveloped in a warm breath and the icy straitjacket began to evaporate in her cosy bedroom in Inish Álainn.

But still, she shivered with fear, her eyes spilling with tears.

"I can't wait to find Lardon. I'm going to make him feel the exact amount of pain that I feel now," Thomas said, his voice cold and distant.

But before Cassie could reply, their Aunt Angel bustled into the room.

"Why, Cassie," she said with concern, "you look like you've been to Hell and back!"

Cassie smiled bitterly as Angel felt her pulse and wiped her brow.

"You'd better stay at home today," said Angel.

"Perhaps we should get Áine to bring some herbal remedies," suggested Thomas.

Angel allowed Thomas and Nancy to go fetch Áine while she tended her ailing niece. She made her a hot drink of honey and lemon and tucked Cassie in with a hot water bottle.

Cassie's brow was feverish, her cheeks burning, but her hands and feet were icy cold. She drifted off in a half-sleep between fire and ice.

Cassie hovered on the brink of a great glacier that crumbled into a great desert of endless miles of sand surrounded by mountains streaked with cobalt and crystal, as old as the world itself. The sun beat down on her like a weapon. She saw in the distance a small oasis of palm trees. Something fluttered in the breeze in the hot desert air. She picked it up from the sand and saw that it was a white swan's feather.

"She's still alive!" Cassie awoke with a start.

Through her glassy eyes, she saw Áine hovering above the bed, wiping her brow. She felt a crystal stone in each of her hands. They were alone.

"Thomas and Nancy have told me everything," she said softly. Tears ran down Áine's face.

Cassie sat up now, alert and focused. The fever had passed.

"Not everything," she said. She told Áine of her vision.

"Then we cannot give up," Áine said intently. She placed her hands on Cassie's head, feeling her aura. "Your encounter with Caitlín at the glacier has weakened you but you still have some power left. Be careful not to misuse it." She kissed Cassie gently on the forehead and left.

She heard Angel coming up the stairs.

"You look so much better," her aunt said brightly as she came through the door with some smelly concoction of herbs. "But I think you'd better rest indoors today. Drink this."

Cassie took the mug and pretended to sip at it while Angel fussily tidied the room.

"By the way," Angel said, as she put some of Cassie's clothes in a drawer, "have you come across a letter that should have arrived from the United States? Lardon keeps pestering me about it. I'm fairly sure the lawyers would have written to Jarlath."

Cassie shrugged her shoulders.

"I must tidy up all the drawers," said Angel, fussing. "There are hats and gloves in here since I was a child."

"I could help you," said Cassie suddenly. She had a vague memory of the letter Muiris had given them days before for Jarlath. She had thrust it somewhere for safekeeping and something told her it might be important.

Thomas and Nancy were summoned into the bedroom but showed no enthusiasm for the task.

"I'm so pleased you want to help, Cassie," encouraged Angel, rifling through an old laundry box. "You never know what you might find."

"Look out for that letter from America," Cassie murmured to her brother and sister when Angel was out of earshot.

None of them noticed Lardon lurking outside the doorway. When they trooped downstairs to get black binliners from the kitchen to store the unwanted clothes, Lardon seized his opportunity. He crept into the attic bedroom and retrieved the letter from the chest of drawers where he had seen Cassie hiding it.

Tidying the drawers took all morning, as the

contents seemed to date back to the sixteenth century. They even found a lacy petticoat that must have belonged to Granny Clíona. But there was no sign of a letter. Cassie gave up, disappointed.

Lunch was a tense affair, as Thomas kept making cutthroat signs at Lardon behind Angel's back. Every time he passed him salad or salt he hissed, "I'm going to get you!"

Lardon was too busy eating to care.

Straight after lunch Angel put on her nanny's cloak that made her look like something out of the Victorian era.

"I'm just off to arrange a little party to welcome Lardon to the island," she said.

Nancy clapped her hands delightedly but Cassie and Thomas didn't look so enthusiastic.

"Come on, children," encouraged Angel, "it will be fun. And I want you to practise those wonderful animal impersonations you performed when we first arrived. Lardon's in charge." With that she headed out the door in a flurry of billowing cloak.

Lardon regarded them with disdain. "So, suckers. I'm the daddy now. You must do what I say and I say we've got to package up those Brussels sprouts. Podge is awaiting my first shipment for export." He threw a pile of sacks at them, with Japanese writing on the side.

Thomas smirked insolently at him and followed him outside. As soon as they were in the open air he began to blow softly between his lips. Lardon's tracksuit billowed in the breeze.

"It's suddenly got windy. My hair!" he said. "I hate Irish weather!" He tried to smooth down his clothes and looked with annoyance at the children who were untouched by the wind.

"Hey, how come it isn't ruffling you creeps?" he shouted in bewilderment.

Nancy looked disapprovingly at her brother as he continued to perform the Breath Feat.

"Just a little game," said Thomas.

"Let me outta here," yelped Lardon as the strange wind continued to buffet him.

"I'm telling," said Nancy sternly.

Cassie shoved her roughly aside. "Just leave this to us," she said harshly. "I'm not taking orders from a kid."

Hurt, Nancy ran back towards the house. Thomas began to blow again. Lardon tried to follow Nancy but was pinioned by the force of Thomas's breath.

"I hate you Shingles! I hate Inishawful! I hate Angel and Jarlath! I hate everybody! You're all mean and poor and stupid losers!" snarled Lardon.

Angered by Lardon's words, Cassie joined her brother in performing the Breath Feat. The twin forces of their breaths carried Lardon into the air like a kite, his gleaming white tracksuit billowing in the wind.

"Put me down!" he shrieked.

The force of their breath carried Lardon out towards Bo Men's bog. They looked at each other with an evil glint in their eyes. The bog was filled with nasty creatures that tickled humans to death.

The smell of approaching human flesh started a faint rumble across the fetid bog. Lardon shrieked in the air. He gazed down at the muddy pools.

"If I fall in there, I'll never be clean in my life again!" he screamed.

Thomas stopped blowing and Lardon fell towards the bog but was kept hovering on Cassie's stream of air. She alternated its strength so that Lardon bobbed up and down. Thomas laughed cruelly.

"OK, that old woman you met the other day. Who was she?" Thomas demanded.

Lardon surprisingly became defiant. "I don't give in to bullies," he said bravely, flapping in the air.

Cassie inhaled and exhaled slowly, so Lardon plummeted and skimmed the bog's surface. He was perilously close to falling in and screamed.

"Who was she?" yelled Thomas.

"How the hell do I know?" pleaded Lardon. "Some ugly old Irish broad with buck teeth and stinking breath. She flashed this diamond in front of my eyes. She said any enemy of the Chingles was a friend of hers. But I didn't mean –"

Lardon's bottom hit the bog with a sickening squelch. But then he was jerked up again on a current of Cassie's breath. Around them, the ghostly laughter of the Bo Men shuddered in the wind. Lardon screamed.

"OK, when she flashed the ring in front of my eyes, I saw my reflection and I was the centre of attention and everybody loved me. I was on a stage receiving an award. She said I could have my heart's desire –"

Cassie increased her breath and Lardon rose suddenly above the bog. She flipped him up so he was standing upright in the current of air.

"What was her name?" demanded Thomas.

"I don't know," wailed Lardon. "We didn't do formal introductions."

"Who do you talk to in the mirror?" Thomas shouted.

Cassie manoeuvred Lardon closer to the bog, so his trainers touched the damp moss on its surface.

"No one," said Lardon in a small voice.

Cassie blew and manoeuvred the current of air streaming from her mouth, so that Lardon turned upside down and his nose was dipped in a muddy pool.

"I'm getting sick of this," said Thomas in a menacing voice.

"I do acting impersonations," Lardon heaved and cried. "I pretend to talk to my mother."

"So she's your mother!" Thomas exclaimed.

Cassie puffed up her cheeks and bobbed Lardon up and down on the current of air, as if he was on a geyser. Thomas was so angry he took a deep breath and joined in. They bounced Lardon between their two jets of air as if he was an inflatable ball. Each time Lardon plunged toward the bog he screamed.

"I don't know!" Lardon sobbed. "It's all in the letter . . ."

The sound of muffled voices disturbed them. Cassie and Thomas turned abruptly round and Lardon tumbled into the bog. He screamed and lay spread-eagled on the mossy surface, as the ground made alarming sucking noises.

"What's going on?" called Connle from Derry's back.

"That's where they're being mean to Lardon," they heard Nancy say.

Thomas and Cassie immediately scrambled to rescue

Lardon, thrusting out their hands to pull him clear of the squelchy bog.

"We didn't mean for you to fall in. Don't you breathe a word about this!" hissed Thomas in a threatening voice.

Lardon slumped on the bank and looked at his formerly white tracksuit encased in muddy peat. He was speechless and numb with shock.

"Lardon fell in," Cassie said sheepishly, not looking Connle in the eye. She had to resist the urge to smack Nancy, who gave them dirty looks.

"I ran into Nancy up at the house," said Connle. "I was on my way over to see how you all were after your adventures last night. She insisted I come and check you weren't throwing Lardon to the Bo Men."

Cassie looked daggers at Nancy.

"I hope there's no funny business going on," warned Connle.

"You didn't actually see anything, did you?" said Thomas to Nancy, mock innocent.

Nancy shook her head. "I knowed you were being meanies."

"The word's 'knew'," crowed Cassie. "There. She doesn't know what she's talking about."

Connle didn't say another word to them on the way

home. Checking that Jarlath was nowhere around, he helped Lardon get cleaned up and sent him to bed with a large bowl of porridge that Lardon said was the best he'd ever tasted. Connle's special magic recipe of course.

"I hope you're telling the truth about Lardon," Connle then said. "I know you've suffered a major setback in your search for Finnen. But it's wrong under any circumstances to hurt or endanger someone."

Thomas and Cassie kept their eyes downcast. Connle gave them a strange look. He could have sworn Cassie was looking rather bullish and Thomas had the distinct look of a donkey.

"We'd better go and practise our animal shapes in our bedroom," said Cassie sullenly

"I hope I can trust you to behave while I go to fetch my tin whistle for the party," Connle warned as he was leaving.

"I don't want to be an animal," said Nancy as the front door shut.

Cassie tried to grab her but she ran off and the others headed up the stairs.

"She's winding me up at the moment. She's such a little goody-goody!" fumed Cassie.

But Thomas said to leave her alone.

Thomas and Cassie slammed the bedroom door and started to giggle at the memory of Lardon floundering in the peaty bog. A pair of cold eyes that glittered in triumph met their laughing reflections in the wardrobe mirror. Their faces began to take on their animal features: Cassie's nose expanded and bull's ears shot up on her head and Thomas sprouted donkey's ears and his jaw elongated as his teeth became large and yellow.

Nancy avoided them and brought a towel into Lardon's bedroom, where he lay listlessly on his bed in a clean new pair of white silk pyjamas.

"Don't be sad," she said gently.

Lardon laughed bitterly. "You know, when that ugly old broad asked me for my heart's desire, I lied to her. It wasn't to win prizes and stuff. I just want my mom and dad to notice me. And the diamond ring was really made of ice that melted away to nothing." He heaved a huge sigh and wiped his snotty nose loudly. "But nobody likes me because I'm ugly and they think I'm a spoiled rich kid."

"I like you," Nancy said and gently flicked her eyelashes on his cheek in what she called her butterfly kiss.

"You're just a stupid little kid!" He turned his back

to her. "Someday I'll show them all," he added defiantly.

Nancy touched his hand.

"Thank you," he muttered, turning his head as she skipped to the door. She turned round and flashed him such a warm smile it lifted a corner of his gloom.

Up the stairs, Nancy peeped into the attic bedroom. Cassie was pawing the ground and Thomas erupted into wild hee-haws. They bounced around the room like things possessed. Nancy didn't like it when they behaved like that.

"We nearly got the truth out of him," brayed Thomas. "I just bet Caitlín's his mother."

"Lardon said something about a letter," said Cassie snorting. "He must have stolen that letter I hid when we got the first postcard. We have to find out."

"But we have to be careful," said Thomas. "We don't want to get ourselves into trouble."

"Let's make up a play. Something to smoke out Lardon!" said Cassie, wickedly.

Nancy tiptoed down the stairs as Aunty Angel returned and excited voices filled the hallway.

The living-room was full of all their friends from the island: Mr Mulally the publican, the twins Macdara and Conán, Mr Guilfoyle the farmer, Donnacha the bodhrán-maker, Mrs Moriarty the knitter. Áine was there with her harp and Connle with his tin whistle. Áine was worried about bumping into Jarlath in case there was a scene but Angel reassured her that he was so busy with his invention he hardly came to the house these days.

Angel persuaded Lardon to join the party and he moped down in his snow-white dressing-gown. The islanders greeted him warmly and Angel was surprised to see that he was actually quite popular.

Upstairs, Cassie and Thomas gambolled about wickedly and dangerously. As Nancy was going to the toilet, Thomas seized her and forced her to wear the stripy balaclava. They dashed around the bedroom and grabbed all the pillows.

Soon music filled the house. Áine's harp and Conán's uileann pipes blended with the high piping tunefulness of Connle's tin whistle and was underscored by the dancing beat of Donnacha's bodhrán. There was something wild and uninhibited about the music that reminded the children of the swirling music of the fairies.

Then Angel clapped her hands and announced that the children were about to put on their play. Cassie and Thomas entered the living-room and bowed low to the audience, then whipped off their hats to reveal their strangely morphed heads: half bull, half Cassie, and half donkey, half Thomas. The islanders gasped and broke into thunderous applause, thinking it some extraordinary make-up. Cassie took to all fours and charged around the room, making such convincing snorting noises that people drew back in alarm, especially Mrs Moriarty who was wearing a big red sweater.

"This is the story of a Bullish Girl and a Mulish Boy!" bellowed Cassie in a deep voice.

Thomas gnashed his donkey's teeth and ate a flower in a vase. "And a giddy little lamb of a girl!" he brayed, pointing his hoof at Nancy.

"I don't want to play," said Nancy. She pulled off her balaclava, her head normal, and sat down stubbornly on the floor. Everyone laughed, thinking it was part of the action. Cassie and Thomas snorted and brayed but Nancy wouldn't budge.

"One day they were playing happily on the island when a strange creature arrived from somewhere else," narrated Cassie. Thomas held up something hidden behind a blanket and Cassie whipped it off, revealing a life-size figure made of pillows and dressed in one of Lardon's trademark snow-white tracksuits. Everyone laughed except Lardon and Nancy.

"This creature was called Streaky Bacon and he told them he came from a magical land beyond the sea where he was a prince. But all the children knew was that he was mean and greedy and spoiled all their fun." Thomas stood behind the Pillow Boy and began to pelt the audience with Brussels sprouts.

"Streaky Bacon told them he was going to become a Bonsai millionaire by selling Brussels sprouts to the Japanese."

At this, Mr Guilfoyle the farmer shifted in his seat.

"But Streaky Bacon was evil," continued Cassie menacingly. "He told a wicked witch where to find the children and stopped them from finding the long-lost sister of a friend." Here Cassie produced ice cubes she had taken from the freezer and piled them into a block. She donned Aunty Angel's black cloak and jumped about cawing and screeching like a madwoman. Then she smashed the ice to smithereens with her foot. People gasped, impressed and a little unnerved by her theatrics.

But Connle and Áine exchanged alarmed glances. Lardon shifted uncomfortably in his chair as Cassie in the black cloak seized the figure of "Streaky Bacon" by the throat.

"But Streaky Bacon had a secret," said Cassie, turning

to the Pillow Boy. "Do you want to tell everyone your secret about what an evil boy you've been?"

Thomas put on a voice for the Pillow Boy – a very bad American accent. "Oh, please let me be! I'm so important and my mummy and daddy are so rich and love me so!"

"But that's not the whole story," roared Cassie, charging at the Pillow Boy and stamping her hoof. "Tell us the truth about your real mother!"

"The one you talk to in the mirror," leered Thomas.

"I think we've heard quite enough," interrupted Angel. "You children are overexcited –"

"But little boys are supposed to tell the truth," grumbled Cassie.

"Evil little boys with evil mothers," said Thomas wildly.

"Stop!" shouted Lardon suddenly. "My mother isn't evil. I don't know. The truth is I don't know who my mother is . . . I'm . . . I'm adopted."

Everyone gasped.

"But your real mother?" persisted Cassie.

"I just told you. I don't know who my real mother is. I was bought over the Internet when I was just a little kid, less than two years old. I don't remember much. I guess I came from abroad," said Lardon, his voice breaking. "My adoptive parents were too busy to spend much time with me and my nannies just plonked me in front of the television. So I learned English from old movies."

"Lardon," said Angel gently. "You don't have to talk about this if you don't want to."

But he ignored her and continued. "The only reason I'm here is that my adoptive parents are divorcing. So Angel is my guardian while the court decides who is to get me."

Nobody moved. They all stared, open-mouthed, at Lardon's revelations.

"Is that the whole truth?" said Thomas cruelly.

"Stop this!" said Angel. "Lardon, I'm delighted to have you with me!"

"You're only saying that because they pay you," said Lardon. "Here! If you don't believe me, it's all in a letter." He thrust a crumpled letter at Cassie and Thomas.

Angel tried to take it but Cassie snatched it from her. It was addressed to Jarlath from a fancy New York lawyer and was accompanied by a cheque. Cassie read it aloud:

"*Dear Mr Mc Coll,*

We are writing to make arrangements for the arrival of our client Lardon B Hackenbacker III who is currently a ward of court in the Guardianship of your sister Angel Verity McColl. While divorce proceedings continue, our client is in the sole charge of your sister. We understand that in a highly unusual situation, neither parent is currently seeking custody. We are sending you this fee so you can make the necessary arrangements for their visit,

Yours expensively,

Ballbreaker Fastbuck, McFee's Law Firm."

There was a stunned, embarrassed silence.

Lardon looked aghast, then sparked into anger. "So now we have the truth. That's just peachy. Neither wants custody. 'A highly unusual situation.' Nobody likes me or wants me. Not my real parents whoever they are or my parents who adopted me."

The islanders regarded Thomas and Cassie coldly and ignored them, making a big fuss of Lardon.

"I was an orphan," said Mrs Moriarty kindly. "I grew up in a convent and the nuns taught me how to knit."

"We're adopted too," said Macdara and Conán.

"You wouldn't want to believe what that thieving law firm wrote," thundered Mr Mulally. "They just said that to increase their fee." He gave Lardon a bear hug.

"Mr Mulally is right," cried Angel.

But Lardon was still upset. "Satisfied?" he shouted at

Cassie and Thomas and ran from the room, followed by Angel and Nancy.

Suddenly Áine began to play her harp, accompanied by Connle on the tin whistle. The music was sad and sinuous and wrapped itself around the listeners, making them drowsy. The islanders fell into a deep sleep. Only Cassie and Thomas remained awake.

Áine put down her harp and confronted Cassie and Thomas, who looked more like a bull and donkey than ever before. She commanded they follow her into the hallway where she made them look in the mirror.

"You have come under Caitlín's sway and your base nature is acting out of malice. It was cruel of you to humiliate that boy so," she reprimanded them.

Cassie and Thomas faced their reflections.

"But we're only trying to find out what happened to Finnen," protested a rattled Cassie. "We had to find out if Lardon is one of Caitlín's servants."

"Even if it were true, you have behaved disgracefully. I am ashamed of you," said Áine.

Thomas and Cassie regarded their reflections. Thomas grinned asininely back and Cassie looked bullish and brattish.

"We're sorry," said Thomas sounding anything but.

He struggled as Áine held his shoulders and forced

him to gaze at himself. His face became more donkey-like but then he saw a vision in the mirror of the time a gang of boys at school had picked on him and humiliated him in the playground. Then it was as if he was looking out at himself and Cassie and their play through Lardon's eyes. He felt a spoke of pain and guilt at their cruelty.

"We won't do it again," he mumbled. His face crumpled and returned to normal.

Cassie glared at her bullish features and saw the time when her two best friends had complained about her in the school toilets, not realising she was in one of the stalls.

"She never brushes her hair," sneered Mary Louise.

"And her scruffy family. Did you ever see her father's car? It's a wreck," crowed Venetia.

"Little Miss Know-all! 'Teacher, teacher!'" mimicked Mary Louise cruelly.

"Thinks she's so clever – bet she ends up a bag lady stinking of pee," mocked Venetia, flicking her long blonde hair.

Cassie's face burned with shame and she felt hollow and empty. That's how she and Thomas had behaved towards Lardon. She realised she didn't like being cruel. It wasn't a nice feeling at all.

The islanders began to wake up as Angel, Lardon and Nancy came back into the room. Lardon's eyes were rimmed with red and his face streaked with tears.

"We're sorry we hurt you," said Cassie. "It was just a silly play. We didn't realise." Lardon didn't look at her. She felt like a louse.

"I'll deal with you later," muttered Angel tersely to Cassie and Thomas. They felt like they'd suddenly developed leprosy.

The islanders started to shuffle towards the door. They showed no memory of anything that had happened. But for reasons they didn't understand themselves, they all hugged Lardon warmly.

Just as Angel was about to close the front door, Muiris dashed up the garden path with a big parcel.

"This is an urgent delivery for Lardon," he said, breathless. "I have to give confirmation to Podge at the ferry by return."

It was from Hackenbacker Studio and contained an invitation and a large brochure.

"*Dear Lardon*," it read,

"*Sorry I've been so busy but I'm inviting you, your nanny Angel and her nieces and nephew to a special studio launch for our newest star. We'd also like to see your photos from the island, as it may be a suitable location for our next film. A helicopter will call to take you to Shannon Airport where you will board our private jet.*

Love, your Dad, Lardon Senior."

The glossy brochure was passed around excitedly.

Lardon's eyes shone.

"Now why would your dad invite you if he didn't want you?" said Angel. "He does love you, Lardon. He's told me so. He's just very busy trying to save the studio."

"I guess you can be my guests," Lardon said magnanimously to Cassie and Thomas who felt about the size of worms.

But even they began to feel excited about a special invitation to Hollywood aboard a private jet. That would impress her so-called best friends, thought Cassie.

Áine sat quietly in the corner with Nancy, who had taken the brochure to look at it. Cassie and Thomas hung back in disgrace as Lardon and Angel began to plan the journey.

Áine suddenly started and took the brochure from Nancy.

The brochure featured a series of photographs of a beautiful starlet with platinum blonde hair. She was shown gracefully arching from diving boards smiling enigmatically, plunging into pools, swimming under -

water. There was also a picture of her with her manager, a dark-haired chic woman with glossy black hair cut in a severe bob. She smiled, somewhat menacingly, like a shark, flashing perfect teeth. One of them, like Lardon's, was studded with a diamond.

"*Newest starlet Fiona Waters and her manager Cath Formor take Hollywood by storm*," the caption read. "*Hollywood's biggest ever budget for the revival of the underwater musical.*"

Nancy stabbed the page at the picture. "It makes my tummy tingle."

But Áine had gone white and let the brochure fall from her hand. "That's my sister!" she breathed.

Cassie heard her and picked the brochure up. She couldn't believe her eyes. The starlet bore more than a passing resemblance to Finnen. And Cath Formor, although pretty, reminded her of Caitlín and she had a diamond tooth!

She handed the brochure to Connle. "We've got to get to Hollywood," she said decisively. "Caitlín has the strength now to take more convincing human form. She could only manage a hideous old hag with Lardon. Somehow, she's got control of Finnen."

"Don't you think it's a bit of a coincidence that the invitation has come just like that?" mused Connle.

"Yes, it's almost as if Caitlín wants to lure us there," said Thomas.

"But it's perfect timing," said Cassie. "We really need to be in Hollywood."

"Excuse me for interrupting," said Angel, catching the tail end of the conversation as she came back into the room, "but you and Thomas aren't going anywhere. You are *so* grounded."

CHAPTER 11

Cassie and Thomas watched in agony as the helicopter spiralled into the sky. They could have sworn they saw Lardon smirk at them as the propellers lifted the craft into a tailwind and headed east. But they just stood there, numb with anger and humiliation.

Despite throwing the biggest strop of their lives, Angel had been unmoved. Only Nancy was allowed take the trip, so Lardon invited Connle and Áine to take their places. But Connle decided to remain behind to keep an eye on the trees. He warned Áine not to go, reminding her of her father's advice not to stray too far from home while she was in an in-between state. Suspended between goddess and human she was neither one or the other and might need the magical energy of her crystal bed to renew her. But desperate to see her sister, Áine insisted on going to the United States. She also confided to Connle that she wished to see the land of Elvis Presley, their favourite singer, and he didn't have the heart to discourage her.

"It's bad for us to be separated from Nancy," said Cassie as they turned back inside. "She shouldn't have to face Caitlín without us. We promised the Sean Gaels we'd protect her and Áine cannot use her powers."

"I can't think how we'd get there," Thomas said downcast. "No one would help, even if they could, we're in such disgrace. And we have no money."

"If only we could shapeshift our way across," said Cassie. "Then we could swim as seals or fish. But Áine told me we don't have much power after our encounter with Caitlín at the glacier. And we've sapped any energy we had left misusing our Breath Feat on Lardon."

"It's true. I don't think I could manage even small changes and anyway we don't know how far our power extends away from Inish Álainn," Thomas said.

"There's no use travelling in dreams," said Cassie in despair. "We don't have the skill to travel so far without magical help and anyway Caitlín has taken physical form now."

"Our only chance would be to smuggle across on some vessel," said Thomas without hope.

"Cassie! Thomas!" they heard as their Uncle Jarlath's clear voice called them in for supper.

There was a tense, silent pause.

Then Cassie and Thomas looked at each other wide-eyed in unison, sparked with the same idea.

"We can't," said Cassie, breathless at even daring to think it.

"We have no choice," said Thomas firmly.

They were so fulsome in their gratitude for Jarlath's offering of cold porridge he was taken aback and looked at them intently.

"Why are you being so nice to me?" He scratched his head. "You're after something."

"We're just glad to see you," said Cassie, feeling a bit guilty. "We've missed you."

Jarlath smiled and ruffled her hair with affection. Shortly after Lardon's arrival, Jarlath had taken to sleeping in the barn with the excuse that he was working late. "I'm glad to see you too. It got a bit lonely in my workshop. But the good thing is I've nearly cracked the Flying Marine. I've ironed out the problem with the sails and I've improved the fuel consumption. In fact, let's go and see it now. It's at the beach."

"How exciting!" said Cassie, suppressing another pang of guilt. It was wrong to deceive Jarlath but what choice did they have?

"How far can it go?" Thomas asked innocently as they put on their coats.

"On the sea, it can go as far as you like, because it's wind-powered." Jarlath screwed up his eyes as he reckoned. "But I believe it could fly all the way from the east coast of America to the west. I've found a way to use oxygen to power the flight. All you need is a little bit of fuel to get it going. Let's get cracking."

"Oh, Jarlath," said Cassie, "there's one thing I forgot! Muiris said you've got to see him urgently. There's a special delivery for you at Stag's Cliff and you've got to pick it up. You'll need Derry the Donkey to help you carry it."

Jarlath looked mystified. "Whatever it is can wait until later."

"Apparently not," said Cassie. "They're delaying the ferry because it might have to go back and it's very important."

"Oh, it must be that new generator I've ordered," groaned Jarlath. "I really didn't expect it so soon."

"You'd better dash," Cassie urged, handing him his woolly hat. "We'll meet you at the beach."

Jarlath saddled up the donkey and set off down the path, turning round to call out: "It's really good to be back home with you! I'm tired of sleeping in the barn."

Cassie felt like a complete rat but as soon as he was out of sight she tore around the house, stuffing a haversack with food and supplies. Thomas left a note, saying they'd forgot they'd promised Angel that they would stay with Connle, who was looking after Áine's house. It was the one place they knew he wouldn't look.

"Maybe we should turn back," said Thomas, his conscience pricking him. "Look what happened when we were cruel to Lardon."

"We've both agreed we have no choice," said Cassie resolutely. "It's too late." But inside she felt very panicky. Then she imagined the three smug-faced Merrows grabbing Jarlath under a wave. That made up her mind.

The Flying Marine was down on the beach tethered to a rock. They examined its inflated rubber platform mounted with the pilot's cage that looked like an old person's Zimmer frame. It still looked rickety but Jarlath had completely updated it. There was a new control panel with a "sail release" button and also a compass and a fuel gauge.

It appeared too clumsy and fragile to withstand a sharp breeze, let alone a trip across the Atlantic. And it was going to be a tight fit for both of them. Thomas donned the helmet and Cassie fixed the life-a-chute on her back. They stowed the haversack in a waterproof barrel affixed to the metal cage.

"You realise we might get sent to prison for stealing this," said Thomas as he pressed the "on" button. The engine spluttered and juddered into life.

"You realise Jarlath will have to become a stupid Merrow and Caitlín will kill everybody else if we don't!" shouted Cassie above the whirr of the engine as she untied the rope from the rock and clambered onboard. The platform toppled alarmingly as Thomas bent down to help her scramble in.

"*Hollywood or bust!*" shouted Thomas as the waves lapped the craft out to sea.

Cassie regarded the compass.

"*West!*" she yelled, feeling curiously light-hearted. "The Chingles go west!" She prepared for flight. "Remember to press down on your toes to tip yourself back and push down on your heels to swing yourself forward. Lean left to go right and right to go left."

They sailed close to Balor's wreck where there was a swirling, unpredictable whirlpool. The craft bounced uneasily on the waves. She would have to focus. But then a shrill voice cut through her concentration.

"Just where do you think you're going?" It was Fand the Merrow who rose out of the foamy waves, confidently bobbing beside the Flying Marine. Mara, the blonde one, was beside her.

"None of your business," retorted Thomas.

"It's very much our business," said Mara, her dark hair flicking out of the water.

"We're going to get Manannán Mac Lir to deal with you," threatened Fand. But she looked rather shifty herself. Cassie narrowed her eyes and saw the flash of a silver tail underwater by Balor's wreck. That must be Sionna, the other unpleasant Merrow.

"So perhaps you can tell him why you're always circling around Balor's wreck," replied Cassie. "Looking for something, are we?"

"You keep your nose out of our business, and we'll keep it out of yours," sniffed Mara cheekily.

"It's a deal. Now sod off!" Thomas shouted.

Cassie narrowly missed the flight button as a squall arose from the sea, tipping the craft.

"The Merrows caused this," Cassie fumed, stabbing buttons. For one sickening moment nothing happened and they watched in terror as a large wave bore down on them. But then suddenly they vaulted towards the sky as if sprung from a trampoline, their legs catching the spume. That's odd, thought Cassie. I didn't press the flight button. But just as quickly, they started to bounce down again beyond the squall. She saw a strong black seal plunge through the water and realised that Lugh's brother Rónán had lifted them beyond the Merrows' reach. They waved back in gratitude. Cassie pressed the right button and they were off.

The sky was filled with grey clouds, tattered into rags by the billowing wind, and herring gulls winged it on the breeze. The engine's propellers whirred into life, their clatter lost in the heaving breath of the sea. The machine rose on a current of air and Cassie and Thomas instantly adjusted their centre of gravity.

It was exhilarating flying above the waves in an open sea, all worry about Caitlín, Jarlath, the Merrows forgotten in the thrill of flying on a current of air. They rocked and teetered, leaned and adjusted until the compass pointed west. Below them the island receded in the distance; horses, cows, Tadgh's Tower, Fairy Fort House became tiny like children's toys. Down in the water, the seals Rónán and his sister Tethra crested a wave in unison and Cassie's heart leaped. She looked at the fuel gauge. It was nearly three-quarters full but she knew they should conserve it so she pressed the landing button and they braced themselves for a bumpy descent. Something whirred and a skirt of short rudders shot out of the tube, cushioning their landing. Cassie pushed the lever to release the sail. There was another clank and behind them billowed out a multicoloured sail. It seemed to be a patchwork of old raincoats and umbrellas but it caught the wind and they were propelled through the water.

They passed schools of dolphins, flying fish, even a startled lone woman sailor in a catamaran who rubbed her eyes in disbelief. But mostly they ploughed along for hours in an endless sea of green waves like a field of dense grass.

"What shall we do when we get to Hollywood?" Thomas speculated.

"I don't know," said Cassie, fiddling with the dials. "Let's get there first. We travel much faster when we fly."

So they took to the air again, all questions forgotten in the exhilaration of flight. The craft was bumpy and unpredictable and they had to concentrate. They found it easier taking it in turns to man the craft while one person sat on the bottom of the platform, their legs dangling over the rubber duct. They didn't rise more than one hundred metres above the ocean and were able to observe the life of the sea.

The sun began to sink on the western horizon, painting the whole sky red. Cassie decided to bring the Flying Marine down into the water so they could get some sleep. They landed in a calm sea just before the sun disappeared. The warm air massaged their faces and the Flying Marine rocked gently under them. They lay out, end to end, careful not to let their legs dangle over the edge in case of sharks, and tried to get some rest. Soon the stars winked overhead in the deep dark cloak of night and they were lulled asleep.

Cassie awoke in the first grey light of dawn from a shivering sleep, aware that they had been drifting for a long time. Her breath hovered in the air, and her eyelashes and eyebrows had begun to frost over. Thomas awoke feeling ice in his bones. The craft was hardly moving. Then they bumped into something. With a start Cassie realised it was ice floes. She looked at the compass and to her horror it pointed north.

A cold mist rolled towards them, blocking sight of any horizon and wrapping them in its clammy embrace. The ice floes sighed in the water and then there was a tinkling cold laugh, like the splintering of a glacier. They'd heard that laugh before, from Caitlín.

Suddenly an undertow grabbed the craft beneath them, rocking it from side to side, making their stomachs heave. They clung to the pilot's cage as the sea boiled up between the ice floes in a sudden squall. Cassie crawled to the control panel and banged on the flight button to escape the clutching waves. But the craft refused to budge. Instead they were buffeted by the ice floes and, beneath them, the water eddied round in a vortex threatening to suck them under.

"This is no ordinary storm," shouted Cassie. She screamed as her head crashed into the bar around the pilot's cage. Thomas raised his hand in the air and to his great relief grabbed hold of the Crane Bag. He pulled out the great white whalebone they had seen before and hung onto it as a twist of sea spray tried to prise it from his hands, sending his stomach crashing into his heart. He could see nothing in the clammy damp but felt he was grappling with a creature of mist. He sat with his legs locked around the pilot's bar, soaked to the skin but holding the great whalebone aloft. The pallid rising sun briefly appeared from behind the clouds, illuminating the scene. The whalebone flashed silver as it pierced the mist.

Cassie gave a cry. As the waves reared up, they took on the shape of a team of ghostly, writhing horses, rising on their hind legs, ready to dash the craft to pieces.

"Darkness visible!" cried Thomas, the whalebone transmitting power to him from the pale dawn sun. "Sea spirits, be gone!"

Thomas leapt from the cage and dived into the spume. He landed on the lead horse's back. The horse pitched and jumped in an effort to unseat him but Thomas held firm and the whalebone extended into a silver sword. He kept his balance and slashed at the horses' heads. Sea spray, red as blood, gushed in all directions and Thomas fell into the blood-red waves. He managed to hold onto the hilt of the whalebone sword as he sank beneath the sea, his nose and mouth clogged with bloody water. He struggled and tried to shapeshift into some kind of sea creature but the water pulled him down. The whalebone was sucked from his hands and sank to the ocean floor.

"Thomas!" Cassie cried as she clung to the guardrail but icy fingers pulled her off and swept her into the freezing water.

Cassie and Thomas sank like stones to the bottom, pushed and sucked at the same time. It was useless struggling and they found their consciousness slipping away as their lungs were squeezed tight in their ribs and their bodies gave in to the sub-zero temperatures. Their legs became entangled in straggling reeds in the black depths of the sea. But they felt themselves pulled back to life as something whipped their faces. Heat emanated from the silken reeds and their blood became warm in their bodies. It was a strange sensation, like being back in the womb, almost as if they could breathe under water. Something was pulling them back to life.

Then Cassie saw coral creatures glinting in the reeds and crustaceans on a piece of old ivory on the ocean floor. She ran her hands through the streaming reeds and realised with a start that she was touching human hair. She gestured to Thomas who swam through the reeds.

The hair was silky-soft as whispers, butter melting on toast, the soft down of a newborn chick. Despite their fear they felt compelled to comb it with their hands, straightening out the tangled reeds into flowing locks. Then at a knotted bit they gave an almighty pull and, to their horror, saw the hair was attached to a human skull. It rose before them from the silt of the ocean floor, the sightless orbs of the eyes glinting with phosphorescent sea creatures, its ivory teeth covered in barnacles.

Skeletal bones, clean of all flesh, jangled into life and formed a net around them. Struggle was useless. They were beginning to pass out with the lack of oxygen. Cassie closed her eyes and drifted into unconsciousness.

But then they broke through the surface of the waves, cradled in the skeleton bones, clinging to the long flowing hair of the skull. They gulped the air, spluttering out briny seawater that gagged in their throats. The bones of the skeleton formed a ladder from the water to the Flying Marine and they clambered to safety aboard their craft. The skeleton fell back into the water, a jumble of bones.

"That strange creature saved us," breathed Cassie.

As they bobbed in the water beside the bones, Cassie felt compelled to rearrange them. She leaned over the side of the craft and began to untangle them, speaking soft words to them like a mother to a child, and soon the bones were all in the order a human's should be. Except for hands that were fingerless and looked like the bones had been chopped at the palms.

Cassie felt tenderness towards this bizarre skeleton

that had saved them from the storm. She breathed on the bones and a tear escaped from her eye, thinking of what the skeleton must have suffered. As the glistening tear slid down the bones, something strange happened.

Eerie singing like the sawing of wind in trees filled the air. Cassie and Thomas realised it was coming from the skeleton's mouth. And as it sang, the body was filled with flesh. It was a woman. She sang herself eyes, a nose, soft skin, a belly and legs. Only her hands remained stumps where they had been chopped. Cassie blew on Oghma's ring that glowed faintly red among the blue-green glacial light.

"*I am Sedna*," the woman sang, "*Inuit Goddess of the Ocean*."

"Thank you for rescuing us," said Thomas. "What happened to your hands?"

Sedna raised her stumps from the water and gazed at them.

"My father chopped them off," she said in a high carrying voice like wind on waves. "He tried to drown me and then cut off my fingers when I clung to his kayak."

The children looked shocked.

"It is a long story. I married the wrong man. My father came to rescue me in his kayak but, when my cruel husband pursued us, my father lost his courage. He thought to save himself by sacrificing me."

Cassie gasped in sympathy. The gods and goddesses did have some terrible relatives.

"But do not weep for me," Sedna smiled. "My fingers became the seals and walruses and fish that feed my people. But I am grateful to people who comb my hair for I cannot do it myself."

"We have been to your planet," said Cassie. "Or at least the planet named after you."

Sedna smiled and they could see that she must have been strong and beautiful in life. "They say all things on earth are reflected in the sea and in the heavens," she said.

"Do you know of the Celtic Goddess Finnen from the other side of the sea, in Inish Álainn?" asked Thomas.

Sedna nodded her head. "We are linked by the water and by the harm done to us by evil men. I have promised protection to those who seek her. Sleep now, children, and you will be guided on your path."

"Do you think we will be able to rescue Finnen?" asked Thomas.

Sedna shook her head. "I do not know but I have a message for you. '*Seek hope in the masks when you are divided.*'"

Sedna blew over the water and a fair wind rose, billowing out the sail to carry them south.

The ocean became a friend and carried them along as if rocking a baby in its arms. As they bobbed on the waves, the sail full of wind, they dreamed that a special escort of sea creatures blessed their journey. A school of dolphins dived alongside them, echoing the bob and weave of the craft. A group of seals took over, surging through the water on their strong bellies. Then for several leagues, phosphorescent fish, their metallic scales flashing beneath the waves, accompanied them. And there were walruses and porpoises, as if all the sea creatures had arisen to guide them on their way.

They awoke to see land on the horizon in the early dawn. Had it all been a dream? Cassie felt a wound on her head where she'd hit the pilot's cage and knew it was real. Thomas checked for the haversack but to his dismay discovered that it had been washed overboard.

"But at least we have survived the ocean," said Cassie optimistically.

"Now all we have to do is fly three thousand miles in a craft with a near-empty fuel gauge!" joked Thomas, trying to keep their spirits up.

And face Caitlín, he thought privately, without the help of any magical beings.

CHAPTER 12

Angel drove through the wide streets clogged with pollution and traffic. The famous Los Angeles smog seemed to be thicker and more deadly than usual.

"Hollywood isn't as glamorous as everyone thinks," she said, swinging into the drab suburb of Burbank in the San Fernando Valley where most of the studios were situated. The squat buildings looked like boring warehouses.

The only glamour was provided by two huge posters of Fiona Waters, in her tiny bikini, that framed the graceful filigree gates to the studio complex owned by Lardon's dad. Áine, who had been in a daze since they'd left Inish Álainn, gave a start.

Angel flashed her pass at the burly security guard and they drove through the tight knot of fans hanging around outside hoping to get autographs and a glimpse of their favourite stars.

"Is there any chance we could get to meet this woman?" Áine asked Lardon, roused from her daze at the sight of the poster.

"I'm going to make sure," he promised.

The studio was a vast, sprawling complex of fake streets and huge sheds like airport hangars. They had to be transported on a golf cart to get to the offices.

First, they had to wait in reception for one of Lardon Senior's flunkeys to take them on a tour.

"Are you here for the auditions?" the receptionist asked, glancing at Áine.

"No," said Lardon firmly. "We wish to meet Fiona Waters."

"But I've been given instructions that nobody can see her," said the receptionist, who was idly filing her long candy-pink nails.

"Do you know who I am?" demanded Lardon, grimacing at her. "Doesn't the name Lardon B Hackenbacker the Third mean anything to you!"

The receptionist rolled her eyes. "Your father is away on location and I'm under strict orders not to admit anyone to see Ms Waters. You'll have to leave. Or do I have to call security?"

"You just wait until I'm head of all this," Lardon spat at her, stabbing his finger. "You're dead meat and you'll have to leave with your sorry ass!"

"I don't *think* so. The whole studio will probably collapse before that," muttered the receptionist.

Áine's face drained. She looked crushed at not being able to see Fiona Waters. But then a tall young man with floppy blond hair, charm dripping off him like grease, appeared around the door.

"Hi, y'all, I'm Daley, Cath's, like, personal assistant. She's *sooo* sorry Fiona can't take any time out of her busy schedule but her manager Cath, who is now Acting Head of the studio, will give you five minutes in her own office. Count yourselves lucky. She's a very important woman."

"Not as important as my father," Lardon muttered darkly. "He owns the studio!"

"For how much longer?" said Daley in a brittle voice. "Let's get a move on!"

Lardon nodded his head in a surly fashion and glared at the receptionist, who returned to filing her nails in a bored manner. They followed Daley back to the golf cart.

Lardon was in his element when they passed through the "backlot", which he explained was the area of the studio where they actually shot the films. They passed a tiny wooded glen that he told them had been used as a jungle and the deep, dark woods of just about every major adventure movie they'd ever heard of.

"You see, it's all make-believe," Lardon thrilled. "Movie magic. We can make anything happen here. Anything at all."

He pointed to trees and boulders on wheels, so they could be moved around more easily as scenery. A group of extras dressed as sea creatures passed by and Daley explained they were working on Fiona Waters' *Underwater Extravaganza*. Although some of the effects would be computer generated, Cath apparently was a fan of old-fashioned film techniques.

"Fiona and Cath are being hailed as the saviours of the studio," Daley told them. "They've mesmerised Lardon Senior. Cath has a vision for a new era of Hollywood blockbusters."

Everywhere there were little clusters of people trying to soothe someone or other throwing a tantrum. They saw a small man wearing high-heeled shoes, sobbing and stamping the ground like a two-year-old.

"I see Chuck Rocket isn't happy," muttered Daley. "I'll have to tell Cath." He spoke into his walkie-talkie.

"Daley to Cath. Operation Exploding Star, Chuck alert."

Around the corner, by the fake waterfall, a large muscular man who usually played super-heroes lay on the ground, gnashing and screaming.

"Gosh, they are behaving worse than usual," observed Angel.

"They're like children," laughed Nancy.

Daley's walkie-talkie crackled into life again. "Daley to Cath, Daley to Cath. Down by the waterfall. Dick Headly alert." He flashed an enormous smile at them and said confidentially, "You know, the only one who can control them these days is Cath. She is simply the best."

"I bet Angel could," said Nancy. "They should be sent to their rooms." Daley let out a laugh, false as tinsel.

They passed through the workshops area where they made props and scenery for the films. In one workshop they were constructing strange flying creatures with knives for beaks and claws. Nancy flinched when she saw them but Daley ushered them through quickly and ignored Lardon's eager questions about what movie they were for.

They drove through the props warehouse, which stored knick-knacks of all description from pretend plastic swords to pretend windows made of spun sugar so the stars wouldn't really hurt themselves when their heads were poked through a plate-glass window. Just outside a factory making moulds, the driver of the cart had to stop to deliver a package. Lardon tagged along with the driver so he could let a few more people know who he was. Daley was distracted, chatting into his walkie-talkie, and Angel tried to amuse Áine by yapping to her about the film stars. But Áine was distant, lost in reverie.

No one minded Nancy as she jumped down from the cart to explore. She was fidgety and felt the faintest tingle in her tummy. She walked down a gloomy corridor and was soon out of sight of the others.

She was drawn to a red velvet curtain at the end of a corridor. Behind it was a door that looked drawn on the wall, like in a cartoon, but when she pushed it, she was surprised it swung open. She ventured in, her stomach doing a cartwheel as if she'd passed through an electric forcefield.

She entered a large room, full of shadows but spotlit here and there by great arc lights hanging from the ceiling that swung back and forth from the draught of the open door. Nancy stood, transfixed and stunned. The room seemed to be filled with people, very still like statues of marble.

She panicked and ran back towards the door but she slipped. As her hand hit one of the people, she realised it was made of plaster of Paris, like the sculpture-making set they used at nursery. Not so afraid now, she peered closer at the statues.

She saw they were replicas and she recognised some of the people. One was the superhero Dick Headly who'd just been screaming on the ground. The other was Chuck Rocket, the man in high heels who had jumped up and down. She ventured further in, her tummy fizzing. There really were a lot of moulds and replicas. She thought she even saw ones of Daley the assistant and the receptionist with pink nails.

She entered a special cabinet, separate from the others, and got a surprise. For here, before her eyes were three life-size replicas of three very familiar faces: Cassie, Thomas and herself! And then in yet another cabinet was a statue of Finnen, hidden behind thick glass. Nancy felt her tummy tingle and she touched the glass. Instantly there was a crackle of energy. The glass shuddered and Nancy was immediately repulsed and thrown across the room as if electrocuted. For a split second a fire alarm sounded but died just as quickly. The room began to vibrate and quiver and hairline cracks began to appear on the statue of Finnen as if there was something inside about to shed its skin. But then a black smoke filled the chamber, causing Nancy to nearly choke. Terrified, she ran from the room, fighting for her breath.

"Nancy, where are you, hurry up!" Angel was calling her. She could hear the others moving around and heard Daley shouting into a walkie-talkie. "Everything's okay, it's a false alarm, there's no sign of entry."

But as Nancy tried to make her way back, she got lost and confused. The corridor seemed to have disappeared and she was in a hall of mirrors that just bounced her reflection back at her.

She called out: "*Help me!*"

She felt little and alone and missed Cassie and Thomas. Then Áine stepped through a door that suddenly appeared in the mirrors and grabbed her hand.

"Why are there statues of everybody?" asked a trembling Nancy. "Finnen and me and Cassie and Thomas?"

"Show me," Áine said.

Suddenly several doors appeared in the mirror walls. They tried a handle, hoping the door led to the hidden chamber. But they were plunged into a bewildering corridor of jagged broken glass.

"This place is not safe!" Áine cried. "I feel dark magic at work." Nancy clutched her hand tightly.

They turned round but the door they had just entered through was gone, replaced by a glass ladder. It was like being in a nightmare they couldn't find the way out of.

"I fear Caitlín is trying to confuse us by trickery," Áine cried.

They climbed up the ladder and found themselves on a balcony. The exit to the balcony was curtained off. Áine tore it down but once more they were met by their own reflections in a mirror. Nancy stood and paused. The reflection was fuzzy and indistinct. She reached up to touch it. The mirror was just a cheap tinsel curtain and gave way. They plunged through, emerging on the other side into a vast room with a stage in the centre.

On the stage they saw a woman in an elaborate dress, regarding herself in a full-length mirror. They approached and as they got closer they saw that the woman had platinum blonde hair and was wearing a tight-fitting dress of swan's feathers.

Áine turned white and gave a start.

"Finnen!" she called out.

The woman turned her head round. "My name is Fiona Waters," she said coldly.

"But you look like my sister, Finnen," protested

Áine. "We've been searching for you for the longest time."

"She's not Finnen!" Nancy cried. "I don't feel a tingle in my tummy like I did with the statue behind glass."

"It's been a long time," said Áine haltingly. "But it has to be my sister." Then she spoke in heartfelt tones to the woman. "I've missed you so!"

"Could someone please call security?" Fiona Waters called out. "Some nutcase is bothering me!"

"We're not bothering you," protested Nancy. "You're horrible!"

"The weirdo's got a kid with her," called out Fiona.

People began to stream back into the set and regarded Áine and Nancy with horror. Two burly security men grabbed Áine by the arm and bustled her outside. A third moved towards Nancy but she ran outside before he could catch her.

"Please tell them I'm your sister, Finnen!" Áine pleaded.

Fiona Waters turned and regarded Áine with contempt. "I've never seen this loser before in my life."

Outside, the golf cart came by, with Angel and Lardon on board, and Daley ushered Áine and Nancy into it to the relief of the security men who didn't want to have to eject a little kid. Daley seemed to believe Áine's excuse that Nancy had just got lost.

"Better if we don't mention the incident to Cath," he said to Áine confidentially.

Áine merely nodded.

"I'm sorry," she whispered to Nancy. "I am weak in this state between human and goddess. Without my powers I can do nothing. Connle was right, I should never have come here." She lapsed into a daze.

She seemed to be in shock and Angel looked at her with concern. But Áine insisted on meeting Cath. Nancy couldn't figure out what was going on. She wished Thomas and Cassie were here to explain it to her.

All four of them were ushered into Cath's office by Daley, who was practically genuflecting with reverence for his boss. Lardon put on a simpering smile but Angel looked severe. Áine gave no reaction and seemed numb with shock.

Cath had her back to them and was on the phone, speaking in a flattering, sweet voice but with a screechy edge, as if she could lose her temper at any moment. Nancy felt a cold stab of fear in her stomach, just like she'd felt at the glacier.

Cath swung round in her chair, her blue-black hair like a raven's wing framing her face. She smiled sweetly but her eyes were hard and cold. Nancy was sure this woman was Caitlín but when she opened her mouth to smile she displayed perfect teeth. She can't be Caitlín, thought Nancy – she's too pretty. Then she saw her diamond tooth glinting.

Cath rose from her chair, strikingly tall and thin, and grasped Lardon's hands. "Why this must be the boy genius I've heard so much about!"

Lardon smiled smugly but then he became tongue-tied despite feeling flattered. There was something unsettling about this woman even to Lardon who was used to important people.

"Where's my d-d-dad?" he stuttered. "This is usually his office."

"He was called away on location. Urgent business," she said. "He told me to look after you." She gazed intently into his eyes.

Lardon reeled back as if hypnotised. Her power didn't only come from her position. She radiated it from a force within.

"If you don't mind," she said coldly to Angel and Áine with a glance at Nancy, "I have private business to conduct with the boy alone. I'm authorised by his father in case you're not sure." She waved an official-looking letter under Angel's nose.

Outside, Nancy said to Áine and Angel, "I don't like her, even if she has nice new teeth. She's a wicked witch."

"Why, Nancy, you say the funniest things," laughed Angel. Then she moved closer to her niece and whispered, "I don't like her either."

Áine looked troubled and ill as if she was about to faint. Then she whispered to Nancy, "Those statues you saw and Finnen's cold reception to me make me fear that she is already soul-split. I am useless here without my powers and have lost her forever!"

Nancy patted her on the hand but Áine looked on the verge of collapse.

Angel decided she'd better take her outside and asked Daley to keep an eye on Nancy.

Daley sat at the doorway, reading a script. Nancy pretended to be asleep. But then Daley's walkie-talkie crackled into life. He ran into Cath's office.

Nancy listened at the door and heard him say something about there being a bigger security problem than he'd realised.

"Impossible!" hissed Cath. "I put my own foolproof security in place in the inner sanctum." Then her eyes narrowed. "You of course are too cowardly to disobey my orders and had our guests with you at all times?"

Daley said nothing and looked down at the carpet. Angrily, Cath threw a paperweight across the room at him – luckily it missed – and told him to deal with the problem. He dashed off, forgetting all about Nancy, who took the opportunity to sneak in the door. She hid behind a filing cabinet.

Lardon was sitting opposite Cath, eating from a big box of chocolates.

"Why, Lardon," cooed Cath, "I'm looking for an island location for my movie. What about Inish Álainn?"

Lardon moaned about the rain and the bumpy roads and the general lack of luxuries.

"And what about children? Are there any on the island?"

"Only three deadbeats called the Chingles," Lardon whinged. "They think they've got special powers and are searching for some old lady called Finnen. But I know they ain't no superheroes. I'm pretty sure they're aliens. The kid Nancy's OK, though."

"And where are the older ones, Cassie and Thomas?" she asked in a voice as sweet as honey.

"They're grounded at home. Hey! How did you know? I never said their names!" exclaimed Lardon.

"My assistants find out everything," she said

knowingly. She held out her hand and in the centre of the palm glinted a tiny mirror. "Now, Lardon, look into this mirror and tell me your real heart's desire. You weren't entirely truthful with me last time."

Suddenly Nancy burst from her hiding place and pushed Lardon out of Cath's range.

"Don't tell her anything!" she shouted.

Cath pushed a button and suddenly the walls flipped around, becoming a series of distorting mirrors like in a fairground. They were surrounded by a series of freakish reflections of themselves. In one mirror they were huge and fat, in another tall and thin, in yet another their bodies became wavy and their heads pointy.

Nancy bent down and curled herself into a ball. She let out a deathly screech. Its impact knocked Lardon off his feet and Cath back against a mirrored wall, cracks appearing in it like a spider's web. She straightened herself and regarded Nancy with a venomous look.

"Nice try, child. But nobody will come to rescue you. This room is sound-proofed. Hah!" laughed Cath. She held up her hand with the mirror in it towards Nancy.

"Come, child, what is your heart's desire? What about seeing your brother and sister again?"

Nancy refused to look at her. "Why have you made models of us?"

"Don't you know your brother and sister are dead?" asked Cath.

"I don't believe you!" shouted Nancy. "And what did you do to Finnen? I couldn't feel any tingle in my tummy."

"Look into the mirror," said Cath. "Why do you feel a tingle in your tummy?"

"Stop!" screeched Nancy. She felt herself weakening. All the blood and energy drained from her body. The mirrors on the wall misted over and, peeping through her hands, Nancy saw faint shapes begin to appear. Comforting faces from home, from Inish Álainn, her grandmother and grandfather. Nancy began to uncurl herself. She felt herself drawn to this woman.

Then suddenly a mobile phone rang. Irritated, Cath picked it up.

"I'm busy Daley!" she yelled at her assistant down the line. Then her expression changed to one of alarm. "Escaped! You mean to say a huge swan flew out of the building with creatures on her back and nobody tried to stop her! They thought it was a special effect in a film! Daley, you incompetent, brain-dead nincompoop! We'll have to find her!"

Cath threw down the phone in a fury, hitting Lardon who gave out a yelp. He was in a trance.

Cath looked at him as if she'd only just remembered him. "Oh, you fool," she said annoyed, "I don't need to waste any energy on you. You already believe any old nonsense."

But she stood over the curled Nancy. "Did you enter my inner sanctum?" she demanded. "That fool Daley didn't want to own up but he finally admitted you ran off on your own in the warehouse. Did you enter my hidden chamber and break the spell? Is that how Finnen escaped with all those wretches?"

"I just touched the glass," whispered Nancy.

"You have a link with her!" Cath cried. "By touching the glass you broke my spell and she has escaped."

"I'm glad," said Nancy defiantly. "And only I can find her with my tummy-tingle."

Cath raised her fist as if she might strike her but stopped as a thought occurred to her. "So you feel a tingle in your tummy when you sense Finnen? This is the magic you used to track her?"

Nancy nodded her head.

"I get it – you are linked through the Star Splinter. It makes sense. That's how she led you to all those clues. So perhaps I won't kill you. Now that she's escaped, you can lead me to her. You are a human tracking device. That could prove very useful."

"What have you done with her?" screamed Nancy.

"Why, I soul-split her of course!" shrieked Cath. "I thought I had her inner soul safely imprisoned in the armour of the replica. But thanks to you she has outwitted me and has flown away in her swan shape, taking those pathetic Hollywood specimens with her. But she is weak because I have split her power and I control her now in human form. Frankly, her swan soul is not much of a threat and will die soon but I don't like to take risks. Now you will help me find her."

"No!" shouted Nancy. "I don't like you! Why have you got statues of me and my brother and sister?"

"I told you they are dead," said Cath.

"I don't believe you!" Nancy yelled.

"Not easy to fool despite your age," purred Cath as she paced up and down. "Why, I have plans for you Chingles. What I want to do with you is weaken your bodies and transfer your life force into my replicas, which are totally in my power. Then your souls can be imprisoned in your, how shall I put it . . . changed bodies. Sometimes I do it the other way round, lock the soul in my replicas and infuse the body with my evil power." Nancy stirred where she was curled on the ground. Cath cruelly nudged her with her foot as if she was a dog lying in her path.

"But I'm getting carried away. I find soul-splitting so absorbing. Don't you?" Cath laughed. "This way will work a treat with you." She paused as she suddenly thought of something. "Of course, little Nancy, your age presents a bit of a problem."

Cath pulled a needle out of a box on her desk. It was so thin it was almost invisible to the naked eye. She held Nancy down by the throat with one manicured hand and with the other jabbed the needle above the child's ear.

"This will make you more likely to do as I say," she snarled.

Nancy winced and held her ear.

Then Cath seemed to change tack. She preened in the mirror and smiled at herself. "Pretty, aren't I?"

"No," muttered Nancy.

Cath frowned and jabbed another needle above Nancy's other ear. She squealed in pain.

"I'm beautiful, aren't I?" Cath demanded.

Tearfully, Nancy nodded her head, crossing her fingers behind her back.

Cath smiled in triumph and snapped her fingers.

The mirrors flipped back to become normal walls again.

Lardon came out of his trance. "Amazing special effects. Wow!" he enthused.

Nancy stood up watching Cath warily. "Where is the real Finnen?" she repeated stubbornly.

Cath bent down and held Nancy gently by the shoulders, smiling at her with concern. Then when Lardon wasn't looking, she jabbed another needle above the child's ear. Nancy flinched and screwed her eyes in pain but when she opened them she looked blankly at Cath who gave her a hug.

"Oh, I'm sorry I was mean. I had to test you," she whispered in Nancy's ear. "You are right, child. Someone has kidnapped her. We've got to find her together. Please, let us be friends. We're on the same side!"

CHAPTER 13

Cassie regarded the fuel gauge with concern. "We'll never make three thousand miles," she said.

Thomas found a lever saying "oxygen input". He pulled it out. Immediately there was a gurgling noise and the fuel gauge began to rise.

"I remember Jarlath saying he'd learned to run the craft with oxygen," Thomas said.

Sedna's fair wind carried the Flying Marine up over the east coast of Canada and across the interior of the United States, which unfurled before them like a chequered counterpane. Below them they saw rocky mountain ranges where snow-capped peaks gave way to lakes and marshes. Then there were vast prairies, fields of ripening corn and cities laid out in strict grids.

"I don't feel like we are in control of this craft," yelled Cassie, as they flew over a wide flowing river.

"I get the feeling we are being summoned," said Thomas, just avoiding getting his feet caught in a stupendously tall redwood tree.

They flew over a rocky crevasse like a great dark wound in the earth.

"That's the Grand Canyon!" squealed an excited Cassie.

From here, the land became more barren and the Flying Marine juddered over desert wastes.

Suddenly they began to lose height and plummeted from the sky. Cassie checked the fuel gauge. It read zero. The horizon raced to meet them and their stomachs jumped to their mouths.

"Hold on tight to me," she wailed. "I'm going to release the life-a-chute." Thomas got into the safety harness with her as she pressed the release button and the life-a-chute shot out of its pack.

They floated in the air. Below them the Flying Marine clattered to earth and disintegrated into a flurry of springs and nails, iron bars and rubber bits. Around it stretched a barren desert surrounded by outcrops of rock, dark violet in the rising sun, shot through with lines of crystal quartz. Here and there tumbleweed blew and great boulders bulged, whipped into sculptures by the wind.

They landed on the desert sands, jolted by the earth. Cassie cried out on impact with the ground, but managed to break Thomas's fall. She thought her leg was broken. Thomas wriggled free of the safety harness. He was covered in bruises but unhurt. A few feet away, lying in bits like a broken animal, was the wreck of the Flying Marine. They looked around the barren landscape scoured by wind, rain and sun – the baked earth, the vast tent of the sky.

They were lost.

Thomas went to see if he could retrieve their water bottles from the wreckage. He stood up and squinted into the harsh sunlight. Despite the vast distance, the air was clear and limpid. At first he thought the violent light had distorted his vision when he saw a figure emerge on the shimmering horizon. But as he continued to look, the figure came closer. It was a horse and rider but to his astonishment he realised the horse was cantering backwards.

"Over here!" Thomas called, waving his arms.

The rider came closer, backwards in their direction. He saw that the rider was a boy wearing jeans and chaps, like a cowboy, with a fringed sheepskin jacket.

He wore a Stetson with a single feather in the brim. Bizarrely, all his clothes were on backwards. Thomas was so relieved to see another human being that he didn't care how odd he looked.

Tears of gratitude came into Cassie's eyes.

"Please help my sister," Thomas said. "She's injured."

The rider dismounted and walked backwards towards them, until he'd passed a point where he faced them. Thomas began to feel slightly irritated by his strange behaviour and then a little afraid. The boy's face was painted red streaked with black paint like lightning. He lifted his Stetson and revealed half his head was shaved but the hair on his left side was long and hanging down.

"Do you have water?" Thomas asked, indicating his own empty bottle. The stranger nodded towards a canister of buffalo skin dangling from his belt but didn't move. Cassie moaned softly in pain. Desperate, Thomas reached out and grabbed the canister.

Thomas helped Cassie to drink, then slaked his own thirst with the crystal water, so cool it must have come from an underground spring.

"Thanks," said Thomas, throwing the bottle back to the boy. He was a little older than them, he guessed, and looked like a Native American.

"*Melbrop on*," the boy said.

"He doesn't speak English." Cassie winced with the effort of talking. She gazed at the ring on her finger and it lit up weakly, giving an intermittent signal. "Oh, no! Oghma's ring lacks power here."

The boy walked backwards towards Cassie. Then in one swift movement, he flung her over his shoulder, walked backwards towards his horse and threw her lying face downwards across the horse's back. A dazed Thomas watched, dumbfounded.

"*Em htiw emoc*," he said to Thomas.

"Should we go with him?" Thomas asked, an edge of desperation in his voice as he moved towards the stranger, thinking to grab his sister from the horse.

The boy made a sad face. He didn't seem hostile, just rough and odd.

"I don't think we have much choice," Cassie whispered, her face pale and sweating.

Thomas felt he had no option but to co-operate. The boy gave Thomas a leg-up to sit behind his sister. Thomas insisted on sitting the right way round towards the horse's head, so he could keep an eye on Cassie. Then the boy jumped up on the horse, facing its tail, and the horse set off, moving backwards.

Thomas was completely disoriented. "Who are you?" he managed to ask.

"*Yob Barc*," said the boy.

"Strange name," said Thomas. "I'm Thomas and this is Cassie."

Cassie put her hand over Oghma's ring.

"Backwards," she whispered.

"Yes, he does everything backwards! Weird!" Thomas agreed.

"Talking backwards," panted Cassie.

Thomas worked it out, spelling the letters in the palm of his hand. "Yob is 'boy' backwards and barc is 'crab'. Boy crab. Crab Boy!" he exclaimed, delighted with himself.

Crab Boy made a strange noise. They realised he was laughing – backwards.

"Where are you taking us?" Thomas asked.

"*Nalc racS eht ot*," Crab Boy said slowly. "*Ouy leah lliw yeht*."

"To the Scar Clan. They will heal you," said Thomas.

The disorientation of travelling backwards and the rocking gait of the horse lulled Thomas into a doze. Cassie drifted into a fevered half-sleep. They lost all sense of time.

After travelling for ages over the dusty, rocky plains, Crab Boy cried "*Pu Yddig!*" to the horse and they climbed up a high ridge.

From the saddle of the ridge they saw a beautiful lake surrounded by lush vegetation, and amidst the fragrant juniper trees and rustling acacias were several wooden structures and tepees. Totem poles carved with masks and ritual symbols vaulted towards the sky.

"*Emoh*," said Crab Boy.

Crab Boy dismounted and reversed the horse down a steep path. Small children scurried over to greet them. A group of men and women, tall and strong, watched while some of them ran to help Cassie and Thomas. Quite a few looked like Native Americans but others seemed to come from all nations and creeds, black, white, Asian, Chinese.

A small boy ran into a tepee shouting, "Grey Wolf, Grey Wolf! They're here."

Strong arms carried Cassie and Thomas towards the tepee and they were laid down on mounds of buffalo skin and given healing draughts and ointments for their wounds and bruises. Cassie's leg was bound in a splint with hide infused with fragrant oils and herbs. Thomas watched Grey Wolf as he administered ointments. He looked like a Red Indian Chief from an old Western movie, except he was wearing jeans and a plaid shirt. He had a long grey plait down his back and wore a feather in his hair. A swan's feather!

"We sent Crab Boy for you," he smiled, his face furrowing into deep lines, his skin like old leather. "I hope he didn't give you a shock. He is a Heyoka chosen by the Thunder Beings. Like a court jester. He does everything backwards to liven things up!"

Grey Wolf lit a fire and fanned the fragrant smoke. Then he chanted songs. They were curiously soothing and the children soon drifted off to sleep.

They awoke refreshed. Cassie blinked her eyes. The desert, the swan's feather. It was the place she dreamed of in Inish Álainn after they returned from the World Tree. She stretched her leg. The splint was gone and, apart from a bit of stiffness, her leg seemed normal. A woman with her long blonde hair in two plaits came in, carrying a tray of steaming food.

"I am Rose with Thorns," she smiled. "Welcome to the Scar Clan."

"Who are the Scar Clan?" asked Cassie, yawning and stretching luxuriously on the buffalo rugs.

Thomas reached over for a pancake and poured on a generous amount of maple syrup.

"We are a tribe. We've turned the desert into an oasis," she said, pouring them each a glass of juice. "Grey Wolf is our leader, our shaman who is a spiritual healer."

"So why are you called the Scar Clan?" asked Thomas, his mouth full of pancake. "You don't even look like a normal tribe."

"All of us bear a scar," explained Rose with Thorns. She pulled up her shirt and revealed a large gash on her belly, like barbed wire. "I lost my family and unborn baby in a road crash. Grey Wolf helped me heal."

"I'm sorry about your family," said Cassie.

Rose with Thorns smiled sadly but then brightened. "I have another family now, the Clan."

"Why are you called Rose with Thorns?" asked Cassie. "Is it because of the scar?"

"You'll find out if you get on my wrong side!" she jested in mock anger. The children laughed and made a mental note to keep on her right side.

"What about Crab Boy?" asked Thomas.

"He was an orphan, abandoned by his uncle in an institution, but he ran away and lived on the streets. Grey Wolf found him and understood him. Some of us have scars on the inside."

"We can't stay," Cassie said with sudden urgency. "We have to find Finnen."

"We know," said Rose with Thorns. "Grey Wolf will help you."

After breakfast Crab Boy came into the tepee

walking backwards on his hands. He flopped down beside them and then stood on his head, making them laugh.

Then he led them out towards a group of trees by the lake's edge and handed them each a knife.

"*Ecnad tirips eht rof sksam ekam tsum ew!*" he sang.

Cassie wrote it down on the soft silty sand by the lake. "We must make masks for the spirit dance."

Crab Boy made a strange face that was a sort of upside-down smile and thumped them on the back in a friendly fashion. Then he took up his knife and they watched as he cut some bark from a living tree. He bade them do the same. Then they followed him back to the central settlement.

They sat at a fire in the centre of a stone circle of rocks, Crab Boy with his back to them. A group of drummers joined them and positioned themselves at the outer edge of the circle and began to drum in unison. To the slow, steady beat, Cassie and Thomas took up their knives. The drummers began to sing over and over again, "*Orenda Manitou! Orenda Manitou!*"

Cassie and Thomas began to carve, lulled into a dream state by the drumbeat and the soft ululation of the voices. The smoke from the fire rose in a steady stream towards a windless sky. The lake lapped before them, deep, mysterious and blue, reminding them of Glimmering Lake back on Inish Álainn.

First they watched Crab Boy as he carved but soon became engrossed in their own masks. Then, abruptly as the drumming and singing had started, it stopped. Grey Wolf loped into the stone circle on his long legs, his grey plait swinging over his shoulder. He regarded their masks with interest.

Crab Boy had carved an upside-down mask, with the nose in the forehead, the mouth in the centre and the eyes where the mouth should be. Thomas's mask had both stag's horns and donkey's ears. The face was recognisably human.

"Two sides of your nature," remarked Grey Wolf. "Which will gain mastery?"

Cassie's mask was even more complicated. One side was of a salmon, the other of a bull.

"Yours is a divided nature," commented Grey Wolf.

Cassie looked at her mask, not liking the bull side.

"Perhaps you need both sides," mused Grey Wolf.

"This is all very interesting," said Cassie, feeling slightly exasperated, "but we really haven't come all this way to do arts and crafts."

Grey Wolf removed the swan's feather from his hair.

He gestured towards a wooden hut down by the lake, made from young willow branches.

"I had a vision in the Sweat Lodge. Swan Woman in the grip of Vulture Woman. Then Swan Woman escaped. Swan Woman dropped the feather to guide you to us."

Cassie gasped. "Do you know where Finnen is?"

"No," said Grey Wolf, solemnly. "You do."

"We think she's in Hollywood with Caitlín," explained Cassie. She told him the story of the search.

Grey Wolf shook his head sceptically. "Come, we must enter Dream Time."

But Cassie drew back, afraid. "I don't think I can have visions here. Besides, it's painful. I feel haunted by them."

"You are safe here at the Medicine Wheel," said Grey Wolf kindly, indicating a circle set out in stones. He gave a signal and the tribal drummers entered the Medicine Wheel, banging out an insistent beat. The flames of the fire leapt up and the children saw the drummers were all wearing masks: Eagle, Hawk, Crow, Muskrat, Otter, Deer, Buffalo, Jackrabbit.

Grey Wolf put on a wolf-skin, complete with a wolf's head. The rest of the tribe also entered, wearing masks. They began to dance, first as if they were being drawn into the ground by the earth's magnetic force, then leaping towards the sky as if pulled by strings from the sun. Cassie and Thomas put on their masks, shy at first, but soon the insistent drumbeat chimed with their hearts and gave their bodies rhythm.

Cassie lost herself in the dance, charging like a bull, then leaping like a salmon, the two sides of her mask joined in harmony. Thomas jumped like a stag and brayed like a donkey. But soon his stag nature overtook him and he whirled around in circles.

Then they sat, exhausted, and sang: "*Orenda, Manitou!*"

"With this word 'Orenda' we name the magical power of the universe," said Grey Wolf, "and with 'Manitou' we summon the shaman's helping spirits."

Then Grey Wolf led Cassie towards the Sweat Lodge down by the lake. It had four openings facing north, south, east and west. They entered through the door facing east and inside were heated rocks brought from the campfire. Grey Wolf poured some cold, crystal water on the rocks to create steam.

"Water, earth, stone, wood, fire, air," intoned Grey Wolf. "Gaze into the steam, Dream-walker, what do you see?"

Cassie breathed hard, the sweat pouring down her face. She felt woozy, her head spun and her eyes became unfocused. She closed her eyes and immediately her mind was assailed by visions.

She saw a steep valley, deeper, drier, hotter than any place else on earth. Ghosts dressed like miners crawled through the barren rocks, combing for gold. The earth was raw and bruised with their digging and scratching. She fell headlong down a deep mineshaft and saw a swan, parched with thirst, surrounded by quivering shapes and howling forms, like in a madhouse. She cried out – "FINNEN!" But on the horizon, the Corra swooped down with Nancy on her back.

Grey Wolf mopped her brow.

"Finnen is in a town of ghosts. A place hotter than a furnace. Caitlín's grown in power and she's got Nancy!" Cassie cried.

She fell in a dead faint.

When she came to, she awoke to a roof of stars overhead. Thomas, Grey Wolf, Crab Boy and Rose with Thorns were by her side.

"You are weak, sister, don't speak," said Grey Wolf, his words echoing in the still night air. "She who you seek is in Death Valley in a ghost town near Furnace Creek. It is one of the hottest, harshest places on earth but you must go there at first light."

"I saw Caitlín as the Corra and she had Nancy, our little sister," Cassie said.

Grey Wolf looked thoughtful. "That explains why I carved three amulets but only two of you are here." He held up three stone necklaces threaded onto leather, then rolled them in sage and passed them through the smoke of the fire.

He gave them to the children. Thomas put on two, one for Nancy.

"Not long ago, a meteorite fell here and I was instructed in a vision to carve three amulets from it for protection."

Cassie examined the stone. It looked like nothing from planet Earth but blazed red and green. There was something in the striations that reminded her of the dusty red planet Sedna.

"These will afford you some protection," said Grey Wolf. "But in protecting you, they will also absorb some of your enemies' powers. They will have to be cleansed and used wisely."

He spoke with confidence but Thomas caught a worried look in his eyes. But there was no time for speculation. They had to leave immediately even though it was nearly dusk. There was no time to lose.

Back in Hollywood, Caitlín was showing the party

from Inish Álainn around the sights – the Chinese Theatre, the baseball stadium, the homes of the stars. She ferried Angel, Lardon and Nancy around in her limousine and catered to their every whim. Even Angel was beginning to like "Cath Formor". But Áine had gone back to Inish Álainn, too ill to stay any longer.

Lardon thought Cath was brilliant. She listened to all his ideas for movies and praised his imagination and creativity.

She was particularly attentive to Nancy. "You are the daughter I never had," she clucked at her.

Nancy followed her around in a daze and hung on her every word.

"Why, Nancy, you've fallen under Cath's spell," marvelled Angel. Little did she know she was right.

After the day's sightseeing, Cath announced she had one more treat in store.

She took them to an Imax – a giant movie screen that showed the landscape of America in giant Technicolor. They were the only viewers in the huge cinema and sat in plush red seats. Cath showered them with popcorn and soft drinks. The screen showed the thunderous majesty of Niagara Falls, the vast blue waters of the Pacific Ocean and the beautiful snow-capped mountains of the North Cascades.

All the while Caitlín watched Nancy closely. But Nancy registered no reaction. Caitlín instructed the projectionist to show film of places closer to Hollywood. Ginormous images of the crashing waves of Big Sur filled the screen, then the giant sequoia trees of Yellowstone Park. Still Nancy continued to watch with fascination but with no unusual reaction.

Then the picture of a dry, hostile valley came on screen. It looked like not a drop of water ever fell there or a plant grew. Nancy dropped her popcorn and clutched her stomach, nearly throwing up on top of Lardon. Angel flew to her, concerned.

"Perhaps we ought to get her back to her hotel," she said. She felt her niece's brow. "Please call a doctor. She's feverish."

Caitlín laughed shrilly and took out her mirror, flashing it at Aunty Angel and Lardon. Immediately they stood up, catatonic.

"You two idiots tell the driver to take you back to your hotel. I can't even be bothered to soul-split you, you're so stupid." They obeyed meekly and left the cinema, barely glancing at Nancy as she writhed on the floor.

Caitlín pounced on poor little Nancy like a wolf

on a lamb, snatching her up with her manicured hand.

"Order my private plane!" she barked at her assistant, Daley. "Get the troops ready. We are going to Death Valley."

All day, Cassie and Thomas rode with Crab Boy on Flying Backwards, his horse. The landscape passed in a blur of jutting mountains and hulking ridges. They were glad that he ran backwards so they couldn't see what they were facing. It was cold and the wind snatched at them, trying to tear them off the horse's back. Crab Boy fed them beef jerky that tasted like old salted leather. But still they rode on, sleeping fitfully.

Towards daybreak, an orange sun like the yolk of an egg broke in the sky, suffusing the landscape with a golden glow. The streaking clouds began to evaporate under its insistent heat. They climbed a steep mountain path and their hearts stopped when they saw the sheer drop beneath them. They felt the effort of the horse through his bony back as he strained up the narrow path, but soon they reached the pass.

Cassie craned her neck round and saw jagged rocks loom above them like skyscrapers that had melted. The wind howled. A sudden crack made her think a thunderstorm was on its way but a shard of rock glanced her arm. She raised her gaze and shouted, "*Look out!*"

Boulders were raining down on them. Crab Boy reared the horse up and abruptly reversed down the mountain path, narrowly avoiding a large rock that crashed just in front of Flying Backward's nose.

They watched, waiting for the landslide to subside.

"*Kcab og s'tel,*" he said. *Let's go back*.

"Wait," said Thomas, pointing halfway up the path where they'd passed earlier. "Look!"

At that moment a shaft of sunlight illuminated a crevasse in the rock-face that they'd missed earlier, halfway up the path but only visible from above. Behind it was rusting machinery and an old wooden ladder. They retraced their steps and came to the eerie entrance to the mineshaft. The old wooden ladder descended into a hole in the ground. There was a symbol etched in the rock face, a straight line slashed with five horizontal lines.

They recognized the Ogham symbol for Yew.

Thomas felt it and realised it was newly done. "Finnen is here somewhere, I know she is," he said, helping his sister dismount.

"*Ecnartne rehtona si ereht fi kcehc dlouhs ew*," said Crab Boy, staying mounted.

"He's saying we should check if there's another entrance," said Cassie.

"I know she's here," Thomas insisted, irritated by Crab Boy's caution.

"*Su esirprus yam seimene ruo ro ecnartne rehtona t'nsi ereht erus ekam tsum ew.*" *We must make sure there isn't another entrance or our enemies may surprise us.*

"I'm not taking orders from someone who does everything backwards!" said Thomas angrily, hitting the horse's rump. Flying Backwards sped out of the crevasse taking a startled Crab Boy by surprise.

"Why did you do that?" asked Cassie, furious.

"This is our mission," said Thomas stubbornly.

"You stupid ass!" Cassie berated him.

A ghostly sound rose from the mineshaft, striking fear into their hearts. Cassie's hands felt clammy and her legs nearly failed her. Thomas's heart beat a tattoo in his breast.

It was the ululating cry of a swan in pain.

And then there were other voices, crazed with anger and longing. Thomas and Cassie stood, motionless in fear.

Thomas felt around his neck and held the two

amulets. His legs shook but he took a stop towards the old wooden ladder that descended into the ground. He beckoned Cassie to follow him.

With Thomas leading they descended the ladder. It was old and creaking. Some of the timbers were rotten and gave way, causing Thomas to slip down several rungs with a sickening lurch. The early morning sun illuminated the beginning of the descent but halfway down they were plunged into darkness as the sun moved on its course. They continued despite the splinters in their hands and their mounting sense of dread.

At the bottom their feet plunged into something sharp. Cassie took out a torch. The tunnel was carpeted with the old spikes of cacti that made the going hard underfoot. But several metres along, a strange, unnatural greenish glow pervaded the tunnel. They waded through the broken cacti, as the swan's cry grew louder and more frantic.

Abruptly, the tunnel turned a corner and led to a chamber lit by the eerie green glow. A hopeless cry rent the air.

Outside in Death Valley, Crab Boy crouched behind a

rock and watched as a large helicopter landed at the top of a ridge. A group of expert climbers descended from a ladder, followed by an unnaturally tall woman, wearing a cloak. She had shining black hair cut in a sharp bob. A child with dark curly hair was lowered after her. The child pointed towards the crevasse where he'd just left Cassie and Thomas but then indicated another place further down the path. Crab Boy cursed (backwards of course) under his breath. The climbers expertly scaled down the rock-face and the woman flew down with the child in her arms.

The child gripped her stomach and the dark woman handed her to one of the climbers. With unnatural strength, the woman rolled back a boulder to reveal another entrance. Crab Boy cursed again. The enemy had found the shortcut.

CHAPTER 14

Deafened by the din of clashing voices, Cassie and Thomas, their legs scratched to bits by the cacti, approached the green chamber. Screeching through the whooping cry of the swan were shouts and roars like in a lunatic asylum.

"*Don't touch me!*"

"*I hate you!*"

"*I wish I was dead!*"

"*Mother, why don't you love me?*"

The air was rife with confusion and tension. Shadows loomed and threatened in the eerie light. Thomas bent down and picked up two rocks, handing one to Cassie. They raised the amulets in their free hands and burst into the chamber.

On a pile of old sacking lay a swan with a broken

wing. Its yellow beak was parted and its tongue lolled out, parched for water. Its plumage was streaked with dirt and clotted with dried blood. An ugly wound in its chest festered with pus and flies.

Around it loomed shapes like the wraiths they'd encountered in Hel's domain except more freakish and deformed.

Green light emanated from a man who looked vaguely familiar. Nearby a great mound of rust-coloured jelly like rotten innards quivered and moaned. The tiny shape of a man with a bleeding head continuously bashed himself against the hard rock-face of a chamber wall. And the ghost of a beautiful woman was barely visible, as it faded away to nothing.

Cassie ran towards the swan with her water bottle and gave her a drink.

"Finnen!" she cried, patting the soft plumage. But the swan choked on the water and winced at her touch.

"Who are you all?" asked Thomas nervously.

The shapes erupted into a wild din that was shattered by a high, piercing voice.

"Ah! What a touching scene!"

Thomas and Cassie swung round to see a woman with a sharp black bob flanked by a dozen super-fit fighters in climbing gear. She held Nancy in her arms.

"I found you!" Nancy said listlessly. "Caitlín helped me."

She looked feverish and ill, like the time she'd been pierced by one of Caitlín's needles. They knew something was wrong with her.

Cassie and Thomas held up their amulets.

"Put Nancy down. Leave her alone!" screamed Cassie.

Caitlín let out a harsh laugh and flung Nancy to the ground. Thomas ran to his little sister and swiftly placed the amulet around her neck. Nancy trembled with the shock of Caitlín's cruelty. She raised her hands to her head.

"She hurt me with the needles," Nancy said in a tremulous voice.

Thomas bent down and pulled out the needles.

"She tricked you!" cried Cassie, stamping the needles underfoot.

"Yes, I did, didn't I? How very wicked I am," purred Caitlín. Her talons reached out. "I even amaze myself with how evil I am."

"Don't cry," said Thomas, embracing his little sister. "You're here with us now."

Caitlín moved forward.

"Don't come any closer," warned Cassie, holding up her amulet, her legs shaking.

Caitlín ignored her and pointed towards the swan.

"So you've found your precious Finnen," she sneered. "Or what remains of her and all these other sad freaks."

The wraiths backed into the wall, quivering and moaning.

"What have you done to Finnen, to them?" demanded Cassie, sounding braver than she felt.

"I've soul-separated her," said Caitlín in a mocking voice. She opened her claws. Her palm contained a mirror. Cassie caught a sickening glimpse of herself, Finnen, Thomas and Nancy cut in two, just like in the vision that had haunted her all year.

"I found the statues and touched Finnen in the glass," sniffed Nancy.

"Horrid child found where I stored my replicas and harvest of souls and broke my spell," Caitlín hissed. "That's how your precious Swan Maiden and her sad-sack friends escaped my clutches."

Caitlín moved towards the wraiths. They quaked and shivered in their strange beings.

"These are the true natures of some of Hollywood's finest." She prodded and poked them with her claws.

"Like this action hero Dick Headley who is really a mound of quivering jelly. No backbone, you see. A total invertebrate. Let no one say I don't have a sense of humour." She laughed harshly. "And this pathetic specimen!" She pointed at the tiny man who held his bleeding head. Cassie recognised him as Chuck Rocket whose face was on the cover of millions of magazines. "That's really how big he feels."

"And as for her," she pointed towards the fading ghost of the beautiful woman. "Snowy's darkest fear of becoming a faded movie star has become all too true."

Cassie aimed the rock and threw it hard at the back of Caitlín's head but it merely slid off her as if she was made of bulletproof glass. Thomas threw his rock but Caitlín caught it and tossed it aside. Her minions moved to restrain the children. Caitlín turned round, becoming more Corra-like, her face morphing into a hag's crooked profile.

"And what about you, my lovelies? What dark secrets do you harbour?"

"We're not your lovelies!" spat Thomas.

"It's a rhetorical question, don't interrupt," crooned Caitlín. "Now let me probe your darkest fears, your deepest secrets, the shameful desires of your black hearts. I could just kill you of course but that would be no fun. I want you to suffer like I have for all these thousands of years. I want to torture you for all eternity. Killing is too good for you."

She transformed herself fully into her Corra shape – large black wings and a hideous hag's face with fangs for teeth.

Cassie recoiled and looked in amazement at Caitlín's followers, who didn't blink an eye.

Caitlín watched her. "I see you're surprised at the total discipline of my followers. They're all willing recruits to my mission. Hollywood hopefuls all, who have fallen on hard times. They couldn't wait to give me their souls for their dreams of stardom. With me, they can rule the world, fulfil their wildest fantasies. They want to command respect and for everyone to look up to them. With me that is guaranteed – more or less." She laughed cruelly. "I extend you the same offer."

She opened her mirrored palm and Cassie saw herself driving to school in a Rolls Royce, dressed in beautiful clothes and attended by a butler. All her school friends looked on in envy, especially Mary Louise and Venetia who had sneered at her.

Thomas saw himself on a private racetrack, at the wheel of his own specially designed racing car, before jumping into his personal helicopter. Then he scored a goal for his favourite team, Arsenal. For a second, it seemed so tempting.

"These visions are not real!" shouted Thomas, clutching his amulet.

"Never!" said Cassie.

Caitlín raised her mirrored talon and a white light like a laser shot towards Cassie. But Thomas and Nancy leapt to her side and together they raised their amulets. The ray bounced through the three stones, ricocheting back toward Caitlín who ducked out of the way. Several of her followers were hit and disappeared on impact.

Thomas tried to locate a rock or a stick but there was nothing. He held out his hand but the Crane Bag didn't appear as it had done in other perilous situations. They were desperately unprepared. In a heartbeat Caitlín's followers restrained them. Caitlín regarded them with malice.

"Try shape-changing," urged Cassie, "into our power animals."

They tried but nothing happened. They felt all hope collapse.

"I've already taken your pathetic powers," mocked Caitlín.

But still they struggled, biting and kicking Caitlín's minions.

"Well, if you don't come willingly, I'll have to do it against your will. Now let me see – what would be most painful for you?" Caitlín mused.

She turned to Cassie. "I know. Let's make your special gift a burden to you. We like to see into the future, don't we? Well, here is your future."

Caitlín grabbed Cassie's hair roughly with her talons and held her head tightly in her grip. She raised the other claw with a mirror in its palm and forced Cassie to look at it. Cassie struggled and screwed her eyes tightly shut but the images on the mirror burnt through her retina.

She saw an old bag lady in a tattered pink coat tied with string dribbling into her whiskery chin as she shuffled along an empty street in ill-fitting trainers with no laces. She carried bags filled with old newspapers, her rheumy eyes half blind. She saw a world of carnage with stumps of buildings and wild gangs of children roaming the streets. The old lady struggled on, stoned and mocked by the children. Cassie looked into the old woman's eyes and realised she was staring at her older self.

Caitlín tossed her aside and Cassie fell down in a slump.

"And what of your brother? So proud of his

shapeshifting. We'll have to find a way of keeping him still," Caitlín laughed shrilly. She grabbed him by the legs and held him upside down. He screamed and shouted but Caitlín spat at him and covered him in some horrible viscous liquid like an insect immobilising her prey. Thomas desperately wanted to try once more to reach for the Crane Bag but he became numb, all feeling and sensation passing from his limbs.

Cassie saw an image of him staring catatonically from a wheelchair, immobile, half dead.

"And you, little Nancy," said Caitlín, ruffling her curls. "So kind of you to lead me to your beloved brother and sister. Now your age presents a slight problem. A bit too young to be properly split in two. I know! Like to talk to animals, don't we? We'll strike you dumb."

Nancy flinched and tried to get away but Caitlín held her firm. She breathed on her, a nauseous stench that Nancy could taste, that permeated her whole being. Nancy became as stone. She tried to open her mouth and cry out but the wail died on her lips. Cassie had a vision of her in a coma on a hospital bed, tubes coming out of her mouth.

"So you've seen your futures," Caitlín laughed. "I'm doing you a favour, for this is how it will end for all of you. You should thank me for ending the pain. What's the point of carrying on when it's all going to go so horribly wrong? Your special powers will not protect you from the infirmities that await all mortals."

She brushed them all with her black wings and they shuddered. She held up her claws and the mirrors in her palms refracted the children into multiple images. She screeched, a nightmarish sound, and, blazing with white light, stepped outside the chamber and sealed it by fusing the rock. Then she was gone.

In the greenish glow of the chamber, in its suffocating heat, Cassie writhed, assailed by terrible visions. She saw a bomb explode over London and her parents burnt to death in a fire. Then cars and trucks crashed and jack-knifed on a motorway and the baby twins were hurtled through the windscreen of a car without a driver. Her grandparents floundered in a river and then sank in the water. A tidal wave washed over Inish Álainn and the Merrows captured Jarlath's lifeless body.

And then she saw another vision. Caitlín in her human shape on television and at movie premieres among thousands of children. Then these children joined serried rows of other children with dead eyes. And they turned on their own parents and anyone who stepped in their way.

"She wants to possess the soul of every child," Cassie realised bleakly in her despair. "And nobody can stop her."

Oblivious to anyone else, Thomas writhed on the floor of the chamber and felt himself turn into a snake. He tried to crawl away but was attacked by another snake. He bit it but realised he'd eaten his own tail. He chewed and gorged on himself until his skeleton stuck out and he oozed green pus. Then he transformed into a stag but, seeing his own shadow, attacked it and dashed his brains out on the wall. The rest of his body became a crazed donkey and feasted on his own brains. Then his rotting tongue became a lizard that bit out his own eye and his front leg turned into an eagle's claw that tore at his own throat. And when he had killed himself, his own body rose from the putrid flesh, more weak and rotten than before, and the cycle of self-destruction began again.

Nancy tried to scream but her throat constricted; her breath was fire and burned her from the inside out. She crumbled and became a child of dust. Then a wind scattered her around the room. But in each mote of dust, she became a child again and burned and crumbled once more, the cycle agonisingly continued.

CHAPTER 15

Lardon spat out his cappuccino latte when he saw Cath emerge from her office. She held Nancy in her arms and was flanked by Cassie and Thomas.

"What the hell are they doing in Hollywood?" demanded Lardon. "Angel grounded them on Inish Álainn."

Angel looked far from overjoyed to see Thomas and Cassie.

"When Nancy told me about her brother and sister being left behind, I moved heaven and earth to get them here," Cath cooed. She gestured to Daley to hand Angel a letter. "I have their parents' permission," she said smoothly.

Angel examined the legal document. It looked authentic. But Angel felt uneasy. She'd felt queasy after the visit to the Imax cinema and couldn't remember how they got back to their hotel. She was beginning to distrust all the attention Cath was paying to Nancy.

"You could ring them but their phones don't work in the Serengeti where I've arranged for them to have a holiday," Cath purred, a look of triumph in her eye.

Angel caved in. Her sister had always wanted to go to the Serengeti, the region of grassy plains and woodland in Africa teeming with wildlife.

Cassie and Thomas smiled at their aunt and ran to kiss her.

"We beg Lardon to come back and be our new best friend," said Cassie sweetly.

Angel eyed her suspiciously. "But I thought you hated him."

"You've taught us the error of our ways," said Thomas contritely.

Nancy ran to her aunt's arms. "Please!" she pleaded.

Angel looked at her nieces and nephew. She'd never seen them so obedient or so sweet. This made her even more suspicious. But Angel always liked to believe the best about human nature.

"I suppose so," she said.

Cath clapped her hands excitedly. "The good news is that we can return to Inish Álainn immediately. We're going to shoot the picture there."

Lardon looked at the children jealously. They seemed to have become Cath's favourites.

"So what's the film all about?" asked Lardon.

"All shall be revealed," trilled Cath mysteriously.

Down the mineshaft, Cassie screamed silently, bitterly, blinded by the agony of the future. Thomas bit so hard on his own thumb that he bit right though to the bone and Nancy sat in the corner, rocking in pain. They felt black with despair and abandoned to their worst nightmares. They were too locked into their private agony to hear any sounds.

At first Cassie thought the dust falling on her face was the debris from a bombed building and the voices were the howls of abandoned children tearing at each other. But the sound at the edge of her hearing became a lilting song and not the stuff of her nightmares.

In her mind's eye, she saw a man approach the old bag lady and embrace her. The old lady turned back into Cassie. The man was Grey Wolf. Soon soft hands were wrapping her gently in furs. "*Orenda, Manitou,*" crooned a voice. Hot tears sprang to her eyes. It was Grey Wolf. He was here, in the chamber, with other members of the tribe. She struggled to get the ghastly visions out of her brain. Grey Wolf placed his hands on her forehead. It felt like a ray of sunshine stroking her brow. He felt for the amulet around her neck and then dropped it as it burnt his hand.

"Thanks to this she wasn't able to destroy you completely," he said softly. "And she doesn't know it but she has given you some of her power. Will you be strong enough to bear it?"

Cassie nodded her head. She opened her eyes but saw nothing. "I can't see," she said weakly.

Thomas and Nancy were also awakening from their nightmares and blinking in the chamber. The tribespeople were holding up lighted tapers to illuminate the cavern.

But Thomas couldn't get up on his feet. He struggled but fell back down again. "I'm lame," he said. "My left leg is paralysed."

Nancy sobbed in the corner. But when she tried to speak, no words came out. She was struck dumb.

The tribespeople helped to carry them from the mineshaft.

Back at the reservation at Lilting Lake, some of the people whose wraiths they had met in the chamber sat around the campfire. They sobbed and shook but were no longer deformed and broken. It was like coming back after a fever.

"When Nancy entered Caitlín's inner chamber she broke the spell that held Finnen and these good people's souls in replicas," explained Grey Wolf. "Caitlín lost interest in their physical bodies so my people were able to rescue them and we have reunited their bodies and souls through our healing rituals. But they are still weak."

"But what about Finnen?" asked Thomas.

"Unfortunately, Caitlín still controls her human shape in the form of Fiona Waters," said Rose with Thorns.

"Where's Finnen?" asked Cassie.

"She is down on the lake with our healers," said Grey Wolf. "But she is fading fast. She will have to return to her own place."

"Caitlín soul-split us," said Thomas, beginning to understand his ordeal in the mineshaft. "That's what happened."

"She tried," said Grey Wolf. "She has managed to steal some of your life-force and put it into replicas. That's why you feel so weak."

"She has also given each of you a physical deformity," said Rose with Thorns, barely suppressing her anger. "That's her idea of a joke."

Thomas hung his head. "I was so paralysed with fear I couldn't do anything. I'm just a coward."

"Shush, don't blame yourself," said Rose with Thorns.

"But all our powers deserted us. We were useless," said Thomas bitterly.

"You have travelled far and have been weakened through many trials," said Grey Wolf.

"We'll never defeat Caitlín now," said Cassie sadly. "She's taken our special powers. I am blind, Thomas is lame and Nancy is mute."

"She tricked you into giving her what she thought you valued most," said Grey Wolf, "and she left you with your worst fears to destroy yourselves. Caitlín is arrogant and ingenious."

"Do you know her?" asked Cassie.

"Soul-splitters all work the same way," explained Grey Wolf, "but she has a very refined evil. You have withstood her. That is extraordinary but you are left with a physical scar. Blindness, lameness and dumbness."

"We are useless now," said Cassie bitterly. "And worse still, she has false versions of us with all our powers under her control."

"Yes, you are useless, if you take your cue from Caitlín. If that is what you think then she really has won," said Grey Wolf.

"We have no special powers and we're all crippled in some way. I think she's done a pretty good job," said Cassie bitterly. "We cannot fight her."

"And have you no other abilities?" asked Grey Wolf.

"I cannot shapeshift," said Thomas dully. "Nor do I want to. Those visions . . . it will end up destroying me."

"Tell me, when you take an animal's shape does it happen like magic, despite yourself?" Grey Wolf asked him, looking him keenly in the eye. Thomas tried to remember what it was like to transform into another shape. But it was a painful memory that sent shockwaves down his useless leg like the sensation people are supposed to feel in an amputated limb.

"It doesn't always happen easily. I have to concentrate and feel the power of the animal I want to transform into. When I am afraid, I have to force myself to do it but in such a way that I don't get so tense I can't do it."

"So you also need courage and skill and judgement," said Grey Wolf.

"I guess so," Thomas admitted.

"And when you have a vision, Cassie, is it always clear?"

"No. It comes in images, in scraps like remembered dreams. I don't always understand it," she conceded.

"So you have also to know how to interpret your visions," said Grey Wolf.

"It's like a crossword puzzle or a jigsaw," Cassie agreed. "I sometimes only see part of the picture."

"It is not the gifts alone that are important but how they are used," said Grey Wolf.

"And what about Nancy?" asked Thomas, looking at his little sister who was playing nearby with some other children. They were competing to see who could hit a tin can with a stone.

"Nancy is so young it is impossible to know with her. Her gifts might come back easily or not at all."

At that moment all the children erupted into applause. Nancy had hit a bull's-eye.

Grey Wolf smiled. "Her aim does the talking."

"You remind me of Scáthach, our teacher," said Thomas. "She was always going on about the importance of learning mastery of many skills."

"So you have more than one talent?" asked Grey Wolf.

Thomas looked thoughtful. A sudden image of Sedna floated into his mind.

"I remember Sedna giving us a message. '*Seek hope in the masks when you are divided.*' Perhaps the masks will help us."

Crab Boy went to fetch the masks they'd made from

the living bark of the tree. Thomas put on his mask with the donkey and stag features. He felt something shift inside him as he breathed in the fragrant smell of the wood. It was if a ray of light had penetrated a dark place in his heart.

"Actually, I'm not really that good at anything else except shapeshifting and maybe puzzles. But I'm stubborn. Scáthach has instructed us in many skills." He remembered Scáthach praising him for his persistence in trying to learn the Rope Feat and the gae bolga despite his lack of talent. He felt a sudden resolve. "I may not be a champion but I can still fight. Even if all I can do is spit on Caitlín, that's what I'll do!"

Grey Wolf hugged him gently. "That's the spirit. Caitlín didn't take your courage. And what about you, Cassie? Why don't you put on your mask?" He handed her the mask, which was half bull and half salmon.

"I've seen our futures," she said dully. "Our lives end in misery. I don't see the point of fighting."

"So Caitlín is all-powerful now," said Grey Wolf scornfully. "Tell me, how do you know it's your future?"

"I saw it," she said.

"You saw what Caitlín wanted you to see. She dug out some fears you have and made it seem real. Did you see us rescuing you?"

"No," admitted Cassie.

"No glimpse of a campfire, no delivery from the mineshaft. So maybe you didn't see the whole story?"

"Remember what the Sean Gaels said about The Morrigan's prophesy?" said Thomas to his sister. "If we change, the future changes. Prophecies can be warnings, one of several possible futures, not necessarily *the* future."

"But it felt so real," Cassie said.

"Yes, but remember at the World Tree, Heimdall the Guardian telling us that the future was unpredictable," persisted Thomas. "And you thought you foresaw us split in two at the glacier but we've survived, haven't we? Come on, Cassie!" Thomas had spent all his life arguing with Cassie and he hated to see her without spirit. Normally she would contradict him just to wind him up. Well, it was worth a try. Maybe if he agreed with her for once in her life, he'd shock her into action.

"OK, you're always right. Caitlín has us well and truly beaten," he said ruefully.

"No, she hasn't," Cassie said in a small voice.

Thomas smiled.

A tear escaped from Cassie's sightless eyes and she put the mask on. Immediately, she fell into a trance. She saw herself in her mind's eye, blind but bearing a sword and guided by Thomas and Nancy.

"We know from the prophecy of The Morrigan there will be a battle where perhaps we will be slain," she said, "but someone has to stop Caitlín. This is not the time to give up." Cassie had caught Grey Wolf's and Thomas's resolution. Her face bore new hope. "Perhaps I haven't seen the future. Perhaps she hasn't won after all."

"You can use what powers you do have to carry on the fight," said Grey Wolf. "No matter how weak and powerless you feel, it's always better to take a stand. And no one who has friends lacks power. I guarantee that."

Thomas smiled gratefully at him. "Anyone got any ideas how we're going to get back to Inish Álainn?"

All the while the Hollywood stars had listened carefully, for once in their lives hanging back from being the centre of attention. Dick Headley, who normally played superheroes but was now a shadow of his former self, cleared his throat. "If any of you can reach a phone, I'd gladly put my private fleet of airplanes at your disposal."

Grey Wolf reached inside his plaid shirt and handed him a mobile phone. Thomas and Cassie looked at it with surprise.

"I never said we were against technology," he grinned.

CHAPTER 16

Back on Inish Álainn, the sacred trees swayed as they inched towards the perimeter fence around Glimmering Lake in broad daylight. The island was in such uproar that nobody paid much attention to a few moving trees. Caitlín had taken over most of the island for the film shoot. Glimmering Lake had been transformed into an outdoor set and Mr Mulally's pub had become a temporary headquarters for Caitlín and her entourage. All over the island, people were renting out rooms to camera operators, make-up artists and actors. The shoot was the one item of gossip on everyone's lips. It was like the invasion of an occupying army.

Thomas, Cassie and Nancy were featuring in the film with Fiona Waters, much to Lardon's annoyance.

Angel wasn't too happy about it but Cassie challenged her with being bitter about her own failed movie career and she reluctantly gave in. Besides, Caitlín wafted their parents' written consent under Angel's nose.

At Glimmering Lake behind the screen of trees, Connle nestled in the branches of Dair, who had grown to almost the size of a mature oak tree over the summer. Connle released Granny Clíona from the bottle. There was so much mayhem going on, nobody was likely to comment on a ghost.

"The Chingles haven't been in contact since they've come back. They haven't even been to see Áine. Do you think, now that they've been to Hollywood, we're not good enough for them?" Connle wondered.

Granny Clíona shook her head. "Something strange is going on. I do not like this modern witchcraft. Our only hope is to talk to them."

A pickup truck driven by a hulking man drove up to the trees.

"Oh no, we're done for!" quaked Connle.

But the pickup truck just scooped up the trees and transported them towards the lake. They'd been mistaken for props and Connle, hidden in the branches of Dair the Oak, breathed a sigh of relief.

A diving platform fitted with camera tracks now

dominated the centre of the lake. Above it was a camera mounted on a crane. And in the waters were several camera operators in diving gear, ready to film Fiona Waters' underwater scene.

Fiona Waters, dressed in her elaborate swan's costume, stood on a platform in the centre of the lake. It was lowered to make it look like she had risen up out of the water. She looked angry and petulant. Daley, Caitlín's assistant, tried to soothe her.

Van Danvers, the action hero who was Dick Headley's greatest rival, emerged from his Winnebago, the special caravans reserved for stars, dressed as an ancient Celtic warrior in a leather tunic and carrying a shield.

"Get ready for a take," shouted Daley into a megaphone. "We're shooting the scene where Lord Balor enlists the help of the Swan Maiden in defeating the evil Sun Goddess. Now remember, Fiona, Lord Balor is handsome and gentle and you fall madly in love with him."

From behind the screen of trees Granny Clíona and Connle looked at each other in amazement.

"'Lord Balor was anything but handsome and gentle!" hissed Connle. "He was evil and ugly and Finnen despised him."

"Och, history is being rewritten!" whispered Granny Clíona, furious.

Van Danvers as Lord Balor walked to the edge of the Lake.

Fiona Waters bowed low. "O Lord Balor, noblest, wisest, gentlest of all, I will serve you forever," she said, batting her eyelids.

"But I love another," Lord Balor said sadly. "The beauteous Caitlín of the Gleaming Teeth. She has sent you a prophecy. In the future three hideous monsters disguised as children, known as the Chingles, will destroy me. You must continue the fight and enlist the help of my wife to resurrect me. Go now into exile and tell no one of the plan."

"I will leave a trail to lead the evil Chingles to their destruction," said Fiona. She raised up her arms. Smoke machines generated a cloud and she seemed to disappear.

Caitlín called, "*Cut!*".

"Let's reposition for close-ups," bawled Daley into the megaphone.

"Why, of all the lies!" fumed Connle, ready to jump out of the tree and thump someone.

"Now," soothed Granny Clíona, "pick your battles. We're here to gather information."

Everyone who had been standing still suddenly surged into action. The make-up girl ran out to Fiona to apply powder and more hairspray. The props people picked up trees to move them closer together and were surprised to get a thump from a branch when they handled them too roughly.

Connle saw the opportunity to talk to Cassie, Thomas and Nancy while everyone else was engrossed in their own tasks. Granny Clíona got back in her bottle and Connle ventured out from behind the trees.

The children were sitting on three canvas chairs with their names on the back and Connle pretended he was bringing them some refreshments. He produced some special treats from his waistcoat: homemade lemonade and Death by Chocolate for Cassie, Starlight Stoppers for Thomas and Brussel sprouts for Nancy.

"Who asked you to get those?" snapped Cassie. "We never said we were hungry."

Connle was taken aback by her rudeness.

She looked at him glassy-eyed, almost as if she didn't know who he was.

"So how did it go?" he asked hesitantly. "Áine said Finnen didn't recognise her. Imagine! Her own sister."

They looked at him blankly.

"Said she'd become a stranger to her. Had her

thrown out of the set and all. Totally under yer one Caitlín's influence."

"That's all in the past," Thomas said mechanically. "Caitlín is a very good friend of ours. Fiona Waters is a star and entitled to her privacy. As are we."

"You've been learning fancy ways in America," said Connle.

Thomas looked irritated and summoned over Daley who ushered Connle away.

"Please leave the talent alone," he said menacingly, in a voice quite unlike the honeyed tones he used when talking to Caitlín and the stars. Dair the Oak was about to thump him on the ear but Connle signalled not to. He motioned to the trees to stay behind and quietly made towards the exit to the set. But when no one was looking he slipped back among Dair's branches.

He watched Caitlín disappear behind a boulder. "Dair, move as close as you can, as quietly as you can," he instructed the tree. He was suddenly glad he'd spent so much time tending the trees and he was thankful for their stupendous growth in one season.

Dair moved stealthily, imperceptibly, through the set and positioned himself by the boulder. It hid a concealed entrance that led to a trailer set into a cave in the rock. Connle could see through the windows that Caitlín was inside. There was one heart-stopping moment when she looked up towards the window and roughly pulled down a blind but she didn't see him and she left enough of a gap for him to peer in.

Caitlín was sitting with an editor, watching the film footage go through on a bank of monitors. They watched the scene that they'd just shot of Finnen meeting Lord Balor on the lake.

"Just as well I can make my own movie magic, Stuart," Caitlín said to the editor. "Fiona's acting isn't just wooden. It's cardboard." She laughed cruelly and held up her hand. It became a talon with mirrored nails and a mirror in the centre of the palm. Connle could see it reflected back on the monitor screens. Light streamed from her talons, weird metallic light. The surface of the picture glittered with tinsel brilliance but then it became a black hole. Even though he was just peeping through the blind, Connle found himself sucked in, disoriented.

"I hate my parents," he thought. "They abandoned me and ruined my life. If I ever see them, I will kill them. Or make them suffer as they have made me suffer. And as for Granny Clíona and all those McColls! They have bound me in servitude and used me all my life. And after all I've done for them, the Chingles have rejected me. I hate them too." Connle began to grapple with the bottle in his waistcoat.

Dair sensed his pain and touched Connle on the brow with a leafy bough.

"We must get you away from here," he said. "I feel evil enchantment in the air." He scuttled along the ground as fast as he could without attracting attention and tipped Connle over the perimeter fence.

Connle ran, gagging for air. His mouth and lungs were filled with the nauseous stench of evil magic. It permeated his clothes, clung to his hair. He wrestled with the bottle of Granny Clíona, threw it away and then retrieved it, crying in anguish. Somehow he managed to let her out of the bottle.

"It's all right, *a stór*," she soothed and guided him to Áine's house.

He staggered in the door and collapsed onto her crystal bed. When he had recovered, they told Áine of the strange goings-on at the movie set.

"Caitlín is back and is determined to wreak vengeance," he said. "She has power over the children and Finnen. And she is filling that picture with black enchantment. I only saw a little bit through a window and when I watched it I was filled with hatred for my parents, the McColls, the Chingles above all. Even

Granny McColl who saved my life and is like a mother to me."

"All those movie people are unnatural. When I was around them, I didn't feel their life force. It was as if they were also ghosts," said Granny Clíona.

The blood drained from Áine's face. "There is only one answer. It is my worst fear. Caitlín has succeeded in soul-splitting all of them. She is growing in power with each soul she harvests. She will not stop at revenge against the Chingles, Inish Álainn, even me, but will move against the whole world. Especially the children. She is very cruel. If she corrupts the children, she will have destroyed the parents anyway."

"What about that film?" asked Connle.

"Caitlín is enchanting it so it makes children hate their parents and puts them in her power," said Áine.

"What are we to do?" asked Connle.

Granny Clíona looked at Áine significantly as if reading her mind.

"I have been in a strange lethargy since coming back but now I see there is only one thing for it," said Áine. "I will have to renounce taking human shape and have my powers restored. I will have to fight her."

"It is the right thing to do," nodded Granny Clíona sadly.

"But Jarlath will have to go back to the Merrows!" Connle let out an involuntary sob.

Áine's expression was set but a single tear escaped her eye and ran down her cheek. "If I stay human, we are all dead anyway. Caitlín will not just destroy the island but take over all the children in the world. If I give up Jarlath it will break my heart but there is a chance he will survive. Perhaps if I can't have him, the Merrows won't want him either and my father can make him forget me. Let us go and tell my father that the Chingles have failed."

CHAPTER 17

Áine stood at the shore near her house and raised her wand of crystal inlaid with diamonds, rubies and emeralds towards the crashing waves. It was high tide. Connle and Granny Clíona watched anxiously. She took a deep breath but just as she was about to summon Manannán Mac Lir from the deep, a screaming sound rent the sky.

A fierce looking military helicopter of pitch black descended and hovered overhead.

A door was pulled back and a load of old scrap, including a rubber doughnut and an iron cage, was slowly winched from the helicopter to the ground. With a start they recognised it as the wreckage of the invention Jarlath had been working on. For one horrible moment, they thought Jarlath had been drowned and had already been returned to the Merrows.

Then to their amazement, three figures descended down a rope. Áine dropped her wand and ran with Connle to the rope and helped Thomas, Cassie and Nancy onto the ground. It was really them! Those other children with Caitlín were the impostors Nancy had seen in the studio.

Connle smothered them in a hug. But then he saw they were weak and injured.

A man dressed in military garb with perfectly styled blond hair and rippling muscles crouched in the hatch and gave them a salute, then winched down a dinghy. Áine ran to the dinghy. Inside was the injured swan. Áine clung to her and wept.

Then the man closed the hatch and the military helicopter circled in the sky and disappeared among the clouds.

"She is near death," said Cassie.

The swan was barely breathing. Her wound had been tended to by the healers from the Scar Clan but the bandage was blood-soaked. Áine suppressed her tears and ran with the swan in her arms into the house. She placed her gently in a bowl of crystal and bathed her wings with water from a jug. She then applied ointments to her wounds. Finnen began to revive, making short whooping noises. Áine spoke soft words to her, comforting her. Then the swan lapsed into a sleep.

Áine regarded the children and realised how changed they were, Cassie blind, Thomas lame and Nancy without the power of speech. She told them of her decision to renounce Jarlath and return to her goddess shape to fight Caitlín.

"No! We must face her even though we have lost our powers," said Cassie.

"I cannot allow it," said Áine. "Even as we speak, Caitlín grows in strength and, weak as you are, she will know of your return. I must act now."

But Finnen burst into a clamorous cry. Áine touched her sister's beak with her forehead.

"If you wish it," she said. She turned to the children. "Finnen says you must face Caitlín to be made whole again. Only if you fail will I enter the battle. So let it be."

"We need a plan," said Thomas. "What if we ambush her?"

"No, it is too dangerous," said Áine. "Ordinary humans will get hurt. You will challenge her to a contest. Caitlín is proud of her battle prowess. She almost defeated the Tuatha Dé Danann single-handed at the last battle of Moytura. She will see three children as no threat. She will not turn you down."

Finnen curved her lovely neck and plucked out a feather from her left wing.

"I'll deliver it myself," said Connle.

The children prepared for battle with heavy hearts. On the lawn outside Áine's house, battle clothes and weapons were laid out – gifts from the smiths of the Tuatha Dé Danann. There was chain mail, the gift of Credne the silversmith, wrought in a silver material yet feeling like feather-down that was not from this world. Goibnu the blacksmith had forged them three blazing swords and large shields of beaten gold that weighed as light as air. Luchta the carpenter had made them lances of black wood as hard as any metal, tipped with silver points so fine it was impossible to see their end.

With resolute hearts the children dressed. To their surprise, before the battle, the Sean Gaels – Lugh, Sennan and Scáthach – appeared.

"But you are all forbidden from aiding us!" cried Cassie. "You risk a punishment worse than death by being here."

Lugh smiled. "I have come merely to sing a song of light with Finnen, my foster sister."

"And we have come to see how well our pupils fare," said Scáthach. "Remember the skills I taught you."

"And I have come to wish you success," said Sennan. "Remember the Crane Bag gives its gifts when you know what you want to achieve. Battles are won by cunning as well as skill. And it's not always the most powerful who emerges the victor."

"But we are weakened," said Cassie. "Caitlín still possesses part of our powers."

"But she has weak spots," said Sennan. "Caitlín's flaw is that she thinks she is invulnerable. She does not rate you as enemies and holds you in contempt. Remember even the mightiest warrior can be killed by a bee-sting."

They set out in Scáthach's chariot, pulled by a ghostly horse. Lugh joined Finnen in a song so mournful it plunged all the humans on the island into a deep, dreamless sleep. Inish Álainn was transformed into a battlefield. There was no trace of ordinary life, no cows, nor tractors nor houses. The island looked like it must have at the dawn of time, hatched out of the sea.

Around Glimmering Lake arose an endless plain surrounded by mountains and punctuated by craggy boulders and stones. In the distance they saw Caitlín's battle camp, a large tent of a material that seemed to be made of shadows and storms. The sky filled with dark leaden clouds, heavy and ponderous.

By a tributary of the River Flesk, they passed an old hag washing laundry and the water ran red with blood. Thomas described it to Cassie.

"This is a bad omen," said Cassie. "Blood will be spilt today. Our blood. One of us will not return from this battlefield."

The hag rose in the sky as a crow and was joined by two others that had been perched on a bush.

"It's The Morrigan, the War Goddess, with her sisters," said Thomas, his heart sinking. There was no going back now. The three crows alighted on the children's shoulders.

"You have their favour," said Scáthach as she drove the chariot on.

They pulled up by the standing stones at Glimmering Lake.

"Caitlín is luring you to her," observed Scáthach. "She expects you to bring the fight to her like a spider playing with a fly. I agree with Sennan. Her arrogance can be her undoing. She believes she is invincible and that is our strength."

But the knowledge of Caitlín's faith in her own power only increased the children's fear. It was eerily quiet and the sky was threatening a thunderstorm. Scáthach departed and, despite all the brave words, they felt little and alone.

Suddenly a Battle Cry, harsh and unnatural, shattered the air. In the distance, a black swarm like a cloud of wasps streamed out of Caitlín's tent.

The children tensed behind their shields.

As the creatures came closer, Nancy gave a soundless cry. She'd seen them before, at the studio. They were the mechanical flying creatures with sharp knives for beaks and grappling-hooks for claws. Their aluminium wings sliced the air.

"Quick!" said Thomas, indicating a large rock. "Let's make it to there." Cassie and Nancy raced ahead and Thomas followed slowly, using his lance as a crutch. With their backs to each other, they held up the shields, creating a pyramid. They heard the mechanical birds approaching, their wings racketing in the air. The first ones dropped stones and rocks at them that easily bounced off the shields from the Otherworld. They heard the birds regroup, their wings clattering and colliding. They felt the next attack as the birds swooped down, glancing off their shields, making them shudder.

Thomas reached out his hand and grasped the soft skin of the Crane Bag. He rummaged inside. What I need now is that rope, Gleipner the Binder, that the squirrel gave us at the World Tree, he thought. Then I could whip those birds out of the sky.

To his amazement he found the rope nestled in the bottom of the bag. Sennan was right: the Crane Bag gave you what you needed when you knew what you wanted to achieve.

"I'm going to attempt the Rope Trick," he said. "I know you're better at it, Cassie, but I can see what's going on."

Cassie took hold of Thomas's shield as he formed the rope into a lasso. Cassie and Nancy hunkered down behind their shields. Then Thomas, with his shield in one hand, the rope in the other, rose up from behind the shields.

"Keep the rope slack in your hand until you feel its tug," Cassie instructed. "The trick is to let the rope dictate how hard you hold it. It's like flying a kite. You have to relax into the wind."

The birds dive-bombed towards him in a V formation. As they drew closer Thomas saw their beaks made of knives, their hooked talons, their vicious ragged wings of gleaming metal. For a second, his courage faltered but then he caught the encouraging expression in Cassie's sightless face, so he cast the rope and swung it over his head. The rope made a whirring sound. He tried to follow Cassie's advice and relax, but thinking too much about it made the rope shudder in his hands and it began to collapse. He abandoned all thought and held it lightly and as the birds approached, it cleaved through them like a cutter, hacking them to pieces. Shards of twisted metal rained from the sky. He dropped back down behind the shields, dodging a severed knife. Metal teeth bit into their shields, trying to find gaps in their defence. Miraculously, their magical chainmail withstood most of the metal rain. The assault came to a sudden stop.

"Hah! Scáthach has taught you a few party tricks." It was the voice of Caitlín, scratchy and evil.

The children were filled with nausea and gagged at the sound of her voice as a poisonous murky fog obscured the battlefield.

"You will soon tire in your weakened state," mocked Caitlín. "But keep up the good work. I'm enjoying the show."

Cassie felt her blood boil and she cursed her lack of sight. If only she could, not just physically see, but look within for a vision to guide them. But nothing seemed to be happening in the still of the battlefield. They began a cautious advance in the direction of Caitlín's distant tent, threading their way between rocky outcrops and stunted trees.

Shapes loomed out of the gloom. At first they looked like the jagged shadows of rocks and boulders in the fog, but then they seemed to advance in a pincer movement.

"Tall men and women with plastic faces are advancing towards us," said Thomas. "They are like the followers of Caitlín we encountered in the desert, soulless and dead-eyed. They must be some of the Hollywood people she has soul-split."

Cassie drew her sword. "I feel there are legions of them. We are outnumbered," she said, an edge of despair in her voice.

Thomas peered into the gloom. "There are thousands of them! A whole army!"

"You will have to split up," said a familiar voice. Standing beside them was Sennan, his sword drawn.

"Please Sennan, leave now. You cannot help us," said Thomas, distressed.

"I'll be the judge of that," said Sennan. He touched Cassie lightly on the arm. "You and I will leap over these wraiths and attack them from the back. Thomas can manage with his lance standing before them. Nancy should stay here and use her slingshot."

Caitlín's wraiths moved closer. Nancy planted her shield in the ground and took aim and fired. She hit a wraith straight in the forehead. Immediately, the flesh flew off the bones and the dead eyes rolled out of the sockets. Then the skeleton got up to continue the fight, lurching towards them with a desperate speed. But Sennan flew in the air, his white cloak flapping, and touched the skeleton on the forehead. It immediately crumbled to fragments of bone.

But something strange happened. A whole battalion fell.

He flew back to the children. "Look into your shields," he commanded. Thomas looked into Nancy and Cassie's shields. Reflected there were not thousands but no more than twenty wraiths.

"It's a trick," shouted Sennan. "Caitlín is using her mirror magic to make it look like there are whole battalions. There are less than a hundred. We can defeat them."

Sennan held Cassie's arm and together they made a salmon leap, vaulting over the advancing line of wraiths. Cassie and Sennan raised their swords and chopped down rows of them from behind. But their swords met fresh air. It was hard to tell who was real and who was a projection. Sennan felt the air. Some of the figures seemed more substantial than others. Sennan concentrated and homed in on one. Cassie felt blood spatter her face. She was glad that she couldn't see so she didn't have to think of them as people. The flesh flew off but still the skeleton rose to fight. But Thomas was waiting for it and aimed his lance. It spun and seemed to bring down several opponents. But there was only one real skeleton.

"Most of the enemy forces are a projection," said Sennan. "But if I can touch the real skeletons, there is a chance the bodies can return to the souls they've been split from."

He whirled around the battlefield like a white tornado, touching the bones of the skeletons of the slain with his sword and mumbling an incantation that was lost in the whipping wind. Once he had anointed them, they disappeared.

"I am sending what remains of their life forces to the realm of shadows and death – the House of Donn," Sennan explained. "Later I will try to reunite them with their souls if I can – or, rather, if I can persuade Donn to let me."

"Is that the God of the Underworld who never takes

his black throne at Tara?" asked Thomas. "I remember Connle whispering his name with fear."

"Yes. He is the dark, mysterious God of the place where the unhappy souls of the damned go to wait their fate. Or so we believe – his kingdom is an enigma. The gods avoid him and no one has ever visited him and returned," said Sennan sombrely.

"We have met his like in the Norse World Tree," said Cassie shuddering at the memory of Hel in her palace of bones in Helheim. "Please be careful."

The children were so busy talking with Sennan that they didn't realise an enemy was creeping towards them.

A wraith that looked like Daley, Caitlín's assistant, advanced towards Thomas and managed to grab his lance, injuring his arm. Thomas stood, petrified, unable to move. The wraith lunged and grabbed Thomas around the neck with his clawed hands. Thomas struggled but the breath was shaken out of him and his eyes rolled in his head. But just as he was about to pass out, the hands released their grip. The wraith gasped and green blood oozed from his mouth as he fell to the ground and crumbled to bone. Sennan withdrew his sword. Thomas gasped in gratitude but also felt guilty. There was no way Sennan could escape punishment now. Immediately Sennan anointed the bones and they disappeared.

There was a lull in the battle and, as the fog cleared, instead of the devastation they expected, there were no battalions to be seen. Within seconds of falling to the ground and Sennan anointing them, the skeletons had disappeared. There were no hacked limbs, no severed heads, nothing.

"I will go now to intercede with Donn," said Sennan, "and see if I can unite their bodies and souls. They are Caitlín's victims too and most did not know what they were letting themselves in for."

"Will they live?" asked Thomas.

"If they recognise their error, they may have another chance. But Donn is an aloof deity and shuns humans and gods alike," said Sennan. "Goodbye. It may be difficult to return from where I am going." And with that, he was gone.

There was a brief spasm in the earth but soon all was still. Eerily still. The children advanced towards the brooding presence of Caitlín's tent, moving slowly from boulder to boulder with heavy hearts. They dared not think of Sennan's departure. Thomas's limp slowed them down. He felt angry and frustrated and slumped against a rock.

"I'm useless," he said. "I'm holding you back. Curse this stupid leg!"

Cassie grabbed him by the shoulders. "You are my eyes," she said simply. "I need you."

They journeyed on for what seemed like hours. Then, as they made their way to a group of low-lying blackthorn bushes, they were surprised by a sudden ambush. Hordes of wraiths began to pour once more from Caitlín's tent. The children saw they were Caitlín's cast and crew from the shoot and they were surrounded before they could react. The wraiths advanced towards them, their clawed hands outstretched.

Nancy hunkered down behind her shield and released a flurry of stones from her slingshot. This pushed the enemy back and bought them a moment.

"We'll have to do the Lance and Shield Feat," said Cassie. "If we get above them we have more chance. Just point me in the right direction. I learned to do this blindfolded."

"I can't do it, Cassie," said Thomas. "I just can't leap up on my shield, with my bad leg."

"We'll help you onto your shield and we'll try to defend your position. But if they come near you, you can fight them."

"I can use Gleipner the Binder to lasso them," he said.

Thomas thrust his lance into the ground and set the

shield spinning on its point. Cassie helped him reach it and he sat atop, the rope in one hand and the sword in the other.

Cassie and Nancy fanned out on either side. Confidently, Cassie thrust her lance into the ground. She knew she could do this. She breathed evenly and talked herself through it, remembering the lesson. "Now land the shield dead centre on the lance." She threw it up like a discus and listened for the even whirr. Then, guided by the sound, she salmon-leaped up to the top of the shield and drew her sword.

"Is Nancy safe?" she roared back to Thomas.

"She's hiding in a ditch," he shouted back. "Look out!"

Cassie heard the tread of the approaching wraiths. She knew she was surrounded.

"They're clambering on to each other's backs," shouted Thomas. "To your left!"

Cassie spun round and hacked with her sword. She felt blood spatter her face but she continued to hack, knowing their skeletons would continue the fight.

"Behind you!" shouted Thomas.

Her sword hit bone. A skull bounced onto the shield but she kicked it away, felling another wraith in his tracks.

"You can come down now," shouted Thomas. "They're all down. I'll throw the Binder to guide you to me and we'll join Nancy. She's managed to find shelter in a ditch. She's been picking off the wraiths with her slingshot."

Cassie jumped down off her shield and held out her hands for the rope Gleipner but at that moment thunder and lightning shook from the tent of shadows and storms, streaking the black sky with a lightning storm. Cassie quaked in the sudden electrical charge. And she screamed when her hand met bone rather than the silken rope she was expecting.

"They've come back, reanimated by the lightning," shouted Thomas. "The skeletons are surrounding you!"

Cassie tried to reach for her sword but bony fingers gripped her legs. She felt a chomping sound near her neck, as sharp claws dug into her shoulders. She was trapped. She heard the slashing sound of a sword. She felt the blade move through the air millimetres from her face. She was finished.

She tensed as she heard blade hack through bone. The grip of the skeletons slackened and was gone. She was saved!

"Thomas, Nancy?" Cassie cried out.

"No," came a familiar rasping voice.

"Scáthach!" she said, alarmed.

Her teacher thrust the rope into her hand. "There is no time. You must reach the tent. Run!"

Cassie hesitated for a second but the sound of Scáthach's sword slicing through bone brought her to her senses. She gathered up her shield and lance and pulled herself to Thomas.

"These skeletons are more powerful than the others," said Thomas. "Scáthach is fighting them off. We have to move forward to join Nancy."

Scáthach, holding two swords, cleaved through the skeletal fighters who had claws for hands. But every time she hacked a skeleton to pieces, the bones regrouped and continued to fight. There seemed no way she could win.

The lightning storm fractured the sky. Thomas and Cassie staggered to join Nancy, who hugged them both. She was unscathed and more excited by the battle than afraid. Thomas looked back to where Scáthach was but all he could see was a mound of skeletal shapes shimmering through the eerie light from the storm. And then he thought he saw their teacher overpowered and sinking into the ground under a mound of bones.

"They've got her," he said in an agonised voice. But a sudden, satisfied roar from the tent of shadows and storms compelled them to go on.

"Caitlin's going to pay for it," Cassie vowed intently, tears in her eyes. Her blood felt hot and she wanted revenge.

The Chingles crawled on their bellies towards the tent. It was much closer now and more hideous than they'd realised, the surface crawling with terrifying black shadows like horrible insects. They soldiered on but the earth shook and stones and rocks moved towards them. A sudden hard rain strafed them from the sky, then hailstones. They sheltered behind their shields. The ground became waterlogged and turned to churning mud. The earth rumbled and a horrible cawing sound came from the tent of shadow and storms. Belching black smoke rose from it. The children clutched their ears and were swept with a wave of nausea.

"We have to face her," said Thomas bravely. "We're very close."

Trying not to retch they pushed forward until they were close by the tent.

But as they got nearer, they walked straight into an invisible barrier. They realised the tent was protected beneath a shield of transparent glass, cold and repellent to the touch. Their heartbeats drummed in their ears. Cassie broke into a light sweat, fear trickling down her back. She raised her sword and, using all her strength, struck the glass shield surrounding Caitlín's camp. But the hilt of the sword was driven back into her hand and the weapon flew from her grasp, tearing the skin from her fingers. The glass wasn't even dented. An evil smoke encircled it, making them cough.

"This is impenetrable," said Cassie, breathing hard.

Thomas examined her bleeding hand. "It's just a scuff," he said.

"But what do we do now?" Cassie panted. "She's lured us here. She's got us where she wants us. We are just sitting ducks."

Thomas helped her retrieve her sword and he told her that the blade was dulled. He leaned on his lance, his leg throbbing. Nancy shook him, mimed a scream and pointed at the glass. Alarmed, he looked at the glass but could see nothing new. He looked back at his little sister. She then made a series of hand signs and he realised she was spelling out Ogham letters.

"It's the code!" he yelled to Cassie. "S–C–R–E–A–M! Scream! She means us to do the Battle Cry. Clever Nancy! Somehow she's picked up Ogham!"

"Yes! A Battle Cry could shatter the glass!" said Cassie. She coughed, already weak from the exertion of striking the glass.

They could barely whisper, let alone unleash a

scream of sufficient power to blow apart magical glass.

Cassie tried to focus her concentration. "Turn yourself to steel, then wood, then air," she breathed. A sudden wind cut through the smoke, dissipating it and giving them a breath of air. Thomas looked up and noticed a falcon circling the glass fortress, its wing-beats creating eddies of air. There was something familiar about the bird. They drew a breath from the breeze and opened their throats.

The force of the cry, like a million birdcalls, rose from them. It burst forth like steam and surrounded the glass. Then the wave of noise crashed into the wall and merged into the deafening sound of glass shattering. There was an almighty crack. The children formed their battered shields into a triangle and hunkered down behind them as a glass rain dashed to the ground, the noise like a million windows breaking.

After a while the sound subsided into the tinkle of occasional shards and Thomas dared to peek out. The ground was now a savage landscape of broken glass shards, gleaming like blades.

As they neared the tent of shadow and storms, a great hissing laugh escaped.

"Why, we are brave, aren't we, little Chingles?" sneered Caitlín, her voice as sharp as the glass. "But now it is time to face your most deadly enemies. Yourselves."

The children felt a coldness in their guts and a sense of foreboding. A look of desolation crept over Cassie's sightless face. They felt exhausted and vulnerable behind their battered shields. Only Nancy seemed to have any energy left.

There was a blinding flash and the sound of carefree laugher, cruel and heartless, burst towards them, mocking them. It was the sound of triumph. Three figures emerged from the tent. For a moment the children froze, not sure what they were facing. Thomas let out a cry with the shock of recognition. Cassie bristled with a sickening feeling. It was unmistakably their Shadow Selves under Caitlín's control.

Their replicas were dressed in black chainmail. They carried blood-red weapons and shone with vitality. All the strength the children lacked was personified in them.

Shadow Thomas was the first to move. He lunged forward and in a heartbeat transformed into a black stag with a ferocious crown of antlers. Shadow Nancy, carrying a spear, made a salmon leap. Cassie's wicked double also performed a salmon leap and brandished the most fiercesome weapon of all – a blood-red gae bolga with the spear point that changed into a thousand barbs when it pierced the enemy.

"We'll never beat them," gasped Thomas. "They have all our strength and skill."

"I cannot see them but I can feel their power," said Cassie, buckling. "But let's think. Thomas, you take my shadow on, you know my weaknesses. Nancy, you take on Thomas and I'll take on Nancy."

"We'll do our best or die trying," agreed Thomas, grimly.

But as they tried to move against the Shadows, they were repelled by an invisible force field.

"Do not try to divide and conquer, weaklings," mocked Shadow Thomas. "We will fight only ourselves."

The three shadows advanced, arrogant and mocking.

"Hold up your amulets," shouted Thomas to his sisters. As they raised their jewels, three beams emerged from them and knocked their adversaries back, stopping them in their tracks. But then the shadow forms, bristling with awful energy, laughed and began to take on the features of their bad selves. Cassie's false form became like a bull, Thomas's a donkey and Nancy's a lamb.

"We have spared you, only so we can fight ourselves," said Shadow Cassie's deep voice. "We want to face our real enemies – our weaker selves. When I master myself, I become twice as powerful."

"And what if I kill you?" Real Cassie cried out.

"Then you'll die without your life force," sneered Shadow Thomas. "So you might as well give up any way."

"I'd rather die than live as Caitlín's slave!" cried Cassie, quaking.

"I have no wish to be an instrument of evil!" yelled Real Thomas.

"So you don't want fame, riches and power?" asked Shadow Thomas. "That is what you get with Caitlín."

"Not at any price!" shouted real Cassie. "Rather death than dishonour!" Cassie and Thomas hid Nancy in a hollow in the ground, determined at least to protect her.

"Perhaps the Crane Bag can help us," said Thomas grasping it from thin air.

But just then Cassie picked up her shield and weapons and stumbled, defenceless and unseeing, towards her Shadow Self. On the point of plunging his hand into the Crane Bag, Thomas hesitated. Perhaps Cassie should choose her own weapon. He waited, ready to throw the Crane Bag to his sister.

I must try to defeat my negative self, Cassie thought. It's what Scátach and Sennan would expect of me.

Shadow Cassie advanced brandishing the gae bolga.

"I am not afraid of you," Cassie said to her Shadow Self.

"Then more fool you!," sneered Shadow Cassie.

Real Cassie was repelled by the hatefulness in her shadow's voice – her own pride and arrogance distorted into monstrous shape. She had to think. Now was the time to muster all her ingenuity to out-manoeuvre this hideous, mocking double.

Shadow Cassie, enjoying the moment of her power, arrogantly swung the bulging gae bolga above her head. Several times she made as if to throw it. Each time, Real Cassie flinched in the displacement of air.

But just as Shadow Cassie dropped the gae bolga to the fork of her foot, Thomas threw his sister the Crane Bag.

At that moment, three black crows seared the sky, trailing thunder and lightning in their wake. Cassie reached inside the Crane Bag and her hand grasped the whalebone. She held it up to the sky as a thunderbolt rent the air. Then a flash of lightning coursed through it. The whalebone, beaten into shape by the sky, lengthened into a spear with a hideous pointed head like a harpoon, sparks cascading from it in points of light as if it had been newly plucked from a forge. It was a gae bolga to match the other one, freshly minted from the sky!

Strength surged through Real Cassie's veins as she placed the weapon in the fork of her foot. She and her Shadow Self matched each other move for move. As Cassie thrust back her foot to cast the gae bolga so did her Shadow Self.

The two bulging spears surged into the air like twin bolts of lightning. They met with a clash in the sky. Real Cassie held her breath, a second lasting an eternity. Then the two gae bolgas merged in a crash of thunder and a flare of lightning. In a split second, the Shadow's weapon disintegrated and Real Cassie's gae bolga rose high in the air. It flashed as a lightning bolt from the sky towards her enemy self. Real Cassie did not see the weapon strike her Shadow but felt a spasm of pain, like her innards were being torn out. It felt as if a barb was tearing into every organ of her body, piercing her with a thousand points. She fell to the ground.

Thomas saw his sister and her Shadow fall but he was powerless. The black stag launched at him on his powerful haunches at a hundred miles an hour. He couldn't run: his lame leg throbbed and his injured arm bled profusely. The stag bellowed and charged, antlers down. Thomas had only one weapon left to him – his voice.

"You can charge and kill me – defenceless! But can you match me, like for like?" he taunted his Shadow Self.

The stag hesitated and reared up in the air. In the blink of an eye it became a fierce boar, then in a heartbeat a ferocious wolf. It ran around Thomas sniffing and growling and cuffed his face with its claw, drawing blood. It was goading him, Thomas realised, as he had done with Lardon. He suddenly felt ashamed of his own bravado.

The wolf became a wolfhound, bounded up on his chest and knocked him down. He slavered into his face and snarled at him. Thomas looked into the gaping maw of his Shadow Self and saw a tongue of fire. He looked into his yellow eyes, at the arrogance and pride in his abilities. There was a wildness there that frightened him but also a wounded desperation at having to do Caitlín's bidding. He saw his own reflection in his Shadow Self's eye. He could not give up on himself. He had to find a way to outwit himself and exploit his own weaknesses, just as Caitlín had done. In a flash he realised why he'd spent all summer battling against his own stubborn nature, his arrogance and pride. He knew he just couldn't resist showing off. And that knowledge was power.

"Clever changes," he said to his double, "but sometimes it is more impressive to become a small thing."

The wolfhound snarled and turned into an eagle. It rose on magnificent wings and circled menacingly overhead before plunging to land on his shoulder. Thomas felt sick as his Shadow Self grew stronger with his arrogance, leaching the little energy he had.

Then the eagle turned round, the talons changing into arms, the beak to a boy's face – his own. He faced his Shadow Self, boy to boy. But soon the Shadow Self's features morphed into a donkey's, hideously half human, like something in a freak show. He saw his asinine competitiveness, his peacock pride. The Donkey Boy grabbed him around the neck, squeezing the air out of his throat.

"Wait!" spluttered Real Thomas. "When I defeated Balor, I transformed into a berry. That's the most difficult of all, to change into a plant."

The Donkey Boy fixed him with a look of arrogant pride. In a heartbeat, the freakish Shadow Self had shapeshifted. On the ground lay a red berry.

Thomas didn't hesitate. He picked it up and popped

it in his mouth. It tasted sour and sweet at the same time, the worst thing and the best thing he had ever tasted. It exploded in his mouth. His insides heaved and he fell writhing to the ground.

All was still on the battlefield. It was hard to detect any signs of life in Cassie or Thomas. Then suddenly figures emerged from the gloom. A grey wolf, an elk with its massive antlers swinging out on both sides of its head like two hands and a falcon appeared beside the children. The grey wolf licked Cassie's face, the elk stood over Thomas and the falcon landed on Nancy's shoulder where she hid in the hollow. The shadows were nowhere to be seen.

The wolf became Grey Wolf of the Scar Clan, the elk Kapo the Ice Age shaman and the falcon changed into Dr Dalgado from Sintra. Grey Wolf held up Cassie's amulet and placed it on her forehead. Kapo did likewise with Thomas. Then they began to sing and chant, a soft repetitive strain, a song older than the earth itself, like the song of creation.

Cassie opened her eyes, blinking with surprise. She could see and she was looking at the calm face of Grey Wolf, smiling at her.

"I'm alive! And I can see!" she gasped. "Grey Wolf! How come you are here?"

"We are also dream-walkers," Grey Wolf said, indicating his companions. "We have come to help you become whole again."

"I can see again!" said Cassie, tears welling into her eyes. "Are Thomas and Nancy safe?"

"See for yourself," said Grey Wolf.

Just then, as Thomas writhed and gagged, his shivering stopped and he awoke to find himself held by Kapo – the cave boy.

Cassie ran to her brother and held his hand.

"You were cunning, my friend," said Grey Wolf. "You have regained your strength."

Thomas flexed his legs and jumped on the spot, turning a somersault in the air.

"Fab!" he exclaimed, running around. But then he stopped. "What about Nancy?"

"Nancy is too young to have been properly soul-split," Grey Wolf said. "Unlike your Shadow Selves, the Shadow Nancy is just a projection of Caitlín's. But the shock of Caitlín's attack caused Nancy to lose her powers and speech. If you, her older brother and sister, call her spirit, she will come. And Nancy will know what to do."

They joined Nancy in her hiding place and called her Shadow Self, which trotted over as a lamb. Nancy patted and hugged the lamb and placed her amulet round its neck. The lamb disappeared and Nancy once more wore the jewel.

"We have to rescue Finnen," she said in a clear voice.

"You can talk!" said Cassie, hugging her, so glad her little sister was restored.

"I love you all," Nancy said simply.

"She knew to treat her projection with kindness," said Grey Wolf, "something that Caitlín would never expect – she understands only conflict."

"But Nancy's right," said Thomas. "What about Finnen? Caitlín still controls her human shape. We have to rescue her."

"Only Finnen can make herself whole again," said Grey Wolf. "She will have to find her own way to integrate, just as you all have done."

A cruel laugh came from the tent of shadows and storms and a belching smoke arose into the sky.

"Why hasn't she attacked us?" asked Cassie. "We have defeated our Shadow Selves."

"Caitlín is drunk with her own power," said Grey Wolf. "It wouldn't even occur to her that you have overcome yourselves. She is keeping her strength for the next phase of her plan."

Thomas looked thoughtful. "Dr Dalgado, if you can fly to bring Finnen here, I think I know what to do. We will bring the fight to Caitlín and fight fire with fire, cunning with cunning."

Thomas, Cassie and Nancy walked straight up to the entrance of the tent of shadows and storms. Up close the surface raged with torrents and conflagrations as if reflecting every storm in the world. They had to swallow to suppress gagging at the corrosive stench from within.

"We have succeeded," said Cassie in a deep voice to the opening in the tent. She kept her head low and let out a bull's roar.

A dry gulping noise and then a blood-curdling laugh came from within.

"Now let us be joined by Finnen so we can help her vanquish her swan nature. We cannot let her escape," said Thomas, his voice braying, with his face concealed behind his shield.

The opening of the tent quivered. They did not dare to go any further in. The shadows subsided and they had to raise their shields to protect their eyes when Finnen emerged as Fiona Waters. She was dressed in a chainmail of thousands of tiny mirrors and they saw their distorted images refracted in the tiny panes.

Fiona let out a harsh laugh. She carried a spear with a silver point and her nails were like silver-pointed weapons. "Lead on," she commanded, her voice shrill.

They walked away from the tent, to the centre of the battlefield. Then Thomas raised his spear in a signal and shouted, "Now!"

Nancy opened her throat and let out the ululating cry of the swan, high and hoping, eerie and strange. At the same moment, Thomas whipped the rope Gleipner the Binder out of the Crane Bag.

Cassie and Nancy held their lances to False Fiona's throat. Together they bound her in the rope of silken cord, just as they'd trussed up the rival Heimdalls at the World Tree. She tore at it with her nails and bit into its softness but it held. She raged and convulsed but was frustrated by hardly being able to see the rope that bound her.

Nancy continued her cry and was met by the echo of another's song. Finnen in her swan shape swooped down and, grabbing the cord around Fiona in her beak, tossed the bundle onto her back. Her great wings hovered in the air and she spiralled into the sky. For the briefest moment, the surface of the tent of shadows and storms cleared and no longer showed torrents and conflagrations. Reflected in its surface were three children and, flying above them, a woman with swan's wings. Finnen had succeeded in reuniting her nature and had become a Swan Maiden again.

The tent quivered and an angry cry came from within. Then the tent of shadows and storms dissipated into a pestilential veil and rose in a black plume towards the sky. The monstrous Caitlín was revealed in the shape of the Corra brooding before them and getting bigger all the time. One of the Corra's wings unfurled and lashed out. The children shrank back.

"You have tricked me," she snarled. "I see you are more powerful than I thought. But so am I!"

She folded back her wings and they confronted once more the repulsive Corra with the hag's face and crooked fangs. Her scaly breast heaved and bristled and she rose into the air, monstrous and looming, bigger than she'd ever been before, like a mountain, blocking the sky. Now they realised why she had seemed to just brood on the battlefield. She had concentrated all her energy into increasing to a monstrous size.

They gasped. They could barely see all of her. Cassie drew her breath and closed her eyes. Her long sight returned to her and she got a sense of Caitlín's dimensions. Her wings spanned the whole of the island, her head was wreathed in clouds and her great talons were as long as a great oak tree. They froze and realised they needed to regroup.

Then the three shamans appeared.

Dr Dalgado spoke. "We will distract her while you find a way to sneak up on her."

"Remember size can be a disadvantage," advised Grey Wolf.

"We will try to crawl up her," said Cassie.

Then the shamans changed into their animal shapes, Dr Dalgado into a falcon, Grey Wolf into a wolf and Kapo into an elk.

Dr Dalgado flew into the clouds as a falcon and pecked at Caitlín's breast. Her scales were hard as bone but she was irritated and bashed her chest with her own talons. While she was distracted, the children salmon-leapt to the bottom of her foot. Cassie took up her sword, Nancy her slingshot and Thomas his lance. As they picked up their battered shields, Caitlín cawed and her great mouth came down from the sky and her talons lashed out at them. They managed to roll aside. Caitlín homed in on Cassie, who was nearest, slashing at her, inches from her face. Behind her shield, Cassie braced herself for the next attack. Caitlín's hag's face came down, gnashing her crooked fangs. But just as she was ready to bite into the shield, the falcon flew up towards her face and tried to peck out her eye.

In a rage, Caitlín reared, then snapped her head back and seized the falcon in her talons, swallowing it whole.

We *must* stop her, thought Cassie. But she found herself pinioned by Caitlín's talons, the vast nails, hard and horny, forming a cage around her. She rammed at a claw with her sword but it was useless. When the wolf and the elk ran at the talons Caitlín swatted them aside. But she had to raise her claw to do so and Cassie rolled free and made a salmon-leap out of her reach.

The elk and the wolf were not so lucky. The elk let out a startled cry as Caitlín's foot stamped him into the earth, his antlers broken and crushed under her great foot. The wolf attacked her other foot but Caitlín lifted him in her talons and dashed his brains out on a rock.

Their friends and helpers were dead. They'd sacrificed themselves to save the Chingles. And they'd lost Scáthach and Sennan. Cassie felt a surge of sadness but this gave way to towering anger. It filled every fibre in her body. She was beside herself with rage.

Her hair shot up as if on fire; her muscles shook like

reeds in a stream. Her eyes stood out on stalks and her heart beat a ferocious drumbeat in her chest. Flecks of fire shot out of her mouth and it seemed the sky was slashed with her fury. She was bathed in a stark white light; her sword shone as if newly forged. The Warp Spasm was upon her and she was inflamed with battle rage.

Cassie rose to several times her size and salmon-leaped onto Caitlín's back. Caitlín shook like an earthquake to throw her off. But in her fury, Cassie hacked her way up her scaly back, plunging her sword in to give her a hold. This inflamed Caitlín further. She writhed around and shook her great back. But Cassie clung on by the hilt of her sword, fury sparking off her.

Thomas saw what his sister was doing. He salmon-leaped away to give him a better range and raised his lance.

Caitlín shook violently but still Cassie clung on by the sword hilt. Caitlín swivelled her hag's head round on her serpent's neck, ready to bite her enemy. Cassie smelt her stinking breath and saw her gnarled teeth come closer. But just as Caitlín made a lunge at her, she was stopped in her tracks. Thomas's lance had found his mark and pierced her eye.

Yellow and green gore flowed from her eye, covering

Cassie, but still she clung on, wading through the vile liquid.

Caitlín swung back her head and reached up with her great talons to pluck the lance from her eye. She pulled out her own eye on its point and in a split second flicked it back at Thomas. He was frozen to the spot with terror.

But Cassie had moved from Caitlín's back to the base of her serpent's neck. Cassie raised her burning sword and with one great swoop hacked into her neck. Caitlín roared and writhed, flailing at her with her talons, but in her fury Cassie continued to hack away at the neck as thick as several tree trunks. With one last great swipe the head was severed from the body.

Caitlín's severed head rolled away. It bashed against a rock and sat on the ground, hideous and deformed. The one eye in her head gazed unblinkingly at the children. Black blood oozed over her crooked fangs and her torn feathers and scales on her headless body, which she'd plucked out while trying to remove Cassie from her back.

The body convulsed and tried to move away but Cassie continued to hack into the neck until it fell over. She salmon-leaped off it and joined her brother and sister.

After a few moments, cautiously, Thomas and

Cassie approached the head. There was no breath, no sign of life. They were soon by her crooked fangs. But at that, the mouth shot open and a red glow blazed from the empty eye socket.

"You think I'm finished," Caitlín snarled. "But you've merely increased my power by splitting me." The mouth opened wide and vomited black bile like lava from a volcano.

The Chingles held up their amulets as Caitlín unleashed a bolt of red light from her eye socket. The light hit the amulets and refracted back, stunning her with her own power. It burnt out her remaining eye. But the impact of the light was so great it tore the amulet from Cassie's hand and it went flying towards the sea. Thomas's cracked on impact. Nancy's fell back to earth and she picked it up.

The great head regarded them with her sightless eyes. The hideous maw of her mouth swung open and her lips peeled back to reveal the snarling fangs.

"I am not –" But she didn't finish her sentence. A great bolt, Nancy's amulet, shot from her sling, shattering the teeth and lodging in Caitlín's throat. There was a liquid gurgle as Caitlín choked on the stone, her teeth gnashing and severing her own black forked tongue.

The head crashed over on its side – lifeless. Cassie and Thomas watched in horror as the flesh on Caitlín's face fell away revealing the skull with fanged teeth. A little way off, the body collapsed in upon itself. The vast wings fragmented into a million motes of black dust. Her bones and entrails collapsed into the soil, a pulsating mountain of liver, kidneys, heart and bone.

Cassie and Thomas wiped the black bile from their faces as the battlefield became suffused with light. They looked up towards the sky.

Finnen's great wings sent a gentle breeze through the acrid smoke rising from Caitlín's remains. She landed before them as a Swan Maiden, carrying Gleipner the Binder in her hands. She began to weave it in her hands into a net.

"I must gather up all Caitlín's remains. She can regenerate even from a fragment," Finnen spoke with urgency.

"But where can we bury her?" asked Thomas.

"Consult the Crane Bag, though I suspect I know the answer," Finnen said.

Thomas reached inside the Crane Bag and pulled out the bones of Assal. They spelt one word, "*Yggdrasil*," the World Tree. A rainbow appeared at their feet, arching over the battlefield in a blaze of colour.

"I shall take her to the Chasm of Chaos where she captured me. It has been willed by the Crane Bag. Little did she know it would become her own grave," said Finnen. "The great dragon-serpent can feast on her innards. Each fragment still contains part of her soul but I think she deserves to suffer for all eternity. The gods of the World Tree can devise a punishment."

"The Norse gods are good at that," said Cassie, remembering the punishment of Loki and the horrors of Helheim when they journeyed to the World Tree.

"You must give me your amulets. They are infected with her power and must be destroyed," said Finnen urgently.

Thomas handed over the cracked burning amulet that throbbed with a dark power. Nancy's was lodged in Caitlín's throat.

But Cassie's had been lost in the fight.

"No matter," said Finnen. "We will look for it later. Let us hope it doesn't fall into the wrong hands."

Finnen gathered up the net of Caitlín's bones and skull. A calm descended on the battlefield.

"I hope now I can have a proper chat with my sister Áine," Finnen said. "How I've missed her!"

"She's worried that you might be mad at her for not

defeating Balor in the First Battle of the Skies," said Cassie.

Finnen smiled wryly. "Oh, only for the first couple of thousand years."

"She has some big news. She wants to marry again," said Cassie.

Finnen laughed heartily. "I'm glad to hear she hasn't changed." Finnen moved towards the rainbow.

Thomas realised that they'd nearly forgotten the whole point of searching for Finnen!

"Before you go, do you vote for Áine to marry our Uncle Jarlath?" he called after her.

Finnen beamed. "I would be proud to be related to you," she said.

"Does that mean yes?" asked Thomas.

"Of course," Finnen said.

The children whooped with delight. For the first time, they felt their sacrifices had been worthwhile.

Finnen plunged into the fiery rainbow. They watched her fly through it on her strong wings, secure in her freedom.

Thomas turned to Cassie. "I'm sad to lose that rope," he said. "It really helped me improve my scout knots."

Cassie laughed. They looked around at the scene of devastation but then bolts of light shot from the sky, clearing the fetid fog from the battlefield. They saw Lugh descend from the sky, golden and luminous and late as usual! Cassie, Thomas and Nancy were blood-spattered and wounded but he embraced them and knelt before them.

"Truly you are heroes," he said, bowing deeply.

Cassie looked rueful. "But we didn't do it alone. There was a heavy price to pay. We lost our teachers, Scáthach and Sennan, and the shamans Grey Wolf, Dr Dalgado and Kapo."

"Can the Merrows object to their help and still claim Jarlath?" asked Thomas.

"No," said Lugh. "Caitlín was more of a threat than anyone realised. As for Scáthach and Sennan, they have divinity in their natures. We do not know what may become of them."

"What about our friends?" asked Nancy.

"Now that Cassie has her long sight restored, perhaps she can see their present," Lugh said, ruffling Nancy's curls.

Cassie closed her eyes. She saw the ghost of a falcon hover over the beautiful pool in Alvide and Kapo in his elk skin writhing on his cave floor, fighting for his life. She had a vision of Grey Wolf surrounded by the Scar Clan, his wolf spirit hovering between life and death.

"Dr Dalgado has returned as a falcon. But Kapo and Grey Wolf are fighting for their lives. Isn't there anything we can do to help?"

"No," said Lugh. "They have to fight their own battles. This is the way of the shaman."

"Our victory has come at a high price," said Thomas sadly.

"But you have vanquished Caitlín," said Lugh. "And for now the forces of darkness have been driven away."

"You sound like there will be more battles," said Cassie, wearily.

"That is the nature of heroes," said Lugh kindly. "But your path can change. I come with an offer from the Tuatha Dé Danann. You have earned the right to live in Tir Na nÓg, the Land of the Ever Young. You need never die, even grow up. You can become immortal."

The children looked at him in amazement. I need never grow up, thought Cassie, never go back to school. She was dreading going back.

"But I want to grow up," said Nancy stubbornly.

The children hesitated.

"You do not have to answer now," said Lugh. "You have the length of four seasons to decide."

He led them off the battlefield as Caitlín's dust swirled and was eaten by the light.

"There is one more thing we have to do," said Cassie. "That film she was making to turn children evil. We have to destroy it."

They found Caitlín's edit suite in the cave hidden behind the boulder at Glimmering Lake that Connle had told them about. Rolls of films lay in cans, locked inside an enchanted cage. Lugh shattered the spell and broke open each can with a lightning bolt from his palm. The films sizzled and erupted and for a brief moment the children caught a stench of the evil Caitlín wanted to use to pollute the minds of children against their parents – against life. He burned the images into oblivion and replaced them with his own.

When the film was shown, no one ever remembered the story, the plot or the characters but everyone said it was the best film they'd ever seen. Any child who saw that film who felt troubled or alone left the cinema full of hope.

CHAPTER 18

For three days, black rain poured down on the island. On the fourth a fine ash fell. But on the fifth, in the morning, winter-flowering jasmine and hellebore burst into bloom. In the afternoon, spring flowers, snowdrops, crocuses and daffodils, grew among the grass and hedgerows. The next day a carpet of summer wildflowers covered the island: betony, iris and mugwort. A flock of Hooper swans arrived on Glimmering Lake and when a tropical wind blew, palm trees and exotic ferns studded the marshy land.

The Chingles slept all through this in Áine's healing crystal room. When they emerged blinking into the light, they felt stronger and more whole than they had all summer.

When they arrived back home at Fairy Fort House,

Angel behaved as though they'd just left the house. Then the children remembered that all the islanders had been slumbering in an enchanted sleep.

Towards lunchtime Angel received a letter from Lardon's father. She began to pack in a flurry. She and Lardon were to return by ferry that afternoon to the mainland.

But Lardon cornered the Chingles and demanded to know what they'd been up to.

"Come on, guys," he said. "I need to know all this weird stuff wasn't just in my head."

Cassie and Thomas exchanged looks.

"You know, despite all that's happened, he never did rat on us about the needles and the Breath Feat," Thomas whispered to his sister.

"And we were totally wrong about him being an agent of Caitlín's," admitted Cassie.

So they told him an edited version of all that had happened by way of apology for their behaviour.

"So you're not aliens. I kinda knew that," he said. "Just some kind of superheroes. That's a neat story."

"But you must never tell," warned Cassie. "An invisible wire will alert us and you will be pulverised in a matter of seconds."

"I'd never rat on a friend," he said, embracing them

awkwardly. "Anyway I'm not going back to Hollywood for the time being. Angel wrote to my father and he's decided to take a year off to go travelling around the world with me. I've been invited to Japan by the Bonsai Federation! Dad's going to meet us at the ferry. We may even try to trace my real parents, somewhere in Eastern Europe I guess."

"Does that mean Angel's out of a job?" Cassie asked.

"She's going to caretake the studio. My dad said anyone who can handle me could deal with anything."

Most of the island turned up to say goodbye to Lardon and Angel at the ferry. As they waved goodbye to him, Cassie and Thomas were surprised to feel sad.

"Will he really be pulverised if he reveals our secret?" asked Thomas as they set off back to Fairy Fort House.

Cassie rolled her eyes. "What do you think?"

As they headed home, Muiris ran after them, holding out two letters. One was from Dick Headley, the Hollywood star. He wrote that he'd made a documentary about the stars' ordeal with Caitlín. But in early viewings, the audience thought it was a hilarious spoof on the vanity and insecurity of Hollywood stars. "So I'm re-billing it as a comedy," he said. "I guess it will have to be our secret."

The second letter contained a postcard of a drawing found in a cave in a place called Pech-Merle near Cahors in France. It featured a horse whose contours followed the natural curve of the rock. It was the drawing that Kapo had been doing when they interrupted him. On the other side of the card was a picture of a grey wolf. They looked at it quizzically. Cassie gazed at it and used her long sight. She saw a vision in the Ice Age of an old man in an elk skin sealing the cave. And then another image of a man with a grey plait descending into the cave in full sunshine.

"Somehow I think it means Kapo and Grey Wolf survived," said Cassie. Tears of relief sprang to her eyes.

There was now only one last mission to accomplish. They set off to the east of the island, with Nancy on Derry and Thomas and Cassie on their bicycles, to find Jarlath in his workshop.

They found him asleep, curled up in the tarpaulin of the Flying Marine. He awoke, in a daze, with a beatific smile on his face. It was clear he was just awakening from the enchanted sleep.

"Why, children," he said, "I've had the strangest dream. It's sad we wrecked the Flying Marine but, oh well, I'll just build a better one!"

"We have a surprise for you," Cassie said. "But first you have to agree to be blindfolded."

Jarlath, still in a daze, did as they asked. They bundled him on to Derry the Donkey and transported him to the northwest corner of the island.

"Where are we?" he asked suspiciously as the breeze from the sea whipped at them on the shore near Áine's cottage. They took off his blindfold.

Áine stood by the Flying Marine – which was broken but with all its parts intact.

They all looked with trepidation at Jarlath but there was no mistaking the look on his face.

"It's not beyond repair?" asked Áine nervously.

Jarlath looked at the children and shook his head in wonder, then broke into a shy smile.

"I'm sure it can be fixed," he said, his eyes shining.

Cassie tactfully dragged Thomas and Nancy towards their training ground to give Áine and Jarlath some time alone. She thought wistfully of their teachers, Sennan and Scáthach.

"Scáthach isn't known as the Shadowy One for nothing," said Thomas reading her thoughts, "and Sennan is so cunning, who knows where he might be."

But Cassie's long sight told her nothing, their whereabouts unknown.

Áine and Jarlath came up the path, holding hands, and ran to embrace the children.

"Áine has sorted it out with her family," Jarlath said. "We're going to marry in a small private ceremony."

"But who will be your best man?" asked Thomas.

"The best man who ever lived," said Jarlath.

The next afternoon, the Chingles, Finnen and Connle stood by the seashore waiting for the bride and groom. Finnen, looking lovely in a silvery dress, was the bridesmaid. Cassie and Nancy wore dresses the colours of the rainbow with blossoms in their hair. And Connle, freshly shaved with his red hair in a splendid quiff, was best man.

Finnen beamed with happiness. With her white-blonde hair and swanlike grace, she was just as beautiful as her sister.

"I have dreamed of returning to Inish Álainn for so long. I am forever in your debt," she said to the Chingles.

"How did you know where to hide and leave clues?" asked Thomas.

"When I first disappeared, I feared Balor and his Formorians would come and search for me, so I sought refuge beyond these waters on the continent where there were tribes who worshipped Celtic Gods," she explained.

"Is that when you moved around and changed your name to Divona and Sirona?" Cassie asked.

Finnen nodded her head. "But in each location I felt compelled to leave an Ogham symbol and a number of feathers. I think it was the Star Splinter that directed my course. I soon realised it was calling me to Yggdrasil, the World Tree of the Norse people. There are many Swan Maidens there."

"It must have been tough," said Cassie. "Not knowing if anyone was ever going to find you or if it might be the enemy on your trail."

"But I never gave up hope that somehow it would all come good. Perhaps someday Balor would be defeated and I would be found by my people. I knew that whoever discovered the Star Splinter would have a link with me," said Finnen, gently ruffling Nancy's hair.

"And that was me!" laughed Nancy.

"Thankfully it was Nancy and not Balor who found the Star Splinter," said Thomas.

"So the Star Splinter also directed Nancy's choices of the tour of the Ham Players," said Cassie, "and helped break the spell in the studio so your soul could escape."

"The Star Splinter moves in mysterious ways," said

Finnen looking towards the sky. The children followed her gaze and, for a brief moment, a shining luminous star flickered briefly high above.

"Why did you hide in the glacier?" asked Cassie.

"At the suggestion of the swans at Urda's well, hoping to outwit whoever found me," she answered. "Remember, I did not know if I would be discovered by friend or foe."

"If only we had got to you in the Chasm of Chaos before Caitlín did," said Thomas.

"Caitlín would have gained power in some other way," said Finnen. "But by getting close to her we learned how to defeat her. So it was well done in the end."

"We still haven't found that amulet I lost in the battle," said Cassie with a troubled look.

"I too have searched high and low," said Finnen. "But it is a small thing. I shall find it soon." She kissed Cassie lightly on the brow. "Come now, let nothing spoil this special day!"

Áine and Jarlath appeared hand in hand. Áine looked breathtaking in a white dress embroidered in gold sun symbols.

Then to their surprise a man dressed like Elvis Presley in a white suit studded with rhinestones appeared out of nowhere to conduct the ceremony.

"It's my present to Áine," explained Connle. "He's her favourite singer." When the ceremony finished the singer launched into "Love Me Tender". He really was extraordinarily like Elvis, the way he curled his lip and tossed his hair. He winked at the Chingles.

"You all be goin' along fine," he said and disappeared into thin air.

Out at sea, three Merrows watched the ceremony from a rock with glowering faces. As it came to an end, Fand fingered a necklace around her neck – the red amulet that Cassie had lost in the battle with Caitlín. It throbbed with a mysterious power.

The Merrows smirked knowingly at each other and dived beneath the waves.

THE END

Pronunciation Guide to "Chingleworld"

The list (using the English spelling system) is to help you pronounce some of the Irish and Norse words and names in the book. Remember it is a rough guide only!

I have borrowed freely from mythology and folklore and made many familiar legendary figures take part in my story – so I hope they don't mind.

On Inish Álainn

Inish Álainn (In/ish awl/ing) –	"Beautiful Island" – somewhere off the west coast of Ireland
Bo Men (Boe men) –	ghostly creatures of the bog who tickle people to death
Boogan (Boo-gan) –	seaweed creature
Clíona (Clee/on/ah) –	sixteenth-century witch in a bottle and ancestor of the Chingles
Connle (Con/leh) –	a *gruagach* (see below) and caretaker of Fairy Fort House
Muiris (Mwir/ish) –	the island postmaster
Rónán (Roe/nawn) –	seal brother of Lugh
Sean Gaels (Shan gales) –	"Old Irish" – name given to an elite group of warriors which includes Sennan, Lugh and Scáthach for the purposes of this story!
Sennan –	druid and member of the Sean Gaels
Tadgh (Tie-ig) –	the island librarian
Tethtra (Teh/trah) –	seal sister of Lugh

Irish Mythology

Áine (Awn/yeh) –	a sun goddess
Balor of the Evil Eye (Bal/ur) –	evil one-eyed Formorian giant
Brighid (Breed) –	Goddess of Fire
Caitlín of the Crooked Teeth (Cat/leen) –	wife of Balor and sorceress
Cairbre (Car/breh) –	God of Satire
The Daghda (Die/dah) –	the "good" God
Finnen (Finn-en) –	a moon goddess, sister of Áine
***Gruagach* (Gruuh/uh/guhk) –**	"The Hairy One" – fairy creature with shaggy long hair
***Geas* (gyas) –**	a binding promise imposed by the Gods
Lugh (Luu) –	God of Light
Manannán Mac Lir (Mon/an/awn mac lir) –	God of the Sea, father of Áine
Merrow –	English form of Irish word for mermaid ("*murúch*" or "*muruach*")
Oghma (Oe/mah) –	God of Eloquence and Letters
Scáthach (Skaw/huhk) –	"The Shadowy One" – legendary woman warrior and teacher
Tuatha Dé Danann (Tuu/ah day dan/an) –	the collective name for Irish gods and goddesses, literally the people of the Goddess Danu

Ogham

Ogham (Oe/am) –	Old Irish alphabet
Ailm (Ahl/m) –	Pine Tree and the letter A in the Ogham alphabet
Dair (Dahr) –	Oak Tree and the letter D in the Ogham alphabet
Gort (Gort) –	Ivy in the Tree alphabet and the letter G in the Ogham alphabet
Íodha (Ee/yah) –	Yew Tree and the letter I in the Ogham alphabet
Luis (Luu/ish) –	Rowan Tree in the Tree alphabet and letter L in the Ogham alphabet
Ruis (Ruu/ish) –	Elder Tree in the Tree alphabet and the letter R in the Ogham alphabet
Saille (Sahl/yeh) –	Willow Tree and the letter S in Ogham

Norse

(In Norse the stress is usually on the first syllable)

Angrboda (Anger/bodda) –	giantess, mother of Hel
Bifröst (Bee/frost) –	"Shining Path" – the sacred rainbow
Garm (Gahrm) –	guard dog of Helheim
Gleipner (Glayp/ner) –	a magic rope

Loki (Lo/kee) –	Trickster god
Heimdall (Hame/dahl) –	guardian of Bifröst, the sacred rainbow
Hel (Hell) –	Queen of the Dead, daughter of Loki
Helheim (Hell/hame) –	the home of Hel
Hvergelmir (Fare/ghel/meer) –	"Roaring Kettle" – the hot spring in Niflheim
Nidhögg (Need/hog) –	"Dread Biter" – the Dragon serpent that gnaws on the roots of the World Tree
Niflheim (Nif/el/hame) –	the Land of Mists, the lowest level of the universe
The Norns (Nornz) –	the Fates, the Three Sisters of Past, Present and Future
Ratatösk (Rat/ah/tosk) –	"Swift Teeth" – the squirrel who runs up and down the World Tree
Skuld (Skule/th) –	one of the Norns, the future
Urda (Oor/tha) –	one of the Norns, the past
Verdandi (Ferr/than/thi) –	one of the Norns, the present
Yggdrasil (Ig/dra/sill) –	the World Tree

Guide to Ogham Alphabet

In this story I followed the legend that the Ogham alphabet was invented by Oghma, the Celtic God of Eloquence and Letters. But Ogham really did exist and has a long and colourful history much disputed by scholars. It is the earliest form of writing in Irish and its real origins are lost in the mists of time, but it was well established by the fourth century. You can still see examples of Ogham today on ancient "standing stones". Most likely, they mark the boundaries between land or are memorials like gravestones. Ogham was also used in Celtic Britain so inscriptions can be found in the Isle of Man, Cornwall, Wales and Scotland. It also pops up in old manuscripts from a later period.

Ogham may have been influenced by the Latin alphabet. It consists of twenty letters that are represented by a series of straight lines and notches carved on the edge of a piece of stone or wood.

Some people think Ogham was used for magical purposes and was a secret language (perhaps even a sign language) used by the Druids, the mysterious priests of Celtic societies. Their religion was based in nature and they believed that trees were sacred. It seems that each letter in Ogham was named for a different tree, though scholars argue about this. The names and their spellings vary a bit and some of the words used have not survived into modern Irish. There is also a tradition that the names had a secret mystical meaning. However, it may be that the names of trees were given to each letter simply in order to remember them better!

Each symbol roughly corresponds to a letter or combination of letters in the English alphabet. However, some English letters are missing because they were not used in old Irish, for example the letter "P" and the letter "W". Other symbols stand for several letters that must have sounded very alike in early Irish. A few more symbols were added to the original twenty as time went by and Irish began to use some new sounds.

The Alphabet

The Ogham symbols correspond to the English alphabet as shown in the chart below.

Note this is a rough guide only!

(The letters that formed the puzzle in this story are marked with an asterisk.)

LETTER	TREE IN IRISH	TREE IN ENGLISH	OGHAM SYMBOL
*A	Ailm	Pine	
B	Beith	Birch	
C K	Coll	Hazel	
*D	Dair	Oak	
E	Eadha	Aspen	
F (V,W)	Fearn	Alder	
*G	Gort	Ivy	
H	Huath	Hawthorn	

LETTER	TREE IN IRISH	TREE IN ENGLISH	OGHAM SYMBOL
*I (J, Y)	Íodha	Yew	
*L	Luis	Rowan	
M	Muin	Vine	
N	Nion	Ash	
Ng	Ngetal	Broom or Reed	
O	Onn	Gorse	
Q	Quert	Apple	
*R	Ruis	Elder	
*S	Saille	Willow	
T	Tinne	Holly	
U	Úr	Heather	
Z, St	Straif	Blackthorn	

The letters were generally written from the bottom up, though sometimes they were written across, left to right. The letters are divided into four groups of five letters. The vowels have notches across the central stem. The consonants have notches to one side or the other, or else slanted across the stem.

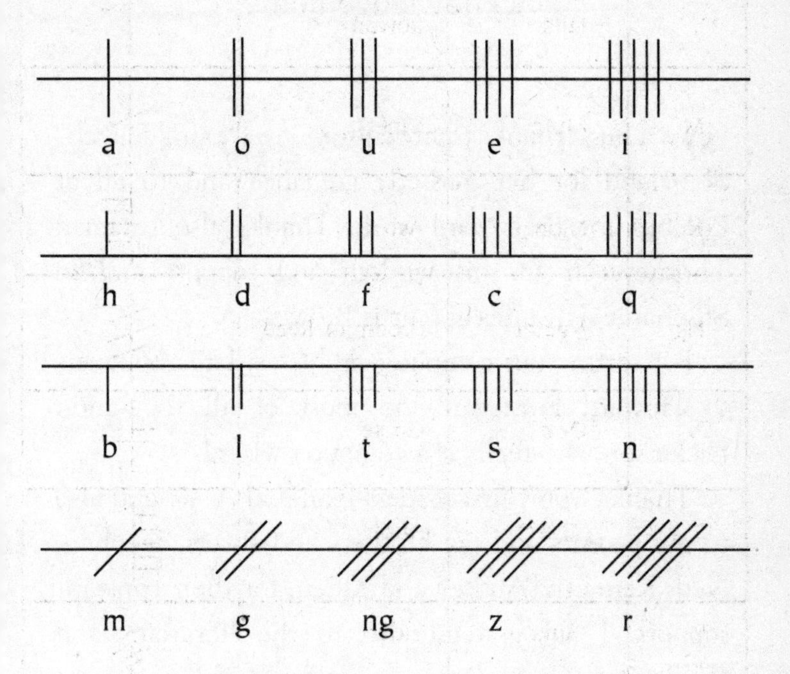

Acknowledgements

I owe a huge thanks to my editor Gaye "Samildánach" Shortland for her masterly guidance and to all at Poolbeg for their hard work. Thanks also to Euan Thorneycroft for his wisdom and support and to Stephanie Thwaites at Curtis Brown.

For sorting out computer problems, large bouquets to Howard Finnegan and most of all to Simon Dickerson who really is a computer wizard.

Thanks to my first readers Ivan and Aoife and also to my parents and my brothers and sisters, Stephen, Neil, Kenneth, Audrey and Karen, for their constant support. I am grateful also to the librarians and children at Cork, Dublin and Wexford libraries for their excellent feedback and encouragement. Special thanks to Eileen O'Sullivan of Cork Central Library, Assumpta Hickey and Paula Robinson of Dublin libraries.

This is a work of fantasy and I take great liberties with mythology but I hope I remain true to its spirit. I am indebted to the *Oxford Dictonary of Celtic Mythology* by James Mackillop, the *Oxford Dictionary of*

World Mythology by Arthur Cotterell and *The Táin* translated by Thomas Kinsella. I also recommend *Ogham* by Crístóir mag Fhearaigh and Tim Stampton and *A Guide to Ogam* by Damian MacManus. Other sources of inspiration were the *White Goddess* by Robert Graves, *Tree Wisdom* by Jacqueline Memory Paterson, *The Encyclopaedia of Native American Shamanism* by William S Lyon, *The Prose Edda* by Snorri Sturrlson translated by Jean I Young, *Favourite Norse Myths* by Mary Pope Osborne and *Women Who Run with the Wolves* by Clarissa Pincola Estés, which inspired the Scar Clan. For information on locks I thank Michael Clinton.

www.luminarium.org is a good website for mythology in general and Irish myths and folklore.

www.mainlesson.com is a mine of information on Norse myths.

Love and thanks to my husband Marc for putting up with all things Chingles. Most of all, thanks to all of you who have responded so enthusiastically to book one. I hope you enjoy the further adventures of the Chingles.

Read another exciting *Chingles* adventure!

THE CHINGLES FROM THE EAST

PATRICIA MURPHY

Here is a sneak preview of Chapter one . . .

CHAPTER 1

Cassie caught her first glimpse of the island from the ferry, in between trying to poke her brother's eyes out. Thomas was really, really winding her up that day, singing that she looked like a monkey and lived in a zoo to the tune of 'Happy Birthday'. Of course, it wasn't even her birthday. Then he started an argument about the colour of the sea. She said it was the colour of green Wellington boots. He said it was the colour of mushy peas. She had just caught him by the throat when the island popped up suddenly out of the sea, like a sponge that had been pushed down in the bath.

Instead of throttling him, Cassie let go and

shouted out: "I saw Inish Álainn first, *na*, *na*, *na*, *naanaa!*" But almost as suddenly as it had appeared, the island disappeared behind a curtain of mist. Instead Cassie's attention turned to the fat little birds with multicoloured beaks that were skimming along the water near the boat.

"Look, look, Pouting, over there! They are puffins!" she called to her brother, forgetting in her excitement that they had been deadly enemies only seconds before. 'Pouting' was her evil nickname for her brother. After 'Doubting Thomas' in the Bible, except her mammy said their Thomas pouted more than doubted. It was true. He did have a way of sticking out his lower lip that made him look sulky. She commanded him to come and stand beside her.

"How can I look if you are going to poke my eyes out?" he asked in an annoying voice that he knew wound her up.

An old lady, who had been enjoying the sun on the deck and was going back into the cabin, gave them both a hard stare. Cassie smiled innocently. As soon as the old lady was gone, she stuck her tongue out. Thomas joined her at the rail. He pointed up to the sky. Cassie looked up. There was nothing there.

Thomas chanted,

"I made you look, I made you stare,

I made a barber cut your hair,

He cut it long, he cut it short,

He cut it with a knife and fork!"

But suddenly there was something there and their mouths hung open in amazement.

Flying over the boat was a strange ugly bird. On closer inspection, they saw that it had no feathers. It had an enormous wing-span and its skin was pimpled like a plucked turkey except it was sooty black. Its big red beak looked ready to gobble them up. The bird was so large that for a moment it blotted out the sun. It looked almost prehistoric and it iced their hearts with fear.

"Ugh, horrible bird!" Cassie shuddered and held on to Thomas.

"Puffins aren't horrible," a voice rang out.

It was their Uncle Jarlath and they were glad to see him. He came up on deck carrying Nancy, their toddler sister, as if she was a sack of potatoes. She wouldn't be three until Hallowe'en but already she had Jarlath wrapped around her little finger. That was an expression of her mother's. Cassie wasn't entirely sure what it meant but had something to do with Nancy's ability to turn everyone into her personal slave.

"Not those birds," explained Cassie. "You missed it. It was an ugly black bird with no feathers."

"It disappeared into thin air," Thomas added.

Jarlath looked puzzled. "We'll have to ask Tadgh when we arrive. He's the librarian and knows everything. Now, puffins," he continued, "they are interesting. They spend most of their lives on the open waves and their young are called pufflings." He spoke facing out to sea with his back to the children.

They forgot their fear of a moment ago and Jarlath now became the butt of their jokes. Cassie mimed blah, blah, blah! Thomas turned his eyes until only the whites showed. Suddenly, Thomas leaned forward and tickled Cassie. They both exploded with laughter.

"My gosh, children, what is so funny?" asked Jarlath, turning round.

"You are," said Nancy.

Jarlath laughed good-naturedly. Little did he realise that Nancy was telling the truth. Nancy always told the truth.

Cassie, Thomas and Nancy were on their way to spend the summer with their Uncle Jarlath on Inish Álainn, a remote island off the West Coast of Ireland. They were to stay in the summerhouse where their mother and her brother and three sisters always spent their holidays when they were children. It was their first holiday without their mum and dad and they felt sick with excitement.

Cassie was desperately hoping to have a holiday adventure although she was secretly worried that she was just too ordinary. Her friend Maya had nearly been trampled to death by an elephant in India, and Quentin, a horrid boy in her class, had spent a month in quarantine after he caught a deadly virus in the jungle. The worst thing that had ever happened to Cassie on holiday was sunburn. But she had high hopes for Inish Álainn despite her mother describing it as 'peaceful', that being the adult word for dull.

Uncle Jarlath was their mother's youngest brother, the 'baby' of the McColl family, although he looked pretty old to the children. He had lots of dark brown curly hair and freckles and was still at university – a 'big person's school', their mother had explained to Nancy. Thomas joked that this was really because he was the most stupid boy in Ireland. But their Aunty Angel, who was an actress, said it was quite the opposite. He was very, very clever and was doing this big long sum that took years to add up and take away and multiply.

Cassie who knew her one hundred times table wasn't impressed. She thought Jarlath certainly looked like a baby who was just learning how to get dressed all by himself. Today, he had on one green sock and one red sock. His jumper was on inside out and, even though it was a sunny day, he was wearing a woollen cap. Thomas thought he looked cool and turned his jumper inside out as well.

Nancy was trying to count his freckles. She pointed and said, "One, two, four, twelfty, seven!"

The island was one hour away from the mainland by ferry and was often cut off by storms but today the sea was as smooth as a mirror. As they got closer to the island the mist cleared and they could make out a few buildings set among lush green fields. Some of the houses had roofs made of straw and Jarlath said they were called thatched cottages. Cassie knew that already. She was just about to tell him this and recite her one hundred times table when a massive black yacht with blood-red sails loomed into view and headed towards them at a frightening speed.

The children screamed. Thomas dropped to the deck and Cassie jumped on top of him to protect him. Jarlath huddled by the side of the cabin, trying to shield Nancy in his arms. The yacht sliced through the water like a killer whale ready to gobble them up.

"Look out!" shouted Cassie, trying to warn the other passengers.

Podge, the captain of the ferry, sounded the

warning bell. The yacht loomed nearer and nearer. Then *WHOOSH!* At the very last moment, it changed course. Everyone on deck got drenched in the backwash of the wave. Cassie looked across at the black yacht speeding away and caught a glimpse of a big fat ugly man with an eye-patch, chomping on a cigar. She could have sworn that she saw fire coming out of his mouth and that big black ugly bird hovering overhead again! Her blood ran cold and her heart pounded with fear. She didn't understand it but she had a funny feeling that this man spelt big trouble for herself and her brother and sister.

"You horrible rude so-and-so!" shouted Jarlath. "If it wasn't for the children, I'd call you every name under the sun!"

The old lady who had scowled at Cassie and Thomas earlier, appeared on deck with towels to help them dry themselves. Luckily it was a warm day and soon there was steam rising off their clothing. Jarlath introduced the old lady as Róisín McGonigal, who ran the island's post office with her husband Muiris. They were bringing back a special delivery from the mainland.

"That blackguard, whoever he is," Róisín said, "if I ever get my hands on him, I'll wring his neck!"

"She doesn't really mean that," said a merry voice. Her husband Muiris appeared on deck. He was smoking a pipe.

"I'll give him a piece of my mind!" she said.

"Is that wise," said her husband, "when you haven't got much to spare?"

"You know what I mean." Róisín glared at her husband. She then smiled and poked him playfully in the ribs.

"Don't mind us fighting," explained Muiris. "It's our hobby. But I'd like to know who it was gave you a free shower."

Cassie told them about the fat man on the deck wearing an eye-patch and smoking a cigar. She didn't tell them that he filled her with dread. Roisín's eyes narrowed shrewdly. "I wonder if that is to do with the special delivery we had to pick up on the mainland?" she said, rummaging in a damp postbag. "I'd ask you to give me a hand," she said to her husband, "except you are a boss-eyed gombeen, who is half blind!"

"No need to mock the afflicted," he laughed, " you bad tempered oul' biddy!"

Róisín took out a notice that was a bit soggy around the edges from the drenching. "These have to be delivered to every home on the island," she said. "By hand, if you please." She held up the dripping notice. It bore a picture of a fat man wearing an eye-patch and smoking a cigar.

"That's him!" exclaimed Cassie.

"Well, more fool him for getting his own blasted notices wet!" pronounced Roisín.

She read it out:

"Dear Islander,

"You are invited to a very important meeting tomorrow at Mulally's pub at 3 pm. Everyone must attend. We have a proposition that will make you all very rich.

From Sir Dignum Drax

The DUM CORPORATION (Drax Universal Media)

Thomas and Cassie were very excited by this. Jarlath looked doubtful and said there was bound to be a catch in it with a wealthy magnate like Drax. Thomas wondered if it was tough being a magnet with iron things sticking to you all the time. But Jarlath explained he wasn't that sort of magnet but someone who owned television stations and newspapers and lots of everything.

"He can stick it where the monkey stuck his nuts," Róisín said with scorn. "Wild horses wouldn't drag me to that meeting even if he was handing out gold bars. I don't care how rich he is," she sniffed.

"Don't mind yer one," Muiris winked at the children. "We'll keep a seat for ye in the front row."

Róisín merely stuck her nose in the air because her attention had turned to the children. "So you must be Theresa McColl's little ones," she said, smiling at them and her face was so crinkly that her eyes disappeared. "Where's your mammy and daddy?"

"They've gone to Sweden. Dad has to search for something – a comet, I think," Cassie replied.

"She means 'research'," Jarlath cut in.

"So you must be Cassie," Róisín said. "I haven't seen you since you were a baby. How old are you now?"

"I'm ten and a half going on forty, my mum says."

Róisín and Muiris laughed.

"He's Thomas and he's nine but we call him Pouting Thomas because he's sulky."

Thomas stuck out his bottom lip and interrupted, "I'm not sulky. I'm changeable."

"You're close in age," Rosin said. "Almost like twins."

Cassie ignored her because she hated when people said that. In Cassie's opinion they didn't even look like brother and sister. For a start she had long nut-brown hair and Thomas's spiky blond hair was like a toilet brush. So she continued, "Nancy is three on Hallowe'en."

"I'm a wish," Nancy pronounced.

"She thinks she's a witch because she was born on Hallowe'en," Cassie explained.

"We are the Chingles from the East," Nancy sang out.

"She means we are children from East Croydon," Thomas piped up. "She can't say 'children' properly."

"I *can* so say ch– them!" Nancy insisted.

"Now where have I heard that word before?" said Muiris, talking to himself. "It's to do with some prophecy about the island but I don't know what it is."

"Pay no attention to yer man muttering away to himself," said Roisín.

"It's only a problem when I answer myself as well," Muiris grinned.

Róisín shushed him. "Go on, tell us more about yourselves," she urged Cassie who needed no encouragement.

"Do you know what?" Cassie rattled on. "Our mother says she's a Roman Catholic, which means she's a Catholic who came roamin' over from Ireland."

"Oh, I've met your daddy before," Róisín said. "He's English, isn't he? He must feel swamped by all the McColls."

"Yes, his name's Ivor Nelson and he's an only child and half an orphan because his father is dead," Thomas volunteered, which was most unusual for him. He wasn't normally chatty with strangers.

"My dad has funny names for all the McColls," Cassie whispered in a confidential tone. "Do you want to hear them?"

Roisín's eyes glistened as she prided herself on being the nosiest woman in Ireland and that was really saying something!

So Cassie rattled off all the family information. How their dad called their Aunty Angel 'Radio 4' because she was always droning on and on and on. And their Aunty Holly 'Aunty-biotic' because she was always ill and her twin Ivy 'Aunty-dote' because she was a doctor and was always trying to make her sister better. Then she whispered very quietly in Roisín's ear that their dad thought Jarlath was bonkers.

"And how are your grandparents?" Róisín asked. "Are they still living on the houseboat on the Grand Canal in Dublin?"

"Yes," said Cassie. "Dad says that it's amazing that two nearly normal people could produce such mad children."

"I'm hungry in my tummy," Nancy said.

Muiris rummaged in his pockets and took out three chocolate bars wrapped in gold paper. "I don't have any gold bars like Sir Dignum Drax," he said. "Will chocolate ones do?"

The children's eyes lit up.

"That's much nicer than gold bars," Thomas said.

"How would you know if you've never tasted a gold one?" Cassie said. She was just about to ask Róisín and Muiris if they'd seen the ugly featherless bird but there was no time because the boat was coming in to land.